THE

WEIGHT

OF

WISHES

STEADYHOUSE PRESS
SteadyHouse Press

SteadyHouse and the logo are trademarks of SteadyHouse Press.

First published in the United States 2024
This paperback edition published 2024

Copyright © 2024 by Tori Weed
Map by Tori Weed
Cover design by Best Selling Covers
Interior art by Miss Vie Book Designs

All rights reserved.
No part of this book may be reproduced or transmitted in any form or by any electronic or mechanical means, including photocopying, recording, information storage and retrieval systems, without prior written permission from the author, except for the use of brief quotations in a book review.
No part of this book, written or illustrated, was created with the use AI technology.

ISBN: PB: 979-8-9897177-1-2

This is a work of fiction. All characters and events portrayed in this novel are either products of the author's imagination or used fictitiously.

THE WEIGHT OF WISHES

A CLARALLAN NOVEL: BOOK ONE

TORI WEED

For Mackenzie—
And those that need a reminder that our stories are written by magic not blood.

GLOSSARY

Clarallan: [noun] The kingdom, composed of five elemental courts.

Sollian Court: [noun] The Sun Court, magic related to nature and the gift of life. Ruled by King Daryn and Queen Hamara.

Lunaan Court: [noun] The Moon Court, magic related to dreams and nightmares. Ruled by King Egil and late Queen Quinlan.

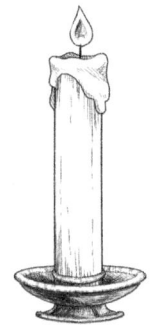

Ocealla Court: [noun] The Sea Court, magic related to control, manipulation, and the waters. Ruled by Queen Aerwyna.

Etiamella Court: [noun] The Comet Court, magic related to fire and mass. Ruled by King Dearil.

Stellean Court: [noun] The Star Court, magic related to wishes and light. Ruled by King Hellevi and Queen Izara.

GLOSSARY

The Verti: [noun] Shifter species of ancient warrior descent.

The Domini: [noun] Leader of the Verti.

Caripers: [noun] Vulture-like species of magical scavengers.

Velis: [verb] Magic of Comets, to move somebody or something immediately from one place to another, to teleport.

Lunaas: [verb] Magic of the Moon, to see glimpses of time, frequently through short visions of the future; sometimes referred to as moon-sight.

Solis Gods: [noun] Creators of Clarallan.
    Shaya: [noun] Sun goddess.
    Kaelu: [noun] Moon god.
    Larir: [noun] Moon god.
    Nephein: [noun] Sea goddess.
    Yara: [noun] Sea goddess.
    Wren: [noun] Sea goddess.
    Vulkan: [noun] Comet god.

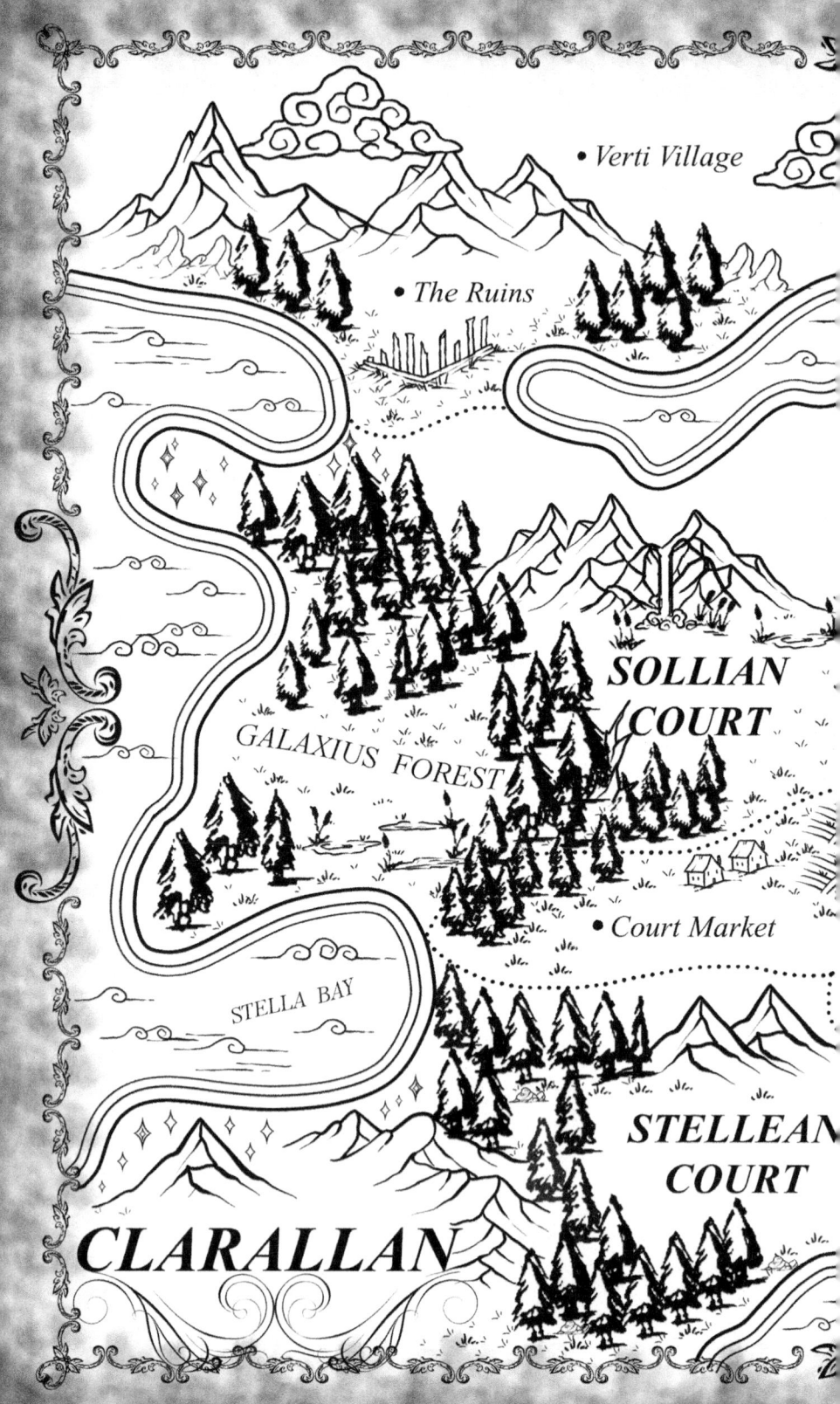

CHAPTER 1

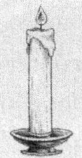

There was blood on her hands.

The only thing left to mourn, the pieces of her she could not save from the Stellean king.

Seren trudged into the empty hall, and the towering gold doors closed behind her. The bright chandeliers a stark contrast to the grim nightmare she had left inside.

A splitting sensation flared behind her eyes and Seren saw nothing but red.

The raw pain of her whipped back. Her helplessness morphing into rage. And the worst of it, the sickly feeling of her own blood covering her skin.

A deep, dry, itchy…

Red.

And still, the monster she had braved lived to kill another day.

The Stellean king allowed Seren to live for one reason only: the pleasure he received from watching her suffer every time he taught her a *lesson*. He wouldn't kill her just yet—that would ruin all his fun. And although Seren didn't want to die, she could not deny wishing for death when at the merciless hands of King Hellevi. A four-hundred-year-old Fae royal, born an only child from the first king and queen of the Stellean court, he had taken the crown after the mysterious deaths of his parents over three centuries ago. The Dark Star court—the perfect place for the wicked king to feed his lust for death and power.

Those minutes with him were days. The hours after—lying on the stone floor, the cold making her bones brittle, waiting for her body and mind to reunite long enough for her to stand—were years.

Trembling, Seren fought the thoughts that always haunted her after his torture. Begging for the end to come, even silently, overwhelmed her mind with waves of disgust. And she could never forgive herself for being too weak to break free of their undertow.

She dreamed of fighting back or escaping, but going against the king was like signing her own bill of execution. There was little she could do, as a human servant, against one of the most powerful rulers in the kingdom.

Seren wiped away the shallow tears blurring her vision with the sleeve of her worn coat, smothered her sadness, and forced herself to walk. A pounding headache throbbed at her temples, and she squinted beneath the glowing chandeliers that adorned the high ceilings. Each step she took was labored, as if she were dragging a body that was not her own.

Carefully, she tugged the worn edges of her jacket together and slipped her stained hands into its thin pockets, grateful for spring's early arrival as her fingers poked through a hole inside the left one. Winters in the Stellean court were cruel, especially for the servants. Seren would never forget the year twelve died of the Winter Fever, during a brutal blizzard when temperatures froze fifty degrees below average. The king had refused to take any responsibility and boasted the pathetic excuse that humans were simply not cut out to live in the Stellean court. As if he was not the puppeteer of their suffering.

Seren averted her gaze from the guards on either side of the last door and left the king's floor. She fought back tears as King Hellevi's words preyed on her mind despite how hard she tried to forget: *I'll never understand how the spilling of your mother's blood wasn't enough for you to learn your place. But how lucky for me—I get to discover how much of your own will suffice.* Even the violence of his favorite leathers couldn't compare to the fear his verbal lashings instilled in her, which never allowed her to forget her eternal debt: her life for her mother's crime.

Aleah, Seren's mother, was freed from Hellevi's punishments by her death fifteen years ago. In turn, the vengeful king claimed her surviving daughter, binding Seren's life to his indefinitely. A fate far worse than death. Her existence, a vicious cycle of servitude and penalty, was infinitely confined to the grim walls of the kingdom's most heinous court. The only crime Seren had ever committed was being born with her mother's treasonous blood running through her veins—something the king deemed worthy of castigation all on its own. And if Seren ever dared to forget her place, the scars on her back served as a constant reminder that she had no control over her dismal life.

She limped down the last corridor toward the servants' chambers, her body aching, and it took physical effort not to stop and curl up on the floor. But if Seren was going to give up, it would be in private. She would never allow the king to see how his cruelty left her.

Her head grew light and her cheeks too warm. She halted, leaned a shoulder against the ivory column at the nearest corner and willed the dizziness to stop, her vision to clear. But when she shut her eyes, white stars still spun behind her lashes, and a warm tingling sensation crawled through her limbs.

As she waited for the strange fainting spell to pass,

distressed, yelling voices down the hall roused her attention. Placing a shaky hand on the pillar, she peered around the corner.

A few yards ahead, a woman's pale face flushed a red so vibrant it matched the dark maroon lipstick lining her serpentine scowl, the color a striking contrast to the skin-tight black gown clinging to her thin figure. Spinning on her heels, Queen Izara began to tromp away, but she threw her hands in the air, peered back at the servant cowering before her, and snapped, "The Grand Room must be ready by tonight. Ardentiella is tomorrow!"

The servant's gaze lifted only after the queen looked away, and a somber expression washed over her taut face.

Seren cursed, grinding her teeth.

Mare's stormy blue eyes chilled the hall with a benumbed glare, her bright red hair tucked behind her tipped ears, shielded beneath the brown hood of her coat.

Leaning forward, Seren's irregular heartbeat paralleled the hitch in her breath. Her heart begged her to interrupt their fight, to intervene before anything bad could happen to her best friend. She and Mare had been inseparable for four years now, but it had taken a full year of friendship before she stopped worrying Mare would disappear. No one else dared to be around Seren for too long, let alone speak with her, afraid that whatever made the king so furious in her presence would somehow rub off on them. But none of that bothered Mare, fear had no hold on her. Her courageousness always surprised Seren, and at first, it had even made her uncomfortable; she was Fae after all.

But Mare's loyalty proved unyielding, and Seren couldn't be more thankful.

Mare had seen what happened after one of the king's punishments countless times, and she'd smeared a wretched scented ointment on Seren's torn back the day Hellevi had been particularly bloodthirsty.

That night, Seren had feared two things equally—that she

would never walk again and the end of their friendship. Her worries convinced her that Mare would come to her senses and do the smart thing: avoid Seren and the plague of pain that cursed her since birth. But Mare never ran away. Instead, the bastard daughter of revered Ocealla warriors had winked and threatened to kill the king for what he had done.

And for that, there was nothing Seren wouldn't do for her friend. But getting between Mare and the queen would only make the situation worse. Decided, Seren sent out a quiet prayer and watched from afar, begging Mare not to be her antagonistic self.

Izara's volatile words cut through the eerie quiet between her reprimands, her sharp tongue complementary to the king's violent temper.

A blur of hands and a small whimper—Seren muffled a gasp.

Raising her hand was unlike Queen Izara; that was behavior only King Hellevi favored.

Mare grimaced, holding her cheek, a swelling smear of red peeking between her fingers. "I'm sorry, my queen. The Grand Room will be ready in time. I promise." Mare's voice was quick, but her words were deliberate and distinct, unwavering. Her glacial eyes stared up unapologetically at the queen; Izara's strappy five-inch heels making her significantly taller than Mare who was already only a hair above five-feet tall.

Seren was certain she had eavesdropped long enough, but she couldn't stop, worried what would happen if she looked away.

Turning to leave, the queen spat her final poisonous words. "Need I assure you, you ungrateful brat, that if the party is not excellently prepared for our guests tomorrow, then the next time I raise my hand, it'll be to issue your exile?"

Without giving Mare the chance to answer, Izara stomped off. The delicate skirt of her glossy gown swirled around her ankles, and her sharp heels clicked against the chilled stone. She slammed her chamber doors with no more grace than a child throwing a tantrum, and the hall loosened a relieved breath.

Seren glanced back to her friend, but the quiet corridor was empty, save for the somber artwork. The only other witnesses to every horrible thing that happened in the Stellean castle.

A metallic click caught her attention. She spotted the nearest door hovering along its lock before latching shut. Shuffling a few cautious steps, Seren hurried inside the small servant room, just barely larger than a supply closet. Its contents comprised a crooked coat hanger, a narrow cot directly under a high window, and Mare, her hunched silhouette shadowing the gray wall.

Dim light poured in from the single window, sealed by bronzed bars to prevent any chance of escape, casting thin strips of pale illumination across Mare's colorless face. Seren studied her tense friend, whose clumsy hands dabbed at her swollen cheeks. One had darkened from a bright red to a bruised plum, marking where the queen had slapped her. Rarely had Seren seen her friend so defeated.

She stepped forward and Mare turned, lifting her potent gaze. Daggers of anger froze in her cerulean eyes, red-rimmed and puffy with tears.

Seren knew better than to ask if she was okay.

None of the Stellean servants were. Settling on an only slightly better alternative, she asked, "Is there anything I can do? Can I get you something?"

Mare hesitated, leaving Seren with enough time to doubt if she would even answer. Embarrassment threatened her friend's expression, and instantly, Seren wanted to apologize for her ambush. She retreated a step and Mare shook her head, clearing away the remnants of her sobs, until only her anger remained.

A heavy silence. Minutes passed before she answered.

"If only you could offer me the queen's death." A typical Mare response.

"Your wish is my command," Seren teased, which painted

color across her friend's cheeks. It wasn't a joke, though, not entirely. Her chest tightened as a memory knocked her off-balance: *I'll kill him, Ser.* That night, Seren had decided she too would risk her life for her friend. Vowing there was nothing she wouldn't do for the only person in her life who cared.

Rising, Mare said, "I hate her." A humorless threat.

"I know." Was the only thing left to say.

One step, and Seren tugged Mare into her arms, wincing as her friend's muscular body followed instinctually. Mare clamped her small hands around Seren's waist, forcing the hug closer without touching her back.

Tilting her head, Seren brushed a long, curled piece of red hair from the edges of Mare's eyes, revealing the welt that pointedly took up her left cheek.

"Why was Izara so mad at you?" Seren hoped Mare wouldn't balk at telling her the whole story. She knew Mare. Her friend was a fighter, a warrior at heart whose worst fear was to be seen as weak or afraid. Something the two of them had in common.

Mare's gaze caught on Seren's hands, where a faint red stain colored her skin from the dried blood she'd been too late to wipe away. "Seren…"

"I'm okay. The queen—"

"What happened?"

As if she had to ask.

"Hellevi didn't like my tone this morning. But it's okay, it already feels better."

Mare glared. "Don't lie to me."

Seren knew how much Mare hated when she shut down, but she couldn't help it. She was used to taking care of herself. "What happened with the queen?"

Sighing, Mare let it go. "Well, I had to tell Izara that some of tomorrow's dinner decorations had yet to arrive, and she took it as if I'd completely ruined Ardentiella. Now, if I don't find new decorations by tonight, the ice queen is going to have my head."

A long-standing tradition, Ardentiella was Stellean's biggest annual party, where every spring all five courts were welcomed to celebrate surviving the harsh winter. It was so grandiose in scale that King Hellevi and Queen Izara began planning the next one before that year's was even over.

It was the one time of year the Stellean court wasn't a complete nightmare. Ardentiella's vivid colors and use of light magic was an anomaly in the morbid court, its usual celebrations hosted only for death and darkness.

"I'm sure the queen won't even notice. She'll be drunk before the first hour is over."

"But she made it my responsibility. I can't mess this up." Mare paced the short length of the room, her hands tangled in her hair, then threw herself on the cot.

Seren gawked at her friend. Mare wasn't the type to get worked up over a party, let alone a few decorations. "Come on, you're the queen's best servant. You'll figure it out."

A desperate sigh. "I don't know if I will this time."

Sitting next to her friend, Seren's back stretched, and she chuckled softly to hide her pain. "Well, even if you don't, though I know that you will, by this time tomorrow you won't even care. Since, you know, the Lunaan princes are expected to attend."

Mare grinned, and the room felt lighter.

The weight of their reality removing its knees from the girls' necks. Mischief simmered across the waves of Mare's beautiful eyes, no trace of the torment that had stormed seconds before. Seren knew mentioning the Lunaan princes would do the trick. Mare always teased Seren for her disinterest in the princes, who she liked to call ravishing sources of entertainment. But Seren didn't see the appeal.

Most Fae males were nothing more than ego-inflated animals who believed they were entitled to anything and anyone. Seren assumed the princes were no different. If anything, they were worse, raised their entire lives waiting to be king. Seren knew firsthand that kind of treatment did nothing but breed entitlement; the frequent victim of the Stellean heir, Jassin, and his ideas of fun.

"You're making that face again." Mare said, wrinkling her thin nose. "The one that means you're thinking about how males are nothing more than entitled assholes."

Seren's disgust broke into a grin, her laughter cramping in her stomach as her best friend perfectly read her thoughts.

"You knowww…" Mare raised her thin brows. "I don't recall you thinking *that* the last time we went to The Shooting Star. Remember, you were all over that Fae guy from where…Sollian? What did you say about him again? Oh yeah, that he had the best—"

Seren rolled her eyes, shoving her friend before she could finish. Warmth spread through her cheeks remembering the last time they had snuck into The Shooting Star, a dancing bar on the outskirts of the Stellean court known for nights of debauchery with creatures from all over the kingdom. It was always a risk, but the girls loved the adrenaline of it all—the sneaking out, the dancing, the people. Seren especially loved the dancing, the blind ignorance to everything save the bodies she melted into—hot and sweaty, their hair down and tangled. Their minds completely free, overdosing on life and music and pleasure. They'd only ever done it a couple times and for a few hours each night, but those were some of the only good memories the girls had together.

"Just because sometimes I want to experience an escape from reality"—Seren shot Mare a sideways glare—"doesn't mean that I'll be fawning over every somewhat good-looking guy in this place tomorrow."

"Come on, Ser. You and I both know the Lunaan princes are outrageously beautiful. Aren't you at least a little excited to see them?" Mare swayed, pleading for Seren to agree.

She could give her friend this one after the day they'd had. "I gueeeessss. But don't get started about how you think you and a Lunaan male would make some perfect match because of that moon-pull-and-ocean-tide connection bullshit. It's confusing." Mare's laughter begged Seren to smile. "And weird," Seren added, earning a playful jab to her side.

They stayed that way for a while, their bodies and smiles intertwined, taking up the entire cot. The more time that passed, distracted by her need to be there for her best friend, the stronger Seren felt, and the less pain vibrated from her hot back.

Again, Mare tried to explain her logic for supporting an Ocealla and Lunaan match, and Seren was too exhausted to stop her. Still, that didn't prevent her from giving her friend heck whenever Mare's lungs forced her to stop and catch a breath.

When Mare finally reached her usual conclusion, silence fell for a moment before Seren asked, "Have you heard who else might be attending Ardentiella?"

Seren knew better than to believe the spring welcoming was the king's only motivation for hosting his annual party. Hellevi loathed the other courts, even more than frivolous events, but he took pride in strategy and war. And there was no better place to move his chess pieces around than a life-size board with all the important players present.

Courts rarely declined the invitation. It hadn't happened in five years; then last year, the Sollian court refused over some scandal involving the destruction of their gardens. The gardens symbolized their magic: their powers of life, nature, and healing, all gifted by the Sun. If the burning of the Sollian gardens had been premeditated, it was more than a symbolic loss. It was a direct attack on their magic—the ultimate demand for war.

Mare scowled. "The Etiamella court, obviously. It wouldn't be a Stellean party without the king's most notorious ally." The former Ocealla servant loathed the Etiamella court. Their magic of fire and destruction opposed everything Mare cherished about her magic's intense connection with the sea and its creatures.

"I heard the Sollian court accepted their invitation this year." Seren shrugged. "Let's hope that a fight between the Sollian and Etiamella kings doesn't burn this place down."

Perking up, Mare taunted, "Or...let's hope that's exactly what happens, and we can finally make our escape."

Seren snorted. Mare returned a blank stare. It wasn't the first time she had proposed the idea of escaping. They had spoken about it plenty of times before. Once, they even devised an entire plan—how they would flee the castle, where they would go from there. Mare wanted to show Seren where she had grown up, and Seren proposed visiting the Lunaan court, where, she was told, her mother had lived before moving to Stellean.

As the joke fell away, Mare's eyes grew distant, a glassy shade of blue that pulled her from Seren.

"Have you heard anything about Ocealla?" Seren regretted asking, but she had to know what to expect—whether the Sea Queen planned on attending.

The first time Seren saw Mare, gray eyed and numb, was in the castle's nursing hall. Her body covered with healed and reopened cuts and month-old bruises. There had been nothing on Seren's mind besides helping the poor girl, who like her was just sixteen years old.

In the time they had been friends since, Mare kept most of the details of her arrival private, only telling Seren enough to understand so she didn't have to relive the horrors. The Sea Queen, Aerwyna, had left Mare for dead on the shores of Ocealla after a brutal beating—Mare's punishment for using magic to free a herd of the queen's Kelpies. A few of King Hellevi's guards had found her, minutes away from death. Hellevi offered her shelter in Stellean in exchange for her servitude. Mare, in her feverish state, had accepted. She never said much else about the whole thing, just that before she'd helped them, the Kelpies' despairing cries possessed her mind for weeks, begging for help.

Seren could count on one hand the number of times she'd

seen someone that broken—someone whose pain reflected her own. The sea witch had stretched Mare's torture until even her Fae body could no longer withstand the abuse. Seren watched over Mare for weeks, the nurses uninterested in helping someone they labeled a lost cause. Sitting with Mare at night, Seren would whisper into the darkness, begging the stars for a miracle.

In answer to her question, Mare's haunted expression exposed everything Seren needed to know. Turning her head, Mare crossed her arms and rubbed her hands along her sides. "I saw the Ocealla acceptance letter on the queen's desk a few days ago." Mare's jaw clenched. "Aerwyna will be here tomorrow."

Seren's stomach churned. The sea witch was wicked, barely behind Hellevi for fabled cruelty. And she was going to be here, in Stellean.

Tomorrow.

The room was unbearably hot.

"Oh." Seren's gaze fell.

Mare wasn't upset about the decorations or even the queen's threats. She was worried about seeing the witch who had beaten her so badly even her Fae healing nearly hadn't been enough to save her.

Mare nodded, a single tuck of her chin.

Ardentiella offered a sliver of protection, assuming Aerwyna would be on her best behavior. A near impossibility, considering the rumors about her. That she enjoyed stealing children from their families—drowning them or locking them into the sea's air cells, and ultimately feeding them to her Kelpies.

True or not, Seren was confident Aerwyna was a monster either way.

Lifting herself from the wobbly cot, Mare stepped to the door without looking back.

"Mare, wait…"

"I have to go, those decorations…" she replied, hurrying out the door, her words too quick to be believable. It didn't matter, though. Seren wanted to comfort Mare and tell her everything would be alright, but she knew Mare would find no comfort in lies.

There was nothing Seren could say to ease the pain of their past. And no one could promise their future would be okay.

CHAPTER 2

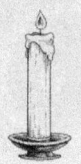

Seren woke up six hours later, a hazy darkness concealing her grim room.

Uncurling her white fists from her damp shirt, she shook her knuckles loose and stretched her stiff limbs. Her joints cracked, and she untangled the soaked, coarse sheet from her legs, pushing it to the floor—the last remnants of her nightmare lingering as the sour scent of stress floated through the air.

The final moments of the previous night were a blur. Seren didn't remember changing into her sleep shirt or crawling into bed, she barely remembered returning to her room after she and Mare went their separate ways. Sometime between then and now, the fiery lashes on her back spiked her temperature, and she had passed out in a feverish state, shivering in agony.

She stood and goosebumps scattered across her skin. Prepared to wince, she peeled her sweaty shirt from her body, surprised when no pain came as the fabric slid over her back. She threw the shirt on the same pile where she'd hastily tossed her bloody clothes yesterday and rubbed her calloused hands over her bare arms.

A few steps to the dresser and Seren opened the bottom

wooden drawer, careful not to drag it across the ground. She dressed in silence, selecting a simple brown top and a worn, ragged pair of breeches, and walked toward her stone sink, avoiding the low-hanging mirror above. She refused to meet her reflection until she had washed her face, rinsed her mouth, and raked through her knotted hair, half-heartedly hoping that after, she wouldn't look as defeated as she felt.

Lifting her eyes, the circles below them darker than usual, her gaze was a weak cage barely capable of restraining the nightmare that had frightened her awake.

It always started the same. Seren stood between two older women, their faces warped by a thick fog that filled the air with smoke. From behind, one woman wrapped gentle hands over Seren's shoulders, the weight of her fear pressuring Seren to lean into her chest.

They hid in a cage of gray walls and darkness—from what, it was never clear. The women spoke quietly, their voices distorted by the fog, their breath heavy with the scent of burned molasses.

"Take her," said the woman holding Seren.

"Come with," the other pleaded.

Smoke whirled, and the dream shifted.

A blanket of darkness eclipsed the fourth wall, a chasm of shadows devouring the stone until a hall appeared.

The woman shoved Seren from behind, pushing her away from the encroaching void. "Take her now!"

Cracking lights flickered to life, exposing a hallway of dark stones and starving shadows. The darkness hunted them, and the monstrous walls pressed in, closing in on their prey.

Tears poured down Seren's cheeks. Her mind begged her to run, but her feet refused to move. The women clawed at her, screaming at Seren, but their cries were lost beneath the thunderous echoes of approaching footsteps. A dark voice, masked by magic, filled the air. It came from everywhere—in front, behind, above.

"Is this what you wished for, my love?"

Seren choked on the smoke, the taste of magic—a burned-molasses-syrup that scorched her throat as the shadows consumed them.

Every night, those were the last words Seren heard right before she woke up from the same nightmare that had haunted her for the past few years—on top of the others that had preyed upon her since her mother's death.

The nightmare never changed, and she never saw any of the others' faces. Even as the sun rose, Seren was plagued with dread, knowing what waited for her when darkness set.

Dreams in Clarallan were supposed to be ethereal, and for most of the kingdom, they were. The Fae could create lucid experiences that captured their mind and body, living out creative fantasies in their dream realms. Clarallan's most-eccentric myths were inspired by dream magic and the incredible things made possible with the right amount of imagination. But without magic, Seren was defenseless against the kingdom's power.

Her nightmares existed the same way as most Fae's dreams, wreaking havoc on her mind. Where the Fae experienced grand fantasies filled with wonder, Seren's dreams were horrid, gut-wrenching experiences too difficult to distinguish from reality.

Shaking her head, she walked away from the mirror and toward her bed. She grabbed her thin coat draped across the end and slid her mattress away from the frame—buried far beneath lay a small silver dagger with an obsidian hilt.

Removing the weapon from hiding, her palm warmed. Her thoughts were taken over by how she wished to wield it, to feel the resistance of the king's body against the hilt of the dagger as she plunged it into him, to watch as the disgust in his eyes rolled into nothingness. She wanted to be afraid of her desires, to feel guilty about wishing to kill the king. But gripping the weapon tighter, Seren felt only cold determination. She strapped the dagger along her calf, hidden from sight, and quietly left the room.

ALERT, Seren kept her eyes high as she scanned the vast fields behind the stables. They were empty save for the horses and other livestock. The stable hands would not arrive to feed and clean until the first light dawned, granting Seren a full hour of peace.

For the past six years, she'd spent nearly every morning training for strength, skill, and speed, thankful for the lackluster feelings of control it gave her. Growing up in Clarallan, it hadn't taken her long to learn that being human put her at a large disadvantage against the Fae. They could take a lot from her, but it was her goal to at least make it difficult for them.

When Mare found out about her training, she immediately invited herself to join. In Ocealla, Mare had been training to become a warrior, her one goal: to make her parents proud. She made easy work of Seren's risible drills, the only ones Seren knew from reading the king's abstruse war novels. Mare quickly moved on to teaching Seren everything she knew, and by now, their skills were comparable in a fight.

As she wandered along the fence of a grassy paddock, a chestnut horse followed her closely. She stopped, and the animal approached, its white muzzle soft under her fingers as she petted the gentle creature.

"You're late," Mare teased, startling Seren as she approached from behind, the brisk spring air fogging around her breath. "I was beginning to think you'd found a better training partner…" Mare grinned, glancing down at herself confidently. "But then I thought how impossible that was, considering you know…me."

Seren groused, rolling her eyes, "Don't doubt me. I could easily do it."

Mare threw her hands against her chest. "You wound me, Ser."

Her dramatic act deserved an award—Mare's ability to lift Seren above the devastating waves of hatred that otherwise threatened to drown her, casting away her lingering nightmare. Over the years, Seren told Mare about a few of her dreams, but she never shared the ones she had yet to make sense of herself. Shaking her head, Seren decided to keep her nightmare private, forcing her attention to her friend. "So, are we going to train, or are you going to stand there and flaunt your superiority a while longer?"

Swaying her head, Mare weighed Seren's proposition before facing the open field. "Race you to the tree line to warm up," she hollered, taking off with a laugh.

Grinning, Seren shucked off her coat and burst into a sprint after the sea warrior, the cool morning air biting at her face. It wasn't unusual for Seren to surrender in hand-to-hand combat. Mare had years of experience over her. But even without a head start, Seren overtook the lead in their race to the trees.

Their warm-up was a little over a mile long. When Seren first started training, it had taken her over ten minutes to complete, longer when she had to stop and ease her gasping lungs. Now her time was somewhere around five minutes, and her body rarely complained.

She pushed for the last thirty seconds—by now, well ahead of Mare—the frozen ground jarring her shins.

Nearing the trees, she stopped, bracing a hand against a rough trunk. Looking back, she smirked at her friend. A few seconds, and Mare slammed to a halt at her side, slipping down to sit at the base of the large pine tree.

Seren joined her on the crisp ground, and her gaze flickered across the spring field. The flowery meadow bordered the omniscient forest to their backs and reached across the front of the stable. The field was flat, dominated by fresh greens and yellows, interrupted by scattered blue-and-white flowers—the new season sprouting generously across the crisp land. The brisk haze of dawn broke behind the brooding castle, its macabre presence a disgrace to the beauty of the kingdom of Clarallan.

Mare rose first, her breathing less ragged.

Standing, Seren shook out her legs and goaded her friend. "Just because I won the race doesn't mean I'm going to let you win the fight."

"In that case, it's only fair I give you a heads-up... I'll be imagining the queen's sweet face during our sparring today." A wicked grin spread over Mare's red lips. Raising her hands, she said, a little too nonchalantly, "I figured you deserved at least a little warning."

"Then, it's only fair if I picture the king's," Seren countered.

Taking their starting positions, Mare chuckled, a contagious sound. "You might just have a fighting chance."

Even when Mare kicked her ass, Seren loved to spar—the intense mind-to-body connection allowed her to work through all the raw emotions of her trauma and release them through the force of her blows. Launching her first attack, Seren kept the king's lashes fresh in her mind.

Trauma was a terrible friend. It begged her to remember it at the worst possible times: whenever she was having a good day or right before falling asleep. So instead, Seren had learned to channel it for training. With her nightmare gnawing on her soul, Seren pulled at the darkest parts of herself, siphoning her rage to her fists as she imagined each blow connecting with Hellevi's loathsome face. Mare returned the same enthusiasm, fighting against the torment of one queen and against the fear of another.

Fear and hatred blurred.

They took no breaks, fighting hand-to-hand, body against body, standing up, and wrestling in the dirt. Until their muscles cried and their anger dissipated, and the glow of the rising sun gleamed against their sweaty skin, calling for a new day to begin.

The girls hurried to the castle, ignoring their throbbing muscles to be on time for work. Parting ways, Seren shook out her coat, and pounds of dust floated through the air, discarding of any signs they had been training. It was safest if everyone believed they had been where they were supposed to be—asleep in their quarters all morning.

Seren nudged open the massive doors of the king's chambers using her good shoulder, the other sore from where Mare had landed an unexpectedly aggressive blow. She made a mental note to get her friend back for that next time. Passing through the golden doors, she dipped her head to the four armed guards blocking the entrance. "Good morning, I'm to meet Hubort in the servants' rooms for work today."

The front guard grunted, cueing the others to let her through as they pressed the golden doors inward.

Hellevi's chambers comprised an entire wing of the castle. The ceilings arched high, with rows of sparkling chandeliers that cast a galaxy of starlight across the patterned navy wallpaper, interrupted by dark oil paintings of past wars, placed opposite one another across the halls in stained, intricately carved wooden frames. Regal and elegant but eerie and haunted all the same—it was a perfect representation of the Stellean court.

Servants shuffled through the halls as the head guard guided Seren toward the main servant quarters. Halting near the door, the gruff male motioned for Seren to enter, a hand secured on the hilt of his sword. "Get to work," he muttered, lurking near her, mindlessly scraping the dirt from beneath his short jagged nails.

She let herself in, and the guard returned to his post.

Inside, Seren could hear Hubort laying into another human servant, madly emphasizing "His Grace" and "will not be pleased" regarding some unfortunate mistake the mortal boy had already made.

Hubort, the head servant of the king's collection, was a brutish creature from the slums outside of the court's estate. Part of the lower Fae, he had slick, pointed ears atop a goblin body and skin laced with burned warts and hardened scars. Often, his words toward everyone were as wretched as the stench of his breath, but mostly he was all talk. Bitter, unpleasant, and displeased talk.

The closer Ardentiella grew, the more vile Hubort became. He snapped at the mortal boy again before pacing from wall to wall, his musty scent permeating the air as he sweated profusely. Hubort evaluated the others' work, displeased with everything and agitated beyond consolation.

"Seren," Hubort warned, noting her tardy entrance. He tightened his glare and his jaw bulged. "Do you know how late you are? What could possibly be your excuse this time?"

"I...I overslept," Seren said, her voice wavering more than she wanted it to. Hubort's lethal face contorted, as if he would devour her right there if he could, but alas, he needed her to work.

"I don't care for excuses." His cracked lips curved upward, revealing the dark gaps in his yellow teeth. "You'll just work extra today to make up for your carelessness. And I expect to hear no complaints from you, you useless girl."

Seren straightened, dipped her chin, and drifted over to her worktable to assess her assignments, holding her breath until she was far away from the goblin.

The previous week, the Stellean servants worked tirelessly, preparing for Ardentiella. Still, there was much left to do, and everything had to be finished in approximately twelve hours. The party would commence at nightfall.

They worked in silence. Some were tasked with preparing the dining room and setting up for the performers, and others attended to prepping the food. Assigned to the latter, Seren shook her cramping fingers and finished her twentieth plate of sweets.

At least thirty more lay waiting for her attention. She swore if she never saw a caramelized persiberry or pine nut-stuffed sweet roll again, it would still be too soon. Her stomach grumbled, and she pondered the best way to eat and drink at the same time. Hubort seriously hadn't been joking when he promised a lot of extra work for her tardiness. The acrimonious goblin had yet to allow her a single break.

She cursed. Distracted, she'd accidentally dragged the steel knife across her left hand, drawing blood from her fingers. Setting the knife down, she rose to rinse her hands under the weak faucet adjacent to her table.

Ignoring the sting of water against her open skin, she remembered how she had once resorted to sneaking dull kitchen knives in her boots. It was all she could think of for a weapon before she'd stolen her dagger. The knives were far from sharp, but with the right amount of force, she always wagered they could get the job done. She laughed at the thought now—her facing off with the king, holding nothing but a simple kitchen utensil. It was comical, really. Even more so that she still kept a slew of them in her room, hidden carefully between drawers of clothes.

Just in case.

Hubort approached, and the scent of stress wafted from behind her. Sneaking a glance at the callous goblin, Seren averted her gaze as Hubort fixed a displeased frown on her hands.

"Why aren't you working?" he asked, not caring to hear her reason, his eyes flickering between her and her chaotic worktable. Before she could explain how important it was to wash her hands when handling food, Hubort complained, "Your work is not done. And since you've taken it upon yourself to take an undeserved break, I'll expect your work to be finished without any further interruptions."

Seren silenced a groan. Hubort would not tolerate any

complaints, and as much as she wanted to retort some snide gripe about his torment, she knew he was angry enough. It wasn't worth it to push him. He nodded off a new list of tasks in an orderly fashion, filling her next few hours with wrapping more sweet rolls, washing the diningware, and shining the wine glasses, punctuating his list with a disparaging remark regarding her inadequate efforts.

After three hours of the repetitive tasks, her aching joints had gone completely numb. Which, near the end of her work, had slowed her down as badly as the tender blister blossoming on the pad of her right thumb.

Few other servants remained as she cleared her worktable. A total of four, including herself and the other human boy Greyson, the one Hubort had scolded that morning. Everyone else had finished hours ago, and she rolled her eyes at the consequence of her tardiness.

Greyson caught her stare and averted his light gray eyes. Roughly her age, the boy had been a servant for as long as she could remember. The two of them weren't close; she honestly couldn't remember the last time they had spoken, but their humanity innately forged an alliance between them.

It was them against the Fae—always.

Surveying the room, Seren approached Greyson. Hubort forbade the servants from talking while working. With the humorless goblin nowhere to be found, Seren asked, "Are you almost done?"

Greyson glowered at the remaining crafts that cluttered his table, his dark brown hair cuffing his round face. "With this, yes," he groaned. "But Hubort assigned a third task for my talking back earlier. I'd only tried to explain myself…" His voice teetered off.

Seren nodded. There was never any use in trying to reason with Hubort and his miserable demands.

Baffled by her courage, she sat next to him on the

workbench. Her stomach had caved in on itself with hunger, and she still needed time to get ready for Ardentiella, but there was no way Greyson would get everything done in time alone.

"Let me help," she said.

His brows rose; he was likely aware he also could not remember the last time they had spoken. He sighed, his gaze falling to his unfinished work, and pointed Seren where to begin. They worked in grim understanding, their silence occasionally interrupted by their mutually growling stomachs, complaining from a long day's work with neither a break nor food. Seren would have bet a full dinner meal that Greyson was as weary and famished as she was.

As they finished, the old clock near the exit chimed, a rickety high-pitched ding. Ardentiella was an hour away.

Standing, Greyson cleared the last of his mess. "Thank you," he said, glancing toward her. Such a mortal thing to say. The Fae never spoke their thanks, too above even the smallest of human decencies.

"Don't worry about it." She willed her voice to be casual despite the hope blossoming in her heart. "Hubort can be a real hard-ass sometimes."

"Sometimes?" A faint smile teased at his lips, but it was gone before Seren could blink. "But seriously, tell me about it. He's actually the worst."

Greyson's words were painfully relatable. Seren hated knowing that even when Hubort was cruel to her, it was possible the boy had it even worse. He seemed to always suffer the brunt of the head servant's cruelties, though she never understood why.

"You know, it would serve you well to stay on his good side every once in a while," Seren teased, drawing a warm chuckle from Greyson.

"If I knew what I did to land on his bad side, I'd never do it again." His wide brown eyes searched hers for understanding, making him appear oddly childlike, just a boy thrown into a world that ate the likes of him for fun.

But maybe it wasn't about what he had done.

Maybe it was just who they were, the cards they had been dealt, or the way the ones in power perceived them. It was their burden to accept the hard truth about life in Clarallan…

The Fae didn't need a reason to be cruel.

They just were.

CHAPTER 3

A late consequence of being only four years old when King Hellevi ordered Aleah's execution was that Seren couldn't remember much about her mother. She had clung to the picture of Aleah in her mind for as long as she could, but over the years, the details—like the color of her eyes or the sound of her voice—slipped away quicker than Seren could resist.

From the few memories she salvaged, her fondest were the bedtime stories Aleah had read to her every night—elaborate tales of lavish balls and epic adventures where the girl saved the day. As a child, Seren had dreamed of being just like the characters in her mother's stories, to wear magical dresses and fight for her happily ever after. Fifteen years later, and the magic had never been lost on her.

Walking down the hall, she couldn't help but wish for something she knew was impossible: to be like any other guest attending Ardentiella. To wear something that made her feel powerful; to drink and dance with her friends; to enjoy the purest of the Fae's light magic.

Annoyed with herself, Seren shook her head and entered her

room, the door handle oddly warm as she twisted it. It was a waste of time to even imagine a different life. For as long as Hellevi lived, it was sure to never happen.

Pink-and-gold wisps of sunset seeped through the window placed high on the far wall, its velvety light pooling across the stone floor. She had under an hour to get ready for Ardentiella, but fortunately, getting ready as a servant wasn't difficult.

Ignoring her dresser, she glanced longingly at her bed.

Her eyelids were heavy and her vision dark, and she was half-tempted to take a quick nap when she noticed a large black garment bag folded over the edge of the bed. Her eyes roamed the room and her heart stuttered. There was no reason for anyone to have been in there.

Studying the item again, she noticed a glossy sheen on the outside of the slick bag, as if it had been dipped in glitter. Besides that, it was similar to the ones in the king's overflowing closet, designed for royal attire. Almost too eagerly, her nerves quickly replaced by childish excitement, she lifted and unzipped the large bag, then tossed it across the bed so her trembling hands held only what it had contained.

The silky gown slithered through her fingers, sending goosebumps up her arms while a tingling sensation warmed her skin.

She lifted it higher, surprised by the substantial weight of the fine material as the dazzling navy skirt stretched to the floor. Gold stitching that mimicked streaks of starlight adorned its sapphire fabric, while the bodice favored an intricate peacock design with animated details of intertwined green-and-gold hues.

Her mind flashed pictures of the ones she had dreamed about as a little girl, but Seren couldn't imagine a more beautiful gown. She rubbed the fine material between her fingers, and panic kissed her skin as tendrils of warmth ran up her arms. She licked her cracked lips, shuddering at the sweet citrus taste of the thick air as magic settled on her tongue.

Years of learning how to avoid magic equipped Seren with the skills to recognize its signs instantly. Powerful magic often had a unique taste or smell, mostly dependent on the user's intention. To Seren, kindhearted spells were sweet like melted caramel, while mischievous tricks smelled sour and made her eyes water.

The hair along her arms rose as goosebumps prickled her neck. Afraid to ruin the fine dress, she promptly laid it across her bed and wiped her sweaty hands on her thighs.

Someone had to be messing with her. It wasn't above the Fae to play with the humans in an attempt for fun; in fact, it was one of their favorite pastimes. But the magic's taste gnawed at her, its sweet citrus flavor her favorite since she was a little girl. She scolded herself for even touching the gown. If it was some part of a deceitful faerie's game… Well, she had volunteered herself to play. Seren paced the length of her bed, cracking her knuckles. She hated letting the Fae get the better of her.

Irritation replaced her fear, and she reached for the middle drawer of her dresser, grabbing her best servant garb. She had officially wasted too much time and needed to get ready. As she slipped out of her work clothes, a chill tickled her ears. The dress buzzed, a faint flutter of fabric, the material calling…begging for her.

Not thinking clearly, Seren grabbed the gown again, and the rich material warmed her hands. Her cheeks blushed, and she closed her eyes as she saved the citrus flavor to memory—a childish ignorance flaring to life.

What would be the worst thing if I wore it? Hellevi would be furious, but that was nothing new. And petty acts of disobedience were her favorite, especially ones that riled the king.

Three more times, Seren set down and picked up the gown, her thoughts in a battle for dominion.

Bad idea.

But it could be fun.

Sighing, she stripped off her stale pants and lifted the lush gown over her head. The silk material alien against her skin and surprisingly comfortable.

With calloused hands, she fumbled over the gold lace used to cinch the corset around her waist. She noted the difficulty of the garment alone, and for the first time, cut the queen a little slack for requiring such an abundance of servants for the task.

Letting her hands fall to her sides, she stepped on bare feet toward the mirror, realizing she had no good shoes to go with the dress. Fortunately, the long skirt reached the ground, and anything underneath would be completely hidden from sight. She laced up her training boots and strapped her dagger in its usual position, their familiarity a needed comfort for the mess she was about to create.

Completely still, she faced her reflection again.

Awe wrapped around her with a smile. The gown was exquisite. Its rich colors complimented her lightly tanned skin and brought attention to her green eyes—their vibrant speckles of gold and brown distinctively more prominent against the dark gown.

She balanced on tiptoes, stretched her arm above her head, and grabbed a thin gold chain from the edge of the mirror's frame. She clasped the delicate jewelry around her neck, and a silver star pendant hung low on her chest. The last day Seren had seen her mother alive, Aleah had taken off her necklace and wrapped it in Seren's small hands, squeezing gently.

She trailed her fingers across the pristine dress with care, tracing the fine patterns that graced the bodice. The tantalizing design revealed glimpses of her chest and figure, drawing attention to her mother's necklace. Lifting her hands away, her fingers tingled, and a prickling sensation zipped through her arms. Magic stitched together every seam and breathed the dress alive with every twirl.

She had never felt more powerful.

Before she could change her mind, Seren hurried out the door. Ardentiella would begin in forty-five minutes, and she had no doubt Hubort was already waiting for her. She sped through the halls, grateful to not be in heels, the dress's magic bouncing along with every step. Gradually, the horror of her decision seeped in, but she pushed it away.

Too late now.

Still, her mind had an itch it couldn't scratch. Surprisingly, it had nothing to do with how a dress magically appeared in her room, or for some unknown reason, why she had decided to wear it. It took her the entire twenty-minute walk to the Grand Room's entrance to realize…

The dress fit perfectly.

CHAPTER 4

Enthralling music carried Seren through the halls to Ardentiella. Ten Stellean guards barricaded the Grand Room's entrance, but they allowed Seren in with no issue. Her stunning gown—a disguise against her familiarity. None of them recognized her, and one even winked, wishing her a good time at the party.

With Ardentiella's grandiose displays of light and life, the night provided a temporary relief from the usual morbidity of the castle. Striding through the heart of the gilded celebration, Seren eased past the gathering Stellean Fae.

Twenty minutes until the guests arrived, Seren pushed through the servant doors, spotted Hubort already ordering around the others, and frowned when she saw Greyson was not one of them. For his sake, Seren hoped Hubort was too busy insulting everyone's work to notice how late her friend was.

The heavy doors slid closed behind her, and Hubort's face puckered as he prepared to shout a demand. But the sight of her dress stole his attention, and he snarled in disgust.

"The party is outside," Hubort said without looking at her face.

When she didn't turn to leave, he stomped a few disgruntled steps in her direction and glared at her. Seren willed her breathing to calm as he glowered at her dress, looking her up and down, his anger vibrating in the small space between them. She shifted her weight between each foot, debating what to say to dismantle the goblin's imminent explosion. She needed to say something... anything.

"Seren." Hubort's jaw ticked, his rage replaced by recognition.

Her hands twitched and warmth pooled in her cheeks. Her mind blanked. She tried to remember the reason she had worn the dress...

Nothing.

It felt like all the times Jassin, the sole heir to the Stellean crown, wanted to show his new magic to his friends. He'd mastered how to grant wishes—a Fae trait present only in the rarest of Stellean bloodlines that allowed him to grant the wishes of anyone he so desired. Which, unfortunately for Seren, led to countless mortifying experiences. Like the time Jassin had wished—at Bower's suggestion—for her clothes to disintegrate in front of their friends. Or when the prince had wished for Seren to trip into a pile of horse manure outside the stables. Seren hated letting herself be embarrassed, but standing in that dress, she didn't know any other way to feel.

Nausea threatened her empty stomach, and regret scorched her throat. Her mouth was dry. Whatever excuse she came up with earlier dissolved on her tongue, and any excitement about how beautiful the gown was or how perfectly it fit vanished immediately. She wanted... No, needed to be anywhere else. But Hubort's lethal stare kept her feet firmly planted right inside the doorway.

She gulped, her nervous breathing the only sound she had made since she'd arrived. Clasping her hands together, she offered a polite nod and forced a tight-lipped smile to spread evenly across her face.

"Good evening, Hubort," she said, a little too sweetly for the goblin's liking.

He snapped, "What in the gods' names are you wearing?" His beady red eyes bulged, punctuating his unnerving tone. "You dare disrespect the king with your obscenities?"

Obviously.

But that wasn't the smart thing to say. She stifled a laugh instead. Hubort was mad if he believed Seren respected the king in the slightest. But he had a point. Wearing the dress was irrational. The king would never allow her to work a party again. And on second thought, she'd be lucky if that was her only consequence.

Hellevi made a lesson out of anything, far too bloodthirsty to even consider missing the opportunity to hurt someone.

Already, the night had gotten to her, and Ardentiella hadn't even begun. The longer she wore the dress, the more plausible the idea became that it was all part of some devious faerie's game. And she had idiotically volunteered herself as a pawn for their entertainment.

"I'm sorry," she forced out. "It wasn't my intention to be disrespectful."

Not a complete lie. Wearing the dress was an honor to her, first, with a bonus of offending the king, second.

Disgust took shape in Hubort's expression as he disregarded her apology. He knew how insincere it was.

She reiterated, "I never wish to upset the king." *That's certainly a lie.*

Hubort's eyes flickered from her dress to the room and back to her, his decision of what he was going to do left unclear. Seren felt her heartbeat near the exposed skin of her chest. It thumped wildly, but she was not afraid. Pride flushed her cheeks. She had gotten under Hubort's skin and would undoubtedly do the same to the king. That was, if Hubort didn't get rid of her right there.

Seren doused her triumph. She was on thin ice. If she wanted to experience Ardentiella this year, she would have to convince Hubort to let her stay. He certainly couldn't know that she was proud of her disobedience.

"I'm sure you don't," Hubort mocked, his stance rigid and shoulders tense. But his bloodshot eyes no longer bulged out of his head. "Impertinence aside, I don't have time to deal with you right now." He huffed. "Get to work. I'll let the king decide how to handle your disrespect."

Seren didn't offer Hubort the chance to change his mind. Scurrying away, she silently listed her responsibilities for the night: serve Hellevi, fetch liquors, clean, be at his every call. That was easy. She only had to work on sealing her lips and staying out of trouble. Which her choice of wardrobe made impossible. There was no way for her to blend in with the other servants. Seren knew the dress was a mistake, yet she couldn't bring herself to wish she hadn't worn it.

Ten minutes passed. Seren and the other servants finished their final preparations, and Hubort led everyone into the Grand Room.

"It's time," he yelled. "Guests will arrive any minute."

Following Hubort, Seren took the chance to admire the lavish hall. Stellean magic had created star-shaped lights that floated above the crowd, casting sparkling galaxies across the patchwork stone floor. Grand displays of towering flora spiraled around the colossal marble-and-gold statues, their roots skirting the polished pedestals, taking up entire corners. Butterflies and sprites, decorating the hall with pinks and blues and yellows, fluttered through air—thick with the earthy scents of soil and blossoms.

Two towering thrones dominated the far side, their skeletal and cruel design a harsh contrast to the festive room. Silk banners hung from the high ceilings, a dark navy embossed with a golden shield brandishing a crown of flaming stars balanced above two crossed swords—the royal crest of the Stellean court.

Across the hall, Seren spotted Mare's deep red hair amidst the sea of bodies as her friend confidently led a group of the queen's servants. Seren waved, catching her attention. Mare stopped and swiveled her head, speaking quick orders at her group. Returning Seren's stare, Mare slipped into the busy crowd. She kept her face tight, a faint grin rebelling against her blushed cheeks.

Seren feared two things as her friend approached: that Mare would be distraught over the risk Seren took wearing the dress and for not including her in the scandal. Mare would have loved to wear a gown, to relive her memories of parties and dances in Ocealla, catching the attention of every eligible Fae in her proximity.

Guilt sprouted in Seren's gut, but Mare's sudden full embrace cut the nasty weed down before it had the chance to grow. Squeezing her hands on Seren's shoulders, Mare pushed her head back to appreciate the gown, a toothy smile taking over her face.

Seren's lips tugged with an insecure smirk. "I know what you're going to say...that I'm crazy, I know. But you'll never guess—"

Mare cut her off. "What I was going to say was...you look beautiful, Ser. Like, downright exquisite," Mare squealed, pulling her in for another long hug. "Who knew a Stellean servant could clean up so well."

Seren beamed.

Eyeing her again, Mare's brows tangled, her head tilting slightly. "But why are you dressed so well?"

"That's what I was getting at. But you'll never believe me...I don't know if I even believe it." Seren's voice trailed off, her mind racking over the magical details.

"What happened?" Mare asked, curiosity carrying her words.

"I found it. In my room when I went to get dressed for

Ardentiella. It was there, on my bed. But Mare..." Seren's body flushed with heat. "It called to me...and it fit like—"

"Like magic?" Mare finished for her. "And you decided to wear it? Seren, you *are* crazy," she teased. "Don't you know what the king is going to do when he sees you?"

Seren dropped her chin.

"I'm sorry." Mare grinned, shaking her head. "I just can't believe you didn't let me in on your plan. You know how I look in a gown."

Mare was gorgeous, her long crimson hair, eyes that resembled jewels, and warrior body all wrapped up with a personality that could melt even a Stellean freeze. It was no surprise that Mare had the attention of anyone she wanted back in Ocealla. Seren's heart lurched staring at the sea-stone pendant tucked behind the collar of Mare's shirt. Her mother had given it to her for Mare's tenth birthday; it had belonged to her grandmother and was the only physical reminder she had of home.

Seren's lips puckered with an apology, but Mare stopped her.

"Don't." She grinned again, but this time it didn't reach her eyes. "Now I can say that I'm best friends with the most beautiful girl here."

"I don't know about that." Seren blushed.

"Seriously, Ser. Am I ever wrong?"

Seren couldn't argue with that...

"Thank you, Mare." Seren hugged her, willing the sincerity of her words to reach to the ends of her fingertips.

Moments like that, they were the only two people in Stellean, in Clarallan even. No cruel kings, no servants, no lessons. No pain. Mare was a lifeline—an essential rhythm that kept Seren from flatlining. Those moments mattered, however far and few between. Their rarity was why they mattered so much, marking the difference between the bad and the good.

"Next time..." *If there is one*, she left out—no point in

ruining the moment. "We'll make sure that you get to wear the gown of your wildest dreams."

Mare's eyes glimmered. "Deal."

Standing near the fray of the crowd, Mare joked that Seren's dress could even catch a special suitor's attention at the party. She was in the middle of deciding which one she would choose for the night, if given the chance, a Lunaan prince or the Sollian princess, when the entire hall fell into an unnerving silence and Mare promptly stopped talking. Not quick enough to escape a few callous glares from the pompous girls gossiping near them— Mare's brazen voice shattered the sudden silence with a comment about the princess's mesmerizing eyes.

Holding in a fit of laughter, Seren's chest ached.

The packed crowd had tripled in size and colors, turning unanimously to greet the Stellean royals—a sea of bowing heads and honoring kneels. The room held its breath as the king and queen strode through the chamber doors and advanced to their thrones. Hellevi dressed in his finest war robes, his presence demanding authority, his sharp silver hair and polished war medals glistening beneath the floating lights. At his side, Izara wore a gown of the darkest navy, drawing attention to her ghastly pale skin and ruby-red lips, her grace complimenting the king's cruelty.

Two shadowy stars who darkened the night sky instead of brightening it.

Leisurely clicking his tongue, Hellevi's golden eyes scorned the assembled crowd.

Hundreds of Clarallan citizens flowed through the sumptuous decorations, the height of their magic electrifying the air which stirred with the overwhelming ambrosial aroma. The hall dominated by Stellean hues of black and blue as Fae from all courts filtered in.

The other royals had yet to arrive, but Seren noted silver armor near the left wall, guards of the Lunaan court. Crimson battle leathers and blades to the right, soldiers of Etiamella. And ladies wearing honey-colored gowns sprinkled in the center marked the presence of Sollian. Most of Ocealla's members were still absent—Aerwyna was always the last to arrive.

Hellevi's voice yanked Seren's attention to the dais; a nauseating grin plastered on his face as he addressed the crowd. "All may rise," he boasted, his voice echoing against the impenetrable silence that had fallen across the hall. Wrapping a brawny hand around Izara's, Hellevi continued, "Tonight, we're here to celebrate and rejoice with our neighbors, to welcome the dawn of a new season. Ardentiella has long been a Fae tradition, honoring the struggles of winter. A night of magic and power." The crowd cheered. "I expect the citizens of Stellean to give nothing but their best efforts as we welcome all of Clarallan into our court."

Izara cut in, throwing stardust over the crowd with Stellean magic. "The rest of the royals will arrive shortly. So, drink, dance, and enjoy. Let the festivities of Ardentiella begin!"

The Fae roared, whooping and hollering as they scattered, seeking fresh liquors and company.

A Stellean performance erupted near the dais. Three Fae jumped forward, two men and one woman. Their skin glittered, revealed by sultry cutouts of their eccentric silver-and-gold outfits.

Teasing the crowd, they picked their victims, their immortal eyes shimmering in shades of yellow and gold. Magic charged the crowd—a feast of sin for the Stellean performers to prey on. They ignited their glamours, the enamored mob heedlessly blind to what tricks came next.

Seren looked away as the female performer compelled a young male to kiss the bottom of his friend's boots. Disgusted, Seren shook her head and looked to Mare.

Mare spoke first, her eyes darting across the hall. "I'll meet you in the servant's rooms if I can get away." She stepped forward, her voice muffled by the rising riots. "Good luck with the hell-king."

Seren giggled at their childish nickname for Hellevi as Mare disappeared before Seren could say thank you. Disappointed that Mare had scampered off in such a hurry, Seren armed her mind to face the king.

Walking the borders of the intoxicating festivities, she kept her distance from the troublesome Fae. But the closer she got to the dais, the more contagious Ardentiella became, the heady magic warring with her immunity to its seduction.

Seren inhaled slowly, steeling her desires. Fae parties were a fatal culmination of untethered and drunken magic. With each step sprang a new threat, and she couldn't help the hitch in her breath every time someone got too close, even as most party-goers paid her no mind. Satisfaction tickled her cheeks, drawing a grin across her lips.

Her gown had granted her wish: kinship with the crowd.

She was just a woman in a dress at one of the best Fae parties of the year.

But her sober movements betrayed the facade; abrupt and rigid, her steps rocked through the liquidity of the tipsy dancers swarming the performances.

Close to the dais, she lifted her eyes.

Standing with one of his most decorated soldiers, King Hellevi knocked back a dark glass of bourbon and sneered. Seren swallowed. She hated the smell of whiskey—the stench of the king's breath every time he punished her and the liquor he poured on her skin after.

Seren stared.

He would see her any second.

She swore to herself she was not afraid. But her clenched muscles and racing heart told a different story.

Her traitorous mind begged her to turn around. To run.

Hellevi's glare stopped her in her tracks. For a second, stopped her breathing.

The king shook his soldier's hand, excusing himself from their conversation. He marched toward Seren, a lethal look in his eyes as he descended upon her. He stopped so close she could see the sweat bead on his furrowed brow as he ran a hand over the stubble of his jaw. He smelled of a tiring fire and pine, overpowered by the scent of bourbon. "You—" His gaze fell, and for a second, Seren swore his features softened. His eyes bore no anger, grief maybe, fogged by a distant memory, but before she could understand, the king snapped out of it. Snarling, he raised a strangled fist. "Do you take pride in disrespecting me, Seren?"

Hellevi's yellow eyes glowed. His face, bestial.

"Your Majesty—"

"After all I have given you, all I have done for you. You continue to disobey me, to laugh in the face of my generosity. And for what? To mock your king?"

Seren held her blank expression through his long-winded threats. *His generosity*, like how he so generously drew her blood any chance he got.

She worked her throat to swallow, tried to make her voice steady. "I meant no disrespect, my king—"

"Where did you even get that dress?" His voice darkened. "Did you steal it? Are you no better than your thievish mother, even after all that I've tried to teach you?"

Seren held the king's wide stare, his questions suspended between them.

Don't make it worse.

She hated when Hellevi mentioned Aleah. It brought out the worst in her, her desire to live swallowed by vengeance.

Seren opened her mouth to speak, but the heavy bronze doors heaved open and Hellevi's head jerked to the entrance.

"Dammit," he snapped under his breath. Seren said a mental thank-you to Clarallan. "I don't have time to deal with your disgrace right now, but don't you dare think this is the end of our conversation."

His tone was drenched with promise, and Seren knew better than to believe luck favored her that way. Goosebumps flooded her skin as she watched the king plaster a sadistic smile over his disdain. "The other royals are arriving," he explained. "Go make yourself useful, and find me something strong to drink."

Seren gulped.

Seething, Hellevi turned away, then paused to enjoin, "And do not return to my side until you can look at your king with nothing but respect."

CHAPTER 5

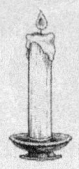

Seren marched as far away from the king as possible. Disappearing into the exuberant crowd, she gave in to the euphoric push and pull of the dancers and reduced herself to the pulsing beat of magic. The tension in her chest lessened and a cold sweat lifted from her body, replaced by heat as frisky bodies bumped into her. She eyed a small liquor table in the corner undisturbed by the crowds, and decided she could watch Hellevi's introductions from there without drawing any attention.

At the front of the dais, the king and queen stood together contemplating the energetic crowd. Hellevi boasted, "Tonight we celebrate Ardentiella as the united kingdom of Clarallan. It's my honor to welcome the royals of the other courts. Please, your respect, dear citizens. It is a pleasure that the courts of Sollian, Lunaan, Etiamella, and Ocealla may experience Stellean at its finest. Tonight, may all your wishes come true."

The dynamic crowd turned as one toward the center hall. Four guards pressed through the golden doors; their gilded armor was embellished with the ten-point bronze sun of the Sollian emblem. Their massive bodies lined the walkway, and two guards from the middle simultaneously stepped backward, creating an opening for everyone's gaze to fall upon the Sollian royals.

King Daryn and Queen Hamara paraded forward, their guards falling into step behind them, their golden heads adorned with circlets of yellow jewels and sparkling, heavy crowns. Warmth radiated from their tanned skin; their long, light blond hair swaying with each stride, as if carried by an eternal summer breeze. Everything about them was bright and beautiful. Waving to the entranced crowds, they donned genuine smiles loaded with kindness. Across the room, members of the Sollian court clapped, eagerly hollering words of admiration for the kindest rulers in Clarallan.

Immediately after, a hoard of ten callous warriors stomped forward—a shrill battle cry escaped the lips of every Etiamella member in the hall. The warriors, dressed in bronzed battle leathers, marched in front of their bilious leader, King Dearil, who stood a head taller than the curvy, dark-haired women following him. His massive body, forged of hard muscle and tough like ancient stone, was perfectly designed for the demands of destruction and war. The room grew too hot, thick with power. Where Sollian magic had caressed the air, Dearil's magic electrified, begging to burn everything it got close to. His incandescent red eyes surveyed the tense crowd, his power amplified by the throng's cowardice.

Seren shuddered and goosebumps rose along her bare skin despite the heat that threatened to overwhelm her. She finally exhaled when King Dearil took his place on the dais; grateful to no longer be close to him.

The crowd's attention shifted when six more guards, their silver armor embellished with an intricately detailed navy crescent moon, stark against the dove-colored shield of the Lunaan court, walked as one through the chamber doors.

The two Lunaan princes marched through the wall of guards,

and the crowd held its breath, anxious to see King Egil appear. But when Hellevi introduced Evander and Casimir as the royals of the Lunaan court, the gravity of the king's illness set in.

Prince Evander, the eldest Lovell son, strode forward, leaving his brother behind. He wore a dark black suit that matched the color of his short, well-kept hair, and his angular face was attractive in a cold way. Looking at him was like viewing a winter blizzard from the comfort of the indoors. He held his head high, his sharp chin tipped up arrogantly as he neared the dais. His movements were tense, and he pinched his eyes in a slight glare, making him appear more uncomfortable than commanding.

Seren looked back as Prince Casimir followed, unhurried, his rugged black hair falling loosely around his face. His light eyes leisurely roamed the hall, ultimately landing on the liquors. He wore a dark, silk tunic unbuttoned nearly too much at the top, revealing black ink tattooed across his sculpted chest. As relaxed as he was, he was still slightly taller than his brother, and his indifferent attitude claimed more attention than Evander had tried to demand. There was an ominous energy about him, the likeness of a deadly thunderstorm imposing on the horizon—beautiful to watch from afar, fatal if you got caught up in it.

The crowd's curious gaze swept forward while slow clapping transformed into genuine cheers for the princes. Aerwyna and the Ocealla court did not follow the Lunaan brothers. It was just like the sea witch to be late, and even more like her to appear when it would cause the most trouble. Even Seren had heard the stories about her most dramatic Ardentiella entrances. Like the one year Aerwyna nearly drowned half of Clarallan by filling the Grand Room with seawater, deep enough that she rode in on one of her monstrous Kelpies. Seren prayed this night would be far less exciting.

"Please, everyone, help welcome the Clarallan royals to

Ardentiella." King Hellevi's voice echoed through the hall. The crowd roared, calling out their individual crown titles. Seren did not join them. No clapping. No yelling. She could think of nothing worth celebrating regarding the Stellean court.

A stumbling Sollian male disturbed her stillness, crashing into her on his way to the liquor. Somehow, she had stepped farther into the crowd without noticing, too entranced by the royals' magic as they posed their power at the front of the hall. Seren felt the rhythm of their magic blend with the rapid beat of her heart, the strength of the room's power seeping into her skin, begging her to join.

The Fae gathered around her, everyone whispering about the attendees. Seren's eyes widened overhearing a young girl chirp something particularly inappropriate about Prince Casimir before laughing with her friends. She couldn't blame the girl, despite her vulgarity.

The prince was gorgeous, almost indecently so. Ineffable, too idyllic to believe, even when he was there, right before her eyes. Her lips twitched to hide a smile. She figured wherever Mare was, she was having to manually lift her jaw from the ground. Seren chuckled; later, she'd ask her friend which prince was her favorite.

Refocused, she lifted her eyes to King Hellevi, who was personally welcoming the various royals to Stellean. A fit of brutish laughter cracked the air as he and King Dearil made their reacquaintances. The two kings built their friendship on a history of war and death, forging their alliance over a shared desire for power. Seren never really understood their friendship—how two of the most power-hungry individuals could come to work together. She guessed it had something to do with Hellevi's willingness to cross even his best of friends for personal gain.

Smiling, Evander approached the kings confidently, his younger brother nowhere to be seen. Clapping a firm hand against Evander's shoulder, Hellevi introduced the young male to his best alliance. The two kings' reputations were well-known, neither the type to keep their conquests, of any kind, private.

The thought of the prince looking up to those two monsters flooded Seren with fear. How they would boast over their greatest tortures and reminiscence about the good ol' days, all while teaching the young male how to be the worst possible version of himself. She sighed. *What mentors they would be.*

Shaking off her worries, she got back to work, reminding herself why she was at Ardentiella in the first place: to serve the king, and unfortunately, he had requested a drink quite a while ago. Seren fought her way through the swarms of drunken Fae, toward the full liquor table. The performances picked up and the dancers grew particularly riotous. Brawny shoulders and slick hands bumped into her with every step. The density of the crowd, on top of the magic-thickened air, was nearly too difficult to wade through.

Near the far wall, a Sollian performance had garnered a large crowd. Dozens of girls clapped giddily, throwing glowing petals in the air as flowers blossomed in the performers' palms. Across the dance floor, a young Etiamella warrior swallowed a sword of flames while the crowd cheered in astonishment.

Her head whipped back—some intoxicated Fae male grabbed for her waist and missed, yanking her hair instead. She braced for her dagger, but before she could do something reckless, the male's friends hauled him into the moving crowd. *Lucky for him.* She glared as he moved on.

Shakily, Seren kept walking, avoiding any more unwanted altercations. She pushed through the last of the crowd and approached the various liquor mixes and magically infused cocktails. She couldn't taste anything to decide what to bring to the king—Fae liquor was laced with magic that would leave her inebriated in minutes. One sip and she'd wave her wits goodbye.

Settling for the darkest of options, Seren lifted the cool glass to her nose. The bitter smell of bourbon and lemon stung. *Surely strong enough.* She tamped down her nausea, the pungent smell reminding her of one of her worst decisions: One night, she and Mare had decided to see for themselves how volatile Fae liquor could be. They'd accidentally downed two entire bottles of faerie wine before it caught up to them. Consequently, Seren spent twelve hours curled around a noxious toilet bowl in the servant's washrooms. She honestly hadn't expected to survive the night.

Protecting the king's drink from the chaos, Seren drained a cool glass of water and surveyed the crowd, searching for the clearest path to the dais. Smack in the center, a circle of Fae women surrounded the younger Lunaan prince, their relentless hands clawing at Casimir's loose shirt as he attempted to shake them away. Seren watched as the prince escaped the crowd and floated to a quiet table, pouring himself a drink, Seren blushed as the prince slammed an entire glass of liquor and swallowed slowly.

She shook her head, waving her hand in front of her face. Half-certain she'd drunk water and not liquor, she turned and spotted Hubort squabbling with Greyson, who was obviously still on the goblin's bad side. She covertly ducked behind a group of dancers, perhaps a bit too dramatically. But running into Hubort was the last thing she wanted to do. She approached the side of the hall, opting to reach the king from behind. It was clear save for a few servants rushing back and forth. All she needed to do was sneak through the back halls and onto the dais, then she could disappear after giving Hellevi his drink. The sooner he was drunk, the sooner she could stow away in the crowd and wait for the night to be over.

Seren rushed around a corner and jumped, her face nearly connecting with the chest of a familiar male descending the dais stairs. Steadying the glass, she took a step back and turned.

A large hand shoved her forward. Her knees cracked against the tiled floor and the glass shattered. Pain exploded in her joints. Grimacing, she forced her anger down, her eyes on the broken glass and spreading liquor.

The two Fae males stepped up from behind and stopped at her side. Seren put her back to the wall and they faced her, cornering her.

Jassin, the one she had nearly crashed into, inched forward, shielded in smugness, his long ringlets of curly blond hair bright against his dark red suit.

Holding the dark gaze of her *favorite* Stellean heir, she drew her tense shoulders back and pushed from her knees to stand. Smoothing the wrinkles from her dress, she cast a threatening glare at the one who shoved her—Bower, the prince's most abhorrent best friend.

A swarm of ill remarks circled Seren's mind, her every muscle flexed as they mocked her. Her hands ached from their cramped position as she clenched them to prevent herself from grabbing her dagger.

She and Mare had been practicing weapon combat a lot recently, and Jassin would make a great first opponent. But that was a mistake she couldn't come back from.

"How pathetic. The creature decided to play dress up," Jassin mused, talking solely to his friend.

Don't engage. They're not worth it.

"Can you believe she thought she could be anything more than a servant?" Bower shifted his weight closer, and hints of sour liquor wafted to her nose. Pain feathered up her arms from where her nails broke the skin of her palms. She wanted to shove him, wield her weapon against his neck, and spit in his vile face. The short distance between them basically begged her to do it. That's what they wanted after all. For her to react like nothing more than a wounded animal.

She refused to give them the satisfaction.

Lowering her chin, Seren mustered the most genuine smile of her life, her jaw throbbing from how tightly she ground her teeth.

"My apologies, Your Highness." The words tasted bitter. She flicked her lashes down and gestured to Bower. "You must forgive my clumsiness. I should've been more careful."

The two males shared a confused glance, cocking their heads to the side.

"I'd expect nothing else from a servant," Jassin leveled, raising his thin brows while his otherwise haughty face gave away none of his irritation. Jassin may have loathed the servants, Seren included, but he always seemed to enjoy their verbal sparring, more than he would ever admit to.

Chances were, Seren was the only one to bite back, to deny him a peaceful submission. She would never forget his sixteenth birthday, when she called him a "feckless, no-good mama's boy" and he immediately ran, crying, to tell Izara. But that birthday changed him, because ever since, he started fighting his own battles. Seren regretted it slightly, only because it made him even more bedeviling; she would never regret a chance to insult the Stellean prince.

"I really should get to your father. He'll be wanting his drink any minute now." Her eyes shot to the shattered glass. "I have to go." Seren pushed from the wall and met Bower's outstretched hands.

Jassin crossed his slender arms against his chest, a serpentine smile snaking across his face. He looked exactly like the queen at that moment, and Seren knew they weren't done with her yet.

"Really? Jassin, I—"

"It is 'Your Highness,'" Bower growled, a twitch in his left eye. "How dare a low-life servant like you refer to him as anything less."

Seren smiled, facing Jassin.

"Oh, does the all-mighty prince need a guard dog?" she cooed, her tone as sweet as honey. *Well, there went the plan of a peaceful submission.* Another mistake added to her night. The list was getting long.

Bower reached for her throat and Jassin shot out his arm, blocking his friend. The prince placed a commanding hand on Bower's chest, scowling at Seren. His eyes were ablaze, the golden rivulets expanding as his pupils contracted. Bower might have been thundering with fury as Jassin held him in place, but the prince was far from angry.

Everyone knew he was having fun.

"Let me handle it," Jassin snapped, cruelty dripping from every word. Bower's chest fell as he forcibly let out a breath, his towering stance still threatening as he glared at Seren.

The air between them was suffocating. One wrong look or breath too loud and Bower would be right back at her throat. And this time, Seren knew Jassin would allow it.

"Let me handle what?" An unfamiliar voice slithered from behind them.

Seren hoped it wasn't another of Jassin's insufferable friends. But she didn't recognize the male's deep, smug tone—a good sign.

"Am I interrupting something?" The voice grew louder behind Bower. "I was only searching for a more private way onto the dais. I'm looking for the king."

Bower widened his stance, his hands clenched near his sides. Arms firmly crossed at his chest, Jassin's grin expanded. Neither male addressed the novel voice behind them.

When no one answered, Prince Evander pressed forward, sliding his eyes over Seren—her dress, her chest, then finally, her face. He asked again, his voice domineering, "Am I interrupting something?"

Seren angled her head, offering a small smile as she looked at Evander. "Nothing worth resuming. I was just on my way to bring the king a drink."

Evander's gaze fell to the splintered glass and he shrugged, raising two bourbons. "Well, it's a good thing I have an extra. We can walk together."

Bower humphed, probably to say something about Evander's disrespect toward the Stellean heir. But Evander added with a slight wink, "We wouldn't want to keep the king waiting any longer, now would we?"

"Oh, never," Seren chimed, twirling away from the near disaster, her smile growing.

Evander offered his hand. "May I?" he asked before lacing her arm through his and steering them toward the dais. Seren nodded, allowing the prince a small "thank you."

They walked down the hall, and a hushed laugh escaped Seren as she overheard Bower mock Jassin. "Seriously man, you're going to let her get away with that? She's a human for gods' sake. You look like a fool."

Even Evander smiled.

"You seemed to have it covered back there. But I couldn't miss the opportunity to wipe that smug look off the child-heir's face." Seren giggled—she also never missed that chance. Intrigue simmered in his hooded eyes, and he added, "To speak to a beautiful lady was a lucky opportunity as well."

Her smile dimmed. The king couldn't see her hanging on the prince's arm. She pulled away and a frown stole Evander's pink lips as their arms unlaced. "If you're bringing the king a drink, I'm no longer needed."

Narrowing his brown eyes, Evander cocked his head and Seren took a few more steps.

"A beautiful woman is always needed." He glanced at the awkward space between them, and Seren felt a wave of heat stretch across her cheeks, her mouth twitching upward.

"You're too kind. But I must get back to the party, I have—" She couldn't say "work to do." Evander clearly didn't think she was a servant, otherwise he wouldn't have intervened. Her mind raced for something convincing. "To get back to my friend. She's probably harassing half the crowd, looking for me. You know how girls get at a party…"

Not a complete lie. Mare was going to freak when Seren told her what happened with the princes.

Disappointment flickered across the prince's sharp face. It probably wasn't common for women to walk away from him. He was, after all, a Lunaan prince, and a decent-looking one at that. He was likely used to getting all that he wished for, exactly when he wished for it. A small part of her wanted to go with him, just to talk a bit more. But she couldn't. Plus, less time with the king was better than more.

Evander considered, probably trying to determine if Seren spouted the truth. "If you're certain I can't convince you otherwise, at least give me your name so I can find you later."

"Oh, no, you don't have to." *Really?* "Your help back there was already enough, thank you." Internally criticizing her awkward attempts at being polite, Seren spun around before she would undoubtedly let him convince her to make another mistake.

Ignoring his response, she called, "Thank you again, Prince Evander." Her heart pounding, she sped into the hall toward the music, away from the prince, who watched her disappear.

CHAPTER 6

Stumbling into the crowd, Seren was overwhelmed by how much had happened in such a short time. The bacchanal's intoxicating energy replaced her nerves as the beat of the music pounded against her racing heart, echoing off the drunken bodies that tried to seduce her. Seren would never have allowed herself to join them, despite her love of dancing, but that was before Prince Evander spoke to the king, nodded, and pointed directly at her.

Blinking furiously, Seren ducked into the wall of bodies, allowing a tanned-skinned warrior to spin her. His broad hands grabbed her waist, sending chills across her exposed skin. She couldn't believe the foolish mistakes she kept making. First the dress, then Jassin, and somehow even a Lunaan prince. She tried to focus on dancing instead, allowing the muscular male, his long hair slicked back to reveal a scarred face and glazed eyes, to take the lead. His warm hands tickled her skin as he drew her into the crowd, shielding her body with his. He brought his rough lips to her neck, and the bitter smell of liquor and magic pierced her nose and made her skin itch.

Hellevi's voice boomed, drawing her attention. "Ardentiella's most honored tradition is about to begin."

The crowd lurched in response and turned to the dais.

Seren straightened, alert. She knew little about Ardentiella's traditions. Peeling away from the drunken male, she whispered in his ear as he tried again to bring his lips to hers. "Thank you for the cover." Seren eased through the crowd, losing the male's slick hands to the drunken woman that pushed into the empty spot she left behind.

Nearing the frayed edges of the party, Seren willed her body to release its desire to rejoin the dance. She closed her eyes, the tension in her muscles relaxing as her mind soothed. She could dance another night. Opening her eyes, she looked at the king, the other royals standing behind him.

Hellevi's words rose above the festive revelers. "Stellean is a court of desire, a land where wishes come true. Tonight, you will all bear witness to our greatest magic as I grant one wish to the royals of each court. A show of generosity, an offering of alliance as we move forward into the next season."

Seren sneered at the king's choice of words. She was sure Hellevi didn't even know the definition of generosity, let alone think him capable of committing a truly generous act.

"King Dearil, would you like to go first?"

The shorter king stepped to Hellevi's side. His red eyes glowed. "An honor, my friend."

"As some of you may know, wish-granting is reserved for the strongest of Stellean Fae, and granting an important wish is no simple task." Hellevi took the warrior king's scaled hand. "What is it you wish for, Dearil?"

Dearil's response was silent, private only to Hellevi. The crowd breathed as one, all leaning forward. Seren's eyes widened as magic floated above various spots in the crowd. The Etiamella warriors hollered—magic erupted around them. They eagerly grasped at their sides, then pumped their fists as they hoisted their new weapons into the air and shouted.

"Once it's granted, it can be spoken," Hellevi said.

"King Dearil wished for a blade, one forged from the power of his land. Etiamella warriors, you will all find yourself in possession of its complementary weapons, a true sign of unity."

Seren shivered. The only reason Hellevi would grant such a wish was because Etiamella was his greatest ally. He would never create such a powerful weapon if he expected it to be used against him.

"Thank you," Dearil and his warriors said in unison.

"Who would like to go next?" Hellevi's smirk made Seren sick.

The Sollian royals walked as one to Hellevi's side, their tan skin gleaming beneath the sparkling chandeliers. Hamara's rose-gold dress clung seductively to her full figure, cascading into a wispy skirt that bounced around her red heels, exposing glimpses of her sculpted legs. Daryn beamed a blinding-white grin as the crowd cheered for his queen, his smiling growing the louder they worshipped her.

It was the same process as before. Hellevi took their hands, and his power surged the hall, seeking their wishes. And as the Stellean king let go, Seren warmed from the inside out.

"It is done. The Sollian gardens will be reborn." Hellevi's yellow eyes dimmed, then glowed as he caught his breath. "But I can't restore their power. You and your court must do that on your own."

Daryn pulled Hamara in for a hug, holding her face to his broad chest. "It's been two cold years without our gardens."

"Thank you," Hamara gushed, her long, curled blonde hair accentuating her sharp features. She nodded hastily, a shiver twitching across her tan face as she was reminded of the destruction to their lands. Seren felt sorry for the Sollian royals. They were fair and kind, even to humans, unlike many of the other rulers. The Sollian court allowed humans to live in peace, as equals, instead of servants.

The way it should be.

Seren watched Daryn and Hamara retreat hand in hand to their place behind Hellevi. To her immense surprise, the Stellean king had restored a piece of their brokenness.

The Lunaan court was next. Prince Evander paraded forward, his vain gaze circling the crowd. Casimir was absent, again. Indeed, he had been absent since the death of their mother, Quinlan. The younger prince had been a prodigy, with magic unlike anything the kingdom had ever seen. But when Quinlan passed, Casimir swore off the crown for good. Seren's heart lurched, for if death of a parent was a thing held in common, they miserably shared that between them.

"Prince Evander"—Hellevi grinned, looking directly into the confident male's eyes—"just you?"

"Yes, sir."

The hall fell quiet, the ripple of silence stealing the warmth they had rejoiced in upon Sollian's granted wish.

Hellevi took the prince's hands, his expression captured by hunger and pleasure. Evander's face was stony, indifferent—a mask to hide whatever truth Hellevi sought in his mind.

"You walk a dangerous path." Evander straightened, taller than the king when he rolled his shoulders. Hellevi tightened his grip on the prince's wrists and dipped his head closer. "You know I can't grant someone's death."

The statement was so guttural, Seren wasn't sure she'd heard it correctly. Shock and fear seized the hall as the crowd recoiled —a sure sign that she had.

Desperately, Seren tried to justify the prince's wish. Maybe he'd asked for the death of the rebels that killed his mother. It was cruel, an eye for an eye, and revenge never satisfied what one intended, but Seren could understand. Every day, she wished for the king to pay for what he had done to her mother.

But any rationale she could craft vanished as she stared at Evander. A sinister grin sculpted his expression, his chin held proudly as he fed off the crowd's disgust.

The heavy chamber doors rasped open, stealing the crowd's attention from where the two monsters' hands remained joined. A wave of dark magic washed over the hall as a new monster prowled in.

The fluidity of the sea witch's steps made her appear to walk on water as she stalked forward. Her inky blue gown, a bright contrast to her dark black skin, trailed dramatically behind her, and her warriors followed in the mist she left.

Clenching her fists, Seren's hands numbed, her blood ran cold, and her heart struggled to pump.

Aerwyna. Queen of the Ocealla court.

Seren fought the old ache in her chest, the memory of what the sea witch had done to her best friend, of what she was capable of. She needed to get to Mare. Hoped that wherever she was, she would be okay until Seren could find her.

Aerwyna never took her gelid blue eyes off the king.

Twirling her spiraled hair, she cooed, "Forget about me, old friend?" Her voice was stunning: youthful and ancient, eerie and seductive, wrapped together—like a siren's.

"Aerwyna, how nice of you to finally join us." Hellevi dropped Evander's hands. Carelessly, he turned to face the Sea Queen, the only monster in Clarallan that rivaled his cruelty. "You're actually right on time. It's your turn if you'd like."

Her almond eyes narrowed with pleasure. "If you insist." Mist rippled from her lips.

Seren blinked and Aerwyna climbed the dais to stand next to the king. Her warriors stalked the crowd, partygoers flinching whenever they got too close. Everyone was keenly aware of the sea witch's reputation, and no one wanted her attention.

Hellevi opened his palms, an invitation. "Your hands, Aerwyna."

"A warning"—she flicked her pointed tongue over her bottom teeth—"do not go wading through my mind, Hellevi."

"Got something to hide?" the king drawled, earning an artful glare from the sea witch.

"I don't make a habit of letting enemies into my mind," she spat.

"Enemies? Come on, Aerwyna, I thought we were friends."

"Flattery looks ill on you, Hellevi." Aerwyna cast her eyes across the crowd, the first time she had shifted them away from the king. "Let's get on with it then." She pointed her head away from the dais. "They're waiting."

Aerwyna laced her hands with Hellevi's, not caring to hide the disgust that puckered her lips as he tightened his grip. This time, the king closed his eyes. Seren imagined the sea witch's mind was difficult to swim through, her truth submerged beneath the current of her violence.

Seren's body ached.

The intense magic, changing temperatures, and her fear taking its toll.

She looked away from the dais; their performance was taking longer than the previous few. The other royals had disappeared, not wanting to be anywhere near Aerwyna.

Dropping his hands, Hellevi inhaled, his tight face the color of his sharp gray hair. Sweat glistened on his prominent brow as he struggled to catch his breath. As if he had held it the entire time he was in the sea witch's mind. His voice thick, he said, "As you wish, Aerwyna."

Silence.

The crowd recoiled, waiting.

Nothing. The two monsters offered no explanation.

Pressure built, threatened to break. Seren's heartbeat, the only sound to crash through the confused silence. The instinct to flee was overwhelming. If fear lived in her blood, she would rather have bled out than stand there any longer.

Queen Izara placed her thin hand on the king's shoulder and chuckled. "Let Ardentiella continue. The party is far from over." Izara guided Hellevi away from the crowd, exhaustion slumping his shoulders. It looked more like defeat, horror even. Whatever the sea witch had wished for left the Stellean king in visible ruins.

Seren shoved the thought from her mind. She honestly didn't want to know what had left Hellevi like that, and it certainly wasn't her problem. For all she knew, the sea witch could have wished for something simple, and Hellevi did look tired from expending too much magic. He would never grant a wish that put him or his power in danger, anyway. He was too selfish for that.

The dais cleared, save for a few lingering guards, and the crowd flickered to life.

Ardentiella would go all night.

Seren refused to endure the party any longer. She wanted to go back to her quarters and pretend the entire night had been nothing more than a twisted dream. She'd had enough of the Fae, their magic, and the king.

She sighed. It would be impossible to avoid Hubort if she went through the servant rooms, and if he saw her, he would put her to work immediately. If she went directly through the main halls, the chances of running into intoxicated Fae were high, but they would be easier to escape than Hubort. If she left the party early, he would just work her extra hard the next day. Still, the latter seemed the better option.

Decided, Seren glided along the shadowy back walls. She spotted Hubort, distracted, carrying a tower of trays full of treats away from the servant rooms. Slipping out a back door that intersected with the main halls, Seren kept her chin tucked and her breathing steady, avoiding the few Fae that snuck off to private rooms and the various servants that busied themselves cleaning.

She rounded a corner and halted when she heard arguing. She

pressed her back against the wall. Unlike the yelling from the Ardentiella crowd, high on dancing and magic and pleasure, what came from the hall was almost hushed, a furious tone just above a whisper. She wanted to ignore it, to give them the privacy they deserved. But that voice—Seren couldn't force her feet to move.

"Where have you been? I've been trying to find you for hours," the familiar voice snarled. Seren's stomach churned at the sound of Evander grinding his teeth.

The second voice was too muffled for her to hear clearly. She could tell it was a male, his deep voice heavy with the effects of magic and liquor.

Evander spat his words through clenched teeth. "You're drunk. Of course, you're fucking drunk."

The second male answered with an empty laugh.

Seren felt power pulse all the way to where she stood, carried through the hall by utter rage. She sucked in a breath at the striking sound of bone against bone. Thinking the drunken fool had hit Evander, she darted from her hiding place and peered down.

Evander towered over the pitiless male. His features were cold and sharp, contorted and emotionless. But he wasn't holding his jaw or throwing a punch.

Seren watched as the other male righted himself, his disheveled black hair curling around the collar of his shirt. Taller than Evander, the male jerked his head back, releasing a laugh that sent magic cracking and Seren's heart lurching.

Disbelief buckled her knees.

"Does that make you feel powerful? Does that make you feel like a king?" The hit had sobered the male's tone, his voice—his voice was horrifically beautiful. "Hit me again, brother."

Brother.

Blood fell from a split in the prince's sharp brow. Casimir

leaned forward, a smile full of hate and satisfaction warping his face.

Seren crept back, suddenly aware she shouldn't have been eavesdropping on a royal conversation. Retreating too quickly, she bumped into a painting with her elbow, sending the heavy metal frame crashing to the floor. The intensity of the brothers' silence was palpable. Not thinking, Seren stepped back, aware they had seen her. Evander's gaze slammed into hers, recognition unfurling in his eyes. Her stomach dropped.

Glancing between the brothers and the mess she had stepped into—crashed into more like—she grabbed her long skirt and ran. Her thoughts swirled, and she raced to her quarters, taking the long way back to avoid being seen again.

Breathless, she closed the door to her room and sat with her back leaning against the door, her dress folded around her on the cool floor.

Seconds stretched into minutes, maybe hours.

Struggling to catch her breath, Seren stared at the dress, begging her tormented mind to calm. She didn't have to ask herself if it was worth it—the answer was clear.

Quickly, exhaustion replaced her panic. Her limbs were too heavy to lift, so she crawled into bed, not bothering to change. Sleep welcomed her eagerly. She didn't remember passing out, her thoughts focused on one thing:

The look on Casimir's face after his brother had hit him.

CHAPTER 7

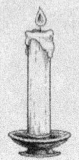

Hazy yellow sunlight slipped through the high windows, its warm touch caressing Seren's back as she sat where no eyes could see her: at a rickety desk in the corner of the royal library.

She and Mare had planned ahead of time to skip their workout that morning, knowing how exhausted the party would leave them. So, when Seren had risen at her usual early time, she'd walked straight to the library to fill her hour before work.

She'd been entranced by reading ever since she taught herself the skill as a young girl. It was the perfect escape from her eternal nightmare. A lifetime as a servant offered a pretty dismal education at best, but after a lot of practice, Seren had gotten pretty good at it. She typically enjoyed faerie myths, romance novels, and combat stories, but today, Seren had chosen texts entirely about the Lunaan court.

Unsuccessful at convincing her rebellious thoughts to release the Lunaan princes, Seren opted for a more productive route; rather than fretting over her new obsession alone in her room.

Rubbing the crusty sleep from her eyes, she stared at the clunky textbooks spread across the table: *The Origin of the Five*

Solis Courts, Policies and Punishments of the Lunaan Court, and *The History of Royal Dreams.*

Leaning into the warmth of the rising sun, Seren dug into the first large tome, *The Origin of the Five Solis Courts.* It offered a detailed history of Clarallan, created by eight solis gods and later ruled by the first High King. She had heard the story plenty of times before. Sometimes, when her mother thought she was too young to remember, between her childhood favorites, Aleah would tell her bedtime stories about the War of the High Kings.

As the story went, Clarallan didn't always exist the way it did now. For centuries, the gods walked the lands. Until eventually, Ares, the first High King, ruled over the entire territory. Back then, there were no separate courts. Ares had a son, an heir to his throne, destined to follow in his father's footsteps and rule the entire kingdom. But the son fell in love with a mortal woman, as centuries ago, the Fae and humans lived in peace. The High King was outraged and forbade his son from ever seeing the woman again, but the son rebelled.

Skimming the next few pages, Seren realized the details of the sequential events were slightly befuddled. Everyone knew the fight that broke out between Ares and his son resulted in the untimely death of the heir. Seizing the opportunity, the hopeful new rulers of the five courts waged a war against Ares, calling for the birth of the individual solis courts.

Skipping the next few chapters, Seren found the first page dedicated solely to the Lunaan court. Unfortunately, the dated text was too old to mention the current princes and only bore details of the court's territory and magic.

Dissatisfied by the text's limited information, Seren stood and walked toward the towering shelves, mostly cluttered by beige-and-cedar-green leather-bound titles. As she returned the useless book, a strange resistance pushed against the spine when she attempted to shelve it in its designated spot. Confused, she removed the book and saw a small tipped-over cover lying horizontally at the back of the shelf. She grabbed the old journal, and a strange heat spread over her skin. Returning to the desk, the pages vibrated in her hands, pulsed, as if the book had a heart of its own.

The navy cover was empty—no title or owner or artwork—and warm in her hands as she cracked it open. The worn spine hissed as she pressed it against the table. Peering down, her hope fizzled with a soft sigh.

Empty. No words. No lines.

Nothing to indicate what it was or who it belonged to. Disappointment settled heavily across her shoulders, and she resigned herself once again to putting the book back where she had found it.

Easing out of the wooden chair, she grabbed the empty journal. An ivory page fluttered to the floor, the hiss of crinkled paper catching her attention. She nudged it with the edge of her boot and waited three heartbeats before reaching for it. The thin material was brittle between her fingers as she rubbed gentle circles over the corners. Slowly unfolding the page, the letter's worn yellow color different from the rest, hints of lignin and vanilla wafted upward.

Reading it, Seren's interest piqued.

Handwritten in black ink on an unlined page, the writer's words had a peculiar style of loops and cursive letters that made it difficult to read. Luckily, it was short enough. The entire letter was a few vague sentences and darkly crossed-out words, signed at the end with no identifiable name.

Whispering, Seren reread the letter aloud.

My Dearest Adora,
I wish nothing more than for this all to be a bad dream. I cannot stand the thought of what you are going through and even more ————— the girl. Tonight, I will visit in sleep and ————— in days I will see you in person. Let this be the

reminder you need that things will soon change and we will go home.

Sanguis et magicea sumus — Q

Unable to see through the darkly crossed-out words, Seren's attention slid back to "*the girl.*" Her best guess: the ink covered a name, one the writer thought important enough to keep a secret. But honestly, the entire letter read like one big secret. And with no prior knowledge of who Adora or Q could be, Seren was at a loss.

With her poor, self-taught understanding of the ancient language, Seren pieced together the quote at the end of the letter: *Sanguis et magicea sumus.*

"We are but blood and magic." Her featherlight whisper tickled the thin paper's edge.

Seren loathed when learning something new left her with more questions than answers. She debated taking the letter with her to study, but although it was clearly old, Seren knew better than to be caught with something like it. Even if she was in the dark regarding the letter's contents, it didn't mean everyone else was. It was possible the king knew who the two correspondents were or what their plan was. She couldn't risk it.

Frowning, Seren tucked the letter back in the journal, keenly aware of the tingling sensation that stroked her fingertips when the pages radiated the same pulsing heat as before. Originally, she'd thought she made that part up.

Returning the journal to its place, her hands went cold, the sensation as abrupt as snuffing out a candle.

She gazed at the golden book titles lining the chestnut shelves, glinting beneath the morning light entering from the east. The looming castle and its inhabitants had begun to stir, and Hubort would be expecting her at work any minute.

Ensuring the study appeared exactly as she'd found it, Seren approached the idle table and tucked in the wooden chair. The hair on the back of her neck stood and a shiver passed through her, infecting her body with anxiety that refused to ease even as she left the library.

To avoid attention, Seren took a back entrance into the servant quarters. Hubort was already standing in the far corner of the room, sharply assigning the others their tasks for the day. The first were two young human girls. Their short jet-black hair and fair skin so alike they could have been twins. As the newest additions to the king's personal servants, Seren had yet to learn their names. And their eyes' frequent liking for the ground made it difficult to warrant any introductions.

Opposite them were two familiar faces, Greyson and an older male from the Stellean slums called Ax. Seren knew nothing about the intimidating male, except what she could tell by looking at him. Year-round, Ax seemed prepared to survive even the most brutal of Stellean winters. Clearly not human or Fae, he stood two heads taller than Greyson, his towering height a perfect match for his gigantic build, all wrapped up with his gruffly braided, long, silver-blue hair. Seren had seen the male around for years, yet whatever he was remained a mystery to her.

Spotting Seren, Greyson mouthed a quiet good morning and walked over to her.

"I see Hubort's already in a good mood today," Seren groused, right as the lead servant barked three bitter insults at the young girls. Their enigmatic presence left Seren wondering—where did they come from? How long would they last? Stellean had a reputation—everyone left broken, if they got the chance to leave at all.

"When is he not in a good mood?" Greyson griped, the impassivity of his tone stealing the lightheartedness of the joke. He turned his gaze to her, his words inquisitive despite barring a question. "You left early last night."

Shit.

Yesterday, Seren had deemed coming up with an excuse a problem for later. And it was now, unfortunately, later. She asked, her high-pitched tone exposing her nerves, "Did Hubort notice?"

Promise filled Greyson's light eyes. "I don't think so, but I'll cover for you if he does. I still owe you for helping me yesterday."

"Do you owe me enough to take king duty for the week?" Seren chuckled, twirling a piece of curly hair in front of her face, her eyebrows bouncing. "I don't really feel like washing his undergarments again."

Greyson wrinkled his wide nose and blinked slowly.

Seren smirked, bumping her shoulder into his. "I'm kidding. And you owe me nothing. I was glad to do it."

She spoke from the heart, extending a branch of friendship —*Clarallan* knew, she needed more friends. Simple understanding passed between them, and Greyson bumped his shoulder back into hers, nodding with an unfaltering smile.

The smell of regret oddly resembled the revolting scent of week-old, sour socks. Seren really should have pushed Greyson to trade her tasks for the day, as Hubort had actually assigned her to king duty. The universe had a factious sense of humor.

She parted ways with Greyson shortly after, dragging her resistant steps through the halls of Hellevi's chambers, mentally preparing herself to see the king.

REPETITION DEFINED THE FOLLOWING WEEK. A monotonous routine with a respectable lack of surprises.

In the mornings, Seren worked out with Mare, then spent her days avoiding pissing Hubort off as best she could. She even persuaded Greyson to admit they were friends halfway through the week, and like a reward from the universe, Hellevi then assigned her to clean his war room over the weekend. Which meant she'd had four days free of seeing him, before he arrived to critique her work.

It had taken hours to scrub the metal accolades and polish the golden plaques. She'd worked until her hands cracked and her joints ached, then worked awhile longer.

Now, her time was up.

Hellevi marched ahead of her, scrutinizing her efforts: a dissatisfied scoff here, an annoyed flick of dust there. Sighing, the king halted, and by the grace of luck, Seren was just able to stop herself from slamming into his back.

"You may be excused," Hellevi said, keeping his back to her.

Seren turned—he didn't have to tell her twice.

"Wait." He paused, turning to face her. "Do you know what tomorrow is?"

She kept her eyes down, unsure if he expected an answer. When she offered nothing, Hellevi asked again, "Well, do you?"

Taking a short breath, she shook her head and braced herself for whatever unfortunate events Hellevi had planned for the day.

"Hubort won't be expecting you tomorrow. You're free to spend the day however you wish."

Hellevi's unexpected kindness felt the same as if someone said "we need to talk," but then walked away without saying a word.

What is he getting at?

She raised her eyes, leveling them to the king's gaze. No signs of anger. But nothing to explain his unusual behavior. The last time she'd had a day off she'd had a magical fever so bad it burned all the way through the layers of her skin and left her bedridden for over seventy-two hours. And the time before that had been her birthday—her annual day off a year.

Seren felt the king's gaze on her skin as understanding wafted through her. She had completely forgotten that tomorrow *was* her birthday, her twentieth: one of the most important birthdays for Clarallan Fae, when their magic reached its fullest potential.

"Since tomorrow is your birthday, I figured you wouldn't want to spend the entire day working," Hellevi hummed. "But, if that's what you would like, I can rearrange with Hubort..."

"No," she said a bit too quickly. "I'd like the day off." He considered her, daring a pointed look. She added at the last minute, "Please, Your Majesty."

Hellevi lifted his chin. "It is already done. You're welcome to spend the day however you wish. Think of it as my gift to you."

Regret tainted her words as she blurted, "Can Mare join me?" She knew how stupid it was to ask. He was never supposed to know of their friendship. It put the two of them at too great a risk. If any harm came to her friend because of her, Seren would never forgive herself.

Hellevi grunted, his mouth curling into a repulsive grin. Before she could apologize, he said, "I will see what I can do. Don't make me regret it, Seren."

Recoiling in unease, Seren had to exert physical effort to hide her reaction. She could count on one hand how many times Hellevi had called her by name. It happened so rarely, Seren sometimes wondered if he even remembered it at all. But if he remembered her birthday... What other things did the king keep secret?

"Thank you, Your Majesty." Her words tasted foreign, but she was pleased with her gift—if she could call one day a year off a gift. She kept her petty thoughts silent and allowed the king to dismiss her.

There was no point in arguing away her one opportunity for a good day.

Hellevi watched her leave, and a sickly feeling washed over her; her scarred back stung in remembrance. She knew the king marveled at his handiwork beneath the thin layer of her shirt.

Retiring to her room, Seren's thoughts were a battle between excitement and unease. All night, she could barely contain her celebratory ideas, but as she planned, a disturbing thought kept her company. It lay in bed with her, rolling the corners of her mind with doubt as her sheets sprang from the frame. Whispering in her ear the absurd notion that maybe Hellevi didn't hate her nearly as much as she hated him.

CHAPTER 8

A crisp breeze cut through the Clarallan court market, carrying warm hints of sweet breads and glazed meats through the alleys lined with rustling birches and oak trees.

Seren inhaled slowly, appreciating the early morning. Soft rays of dawn reflected against the bright shop signs and gently cleared the fog that stretched across the cobblestone streets. The spacious market was quiet, the vendors not yet bothered by the bustle of rushing customers that would undoubtedly arrive later. Patiently, two shop owners talked near a tender fire, waiting for their tea to steep.

Seren loved the simplicity of the court market—it was why she visited every year on her birthday. But this was the first time she had been lucky enough to bring anyone with her.

Something tightened in Seren's chest as she watched Mare take in the market for the first time, her fair skin gleaming beneath the rising sun, her normally deep blue eyes light with wonder as she hummed a harmonic melody. Seren's heart overflowed with joy; no one could have wiped away her smile no matter how hard they tried.

A short figure appeared from the smoke. Older, but full of radiance and surprise, she spoke in a lovely tone. "You ladies surely are awake early this morning. Would the two of you like any tea to warm up?"

The older woman held two steaming mugs. Her graying hair, curled neatly around her soft features, held down by a handcrafted wool hat, to which she wore the matching rust-colored sweater.

Seren extended two silver coins in exchange for her kindness.

"Save it," the woman said, smiling. "I always make extra. I like to enjoy my mornings with good tea and even better company."

"Thank you," Seren and Mare said in unison.

She took a small sip, and hints of honey and cinnamon coated Seren's tongue as she lifted her gaze to the homey building at their side. "Do you own this shop?"

"My late husband bought it as my wedding gift some twenty years ago, and we ran it together before he passed away last winter. That's why I appreciate the morning company. It gets lonely after a while, but I'm much too old now to go anywhere else."

"We're so sorry," the girls said, sharing a concerned glance as sorrow glossed over the woman's gentle eyes.

Seeking a distraction, Seren gestured to the shop again. "What do you sell?"

The woman shook off her solemn memories and pointed into the hazy window to her left. "Antiques, artwork, old books. Anything of the like. My husband was a terrible salesman, a collector at heart. He always kept more than he sold." She took a small sip from her tea, her brows knotting together. "Now that he's gone, I have a hard time letting things go. Everything reminds me of him, and selling anything feels like I'm losing pieces of him too."

Pain bit at the bottom of Seren's throat, and her tongue tied in knots. There was nothing she or Mare could say that could ease the woman's suffering. Seren toyed with the delicate gold chain of her necklace—she knew exactly how it felt to want to hold on to anything that reminded her of someone she had lost.

"Thank you for sharing with us..." Mare's gentle words blew away the frigid air permeating their silence. Like always, her friend had a charming way of setting any building tension at ease, a natural reflex more than a practiced skill.

"Rosella." The woman's smile buried dimples in her cheeks. "It's been a pleasure to meet you two..."

Mare placed a hand over her heart, and held her tea with the other. "Oh, I'm Mare and this is Seren."

"So, girls, what brought you to the market today?"

"It's her twentieth birthday, and I'm going to find her the best gift." Mare nearly squealed, and she and Rosella shared a laugh. Seren was grateful Mare was so good with people, so at ease with genuine conversation. It was harder for Seren. She didn't have a lot of practice, not when she'd spent her entire life in a castle where everyone purposefully avoided her.

"Twentieth, you say? That's a very special birthday in Clarallan. The stories go that upon a child's twentieth year, their magic is revealed to them in full. What has your birthday brought you thus far, dear?"

"Oh, I'm—" Seren's words fumbled out of her mouth. "I don't have magic. I'm human."

Rosella cocked her head to the side, her gaze focused entirely on Seren as she looked her up and down.

"I know a woman, a Seer—she might be able to help you find the perfect gift." Rosella paused, her maroon mug halfway to her lips, warm steam circling her thin mouth. "Her name is Prue, and she occasionally works near the far end of the market."

"How do we find her?" Seren asked.

"It's much more likely she will find you." Rosella chuckled.

"You're welcome to come back later when my shop opens. I'm sure I'd have a great gift for you in here somewhere if you don't find what you're looking for."

"Thank you again, Rosella." Seren beamed. A chill scurried up her arms as she returned her empty ceramic mug to the kind woman. She hovered her stiff hands over the mellow fire for a few breaths before gesturing to Mare to go.

The market bordered the edge of Stellean and welcomed citizens from all five courts—Fae, humans, and creatures alike ventured far to experience the heart of the magical kingdom. Besides Ocealla citizens, the Lunaan Fae traveled the farthest: roughly a three-day cart ride in good weather. The Stellean castle was visible from the skirt of the market, it's dark, looming presence—dour and frigid—a brutal contrast to the festive kingdom's center, lit with life as spring wished Clarallan her warmest welcome and waved the pestilent winter goodbye.

Unhurried, the girls walked down the alley, tucked away from the bustling shop vendors rising with the sun. The main street was filled with early shoppers eagerly lining the cobble roads. Horses stood saddled and tied near tall wooden posts, and stray animals rooted around worn bins in search of leftovers from breakfast tossed out by the passing shoppers.

Mare took every opportunity to absorb the quaint village, stopping at nearly every vendor as they searched for the Seer and Seren's perfect gift—whichever came first, really. Surveying the busy street ahead, Mare exclaimed, "I can't believe I've never been here before. It's amazing!" Seren's heart warmed, and she saved the feeling to memory.

She desperately wanted to ask Mare about Rosella's peculiar behavior, but she couldn't bring herself to ruin that feeling. They could pretend, for one day, that everything was as it was supposed to be, even if Rosella's odd reaction lingered in the depths of Seren's anxieties, raising doubts in her logic. Rosella's contorted expression had been telling, barring no words. The woman had looked like she wanted to argue, to tell Seren she was wrong, or laugh as if there were some joke Seren wasn't in on.

But she refused to let what was out of her control ruin her birthday. Distracted, she shuffled her tenacious worries to the back of her mind, then jolted at the nearness of an uncanny voice whispering in her ear: "*Looking for me?*"

She spun, fear grabbing her by the throat. No one was there. But she knew what she'd heard.

"Mare!" She scurried her eyes from the empty street to her friend—Mare's attention was captured by a charming young woman attempting to sell her intricately handcrafted pieces of jewelry.

"Mare," she called out again, louder this time as annoyance and panic tainted her tone. Whatever game some faerie was playing, she certainly wanted no part of it. Her hand slid to her thigh, reaching for the dagger that was always there, and she turned again, irritated.

"Whoever is messing with me, just know—" She came face-to-face with a spindly, dove-skinned woman, long black hair dramatic against her fair wrinkles, time intricately woven within her expression. "Who are you?" Seren asked.

"My child, I am Prue."

Seren's eyes widened. Prue's girlish voice—somehow, at once, the woman was young and old, aged and timeless. The devastating years of their broken kingdom carved a narrative on the woman's skin; Clarallan's stories shone through her wondrous eyes.

"The Seer." Seren's mouth gaped.

Nearly singing, Prue trilled, "The Seer, the witch, the daughter of the moon. Whatever you wish."

"I was told to find you." Seren couldn't decide if the woman was captivating or terrifying. "Or more so, you would find me."

"Find the girl, stop the war. If she fails, it is sure." Prue's arcane words chilled Seren to her core as the Seer's melody seeped through her skin. Something about how the Seer spoke made her incredibly nervous despite her usual confidence. She debated calling out for Mare again, but one quick glance and Seren knew her friend would never hear her over her own distracting flirtations: the twirl of her silky hair and the gleam of her bright eyes as she amplified her charms toward the vendor.

Mare had yet to notice she'd left Seren behind. But Seren couldn't have been any less surprised. Leave it to Mare to be distracted by a pretty face when Seren needed her.

Seren looked past her friend, at an older Sollian couple browsing a quiet vendor of beaded jewelry and hand painted vases. Too far in the distance to hear her call for Mare as they began to leave the alley.

She met Prue's gaze. "I'm not sure I understand."

"Unknowing star, dark and bright. Oh, kingdoms will fall, and kingdoms will fight." Prue's eyes were a glassy, unseeing lavender. If she wasn't sure before, Seren was then—the woman was mad, certifiable even.

She reminded herself running away was always an option.

"Ma'am, please." Seren stepped to the side and met the woman's cold grasp. "I really should go."

"Don't you wish to know your fate? An evil is coming, and there's only one way to stop it." Prue's eyes grew clearer, her words less riddled.

"I think you have the wrong person. I'm—"

"Seren." She balked at the sound of her name coming from Prue's lips. She hadn't told it to the woman, but of course she already knew. She knew everything. Saw the past, present, and future, life, death, and destiny. "You are who I was supposed to find."

Seren blinked slowly, her nerves settling. The Seer didn't appear to pose any real threat; the only danger Seren could find was in believing the insanity of Prue's harmonic riddles. She was certain the madwoman had no lack of loose screws, but Seren would too if she had spent her entire life experiencing time the way the Seer did. With a racing heart, Seren asked, "What do you want from me?"

"The Clarallan you know is broken, shattered since the Great Wars of the High King. This kingdom was never supposed to exist this way, under the separate rules of the courts. Its magic is tempered, and the lands...they're weakening." Prue stilled, inhaling deeply. "Before the Wars, Clarallan was magnificent. Its magic absolute, boundless even. The lands thrived, and the people were united. It was at real peace."

"That sounds"—Seren was at a loss—"unreal."

"When the High King murdered his only son, he set Clarallan on a desolate path. He made the kingdom vulnerable to the greedy and the traitorous, providing the new rulers with the perfect opportunity to seize the power they so desperately craved. Ares, he's who let Clarallan crumble into the broken fragments we know today."

Seren's face tightened. "I don't understand what any of this has to do with me."

"Your king... King Hellevi, he's the greediest of them all. He must be stopped."

That explains nothing beyond what I already know. "Why are you telling me all this?"

Wagging her finger, Prue continued. "He's planning a war—that Hellevi. One that will bring our kingdom to its knees given the chance. He won't stop until he's become the High King of Clarallan."

Seren pushed. "Shouldn't you be warning the other courts, then? If what you say is true, why waste your time with me?" Darkness crept from the alley's edges, veiling them in shadows and hiding them away from the public. Agog, Seren watched the Seer nervously as she closed her eyes, lifted her frail hand, and tilted her head back until her gaze pointed to the sky. "What are you doing?" Seren stammered.

Prue did not answer.

Seren's skin took flight with goosebumps, as Prue raised her curled hands above her face, opened her palms, and whispered an eerie melody. From the murky shadows, came vibrant colors that flickered through the gray air—pictures flaring to life against the darkness; twisted and warped. It took a few seconds, but with the air as a canvas, the Seer's magic painted a familiar memory.

"Is that…" Seren took a hesitant step forward. The stone walls, the long arched hallway, the silhouette of three figures huddled together in smoke. "My dream?"

"Oh, child, that is you." Prue said emphatically, waving her thin hand through the vision, scattering the colors, and causing the scene to change again. "Well, your memory at least."

Desperate, Seren asked, "Who are those women? Do you know them?"

Prue, neither hearing or caring, ignored Seren's question and continued working her magic until a new vision enveloped them.

"Do you know who those women are? Tell me," Seren demanded, but Prue didn't even flinch, wielding her magic until a new picture burst to life.

Seren froze, unable to tear her eyes from what the Seer had created.

Hellevi, wearing a full suit of armor, dominated the new vision, kneeling the entirety of his heavy weight on the chest of a small child, the tip of his blade begging to draw blood from the base of her neck.

He twisted his head, and a shudder passed through Seren. It was as if Hellevi looked directly at her, a wicked smile plastered on his cold face, his thin lips red with blood.

Was Hellevi the voice in my nightmare? And if that was me, why can't I remember?

Again, Prue twirled her fingers through the colorful air, moving the hands of an invisible clock forward in time. Slowly, she guided the memory into a new perspective, unveiling the hidden figure's identity.

Seren gasped, recoiling. She saw herself reflected in the innocent eyes of four-year-old Seren. A perfect mirror image, barring the age difference of the memory. Her curly dark hair fell over her youthful face and tumbled down her small shoulders, covering a bloody cut that stretched the length of her cheek, kissing the freshly purpled bruise under her eye.

The king spoke, but the memory offered no sound.

"What is he saying?" Seren asked.

Prue paused.

The silence nearly worse than what she confessed. "That he's going to kill you, Seren."

Fear overwhelmed her from the inside out. She wasn't even sure she believed the old crow of a woman, but if Prue spoke the truth, then why was she so afraid? Seren was entirely aware of how much the king hated her; it was no surprise that he wanted her dead too. But in twenty years, he had yet to make good on his word.

"I don't understand," Seren pleaded. But there was no time for Prue to explain.

Rage—undiluted, untamable rage—ravaged Seren's heart as she watched Hellevi lift his armored hand and slap it across the child's face, watched her young body, in pain, ricochet off the stone floor right before the king shoved his knee farther into her chest, pinning her down once more. Seren didn't care if she couldn't recall the horrific memory. She remembered the fear. The helplessness. How vulnerable and weak she had felt, even as a child.

Sixteen years later, and those torturous feelings had never offered her freedom. Having spent years beneath their unbearable weight, there was one thing Seren would never forget: she wanted the king dead.

Prue's melodic voice floated through the tense air, but Seren couldn't rip her gaze from her own reflection. "I saw you when you were born, my magic unveiled for the first time in decades. I've watched you ever since, fragments of your life shown to me by the stars, time whispering about your fate."

The child's speckled eyes stared at Seren, piercing through the hazy memory. Something had changed. An inky black now diluted her normal irises, replacing their hues of green and brown with dark shadows and flecks of white until eventually they held nothing but a star-encrusted night sky.

Seren gasped, and a ripple of warmth coursed through her veins, stealing her breath. "What's wrong with my eyes?"

Dragging her fingers through the smoke, Prue tightened the gray veil around them, and the hair on the back of Seren's neck rose.

"You still don't know who you are, and neither does the king. But that won't last for long. He'll figure it out soon, and when he does, he'll use you to win his war. You must discover the truth before he can use it against you."

Typically, Seren liked to hold her dignity above begging, but there were always exceptions. "Please, I still don't understand." Her voice cracked. "Why won't you answer my questions?"

Prue closed her eyes. Her high-pitched voice darkened until a more ancient one—scratchy and morose—crawled from her pale lips, her eyelids fluttering violently. "A star's light to end the fight; through trial and test, the kingdom is blessed. Your magic seeks the destruction of peace; through five tribulations, all is complete."

Seren's heart thudded wildly in her chest, and the scent of burned earth and ash assaulted her nose. "Answer me!" She threw her hands into the air, frustration flooding her veins. "Please, answer my questions."

Twisting her head to the side, Prue remained utterly silent.

"You don't know what you're talking about," Seren snapped. She'd had enough of the Seer's inscrutable riddles and annoying half-truths. If Prue couldn't give her the answers she needed, she refused to waste any more of her birthday by listening to nonsense. "I need to find my friend."

This time, she wouldn't take no for an answer.

Seren shoved at the haunting smoke that pressured her to stay, pushing and pulling until its murky fingers finally released her. Before she was completely out of its phantom grasp, the Seer spoke, slow and prophetic, once again in her harmonic pitch, smoke twirling around her lips. "Let what you do not understand guide you. The truth about you, daughter of the universe—"

Enough.

Writhing out of the magic's hold, Seren shook her arms and patted her clothing, casting specks of glittering dust and ash into the air. She squinted, the bright sun glistening off her warm skin, and darted her eyes between the empty space behind her and the alley ahead. Mare was still enamored with the beautiful seller, lost in time to her tantalizing charms. And the same Sollian couple Seren had seen leaving before Prue ambushed her waved their thanks to the vendor across the street.

For a moment, the world fell still.

Trapped with the Seer, receiving so much and yet so little colliding information—it felt like hours had passed, and yet, it appeared no time had passed at all.

As she faced the still-rising sun, the morning light casting warm shadows behind her, it dawned on her—the Seer had stopped time.

She added that to the list of weird things that had happened that day and shoved the thought from her mind, determined to enjoy the remnants of her birthday with her best friend. Running her hands through her disheveled hair, Seren walked, chin high, toward her friend, calling her name when she got close. "Mare, hey."

"Seren." Mare's head turned, her wavy hair cascading over her shoulder. "Get over here, will you."

By the time she approached, Mare held a gilded star ring in her palm, its band a dark opalescent.

"It's stunning." Seren breathed, lifting her gaze to the young female vendor, a short, sweet-faced girl with bright golden hair cuffed loosely around her chin. Her dazzling green eyes beamed radiantly against the warmth of her unblemished, tan skin and immediately, Seren understood Mare's attraction.

"It's perfect," Mare countered. "For you, especially, but she won't budge from five gold marks, even for your birthday."

"Five gold marks, you say?" Seren slid the thick banded ring over her finger; it was lighter than she'd expected. "Seems a bit high, don't you think?"

"It's worth more than that. Five gold marks is a deal, even for your special day," the girl rebuffed, her tone laced with sweetness despite her adamant haggles. Glancing to Mare, Seren stifled a giggle. Her friend flashed her best smile and soft doe eyes. Nothing worked. The girl was sweet, but certainly stubborn.

"Please," Mare implored, switching to a covertly alluring tone and blinking slowly. "Not even for me?" She clasped her hands together with an impish grin, punctuating the gesture with a wink.

"Sorry." The young girl swiftly shook her head, unable to hide her sheepish grin. "But no, a girl's got to live."

"You're sure?" Seren asked.

Again, the girl shook her head, resisting their vain attempts at bargaining.

"I'm sorry, Ser, I don't have enough." Mare's eyes fell.

Seren pulled the ring from her finger, handed it back to the kind vendor, and placed an assuring hand on her friend's shoulder. "It's okay, Mare. We'll find something else, I swear."

Seren looked at the seller and offered a polite hand. "Thank you for your time." She paused. "I didn't catch your name?"

"Imrie," she supplied, returning Seren's handshake. "It was nice to meet you, and happy birthday. I'm sorry I couldn't budge on the ring."

Seren simpered and shook her head gently. "Don't worry about it. We get it." She bumped shoulders with Mare. "Life's not easy, and everything has its price. Nothing wrong with setting yours."

Imrie's genial manner was contagious against the immunity of the girls' disappointment. The ring didn't matter, but maybe they could still make a new friend.

"Since I couldn't help with your present, can I offer a girls' night in the market square? My treat." Imrie beamed.

Mare blushed and Seren giggled. In their friendship, a "girls' night in the market square" was code for reckless debauchery in esoteric spots like The Shooting Star.

"Oh. Maybe some other time," Seren deflected, her mind blanking.

Shrugging, Imrie cut her off before it got too awkward. "I get it, some other time, then."

"Yes, please." Mare clasped her hands enthusiastically.

"Thank you again," Seren said, turning to lead Mare away.

Allowing Seren to pull her along, Mare smiled brightly and, last minute, lifted her head over her shoulder to add sweetly, "See you soon, Imrie."

"She was cute," Seren chided, wrapping her arm briefly around Mare's shoulders, squeezing lightly.

"I hope we see her again. You know, if we're ever up for another risky midnight at The Shooting Star." Seren agreed eagerly, but still, Mare's shoulders fell. "I'm sorry though, Ser, I wish I could've gotten you that ring. It would've paired perfectly with your mother's necklace."

Seren hummed, her voice not entirely her own. "It was beautiful, but it doesn't matter. Spending today here, with you"—she waved her arms briefly before grabbing Mare's hand and swinging their arms together—"is the best present I could've asked for."

Mare grinned, lopsided, and squeezed Seren's hand. Drawing her words out slowly, she said, "I still wish we'd gotten that ring. It was *so* perfect."

Seren's palm warmed, and a tingling sensation zipped through her arm. She dropped Mare's hand, prepared to ask her friend if she'd felt that, when a metallic *tink* stole their attention.

Kneeling, Seren plucked the golden star ring from the ground and faint heat buzzed at her fingertips.

Mare paled. "Is that…is that Imrie's ring?"

Twirling the metal band between her right thumb and pointer finger, Seren raised the ring to the light, examining its exquisite craftsmanship. "It's the same. Either that, or perfectly identical." Seren turned, presenting the ring to Mare.

"Seren, you—" Mare eyes widened. Blinking slowly, puzzled, her smile dimmed.

"How did—"

"How did that happen?" Mare interrupted. "Seriously, Seren, how did you do that?"

Seren put her hands up. "I didn't do anything."

"Well, neither did I," Mare retorted.

They stared at each other in silence.

Mare swore and kicked a small rock down the alley. "Did you steal Imrie's ring, Seren?"

"Really, Mare? Are you actually asking me that?" Mare stared at her blankly. "Come on, you know I would never do that. And I really liked Imrie." Seren's voice lifted rebelliously high.

"We should go."

Is she seriously mad at me right now? "Mare, hold on. You know I would never steal the ring. And seriously, I'm just as confused as you are."

Her friend lifted her chin. "You promise you have no idea how that ring appeared?"

"I swear." With a wink, Seren drew her finger in an X across her chest, then in a line down the center. "Cross my heart, may the king die."

Mare smirked.

That saying was the first inside joke they'd ever come up with, the same night Mare had vowed revenge against the Stellean king—an X for "cross my heart" and the last line to draw a star, marking the king's fate.

Sighing, Mare apologized. "I'm sorry I doubted you."

Seren simpered, examining the ring again. "I don't blame you."

"Any ideas how it happened then?"

Magic.

Nonsense. Shaking her head, Seren lifted her shoulders. "Not any good ones. You?"

Mare shook her head too, her expression long and confused.

"We should go," Seren said.

Together they glanced down the alley, and Seren stepped forward as if to leave.

"Ser, wait."

She glanced back sideways.

"I think we need to talk about something."

Seren's stomach dropped. Those were the last words anyone wanted to hear. She raised her brows, feigning composure. "What about?"

Mare blurted, "Do you have magic? I mean, that's crazy, right? Humans don't have magic, that's impossible." Her words fell out of her gaping mouth quicker than she could catch her breath, and her eyes bulged with uncertainty.

Seren wished for something good to say, anything to explain how the ring appeared, but she was just as lost. Mare wasn't the first to ask that question. But...

"No...I don't know. Maybe? But it's impossible, you know, I'm human. I—"

"What do you mean, you don't know?"

"I mean, I don't know." Seren's hands clenched, a strained grasp. "I have no way to explain the ring or any of the weird things that keep happening."

"What other things, Seren?"

"Where to begin?" She hesitated. "Okay, you know the dress? From Ardentiella? There was definitely something off about that whole thing—honestly that whole night, but that's beside the point. And my back, right? My scars? You've seen how bad they are. I should be laid up with a nurse for weeks, but they always heal—"

"Really fast." Mare finished for her.

"And the woman we met in the market, Rosella, did you notice how she reacted when I told her I was human?" Seren couldn't tell where Mare's head was. She added, "Almost like she didn't believe me?"

Mare picked at the dry skin on her lips and paced back and forth as she nodded, her eyes bouncing up and down, at each question Seren asked. She stilled long enough to ask, "Do you think we should go back and find the Seer? Maybe she could help."

Seren's mouth gaped. "About that..."

Mare lifted a brow, her lip curving.

"Well, the Seer, she found me, okay." Seren let her confession hang in the air between them while she scripted her next few words.

"Seriously, Seren? When? You were with me the entire day. So how did it happen without me knowing? And when were you going to tell me?"

Seren kicked a rock near her boot, emphasizing the silence between them. Mare was technically right. It was true. She *had* been with her friend the entire day, barring those odd minutes in time the Seer controlled—when she had stopped and started their lives, unbeknownst to everyone but the two of them. Chewing on the inside of her lip, Seren elaborated, "Prue found me in the alley before I met up with you and Imrie. I tried to call out for you...but you were distracted, and then the Seer, well, she stopped time, and you couldn't hear me. I know how I sound, but Mare—"

"What did she say?"

Mare handled that better than she'd expected. Seren stepped closer, leaning forward.

"She was mad. Insane actually, and I'm pretty sure she only knows how to speak in riddles and lies and that's why I haven't brought it up yet. I didn't see the point because I didn't even believe her myself."

"Seers can't lie, Seren." Mare's voice was soft, apologetic. "Their magic is bound by the truth."

Seren choked, her heart suspended from beating inside her tight chest. If what the Seer said was true, even partially true... She blurted, "The Seer said Hellevi is starting a war. Apparently, he wants to become the next High King of Clarallan, and if he finds out who I am"—Seren gritted out the last part, not convinced the Seer hadn't worked around her rules of truth—"he'll somehow use me to do it."

"What do you mean if he finds out who you are? You're one of his private servants. Don't you think he already knows?"

Frustrated, Seren groaned. "I have no idea what she meant, Mare. Or what any of this means."

Everything had made so much more sense before the day's events had transpired.

But if the Seer was telling the truth?

Seren shuddered.

They were in danger—the entire kingdom of Clarallan was.

Silently, Mare wrapped her strong arms around Seren and pulled her close.

Seren returned the gesture, her hands lost in the endless knots of Mare's long hair. Latching onto the few strands of logic Seren managed to follow in her mind, she compiled a plan. Without breaking their hug, she eased her head away and said, "I have an idea. But I'm not sure you're going to like it."

Mare winked. "I will if it's a bad one."

CHAPTER 9

Later that evening, Mare waited for Seren at the end of King Hellevi's chambers, down the lavishly decorated gold corridor, a few doors away from his private study.

Seren appeared around the corner.

"It's clear. The guards sweep the halls every ten minutes." She inhaled quietly, catching her breath. "But no one ever goes into the study."

"When I said I'd like a bad plan, this isn't what I had in mind." Mare furrowed her brows, her eyes scanning the empty hallway with cool determination.

"It's not *that* bad, come on."

"Yes. It is," Mare said pointedly, not caring to hide the frustration in her tone. "Your plan is to sneak into the king's study, alone, and I'm supposed to, what? Wait here?" Mare glowered, telling Seren exactly how little she trusted her aleatory plan. And to be fair, Seren hadn't exactly worked out all the details. She just knew she had to do something, and quick. Before she either lost the courage or her scheming was exposed to Hellevi.

Seren shook her head, eyes wide. "I need you to watch for

Hellevi. If you see him coming before I get out, distract him. I'll listen for you. Just keep him busy until I know if I need to hide or run."

"This is foolish, Seren. What are you even hoping to find?"

Anything that proved whether the Seer was telling the full truth—maybe something incriminating regarding Hellevi's war plans.

Seren shrugged. "I'll know when I see it."

Mare rolled her eyes, looking back to the study. "Ready?"

Seren flitted across the hall. With gentle hands, she pressed against the heavy door, opening it slowly. Soft light escaped, cast by hazy yellow sunbeams illuminating the study, which stirred velvety shadows across the dark navy walls and slipped delicately over the tall shelves brimming with books.

Stepping inside, the door closed softly behind her. The stiff air—walking through it felt like wading through warm water—overwhelmed her with scents of aged, yellow pages and mahogany wood. Seren glanced around the room. The back wall, made almost entirely of impenetrable glass windows, reached from the patterned-rug floors to the high ceiling, looming behind an antique wooden desk. The sturdy desk dominated the center of the room, its surface cluttered with papers, letters, and maps, fresh charcoals, and half-empty bottles of ink. A dried circular stain from the repeated placement of a cool whiskey glass punctuated its use.

The noiseless study was so quiet, Seren imagined she could hear the erratic rhythm of her own fussy heartbeat. It was a problem for later, but if Hellevi showed up, there was no way she'd be able to hear Mare.

Seren stepped around the leather chair, cracked and worn, a silent witness to the study's kept secrets. She groused at the messy surface. She had no idea how Hellevi managed to find anything in the clutter—it would take hours to even sort. Whatever she touched, Seren was careful to leave exactly how she had found it. Hellevi was no fool; he'd notice even the smallest detail out of place—despite the mess.

Every word she read felt like a waste of time. Militant budget this, new weapon order that. But absolutely nothing that even hinted at a potential war.

Either the Seer was wrong, or Hellevi was already too many steps ahead.

Seren surveyed the rest of the room; besides the desk and three chairs, the study comprised a few mammoth bookshelves and an elegant wooden armoire, possessing few places to conceal much of anything, let alone something important.

She approached the bookcase. The lower shelves were of little interest to her, but balancing on her tiptoes, Seren scanned the ones above eye level. On the tallest shelf, dust lined the wood in front of each book, barring one thick spine. Twisting her head to the side, she tried and failed to read the title, written in an old Fae language she had yet to learn. She placed her left palm against the sturdy frame of the case and stretched her right hand above her head, reaching to pluck the strange book from the top shelf.

Tick, tick. Seren froze, her fingers barely gracing the worn spine before the clicking of metal drummed in her ears, and panic flooded her veins.

A few seconds and the door would open.

She would be seen, caught, and certainly punished.

Her eyes roamed the room. The tall windows were sealed shut, and the only way in or out was the door—the one about to open.

Three.

There was nowhere to run. *Hiding it is, then.*

Two.

There. The armoire—her only chance.

One.

Seren's heart raced as she leaped across the study, opened the armoire's rickety wooden doors, and eased her body inside. Carefully adjusting her back against the massive amounts of hanging weapons, she sealed the doors shut in front of her.

Stiff darkness surrounded her body, and Seren willed it to still, her ragged breathing to quiet. The only source of light was the bright wisps of daylight slipping through the thin crack between the armoire doors that she used to peer out.

Footsteps echoed in the study, two distinct pairs.

"My apologies for the interruption. The servants, they sometimes forget their place," Hellevi griped, annoyed, taking a seat at his desk while gesturing to his guest to sit. Seren smirked, lopsided. Mare had done what she'd promised and bought Seren enough time to hide; without her, she would have been caught.

Hellevi's guest huffed a low chuckle. "It's not an issue, but I believe we have important matters to discuss."

"Yes, yes, I know. We got cut short at Ardentiella."

Who is he talking to?

Curious, Seren strained her neck and pressed her ear against the front of the armoire, careful not to put too much weight on the doors. If they fell open...

Hellevi's guest kept his back to the armoire, casually taking a seat across from the king. "Well, like I said before, I wish for a change in Clarallan, and I believe you're one of the few who share the same wish."

"And what is this change you have in mind?" Hellevi feigned intrigue, a hint of stiff boredom carrying his deceit.

"I've heard rumors." The second male paused, weighing his quiet words before the king. "That a war is coming."

"And what is it you'd like me to say about this supposed war?" Typical Hellevi, the type to never show his hand without knowing his opponent's first.

"That I can join you." Seren stifled an alarmed gasp as the visitor's voice grew louder—clear and recognizable as he continued, "Create an alliance as you may and offer the full forces of the Lunaan court in your parliamentary pursuits."

Seren heard the prince's words, studied them, processed them even, and still could not believe her ears. To know Evander wished for an alliance with the cruel king was one thing. To believe that anyone could truly want that was impossible.

Uneasiness settled over her shoulders, her stomach roiling in remembrance of Evander's perverse request at Ardentiella. Desperately, Seren had attempted to rationalize his depraved desire in favor of the charming prince, but now, every word was added fuel to the fire of her distrust.

Hellevi yawned. "Evander, as much as I appreciate the enthusiasm, really, what is it that a prince can offer me? What power do you hold? What do you have that I can't take for myself? Unrivaled, I'm Clarallan's greatest ruler"—he snorted—"and you, you're not even a king."

That was all the confirmation Seren needed.

Though Hellevi didn't state his participation, he certainly didn't deny it, and even implied the war's existence.

Evander trailed his finger over the arm of the leather chair. "Ah yes. That pesky little problem is what I tried to discuss at Ardentiella. I wish to join your side, to offer any assistance, but to do so I need to be king." Evander dismissed Hellevi's concerns with a bemused chuckle, flawlessly mirroring the coldness of the king's cruel tone.

"Evander," Hellevi mocked, pretending inflated horror. "You know there's nothing I can do to make you king, right, boy?"

Seren didn't need to see the prince's face to know he sneered a loathsome, vile grin as he spoke. "But isn't there? My dear father, ill as he is, is still alive. And all that exists between me and the crown is one vexing little life." Evander shook his head. "Now, has that ever been a problem for a king like you?"

Hellevi scoffed, unamused by the young male's conniving ploy. "And what of your feckless brother? The golden prince that dear dad wished to one day inherit the Lunaan crown? I can't afford to bear the weight of your disappointing familial affairs on top of taking a chance on you."

Evander vibrated with rage—envious and overwhelming. Seren swore even the blades behind her rattled from the force of his ire. Hellevi had certainly discovered a sore spot in the prince's otherwise meticulous defense.

"I can handle my brother," Evander spat, more hesitant than he'd likely intended. "But you must not worry about Casimir. He's made it *very* clear he has no interest in our father's title."

"And still you wish for me to handle your father when you could simply—wait?" Hellevi tapped his fingers. "If he has no interest, your plan sure involves an awful lot of unnecessary risk."

Seren's eyes widened. *Handle King Egil how, exactly?*

"Anything worth anything involves a little risk," Evander mused. "But no risk—no reward. Besides, Casimir won't be a problem. All I'm asking for is a little help with my father, but apparently, I thought too highly of you."

"What's that supposed to mean?"

A shrug. "I guess I imagined my father would pose no threat to a king like you, unlike myself. I thought I asked a favor not difficult enough to warrant any risk to you. But if I was wrong…"

Seren's stomach twisted in knots. What Evander implied…

Hellevi boasted, "Why risk anything when you already have everything you need? And besides," Hellevi said dismissively, "you're young, ambitious. Bloodthirsty, even, and I respect that about you, but I don't *need* you."

A tense silence—the room became unbearably warm.

Seren leaned her head against the back of the armoire, carefully fanning her face with her hand as nausea roiled in her gut. Inhaling slowly, she leaned forward again.

Evander asked, "How can I change your mind? There must be something you need, something you want?"

Hellevi scoffed, stretching over the arm of his chair to slide open the bottom left drawer of his desk. Leaning back in his seat, he lifted an almost empty bottle of dark liquor and poured himself a generous drink without an offer to the prince.

His eyes on the glass, he swirled the noisome liquid, slowly contemplating. Abruptly, he met Evander's gaze with a smirk. Then promptly drained the entire drink, slamming the glass on the desk.

"Alright, son, I'll cut you a deal. In one week, you bring me something, anything really, to prove you can be an asset to my court. Then, and only then, will I consider helping you. And, please, make it interesting. Consider boring me akin to treason—sure, you *can* do it, but it'll never end well for you."

A shudder.

The king's words were his deadliest of weapons.

The prince quietly clapped his palms together and dipped his chin. "Thank you, sir. I won't let you regret it." Evander stood, dusted the ends of his silver suit coat, and offered the king a respectful hand.

"I know." Hellevi lifted his chin. "But it's good for me, even if you do."

A promise.

Evander walked to the door, shoulder blades drawn together. Pausing halfway into the hall, he insisted once more, "You won't regret it, sir."

Seren's blood chilled, raising the hair on her arms. She wouldn't dare let herself imagine whatever plan thrilled the vile prince. Glancing at Hellevi, she silenced a groan—the king refilled his glass with another long pour, finishing the healthy bottle.

Time to get comfortable.

Leaning back against the armoire, Seren cursed, a sharp prick of a blade nicking the nape of her neck. She flinched, an innate, rebellious reaction that cost her.

The blade thudded loudly against the thick wood, echoing the sound of Seren's heart as it beat fiercely in her chest.

"Who'ss there?" Hellevi slurred.

Out—there was no way out.

Regret poured down her throat. Why did she ever think this was a good idea?

She held her breath and forced herself to look through the thin crack. Hellevi rose, his palms placed threateningly on his desk.

"Come out," he demanded. "I know ssomeone'ss in here."

Seren squeezed her eyes shut, cursing her reckless tendencies.

Prue's words rang through her head, and a frisson of fear coursed her veins... *He's going to kill me.*

She didn't want to die.

But when he found her...

She was no stranger to his carnage. At his hands—it was enough to make anyone wish for death.

But even that was a kindness too sweet for Hellevi to grant her.

The king marched drunkenly toward the armoire, slurring and elongating the ends of his words. "Now, now, who'ss there? Who'sss foolissh enough to spy on their king?"

No, no, no.

Squeezing her eyes shut, Seren made sympathies with the universe, begging Clarallan—her life in exchange for anything.

She wanted to live.

Would do anything to live.

Painfully bright light stripped the armoire of shadows, exposing Seren in all her horror. Hellevi stumbled backward, his drunk strength overpowering his balance.

The door. She had to get out.

Seren jumped up, her stiff limbs numb as she leaped from her crouched position toward her only escape, refusing to look back.

Hellevi reached out an open hand as she dashed past him, clenched his fist and hauled her backward, his Fae strength amplified in his inebriated state. The roots of her hair cried in agony.

He wrapped rough hands around her neck, and she yelped, tears welling in her eyes. His grip tightened and pain erupted behind her eyelids.

The king's breath—uncomfortably warm and heavy with liquor—sent a chill down her spine. "Oh, Sseren, *gotcha*."

He used two hands—her vision went dark around the edges, her chest slammed into the ground as Hellevi shoved her to the floor. Seething, his golden eyes lined with red, he stomped a booted foot hard on her chest. Clawing at his leg with shaky hands, breathless, she gasped.

Hellevi backed away, removing the pressure from her airway. "Why were you hiding?"

Seren gaped, sucking in barely enough air to spit out, "I know what you're planning."

"Obviously." He stumbled. "So…what should I do about that?"

He was wasted.

She could take him.

Pressing herself from the floor, Seren glared, resisting the urge to rub her neck. She swallowed, her throat like sand, but she remained silent, determined.

"Have I ever told you how much you look like your mother?" He chuckled, swaying.

Unrecognizable rage flared within her and deepened her scowl, provoking him further, the sickening sound of his laughter igniting something in her core.

"I hate you."

He slapped a hand across his chest, his bemused laughter

deepening. "You sound like her too. But Sseren," he stuttered, "you're worse than even her."

Hellevi—Seren's nightmare in physical form. Everything he'd done to her. Her chest tightened, her trauma rooted deeply inside her.

She charged.

She hated him, she hated him, she hated him—

Hellevi raised his fist, coiling his Fae strength.

She could take it.

He struck. Starlight exploded inches in front of her eyes, magic braced firmly against Hellevi's fists.

Her blood heated remembering all the times he'd hurt her.

"How?" he panted.

Magic filled the air, thick with sweet hints of citrus that smothered her senses.

Reeling his fist back, Hellevi lunged again, aiming for her head.

His fists cracked against the same blinding light that shielded her. Magic snapped across her skin. Grabbing for her neck, he hissed, and then stumbled as he recoiled from the burning light.

A sickening wish blazed through her thoughts, a morose cerebral comet.

She didn't know *how*, but she could get her wish.

Memories of her lashes blurred her vision; her scars, her pain. The king choked. He grasped at his back, falling to his knees. Nothing—no—everything but this magic protecting her made sense.

This feeling.

This power.

No.

Her heart pleaded with the conscience that shaped her soul, showed her where her morality was written in the lines of her ribs.

Out—she needed out.

She had to stop.

Metal clanged outside the hallway. Guards shouted, thundering toward the study.

Run.

Her limbs tingled with the quality of a dream. Seren demanded her body to move. Begged her mind to focus.

She had no control. Her feet ran without her telling where to go, her breath in rhythm with the rapid beat of her heart. Comforting light whirled around her, urging her on.

Hellevi yelled, his garbled words a distant echo cutting through the fog of her mind, "I will kill you, Seren."

CHAPTER 10

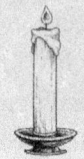

Seren ran into the night.
    Her only focus: putting as much distance between herself and the Stellean castle as possible.

She approached a busy road and slowed, hiding in the shadows far from the revelrous Fae enjoying a night out in the court market. Bright moonlight illuminated her path between the lively bars and brewhouses overflowing with Fae from all courts —eating and drinking, laughing and cheering. All too distracted by their fun to notice as Seren passed through, unseen and unbothered.

All utterly oblivious to what was to come.

A blessing. Seren walked, invisible beneath the cloak of their ignorance. Weaving through the gracious crowds, she slipped behind the farthest bar. Her eyes skimmed the bar's lopsided sign as she approached a humble set of oak stairs.

Exhaustion pressured her to sit, and she settled her aching limbs against the damp wood, following its command. She closed her eyes, rested her forehead against her knees, and wrapped her arms around her chilled body.

What a mess.

Only a few hours remained of her birthday, and Seren had used the entire day—her one day off a year—to create more problems than she'd ever had her entire life.

She tugged at her sweaty dress, clenching the wrecked material in her fists. Sighing, Seren remembered the smile on Mare's face when she'd given it to her as a present for her eighteenth birthday. A stunning midi dress that cuffed around her calves. Its simple pastel fabric a complement to a warm spring day, with wispy hems of orange and peach. Guilt gnawed at her hoarse throat, and she pawed at her sorrowful tears, her heart lurching at the thought of Mare—and how she had left her alone in the Stellean castle.

Seren had to go back.

Hellevi's last words clamored in her mind, shocking her heart into flight. She couldn't. Already the king would have instructed his guards to search for her. There was no way she could sneak in undetected.

Returning was a death sentence.

During her escape, Seren hadn't seen Mare, but there hadn't been time to stop. She prayed her friend had fled the halls before the guards stormed in. If she was smart, she'd drop it and keep her head down. Seren's heart ached—she knew her friend too well, loyal beyond fault.

She'd never made a decision like this before.

The unbearable weight of her guilt—quite foul company.

Thud, thud. The bar's back door slammed open. Seren scrambled forward, scraping her palms against the jagged gravel. Regaining her balance, her face inches above the hard ground, Seren lurched, then whirled as three intoxicated Fae males barreled toward her. Their sultry laughter tainted the brisk air.

She scowled. The tallest, a broad, buzzed-headed male, stumbled through the door. He clapped a rough hand on his friend's shoulder, bragging boisterously of his evening plans. Earning a playful jab to the side from his friend—a shorter, blond male who reeked of wealth and entitlement, his pristine suit accented by a surplus of gold bangles. Seren's favorite type of male—to cut—due to their perturbing expressions and disgusting disregard for boundaries.

A third Fae staggered forward, rounder than the rest. His intimidating stature towered behind his friends. All three permeated the air with their sour sweat, the bitter smell of aged whiskey pouring from their lips as they howled with laughter.

Clearing her throat, Seren stood her ground. The tallest male, his pale autumn eyes reflective against the dark night, noticed her then and, shoving through his friends, stalked closer. Peering down, he brought his face disturbingly close. His rancid breath smothered her senses, and his clumsy hands made for her hair. "Well, boysss, what do we have here?" he taunted, sloshing his slippery, liquor-laced words,

"Don't." Seren knocked his hand away. The fatality of her tone surprising even herself. Without thinking, she brushed her fingertips over the hilt of her dagger, its enticing zeal teasing her through the thin dress.

"Oh, come on now, little lady, no need to ruin the fun night we're having." The male gestured at the others for support with a ragged crack of laughter. "Why don't you help show us a good time?"

"Why don't you all screw off?" she spat.

"Ooh, she's got a mouth on her." The shorter male snickered, elbowing his friend. "Just your type."

"What else can—"

"Ask me what else it can do, and I'll cut out your tongue."

His friends howled, but the seething male refused to laugh. Violence and lust circled his golden eyes, a wicked grin pulling at his face.

Seren pivoted and took two steps, determined to flee. "How about you find your fun elsewhere…and if you're struggling for something to do, might I recommend you go fuck yourself."

Infuriated, the male lunged.

His beastly hands clawed at her waist. Catching her arms, he hauled her backward and slammed her body into his stern chest, pinning her against him. His powerful hold—an impenetrable defense, regardless of how hard she writhed or kicked.

Seren whipped her head back and glared. Almost spat in his face so he would have a reason to wipe away that foul expression. Then she thought better of it, dread stirring in her gut.

A silver blade gleamed against the male's throat, inches before her eyes.

"I would do as the lady says," a voice as dark as the night purred. "That is, if you want to live."

An imposing figure loomed behind the wasted monster that held her. Pure predatory power electrified the air. Seren choked on the magic the figure exuded with every word as he pressed the knife into the male's bobbing throat.

She struggled against her attacker, straining her neck to see the stranger, but he kept his face hidden beneath the moon's velvety shadows, darkness distorting his sharp features. Seren felt the male's panicked heartbeat through his desperate palms. She kicked upward, connecting with a sensitive area, and he released her. A high-pitched shout escaped his lips, and with greedy hands, he shot forward. Interrupted, the figure behind him dug his blade deeper, drawing droplets of blood from the Fae male's neck. His friends stilled, wide-eyed, their movements arrested by fear.

Seren jumped free of the grimy male's reach, reeling to face him.

"You have five seconds to be out of my sight. Make it quick," the stranger scolded, a guttural command.

Her knees buckled.

He began to count. "Five…"

Recognition flared. The bitter taste of fear drenched her tongue.

The males behind her gulped.

Did I simply trade three monsters for one who is much, much worse?

Cursing her bad luck, she froze. Her stomach dropped, her balance swept away.

"Four…" He stepped forward.

The two males behind her disappeared in seconds. Seren smirked, imagining their tails tucked between their legs as they ran.

She got it now—how one male struck such fear into the hearts of her attackers.

Lifting his brows, amused, he pressed his blade even deeper into the first one's neck. "Three seconds before I let her carve you up herself."

Seren watched him draw the serrated edge along the column of the male's throat, leaving a trail of blood as he went.

"Two…"

Seren gulped. The male jerked, shoving away from her bloodthirsty savior, and disappeared into the murky night before the Lunaan prince could say "one."

Lowering his blade, Casimir's silver-blue eyes gleamed against his starving expression. His tongue flicked across his full lips, his predatory gaze locked on his lucky victim. For now, he would let him live.

Turning to leave, the prince said nothing to Seren.

She blinked, dazed.

Does he seriously think he can sweep in, rob me of the fun of dicing those males myself, and leave without a word?

She sprinted, catching up to Casimir as he neared the end of the alley, and blurted, "Not even going to ask if I'm okay?"

Obviously she was fine, but he didn't know that.

"That's a horrible way to say thank you." The prince kept walking, his voice gravelly as he turned his face away.

"How was I supposed to say thank you when you left?" Seren looked back to where the males had attacked her, unsure why she was speaking so boldly to the terrifying male who maybe just saved her life.

"I have no need for your gratitude. But you, you need to leave. Now."

Seren's pace faltered behind him, the events of her day slamming into her mind.

"I...I have nowhere to go." She couldn't believe she'd admitted that to him—a stranger. At least it got his attention for a while longer.

The male halted, the streetlights dancing across his tightly drawn back. Black hair fell across his face as he turned, and Seren noticed the endless tattoos inked across his muscular chest, the rest of his skin hidden beneath an all-black outfit. He lifted his gaze.

She knew the prince was beautiful. But seeing him up close...

He was gorgeous, his prominent features highlighted by the harshness in his eyes, stunning in the way one would appreciate the cruel beauty of a broken statue.

Seren knew she was staring, and honestly, she wouldn't have been surprised if she was drooling too. She shook her head and swallowed. "Can you—"

Casimir cut her off, a dark tone in his words. "I can't help you. Find someone else, anyone really."

She took a step. The male tracked her every move, her every breath. She didn't understand how she could be so afraid and captivated at the same time. Her eyes slid down the lines of his tattoos once more, her attention snagging on the inked phases of the moon crowning his chest.

She glanced up to meet his gaze again. Her breath caught as she became aware of the male staring at her, as she stared at him.

"Like what you see?" he taunted, his voice a sensual whisper.

Unable to find her words, she wished she had something clever to say, wished she could do anything besides stare at the unnerving male before her.

"I-I—" she stammered. *Seriously?* That was all she could manage? Seren scolded herself for letting a beautiful face get her so out of whack.

"I?" He raised his brows, curving his lips into a lethal smirk. "I, what?"

Gods. He definitely knew he was getting to her.

"I have to leave." Her words felt rushed. She forced herself to turn around, painfully dragging her gaze from the prince.

"I thought you had nowhere to go?"

"I'll figure it out," she spoke over her shoulder. Determined to not make a fool of herself again.

"I have no doubt that you will."

Seren couldn't help herself. She halted, turned once more, and asked, "What were you doing here tonight?"

"I could ask you the same thing." His eyes searched hers. No doubt noting her rugged look after the day she'd been through. But his expression held no judgment, his gaze merely amused. She didn't tell him the reason she was out that night involved his brother. When she didn't respond, Casimir continued, gesturing at the space between them with a smirk. "See, you and I? We're nothing but strangers. And I don't make a habit of telling strangers the likes of my personal business."

"But don't you have, like, I don't know, princely things to be doing?"

The prince mocked, "And what is more princely than saving a damsel in distress?"

"I am not—"

"Am not, what? A damsel? Or in distress? Because from where I stood, you were both."

"I had it covered." Seren wanted to shout.

"Did you?" the prince continued officiously. "How so? Because from what I saw, you were about to be the victim of whatever nasty plan those odious males came up with. You're lucky I stepped in. Don't make me regret it now."

Without thinking, Seren wrapped her dagger in her hands and pressed it against the prince's throat, donning a smirk that matched his. She whispered into his ear, "Like that."

Her satisfaction cost her the win. In seconds, Casimir pinned Seren in front of him, her own knife pressed against the base of her neck. "Nice try." He tapped the hilt of the blade. "But it'll take more than that to best a prince."

Asshole.

"That was not a very princely thing to do," Seren murmured, earning her a slight prick of the blade against her skin. Her heart pounded relentlessly, so loud she was certain the Fae prince could hear it.

"If you haven't realized yet, I'm not a very good prince."

Seren slipped from his grasp and faced him. He twirled her dagger between his fingers, his eyes daring her.

She reached out her palm. "Can I have that back now?"

"I could keep it. Say, the price of saving your life." His grin was devilish, sinful and beautiful. He danced the blade between his palms, his eyes never leaving hers. "Or, you could at least say 'please.' Or how about, 'please, Prince Casimir'?"

It was a conscious effort to stop her eyes from rolling right out of her head. "I'm not the begging type."

"I bet I know a few ways to make you—"

"Finish that sentence and you'll regret it." Her threat only made the prince's eyes burn darker. The wicked male enjoyed her violence.

"Those males were right about one thing. You do have a

mouth on you." *And I like it,* his expression said silently. He prowled closer and her nerves begged to retreat. But she held her ground, and eventually, the prince extended her dagger.

Seren bristled at his arrogance, her hands greedily wrapping around the weapon. She had half a mind to stab him with it as she turned from the infuriating prince. She should have walked away earlier. "Thanks again for your help. I guess."

"I'll see you again, Seren." He laughed under his breath.

Her head spun. *How does he know who I am?* She turned back, her eyes gracing the empty place where the prince had stood.

Nothing but cold night air existed before her, the alley left dark without the Prince of the Moon to light the tragic sky.

CHAPTER 11

By the time Seren approached the familiar shop front, the rising sun warmed the Clarallan market. It had taken hours to find it in the dark. The break of dawn was the only reason she had managed to find the shop again. She braced her knuckles to knock, but the door swung inward before Seren gathered the courage. Rosella's affectionate smile beamed her greeting, and she ushered Seren inside without questions.

Leading Seren up a swirling staircase, Rosella welcomed her to her home directly above the shop.

It was peaceful despite the clutter. Tidy nests of leather journals and aged books sat stacked at various heights along the walls. Rosella drank from her cup of steaming tea and gestured to her to take a seat in the living room. Seren eased into the worn plum couch facing away from the open window, warm morning light caressing her back as the songs of waking birds filled the quaint room.

Rosella hummed gently, handed Seren a hot mug, and sat in a rickety wooden chair across the green rug. The woman had yet to ask her why she was there, or if she had noticed, why she was wearing the same clothes as the day before. They sat in silence, long enough for Seren to finish her drink, its spiced contents warming her from the inside out.

"I don't know if I should be happy or worried about seeing you again so soon," Rosella mused. The woman's words were gentle, but her gaze lingered on Seren's day-old dress, torn from her fight with the king. Seren slid her hands over the soiled fabric, embarrassment preventing her from meeting Rosella's concerned eyes.

"I'm sorry to have bothered you again so early." Seren chewed on her bottom lip.

"It isn't a bother. I enjoy sharing my morning tea, remember?"

Seren didn't deserve the kindness the gracious woman extended. It had been risky to even come, especially if Hellevi ordered his guards to search the market. Her heart dropped at the thought of the danger she was putting Rosella in.

As if sensing Seren's worry, Rosella smiled, washing away her negative thoughts with a subtle change in conversation. "What brings you here, dear?"

"I ran away. From Stellean, I guess." Seren didn't dare mention her fight with the king. The poor woman was already harboring a castaway. She didn't want to frighten her more by explaining she was a reckless one at that.

"I see."

"I came here because I don't know what to do or where to go." It was a stupid idea. Seren pressed up from the couch, ready to walk out. "I'm sorry—"

Rosella didn't let her finish. "Sit, my child."

Seren flicked her eyes between the couch and the door. She had nowhere to go, but it didn't feel fair to ask the woman for help, and she didn't want to be a bother. Losing her internal debate, she sat, propping her arms on her knees as her face fell into her hands.

"Did the Seer find you?" Surprise drew Seren's gaze to Rosella. She nodded, thankful for the change in conversation. "And what did you learn?"

Nothing. In the past day, she'd found only questions, not answers. She wasn't sure she knew anything at all. Everything the Seer said spun in her mind—the war, magic, her memories, her fate. She scoffed at the last part. It was still impossible.

"Can Seers lie?" Was all she could ask.

Rosella's expression was inquisitive, her brows high. She shook her head back and forth. "Seers are bound by the truth, whatever that may be."

Great. Seren hadn't wanted to believe Mare when she said the same thing. But she didn't think her friend, or even Rosella, had any reason to deceive her. Not when they didn't even know what the Seer had told her.

"How do I find her again?" Seren hated herself for asking, but she had to know the truth.

"The Seer finds all who need her."

"You sound just like her, riddles for answers."

Rosella chuckled. "I take that as a compliment. The Seer is wise, a being of time and knowledge. She'll find you if she believes you're ready to listen."

That could be a problem. Seren still wasn't convinced she trusted the Seer or believed any of her madness. *Right*, she mocked herself—truth not madness. She would have to work on that if she wanted Prue to believe she was ready to listen. And she was. She needed the truth.

"The Seer won't find you in this house. It's enchanted against magic like hers, but you are welcome to stay for as long as you wish. But if you wish to stay, you must change"—Rosella smiled—"and shower while you're at it."

Her attempt at humor forced Seren to chuckle. It wasn't a joke, though. She knew she looked a mess. She crinkled her nose. "A shower sounds great."

Rosella led her down a hall, past a thin closet, where she grabbed a plush towel, and pointed to a bathing room. "You can shower in there. I'll leave a change of clothes outside the door when you're done."

"Thank you." Seren smiled, closing the door after Rosella walked back to the living room.

Staring at her reflection, she saw her fears outside her body. Purple shadows rounded under her eyes, and her dress was as shredded as she felt. She slipped the once-beautiful gift off her shoulders and it cascaded to the floor, cold air biting at her pink skin. She turned the water on and waited until the room filled with steam.

Her chill was immune to the scalding water as she stood beneath the pressure, her eyes closed for what felt like hours. She rinsed soap through her tangled hair and opened her eyes, watching as the water speeding down her body turned a pale red and circled into the drain. The king's last words burned her memory, numbing her senses.

She hadn't thought about what had happened—the insanity of it all.

Hellevi. The war. The magic…

It had saved her.

She didn't care how long she spent in the bathroom, but she knew she couldn't make sense of everything in one day. Her skin glowed red by the time she emerged from the steam. She cracked the bathroom door open and saw a fresh pair of clothes from Rosella. Seren grabbed them, and the smell of rich teas and herbs swelled from the fabric as she dressed. They fit well despite the size difference between the two of them, and she wondered if Rosella and her husband had any children, maybe a daughter the clothes belonged to. But it was possible she'd just helped other young women in the past.

Walking down the hall, Seren saw nothing that hinted anyone

lived there besides the kind woman, nothing but memories of her life before her husband passed.

The living room was quieter than before—no hum of Rosella or brewing tea. Seren supposed she could have gone downstairs to open the shop, but it was odd she hadn't said anything. Vibrant blue skies outside the opened window welcomed a warm spring day, brightening the comfortable home. The streets below were empty, none of the usual shop vendors haggling a deal with bargaining customers, the shutters were all drawn, and even the stray animals lay sullen behind the humble buildings.

Dread held her hand as she walked in front of the windowpane, the room too small, her palms sweaty as she angled her head to get a better view of the street leading to the Stellean castle.

Tens of soldiers advanced from the far end of the street. Their metal armor clanged a deafening call for violence amidst the desolate market. Seren ducked behind the maroon curtains.

Where was Rosella?

Clearing the upstairs, Seren swallowed, forcing her panic down, and found her dagger. She crept close to the spiraling staircase. Each step was an audible crack as she descended, begging her to stop, to turn around, to hide or run.

Splinters of daylight fluttered across the dark shop. Rosella must have come down to close the blinds and lock the doors.

"Rosella?" she whispered.

She wove through every tall shelf, checked below every cluttered table and behind any closed doors. Her search was fruitless.

Rosella was nowhere to be found.

Seren tried calling out the woman's name again and again, but the only response came from clanking swords as soldiers swarmed the streets close by. Seren stilled. Soldiers banged on doors, demanding owners come out and give information on a missing servant.

It wouldn't be long before they beat on Rosella's weary door.
There was nowhere else to look.
Nothing else to do but run.

Sneaking past the shuttered windows, Seren tried to gauge how far away the soldiers were, but it was impossible to get a good view without giving herself up. She crawled in the shadows behind the door, then stood on her toes to see if there was a peephole.

Nothing.

A pinned note caught her attention, folded over itself where it hung above the handle. Likely a reminder Rosella wrote about something she needed to do or remember.

Seren grabbed it anyway.

Run… I will buy you some time.

The scribbled words disappeared as Seren read them, a spell placed on them to prevent anyone from ever knowing they were written.

The paper shook in Seren's tight grasp.

She couldn't believe how quickly her life had fallen apart.

The shop door rattled, jarring her from her stupor.

Seren stumbled back, her every instinct demanding that she flee.

The soldiers knocked harder, calling for the shop owners to open or else they would enter themselves.

"Can I help you?" Seren's heart choked at the sound of Rosella's familiar voice. She spoke again. "I know nothing of the girl. My shop has been closed all morning." A pause. A rustle of bags. "Errands."

"No matter, we need to check your shop. The girl could have stowed away while you were out." The soldier's voice was still, almost bored. Goosebumps rose on her skin at the male's callousness.

Why am I still standing here?

Waiting for the soldiers to barge in despite Rosella's refusals would only get them both killed. She didn't want to leave without saying goodbye…

But Seren knew the best way to repay the woman who had saved her life was to return the favor.

The soldiers could never know she was there.

CHAPTER 12

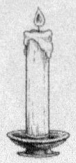

For the second time in twenty-four hours, Seren ran for her life.

Exposed in the barren market and without the shadows of night to conceal her, she had to be quicker, more alert.

She raced toward the forest—her only chance.

She had trained for this. Yet despite her effortless lungs, pain welled in her chest, her guilty heart inflicting the worst of it. Seren owed Rosella a hundred thank-yous, and she prayed one day she would get the chance to give them.

But she had to survive to do that.

Even if she wasn't sure she'd live where she was going.

She didn't have a choice. She couldn't risk being on the roads, too many traveling traders between the courts. Her mind rallied. She ran faster, vanishing beneath the ancient trees of the Galaxius Forest—Clarallan's sacred woods.

The sound of her boots smacked against the eerie quiet as the darkness took interest in her. Shadows bit at her heels, and the trees leaned in. No one traveled through these woods willingly—home to the kingdom's most primitive monsters, which even the

Fae feared. She was as much prey inside as she was out, but at least these predators were acting on instinct if they attacked. Hellevi was not as pure. Anything that happened in Galaxius would be far more humane than with him.

She pressed on.

If twenty years had taught her one thing, she never gave up when things got hard, because things had pretty much always been hard.

The air was damp beneath the stygian shade of the forest and thick with magic—a heavy scent of rotting fruit. She wove between the trees, ancient blackwoods that soared hundreds of feet above her, eclipsing the sun. Leaping over the uneven ground, Seren followed what little light penetrated the canopy.

The colors of Galaxius presented themselves like a mirage, dark hues of green and brown blurring as she ran. As she waded through the shadows, thick magic dampened her skin, and the wind picked up, forcing a gust of leaves to swirl in front of her.

Whispers echoed in the darkness—from who or what, Seren didn't want to find out.

The magic in Galaxius was lawless; its essence and the monsters who called it home drew their magic from the entire universe, ungoverned by the magical rules that protected Clarallan's kingdom. For centuries, the creatures had been trapped inside the forest, bound to the darkness by the gods. The Fae had their stories, legends of what lived and ruled the woods, but most myths remained unproven.

Because those that went in rarely came out.

Low brush ripped at her ankles, and her new clothes were torn and sweaty. Seren slowed to a walk. A bright stream curved ahead, its opalescent water shimmering as it caught the faint streaks of sun. Its motion was unnatural, flowing with the quality of a brush stroke, like an oil painting rather than a real current.

Seren sank to the muddy ground, moss clinging to her skin. The tall branches above stitched together, leaning in to study their unexpected visitor. A cage, not to keep the monsters away, but to trap her for them instead.

Her muscles lured her to rest and her mind was unable to resist. A small primal part of her thrashed against the wave of sleep that flooded her mind, begging her to stay awake, to run. But the whispers of the woods were too sweet a lullaby and there was nothing she could do to stop it.

AN INFINITE STARRY sky existed above, below, in front, and behind—a void of twinkling obscurity. The night was illuminated by eight moons, each in a different phase. They circled the dream realm, drawing lines of light as they spun through the stars.

Seren had never experienced a dream like this before.

It felt light.

Real.

Like she could reach her hand through the sky's embrace and touch the moons.

She pivoted slowly, and tendrils of velvety shadows swirled at her feet.

Pressure budded in her temples, spreading. She squinted, glancing around the dream realm. Movement split the darkness at her side, and she jolted.

Eyes the color of ice froze her in place as the Prince of the Moon stalked toward her.

"Seren," Casimir said sharply.

"Casimir?" His name was a question she willed not to tremble. But her name on his lips had kissed frostbite down her spine, and her voice shook despite her efforts at control. "What's going on?"

The prince stepped closer, trailed by the familiar wisps of mint and rain. He glared at her, his fair skin glittering as the moons' light brightened for their prince. With hesitant hands, he reached out, stopping before he could touch her, his expression contorted by what looked like guilt. Trails of silver light followed his movement, illuminating his unreadable expression.

He pulled his dark brows together. "I don't know."

Seren shook her head, forcing away the urge to touch him. He wasn't real, none of this was.

For a second, Casimir jerked his eyes away, returning them twisted. He towered over her, his dark presence setting her on edge. "We need to leave."

"What is this place?" Seren asked, eyeing the prince's disheveled clothes—the same ones he had worn in the alley the night before.

He shook his head, and his jet-black hair parted over his arched ears. "It doesn't matter."

"I want to know."

"No."

Seren gulped. "Why are you acting like this? It's just a dream."

"Wake up."

"What? Lighten up."

"Wake up, Seren." His tone was lethal.

One at a time, the eight moons dissolved into darkness. The stars blinked out until the once-limitless sky was nothing but a hollow veil of black.

She couldn't see anything. But—the prince's hands were on her shoulders. Pressure drummed in her ears. She felt the heat of his skin.

He shoved her. She braced for an impact that never came.

Shadows consumed her, and she was falling and she didn't understand.

Her attention ravaged by Casimir's last words as he yelled...

"WAKE UP NOW."

DAZED, pressure throbbed in Seren's head, splitting her temples as beams of light thumped across her eyelids.

She opened her eyes, her crusty lashes ripping apart. Her neck was stiff, and she stared at the passing tree canopy. A dull throb swelled in her left cheek, and her back scraped relentlessly over fallen branches and rocks. She strained to put her hands out, to stop herself from…

Am I falling?

No—her arms were bound above her head.

She was being dragged.

The last thing she remembered was falling and…

Wake up, Seren.

She strained her neck but couldn't get a good look at her captor, his back to her as he marched. Seren faced the path they left behind. No wonder her body ached—the path he chose could best be defined as a jagged ditch lined with thick, unearthed tree roots.

She couldn't tell how long she'd been out, but they were still in Galaxius. Light trickled down through the twisting branches high above. She guessed it was morning, which meant she'd either slept through the night or had been knocked out ever since. Maybe longer, she supposed, if her pounding headache was any sign of how hard she had been hit.

Seren's voice cracked, her throat hoarse as she tried to speak. Her captor halted.

"You're alive." A male's voice, rugged, and full of disdain. Seren coughed, and the male continued, "I thought you were dead, and you would've been if I hadn't chased off those Caripers. I was walking when I heard their screeches. Found you near the water, right before they lifted your body from the ground." He jerked his head at the sword on his back. "A few good swings and they dropped you. You can thank that for the nice head wound."

Blinking slowly, Seren thanked her lucky stars instead. She couldn't remember anything besides her dream. A cut was nothing. If Caripers had really attacked her, she was lucky to be alive. They were vicious scavengers, their chimeric bodies adorned with membranous wings powerful enough to carry even the largest prey. Helpful, as they preferred to feast in private.

Clarallan parents loved to use myths about Caripers to scare their children into submission. They claimed if the children sinned, the monsters would steal them and eat them slowly. Besides being a poor parenting tactic, the stories were pretty accurate. Caripers kept their victims alive for days while they feasted—shredding their skin and crushing their bones. A slow and torturous death.

Seren's mouth gaped; she was about to say thank you when her dazed mind remembered she was still tied up and being dragged across the forest floor, nonetheless. She shut her mouth. It wasn't safe yet, and she certainly wasn't thankful.

As if sensing her thoughts, the male dropped her hands. Her knuckles cracked against the rocks.

"Ouch." She mewled.

"You're welcome."

Seren's mouth begged to spew every hateful curse she knew at the arrogant male. She'd had enough. Enough of the running, the fighting, and the near-death experiences. She lifted her chin and hands. "Untie me."

"Why should I? You haven't even thanked me for saving your life."

"Why should I thank you? You tied me up. Dragged me like waste across the forest—"

"Fine." He turned. Seren pulled her knees into a sitting position and again stretched her bound wrists.

Amused, he didn't move. Golden hair fell across his tanned

face, exposing the jagged crimson scar that extended below his left eye. From the Sollian court, she guessed, but his brown eyes glowed a faint yellow, and his black pupils were unusually small.

Seren jerked her chin at her wrists.

"Fine," he repeated, losing the smug curve of his smirk as he knelt.

As soon as her hands were loose, Seren scrambled to stand, and the male stepped away. Her head throbbed, and she shook her wrists, her joints cracking from the however many hours they were bound.

The male gestured at her free hands.

"Uh, one more thing." Seren stared at his boots, her palm stretched out.

"What are you doing?"

"You really think I'm that dumb?"

The male shot her an impish smile. "Not dumb." He pulled her dagger from his boot and handed it to her. "I was just hoping the head wound would've been enough to make you forget."

"Thanks," she said, not caring about the bite in her tone as she gripped the weapon.

He turned on his heels and said, "With that attitude, I'm inclined to leave you here." Making a show of it, he took a few exaggerated steps.

Seren watched, blinking slowly.

Take her chances alone in the forest again or with her aggravating captor turned lousy savior? The former had clearly not worked out too well the first time...

She rolled her eyes and leaped to his side—the latter it was then. His grin returned.

Matching his pace, Seren glanced sideways. The unusual male wore dark brown leathers that reminded her of Etiamella warriors, his tanned arms exposed—muscular and scarred. He stared ahead, his rugged golden hair concealing his ears and face. She asked, "Who are you?"

"That's unimportant."

"Huh, I've never heard that last name before. Where's it from?" The male didn't respond, didn't even pity laugh at her attempted mockery. "Where are we going?"

"You ask a lot of questions."

True, but she was tired of not having answers.

"Are you going to answer any of them?"

The male glanced sideways, his innocent expression full of false contemplation. "Probably not."

"That wasn't a no." Seren raised her brows. Her headache stretched further, and she squinted, eyeing the heavy pack strung over his shoulders, a fine-edged sword peaking above his tall frame.

"Then, no," he said, riling her further. "Your talking is going to alert the creatures of these woods to our presence."

Seren's confident annoyance wavered. She lowered her voice and asked, "One question, one answer, and I'll be quiet. Deal?"

The male sighed his contested agreement. Clearly not favoring her persistence.

"What's your name?"

"Rae," he said, his look adding a silent *Are you happy now?*

"I'm Seren."

"I didn't ask."

She bristled. His complete disregard was almost offensive, but she shut her mouth. A deal was a deal.

As they walked down the path that seemingly only Rae could see, Seren knew three things: One, the Galaxius Forest was never-ending. Two, Rae was a terrible travel partner. And three, they were certainly lost.

Again, passing a massive tree with a low-hanging bough, Seren broke the silence. "I've seen that tree three times in the past hour. Admit it. We're lost, aren't we?"

Rae held a finger to his lips, and Seren couldn't help but roll her eyes. "I'm sorry if it hurts your big male pride to admit it, but we're walking in circles."

"Be quiet." His tone allowed no room to argue. "We're being followed."

She shuddered. "Caripers?"

"I don't think so. They don't attack their prey unless they're already vulnerable or dead. Scavengers don't like the fight."

His words were almost a relief until she realized what they meant. They had no idea what they were going to face if the creatures attacked.

"We should run," Seren suggested.

"We won't make it." His honesty jarred her, and his expression was paralyzing. Rae believed he was telling the truth. "We have to fight."

"You really believe that's a better idea?"

He stiffened but said nothing, fists clenched at his sides as he stared.

For the first time since they had met, Seren was thankful for his silence.

The darkness circled closer, a cold breeze carrying whispers from the forest. Tendrils of shadows flickered toward them, caging them in. The whispers grew louder, morphing to screams and cries. It was deafening. Impossible to make out any of the words. Rae gave nothing away despite the cries that chilled her blood. His defense seemed impenetrable, unaffected by the fear that ravaged Seren's mind.

My forest has brought me a gift.

It was a terrible idea, but Seren asked, "Did you hear that?"

Rae looked at her, never turning his back to the forest, wrinkles creasing between his eyebrows.

You're afraid.

The voice was wholly inhuman and sounded like it came from inside her mind. It was masculine, feminine, young and old, cruel yet moral.

Seren jumped. "That! Did you hear that?"

"Stop messing around."

I speak only to you.

Seren's mouth opened to scream, but her throat was strangled by fear and only a mangled gasp escaped. Rae looked over his shoulder, drawing knives that pointed at nothing.

Can you see me?

There was only darkness.

Can you feel me?

Crying out, Seren fell to her knees, dropping her dagger. Talons scraped the inside of her skull, tearing at her mind. Her hands clawed at her head. Rae reached for her, his other hand blindly brandishing a blade. Agony forced her eyes shut. At least Rae couldn't see the monster either.

"Seren," Rae yelled, trying to hold her as she writhed against him.

There was nothing he could do to stop the monster in her mind.

Rae's warmth disappeared, and Seren could vaguely tell that he wasn't there anymore as she thrashed on the damp ground. He was leaving her—escaping while the monsters hid in the shadows and turned her mind to nothing.

No.

This wasn't the way she was supposed to die. She rallied everything within her.

She had stared evil in the face thousands of times and lived. She wouldn't let some monster she couldn't even see kill her.

Grasping at a thread of hope, Seren pulled.

A primitive feeling poured from her heart, commanding her body. She zeroed in on that feeling, let it wash away the pain that collapsed her. A whisper mused in her ear: *let what you do not understand guide you.*

Everything stopped.

For a second, warmth radiated around her, gone by the time

her vision cleared. Seren pawed tears from her cheeks, her hands filthy with mud. Her ears rang and her mind felt foggy as it meticulously pieced together the parts of her shattered by fear. She glanced down; physically, she'd live. There were no wounds to represent the battle just waged, only tears and mud. And her soul, the poor graveyard for every time her heart broke or her mind bled at the cruel hands of magic and monsters.

She forced herself to stand, knocking clumps of mud from her clothes, and grabbed her dagger. Everything else was the same as before. The forest left undisturbed. No traces of the monster that attacked. No—

"Rae?" Her voice cracked. Panic threatened at the thought of being alone in the forest again. "Rae?" she called louder and took a few steps in the direction they'd been going before the attack. Or at least she thought it was the same direction. Her brain was a thousand-piece puzzle, and the monster had flipped the table. Everything was still in there, it was just a scrambled mess.

Gold light flashed in the murky shadows, and Seren rubbed her eyes, begging for no hallucinations. Galaxius was nightmarish enough with its real monsters. She didn't want imaginary ones too. Blinking fiercely, her vision cleared. The woods were dark; whatever had been there was already gone.

Determined to find her way out of the dreadful forest, Seren marched over the rugged terrain. Minutes passed in silence.

She jolted, whipping her head to the side at the sound of splintering branches. Her eyes were still unable to pierce the darkness. But she knew something was there. She was no stranger to the feeling of being watched by a predator.

She thought about calling out for Rae again. But he'd left her, saved his own skin when the monster wanted nothing to do with him. She couldn't blame him—they were strangers, she might have even done the same thing if the roles had been reversed—but a small part of her wanted to.

The monster's words scratched her mind, *I speak only to you* echoing in her skull. Rae had been right, it definitely hadn't been Caripers that attacked. It had been something much worse, something that had the power to disable her without her even getting a glimpse of it. The possibility of it happening again energized her steps, and her breath quickened.

She kept her head straight as branches snapped at her side, followed by the sound of claws scraping over rocks.

Seren stared at nothing as she walked. Whatever was stalking her didn't care to keep its presence a secret, and that was scarier than the reverse. Occasionally, her eyes scampered across the darkness pressing at her sides, but it felt better not to look. She spoke quietly to herself, a series of swears and questions about what the hell she was going to do. The monsters clearly already knew about her; she didn't have to worry about being quiet. Maybe they'd even feel bad for her if they heard about the day she'd had. Seren swallowed, shaking her head. Pity had a vile taste.

"You ask a lot of questions."

Stumbling, Seren barely caught herself in time.

The forest had responded.

"Careful," the animalistic voice mocked, a familiar purr as it continued. "Even when you're alone, you can't seem to shut the hell up."

"Rae?" Seren's jaw cracked. An assault of questions armed her mind, but she sealed her lips. He'd left her. She still wasn't even sure he was the one speaking. She couldn't see into the darkness. For all she knew, a monster was playing with its food, softening her up before it feasted.

"I thought I told you, the more you talk, the more monsters you'll alert to your presence." The voice loosed a rough chuckle, stirring the dense brush as it stepped closer.

Seren peered into the woods, jumping away when two golden eyes stared back, their round black pupils dilating as they zeroed in on her. The eyes shrank and the figure grew taller.

Like a jab to the throat, Rae stalked out of the darkness. Seren gasped, her eyes widening as she studied him.

"Rae—" she said for what felt like the hundredth time, her gaze catching on his clenched fists. "You're bleeding."

He squeezed his fists tighter. "It's nothing."

Feigning disinterest, Seren asked, "Where have you been?"

"I've been with you."

She couldn't stop her eyes from sharpening. "I think I would have noticed that. Last I checked, you ran when you had the chance."

"I might not have been at your side, but I've been here." His voice was low, stern. He sounded like he believed what he was saying. Seren's mind cleared. The snapping branches, the claws against stone, the monster that stalked her. She was so stunned by Rae's appearance, she had completely forgotten about the last hour he'd been gone. Or not gone—Seren tried to make the pieces fit together, and anger filled whatever didn't. She asked, "That was you following me?"

Rae opened his mouth as if to speak.

Seren cut him off. She wanted to yell but checked her tone. "You ran, you didn't have to come back. So why hide when you did?"

Her rage coiled, prepared to strike. She wouldn't show him all her cards yet. He didn't deserve to know how furious she was that he'd left her to die. That would imply she needed him.

He held her stare. "I couldn't."

Seren scoffed. "Whatever."

"Seren, I—"

"I don't want some pathetic excuse," she snapped. But why? They barely knew each other. They owed each other nothing. And she certainly didn't need him. Her gaze fell to his bloody fists, clenching and loosening, again and again, never opening fully. "And can you stop doing that?"

Rae gritted his teeth, his eyes in turmoil as he raised his hands and uncurled his fingers. Tan, thorn-shaped claws protruded from his fingertips, curved to a serrated, bloody point. Seren hadn't known it was possible to feel horror and awe simultaneously. Her mouth parted…

A shiver spread through Rae's body, and he winced, snapping his fists shut. His arms were taut, flexed muscle all the way to his stiff shoulders. There was a power around him, enough to shield the predator that lurked beneath thin skin.

She asked, "You're not Fae?"

"No." Rae paused, inhaling slowly. "My kind…have you heard of the Verti?"

"But I thought—"

"That the Verti were extinct?"

Seren nodded, eyes wide as she stared ahead at the hundred-foot trees that veiled their path in murky shadows. She considered his words, disbelief fogging her thoughts. By now, the Verti were a myth—ancient warriors of Clarallan preceding the Great Wars, their magic heightened by their ability to shift into the kingdom's greatest predators. Little in the library was written about them, but Seren knew the legends. And what Rae was saying… She shook her head.

Rae pushed, "That's what the Fae wanted everyone to believe, so no one would ever challenge them. Once, the Verti protected the High King and his kingdom. But when the wars broke out, Ares's warriors were killed first. The Fae wanted to expel Clarallan of all creatures that rivaled their magic. To create the court system. If the Verti lived, Ares could have rallied against their treason. The Verti fought until the end to save Ares, but the court's rebellion proved victorious." Rae's eyes glowed a liquid gold. "But not all the Verti were killed. Most of them were, yes, but many were captured. The Fae kept them caged, and used manacles that tapered their magic. They didn't let them shift unless they were torturing them. They wanted to study our magic, learn how we shift."

Seren shuddered. She knew the Fae were cruel, but this went beyond even what she thought them capable of. "Why?"

Rae paced, his lips puckered with disgust. "Do you even know the true history of Clarallan? What it was like before the Fae destroyed everything?"

Seren shook her head.

"When the gods ruled the kingdom, before the court system, Clarallan was home to more creatures and magic than you could ever imagine. But the Fae ruined everything. Too power hungry to care who lived and died in their selfish wars."

"I didn't know." Seren's words were quiet. If she was honest, Rae was starting to worry her.

He loosened an irritated chuckle, and Seren sensed it did little to diminish the anger coursing through his veins. "Of course you didn't. How could you? The Fae destroyed everything. Even rewrote Clarallan's history to support their claim to its power. Killing anyone who rebelled against them."

Learning too much devastating information at once had the same effect as eating something rotten. It felt like Seren had been poisoned, and it made her want to puke until even her insides were out.

A crack of wood and stirring of foliage caused Rae to snap his head to the side, and his anger cooled. "We need to go."

Just in time. Seren winced. She couldn't take anymore. Not right now.

"I don't know about you, but I don't want to spend another second in this damn forest."

Agreeing, Rae walked on. Seren followed, her mind reeling. She wasn't even convinced she should be following him after everything he'd told her. And how angry he'd been—

Seren chased her doubts to the back of her mind. The more

she learned, the more questions she had. Everything she thought she knew was a lie, and the truth appeared to have never even stood a chance against the Fae's deceit. But now that she had gotten a taste of the truth, she knew what she had to do. Even if it meant going up against the king.

Determination strengthened her steps.

CHAPTER 13

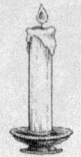

Time was a secret beneath the ancient trees. Seren couldn't tell if they had been walking for one hour or five, trudging through the perpetual night. Time belonged to the living, a way of symbolizing important moments in life, and since life didn't exist within the forest, neither did time. The dead had no use for it, anyway.

She kept track of every time she wanted to ask Rae how much longer—adding to eighty-seven—until his pace quickened.

The air grew thick, the shadows anxious.

Seren couldn't see one foot in front of her, let alone up ahead. She hurried after Rae, refusing to lose him again.

The shadows pursued them with inky fingers, grasping at their clothes, their hair, tickling their skin. Seren wrapped her hand around her dagger, thankful that despite everything, she still had it with her.

The darkness was unforgiving, whispering desperate pleas, begging them to stay as shadows pressed in on them, slowing their escape.

Seren raised her dagger, waving it through the murkiness.

Rae hollered, "Over here." He coughed as the shadows lunged.

Clawing forward, Seren kept her mouth shut, wincing as her outstretched hands ripped through barbed branches. Rae was at her side, a blade in each hand as he sliced through the dense foliage bordering their cage. A wall of vines and thorns and branches. Their skin tore, but they didn't stop, the relentless brush regrowing nearly as fast as it was cut.

Rae grabbed her hand. "Come on," he said, jerking her through an opening.

Scrambling, Seren stumbled, falling to her knees as sunlight washed over them. The light was blinding. She pressed her palms into the warm grass, panting as she closed her eyes. Her skin cheered, and she reveled in the sun's warmth, willing it to spread through her every limb. The forest had planted a weed of fear within her, and untamed, it chilled her core. Seren shivered. It would take a lot more than sunshine to cut it down.

She stood, squinting at Rae, who observed her, oddly amused. She glared a bit, her eyes adjusting slowly. Behind him, miles of verdant grass stretched to the base of a mammoth mountain, its points visible where they soared through the mist of cirrus clouds. From such a distance, Seren could just make out the trees peppering the steep slopes before giving way to a spring snow that froze the jutted crests.

The landscape had the quality of a dream: a clear sound of a brisk stream, when Seren saw nothing beyond the valley and mountain range, the thigh-high grass waving, but again, Seren didn't feel any wind. She dampened her dry lips, cracking her jaw to ask—

Rae cut her off with a low chuckle. "Before you ask, we're at the Ruins."

Shaking her head, Seren rubbed her eyes. Had Galaxius gotten to her more than she thought? She didn't think she was hallucinating...but was it possible that what she saw differed completely from where Rae had taken them? White stars blinked away, and her vision cleared. She scanned the glorious meadow again, its delicate bursts of pinks and yellows skipping between the thick green.

Everything was the exact same. Bright, colorful, and teeming with light magic.

If Galaxius was the land of death, the Ruins were the land of life.

"It doesn't look ruined to me." The words felt as stupid as she'd expected them to.

Rae turned his back to her and said over his shoulder, "Come on, I wanna be home by tonight."

Home? Seren's brows shot up. She obviously knew he was taking her somewhere, she just hadn't thought that far ahead yet. Too busy trying not to die and all that. Shrugging, Seren kicked her sore feet forward and followed Rae toward the mountain.

They walked through the meadow, the grass tickling her filthy skin through the tears that littered her clothes. She hoped wherever home was it had a real shower—her stomach rolled—and a lot of food. Seren distracted herself by studying the foreign land. Based on her studies in Stellean, running through the Galaxius was supposed to spit her out somewhere near the Sollian court. But the harder she imagined the maps of Clarallan, the harder it became to picture where Rae had taken them. She had never even heard of the Ruins before, let alone knew anything existed beyond the dreadful forest.

"Where did you say we were going again?" she asked.

"I didn't."

"So where's home?"

"About a five hour walk north." His tone was satirical, not secretive.

Seren scowled, if only to make herself feel better. Rae never looked back. Her expression dimmed. "Five hours?"

"It'd be three if you weren't slowing us down."

Seren snorted. She was slowing them down? They hadn't taken a single break since they left the meadow, and she'd kept up with him the entire time. However long it took was not on her. "Typical really, the guy blaming the girl for something entirely not her fault."

Rae peered over his shoulder and his pupils dilated. "If I were alone"—his eyes glowed—"I wouldn't be walking."

She stiffened, sealing her lips. No need to further irritate the prickly predator. She still couldn't believe Rae was a member of the Verti. Which after what Rae had said about the wars... Seren shivered. The Fae had done everything in their power to help Clarallan forget their crimes against the kingdom and its creatures.

They walked in silence, leaving the foot of the mountain behind. From afar, its beauty put on a show. But as they hiked, the dense forest transformed into a perilous mountain range with no trail. Rae simply stared straight ahead, occasionally veering one way or another, dragging them down vertical drop-offs and scrambling over mounds of boulders. Seren couldn't have talked if she wanted to. Too focused on making sure the ground didn't give way beneath her. Two hours passed, and they had long ago lost sight of the meadow boarding the Galaxius Forest. If for some reason she had to find her way back on her own, Seren wasn't sure she'd be able to. Her sense of direction was shattered.

Her feet ached and she stumbled. Cursing, she clutched desperately to splintering branches that couldn't bear to save her. They snapped, and her knees cracked against the cold boulders, her palms burning with gravel as she saved her face.

Rae lurched. "You alright?"

She glared at him from her hands and knees, sneering sweetly, "Never been better." Groaning, she stood. Rae resumed his hike, and Seren followed a few steps before stopping. Wiping her knees, she sat on a fallen trunk. Rae kept walking, long enough to make Seren wonder if he even knew she had stopped. Maybe he did and just didn't care enough to force her to get up and continue. Inhaling, Seren hauled her body off the tree and trailed after him, mocking him under her breath—Rae halted, at least fifty feet ahead of her.

He stared at her, a derisive expression. "Quick insults do a better job. Short and sweet, you know. That was just a compliment mistaken for a mouthful."

Seren gaped, boggled and out of breath. "How did you—" His eyes glowed. "Verti, right. I hadn't forgotten since the last time your ego flared."

A chuckle. "That was better."

Seren smirked. Why? She didn't want his validation.

This time, Rae waited for her to catch up, his arms folded across his chest.

"It wasn't a compliment by the way," she said by way of greeting, stepping directly behind him.

"Seemed like one to me, even if it was a bad one."

"How?"

He smirked. "Rae something something, annoyingly athletic, amazing self. You mumble too much, but I got the gist."

Chuffed, Seren sharpened her gaze. "Ah, you misheard me. It was 'Rae and his annoying, arrogant, animalistic self,'" she amended, with a nod for each insult.

He rolled his eyes, and Seren had the sneaking suspicion he'd heard her perfectly fine.

For once, Rae continued the conversation, pointing ahead as he walked in front of her. "About two more miles of incline, then we're gonna veer left. Think you can keep up this time?"

Seren groaned. "You're infuriating."

"Thanks." Rae's tone was cheery enough that Seren pictured grabbing her dagger and throwing it at him—see how quick those animal reflexes really were.

"Again, not a compliment."

He tittered and quickened his pace. The sun neared a hazy descent, laying its warmth to rest as the last of its light gleamed against the damp forest. Sweaty, the warmth from their physical efforts turned into a tragic chill. Seren peered ahead, shivering and clenching her fists as she hurried. Miles above, spring snow crested the jarring mountain peaks, their harsh summits casting ghastly shadows that collided with the dense trees.

Rae turned left, and in front of them, a vast slope dropped to a wide clearing, its surface overrun by a crumbled kingdom, a plateau littered by devastated homes, ancient architecture wearing centuries of weight. Seren flinched, a shiver coursing through her at the sight of the true Ruins.

Crossing the dark valley, Seren trailed closely behind Rae. He moved quickly, the frigid night air settling as they walked beneath a massive stone archway and into an ancient courtroom, the crumbling stone the humble bones of a once-great castle. Moonlight slipped through the caved-in roof and airy colossal pillars, flickering across the cracked stone. Broken marble statues—once at least fifteen feet tall—littered the floor in pieces. Dark ash scars coated the art, climbing the few standing walls, distorting the fractured murals—and scattering the story of what happened centuries ago.

Wonder and sorrow stirred queasily in Seren's gut as Clarallan's magic held her hand, sharing pieces of its past glory. If she closed her eyes, she could hear the whispers of the crippled kingdom. Could see the extravagant life that had thrived within the profound purlieu. The magic didn't speak of the decimation, but...

Something terrible had happened here.

Now, just a forgotten battlefield grieving the spirits of the past.

Seren kept her questions to herself as they wandered through the disintegrating halls. It felt wrong to disturb the spirits resting in the darkness.

Rae walked with his head down, his face dark as he led them through the haunted corridors. He followed a long hall, stopping as he approached a broken wall. Crawling over the jagged rubble, they faced a dirt trail leading away from the forgotten castle.

Far off, flames penetrated the darkness, lighting a path through the trees toward a large village. Cloudy moonlight faintly illuminated the woodsy town as fire posts blinked a clear trail for their arrival.

For the first time since Seren ran from the market, she heard life flutter toward her, laughter and conversation echoing through the twilight. Footsteps shuffled over gravel ahead, and creaky doors opened and closed. When they broke through the trees, she saw dozens of humble houses stamped across the valley and nestled in the woods. The two of them walked in the company of the lively citizenry, the sweet smells of late dinner welling in the brisk mountain air: honey-roasted meats and campfire smoke.

Seren's mouth watered in time with the growling of her stomach. Rae had shared his limited portion of food and water throughout their journey, but they'd finished it off before they even reached the mountain. She had survived their journey off adrenaline alone.

Hope sprouted within her at the sight of the town. "Where are we?"

Rae kept his eyes straight and said, "My home."

A feeling Seren didn't recognize made her heart swell. From everything she had learned about Rae so far, she guessed it took a lot for him to bring her there. He had no reason to help her, and he especially had no reason to take her to his home.

"Thank you." Seren had yet to really thank Rae for saving her, but she meant it this time.

"For what?"

Seren tilted her head back and forth. Despite Rae's ability to provoke such indignation in her, she did have a lot to thank him for. He saved her from the Caripers, helped her escape Galaxius, and now had brought her to safety. "For everything, I guess." She met his gaze, a half smile on her lips. "I mean, you did save my life. And we don't know each other...you didn't have to."

"I did."

Rae's answer confused her, and he didn't offer any elaboration—typical, as he seemed to loathe conversation. Seren didn't ask anything else as the secretive male led them through the town. Instead, she studied its inhabitants. The town reminded her of the market in ways: unique homes, wooden and slanted and colorful, fire pits placed amidst gatherings full of easy conversation. Their arrival earned curious looks, but eventually folks waved to Rae a welcome home. They neared a charming two-story building crafted of wood and stone. A group of males sitting in the grass around a generous fire hollered for Rae, their laughter gliding over the flames.

Rae lifted a hand and gave a half grin. His demeanor was suddenly more relaxed than Seren thought possible for the serious male. He'd been so rigid, so alert their entire trip. Every action was primed and ready, a warrior with every step.

Seren stayed behind Rae and eyed the group as she and the Verti stepped on the liberal lawn. There were four males in total. Two of them jumped up, eager to greet their friend, while the others stayed lounging around the fire. A large male drew Rae into a messy hug, and Seren took a breath.

Clapping Rae's shoulder, the tall male shook his dreads, and asked, "Where have you been, mate? You were supposed to be home days ago."

Rae taunted, "Aw, Carr, did you miss me or something?" That earned an eye roll from the male that hugged him, Carr, and a huff of amusement from the others.

Seren's lips curved up. At least Rae appeared accomplished at annoying everyone.

The second male that stood gave Rae a side hug and added, "Seriously, Rae. You had us worried."

"I'm okay, Tait. I just made a slight detour on my trip." Rae pointed his chin at Seren and four keen gazes landed on her, all looking at her for the first time. He strolled forward, sitting in the grass with his friends as the other two rejoined the group, then leaned on one arm behind him and pointed with the other. "Guys, meet Seren. Seren, meet my friends."

She felt on display, and it took everything in her to not turn around and walk back into the darkness. Instead, she stilled, mortified by the intensity of all four pairs of eyes.

Rae assured her, "You can come sit, you know. They won't bite."

Seren's eyes widened. That was a terrible joke if they were all Verti. The one thing she did know about their kind was their most prominent magic ability—shifting.

"Speak for yourself, Rae," said Carr—a muscular, pretty male with dark brown skin and shoulder-length dreads with the occasional blond highlight. His smirk was sinful as he bared his unusually sharp white teeth and waved for her to join.

"Don't scare her, Carr. It's not often Rae brings a woman around," the male sitting next to him teased, his emerald eyes glinting in the firelight. Besides Rae, everyone laughed, Seren included.

She stepped toward the fire, debating the best place to sit. She didn't want to pick a seat next to Rae and encourage the males to make assumptions. So, instead, she sat down opposite him, closest to the one who had just spoken and the shorter blond male Rae had called Tait.

Rae leaned back on both arms, which were taut as he propped up the weight of his large body. In the Galaxius Forest, it had been too dark to truly study him, and trudging through the mountain had been too difficult for Seren to get a good look.

He was stunning in a rugged way. His tan skin was scarred

over his muscular arms, adding to the gravity of the jagged vermilion line under his left eye. Curly golden hair fell loosely around the harsh edges of his face, emphasizing his golden-brown eyes and softening the history spilled across his body.

Seren drew her attention away and forced confidence into her voice. "It's nice to meet all of you."

Sprawled back on his arms, Carr grinned lazily. "It's our pleasure."

"That's Carr." Rae rolled his eyes, gesturing at the other males, losing the cheek in his voice as he went. "And that's Dax, Tait, and Izzac."

Seren let her eyes linger on each male for a moment, scoping out the group. There was an easiness among them, like they had all grown up together.

"So, Rae, you gonna tell us what happened?" Tait asked. He spoke with Rae's same slang, almost looked like him too. Like a younger brother. Tait had short blond hair, light tan skin, and golden-brown eyes. But his expression was more inviting than Rae's, and there was an almost childish innocence to his demeanor, despite his mature build.

"Yeah, did you kidnap this girl on your detour? She's way too pretty to go with you willingly." Carr egged them on, and Dax sneered at his side.

Seren wasn't sure if she liked or loathed Carr and his nonsense, but she smiled despite herself.

"Actually," Rae gave them each a pointed look, "I saved her life."

"I don't believe it," Dax grumped.

"Me neither," Carr interjected. "Come on, girl. You can tell us. Did Rae kidnap you?"

"Rae's right," Seren admitted. The males whooped, and Carr slapped an approving hand on Rae's shoulder.

"Of course I am," Rae insisted, his voice prideful.

"I still don't believe it," Dax muttered, tossing more wood on the fire. He was tall and lean, but in a way that Seren suspected he was stronger than he looked. And his dark pronounced brows brought attention to his striking green eyes and buzzed blond hair.

"So how did he save your life?" Izzac spoke bluntly, the first words she had heard him say since they'd arrived. Seren drew her eyes away from the captivating tattoos swirling over Dax's arms, an intricate pattern of lines and circles inked in his olive skin.

Seren lifted her gaze over the fire; she had all of their attention. "Uh…in the Galaxius Forest. Something attacked me when I was sleeping, and he—"

Rae interrupted, "And I swooped in like the hero you all know and love, and I saved her."

"From what?" Tait asked, his wide eyes full of wonder and worry.

Seren gulped. "Caripers."

"She was about to be carried off for dinner when I found her." Rae stared at her with confused pity. "It was foolish of you to sleep in the forest."

Seren's shoulders curled forward.

"Why were you in Galaxius?" Izzac asked, his tone jarring.

"I was running." The memories of the king seared her mind. Everyone leaned forward except for Izzac. She hesitated, unsure of how much she wanted to share with strangers. "Something bad happened, and I ran. I had nowhere to go besides…"

"That something had to be pretty bad if you thought the Galaxius was a better alternative," Izzac leered, suggestive.

Seren swallowed. They had been trusting of her thus far; it was her turn to extend the gesture. "How much do you guys know about the courts?"

All five males tensed. Anger rippled toward her and the fire cracked. Seren jolted. Of course they all knew plenty, Rae had taught her more about Clarallan in their brief time together than she had learned in twenty years. Regret scratched her throat and she choked. "I'm sorry, I—I was a servant for King Hellevi of the Stellean court. I was running from him."

"Why?" Rae's eyes burned, and Seren regretted looking away from the fire.

Seren continued, "He's evil. The cruelest of monsters I know, and he's hated me my entire life." She swallowed the vile taste of vulnerability. "I've been bound to him in servitude since I was a child. We got into a fight on my birthday, and for the first time, I fought back. That didn't go over very well, and he swore he was going to kill me. So I ran, but he sent soldiers after me. There was nowhere else to go."

Grumbles of hatred weighed down the air, and even the fire seemed to dim. But Seren's confession breathed oxygen into the flames, and everyone took a breath. Once again, the fire roared, but the heat couldn't compare to the shame burning inside of her.

Carr bristled beside Rae, muttering nasty swears along the lines of "fuck the Fae" as Dax and Tait nodded. Rae was completely still as he stared at her, and Seren couldn't help but watch the flames reflect off his golden-brown eyes, the illusory reflection of his rage. She tore her eyes away, glancing at the others. Izzac was gone. She searched the open yard, but the smaller male was nowhere to be seen. He had walked off quietly, his steps inhumanly light, like the air had carried him just above the earth.

He had been completely unreadable all night, only interjecting his judgment with prying questions. Seren couldn't tell if he was always like that or just keenly bothered by her presence. She reasoned he could be severely distrusting, but Seren was still unnerved by his undertones.

The others didn't seem to mind that Izzac had wandered off without a word, and Seren—distracted by her unease—jumped as Carr and Dax sat on either side of her, the former slinging his heavy arm over her shoulders.

"I like a beaut who can fight, you know." Carr spoke close to her ear, but loud enough that the others could still hear. Rae's eyes tracked Carr's every move, sharpening at the close contact he had with her. Dax slapped at his friend's hand, but Carr only gripped her shoulder tighter. Seren was sure Rae's breath hitched.

"Violence turns him on," Dax groused.

"That's twisted." Seren laughed alongside their brotherhood. It was unusual, but she enjoyed their company. Felt safe in their presence now that they seemed to have accepted her. It was a feeling she only ever had with Mare, and she wished her friend could have been there to experience it with her.

Carr slid his free hand to his chest and said with a wink, "The heart wants what the heart wants. I can't control it."

"You're shameless."

Carr gave her a grin of pure trouble.

She asked, "Do you flirt with every new woman you meet?"

"Only the pretty ones." Care feigned innocence, and Seren laughed anyway, rolling her eyes.

"By that, he means everyone," Dax harped on his friend. He and Carr seemed the closest, their brotherly relation branded by constant mockery and insults. Seren could see the deeper bond there, through the entire group even. Her heart ached for Mare, the one person she had a relationship like that with. She swore when the time was right, she'd find her way back to her friend. And hoped that when she did, Mare forgave her for leaving.

Seren asked, "So, how did you guys meet?"

The four of them shared a glance, a silent question. Rae lifted his chin, a sign they could trust her.

Carr opened his mouth, prepared to start. He really seemed to like the sound of his own voice. But Rae cut in, and Carr presented an exaggerated gesture that meant Rae would tell the story instead.

"I met Dax and Carr when I saved their lives. You guys have

that in common." Rae laughed at his own cleverness. Carr rolled his eyes, implying that was definitely not the way he would have told the story. Rae continued, "Like I told you, many of our people didn't survive the Great Wars. It took years for them to rebuild and even longer before their lives regained any normalcy. But after a while, many of the Verti found their way back here—"

All three of his friends pounced.

"You told her?"

"Rae!"

"Bloody hell, mate."

Rae raised his hands. "Easy, guys—"

"Seriously, you told her?" Carr asked. Carr fell away from her side in an exasperated motion and threw his hands in the air. Dax went still, and even Tait looked nervous.

"I had to," Rae complained.

"Why? How?" Dax and Carr asked in unison.

"It came up." Rae's nonchalant behavior only riled his friends further. "Moving on." Rae leaned back, his palms in the grass. "Many of the Verti found their way back here and started to build anew. Our community, nearly decimated by the wars, had to adapt to survive. We needed to be stronger. Our enemies knew how to defeat us, so we focused on our magic. The Verti began to train everyone, even the children. Everyone was required to learn about our kind, our magic, and our history. But most importantly, the Verti were training warriors. In case the Fae ever discovered them again. To complete our training, all the Verti must endure the Cere in their twentieth year—a final test that celebrates those who have mastered our skills, thus granting placement among our people. But the Cere is no ordinary test. It's a lethal ritual that results in either your gift or your death."

"Your gift?"

"Our shifted form," Carr clarified.

Seren nodded. So it was true, they were all shifters. She couldn't believe it.

Rae's face tightened. "Dax, Carr, and myself were all a part of the same Cere. A usual Cere has an average of ten Verti competing for their forms; ours had eighteen. Each year, only half are chosen to earn their gift. The ancient ritual can last for days or weeks or even months."

"How long did yours last?" Seren asked.

Dax clenched his jaw. "Five weeks."

"Each Cere has two stages. The first stage takes the longest, when the group fights to get down to half the number of Verti they started with. So for us, that was nine. The second phase happens immediately: a soul test of your magic and your compatibility with the Verti's gift."

Seren swallowed. She wasn't sure she wanted to know what these males could shift into.

Rae lounged backward. "I found these two bogans over four weeks into our first phase. They were two of the most powerful males in our group, and they'd allied themselves, putting a target on their back immediately."

Carr raised his fist to Dax, who shook his head begrudgingly and raised his own to fist bump his friend.

"The Cere has almost no rules against what the participating Verti can do to earn their gift. Fighting and magic are encouraged, and death is absolute. Because only half of the forms are granted in the second phase, many of the competitors have no problem killing to ensure their placement." Rae's throat closed up, his voice hoarse. "The year of our Cere, a few others created an alliance of five savage Verti. Their leader, Blaise, convinced the others that to survive the Cere, they had to kill at least four other competitors."

"He was a monster," Carr spat.

Was.

Dax carried the weight of speaking their trauma out loud,

explaining while Rae took a moment. "It wasn't unheard of for the Cere competitors to be killers; it was a common method used every year. But Blaise was different. No one before or after him has committed the same level of atrocious abuse that he inflicted on the Verti community that year." Dax's vibrant green eyes dulled a sorrowful sage, and regret pressed on Seren's chest. The Cere sounded intense, and the severity of violence they had lived through… She hadn't meant for her curiosity to force these kind males to relive such horrors.

Rae took over again. "By the time I found these two, Blaise and his cohorts had killed three Verti. His methods were brutal—not in the way he took his victims' lives, but in how he disposed of them after." A shudder crawled through Rae, infectious, and the others flinched. "He dropped the bodies at the front doors of their families' homes to make a statement. He wanted to ascend the ranks of the Verti warriors. The Verti community was outraged. Some even tried to get the Cere canceled permanently, rioting against the old tradition and its barbaric practices. But their efforts were unsuccessful, and the Cere continued as always. Our people can't risk not training their children. We need warriors."

Seren shivered despite the fire's warmth, and Carr returned his arm around her shoulders. His right hand mindlessly rubbed soothing circles over her skin. She guessed it was as much a comfort for him as it was for her.

Poking at the fire, Rae lifted his chin. "At that point, I was the only one left without an alliance. I worked alone the entire time before that final night of phase one. For weeks, Blaise's group was unbeatable. In that last week, they had rallied nine members, and only the three of us remained. I tracked both groups for days. Just three more deaths and the Cere's final phase would begin, and the remaining competitors would get their chance to earn their gift."

Seren's mind spun as she followed the story. She had so

many questions, but she picked one. "So, even when there's only half of the Verti left, not everyone will pass the final test?"

Dax explained, "To earn your final form, the Cere tests not only your magic but also your compatibility with the gift of the Verti. If you want to be chosen, both your body and mind must pass the test—but so must your values and soul. The Verti don't grant their gift to everyone, but that's a secret to all before completing their own Cere."

"A secret?" Seren asked, tilting her chin.

"They don't want it biasing the competitors' actions. Everyone swears to secrecy at the completion of their Cere," Carr added.

Rae elaborated, "Before you complete your own Cere, you're told that to earn your gift you just have to survive long enough to be one of the remaining half of the competitors. They offer no advice on how to do so, declare no rules on how you may decide for yourselves who earns the privilege. All that you know is if you want to earn your Verti form, you must be part of the final half."

Seren began to understand the Cere. Phase one was lawless, a chance for the competitors to act on instinct and make their own decisions, unaware of the fact that their decisions sealed their fate in phase two. It made sense that the Cere would not grant its gifts to all the remaining competitors, even if they survived phase one. The Verti designed the test to discover warriors of physical strength and mindful magic but also those with strength of the soul. Only those who truly deserved to win would earn the Verti's gift.

"Because I worked alone, I would have been the easiest first target," Rae reasoned, looking at his friends. "But Blaise was furious after those two killed a member of his alliance. I knew he was too vengeful to let it go…that Blaise would go after them. I sought out Dax and Carr immediately. I didn't know either of them well, and they had no reason to trust me, but I was willing to do anything to stop Blaise, and fortunately, when I found these two, they were too."

The guys shared a long glance, their breaths perfectly in sync. Seren was in awe of their connection. They were brothers bonded by blood, if not the blood that ran through their kind, the blood they'd shed in battle.

"I tracked them to the old ruins of the ancient kingdom, and watched for a while to get a sense of how they would react when I approached. I needed to ensure they wouldn't kill me immediately. But I waited too long, and didn't expect Blaise to catch up so quickly."

"It was an ambush." Carr shuddered.

"A damn good one too," Dax added.

"Blaise and his remaining allies attacked from different angles, getting the jump on Dax and Carr. These two were far more trained than Blaise's entire cohort combined, but the time it took for them to react cost them. Blaise went for Carr since he was the one who killed the female in Blaise's group, supposedly the woman Blaise claimed to love. The rest of his group teamed up on Dax."

Seren leaned against the warmth of Carr's heavy arm and placed a hand on Dax's knee, squeezing slightly. She swayed her head, glancing at them both. Guilt wrinkled their brows and suffering glazed their eyes. She felt awful for dredging up such a story, the horrors these males were forced to remember. Carr's lips quirked to the side, a silent reassurance.

Rae tossed the stick he had been poking the fire with and the flames soared. "I'd never killed anyone before that night."

His words were the venom that stopped Seren's heart. Rae looked about as good as she felt, his gaped lips still as his words failed him.

Carr took over. "Blaise had me on the ground. His boot stomped on my chest, and his sword jutted into my neck as he bragged about being the strongest Verti in decades." Violence shivered through his body. "I heard Dax cry out, and I had a terrible realization—that sound was going to be the last thing that I ever heard. The crack of metal against bone as Blaise's friends beat my best friend, and the pain in his screams as my brother and I watched each other die." His voice cracked on the last sentence. "One second, I was a dead man, the next I was staring at Rae, a stranger covered in blood standing over me as Blaise collapsed to the ground—a dagger pierced straight through his throat."

"I wanted him to shut up," Rae added. "Forever."

"I killed Blaise's second right as he made to kill Dax. With those two dead, the first phase of our Cere was complete. Nine of us remained, and six of us passed phase two. Myself, Dax, and Rae obviously, and three members of Blaise's group that had allied themselves simply to survive. They'd been too frightened to go against Blaise, but they'd never physically participated in his crimes. The other three didn't make it. The final test failed them because of their actions in phase one, their souls broken by inconceivable values. They didn't stand a chance of receiving the gift of the Cere."

"The three of us have been friends ever since." Rae grinned and the air cooled. "The next year we started to train other young Verti for their Ceres, and that's how we met Tait."

"He never would have made it without our help." Carr smirked at the younger male through the fire. "He was powerful, sure, but naive enough it would have gotten him killed."

"That's not true," Tait fussed.

"We took him under our wing." Dax's pride swelled. "Then we hoped he'd learned enough to come back to us after his Cere."

"Which I did," Tait said pointedly, his own pride rivaling his friend's.

The bond between them went beyond blood and death. It

may have been forged through survival, but it was maintained by love and life. Seren asked, "And Izzac?"

Rae glanced sideways, his speech shallow. "That's a long story, one he doesn't share too often. Things were really bad when we met him."

"He'll tell you when he wants to." Carr squeezed her shoulder.

"If he wants to," Rae emphasized.

A story for a different time, then. Seren nodded, yawning. How long had it been since she'd last slept? At least a day or so.

Carr chuckled. "Did our morbid bedtime story put you to sleep?"

Seren couldn't help but yawn again.

"We should probably call it a night, guys." Rae and the others jumped up.

The fire was nearly out, and Seren let herself accept how exhausted she was. Carr offered her a hand, and she took it immediately.

Walking to the house, Dax asked, "Where's Seren going to sleep?"

"She can take my room. I'll take the couch," Rae said.

"Or...better idea: Seren can sleep with me." Carr flashed an impish smile. She would have smacked him if she wasn't so tired.

"In your dreams," she mumbled.

"Oh, I'll definitely be in your dreams tonight."

Another wink from the facetious male. Carr was relentless.

"I can take the couch," Seren offered. Rae shook his head, and her exhaustion stopped her from arguing. She followed the four males inside, and Dax and Tait said their good nights, disappearing into two rooms on the main floor. She walked between Carr and Rae up the stairs, her gaze skipping from side to side, painting to painting. At the top, Rae stopped and opened the first door on the right. "This is my room. Come find me if you need anything, I'll be downstairs in the living room."

He retreated down the narrow stairway, and Carr whispered in her ear, "My offer still stands, you know."

"Not a chance, Carr."

He walked to the farthest door, opened it, then paused. "See you in your dreams, Seren."

Another wink and he was gone.

CHAPTER 14

Seren woke up from a nightmare-free sleep.

Stretching her arms above her head, she drew her body into a sitting position and leaned against the headboard. A small window brightened Rae's room, putting a spotlight on his barren furnishings: a bed, a desk, and a closed closet door, with a short stack of books placed between the first two. The desk was cluttered with bundles of papers, scribbled on and folded, and a few clean knives and jars of polish. It felt just like Rae—vague and abstruse.

She rose, and the wood floors warmed her bare feet as she swayed in the sun. She took a few steps—a knock sounded on the bedroom door.

"It's Rae."

Seren walked to the door, swung it toward her, and said, "Morning."

"Good morning—" Rae drew his words out slowly, his eyes screwed up and his jaw clenched as he looked her up and down. Seren's cheeks flushed under his gaze. His hair was loose and disheveled, and his sweats hung low on his hips. Did he always look like that in the morning? Maybe he was staring because she had something on her face; she was known to sometimes drool in her sleep. She rubbed the back of her hand over her lips and looked sideways.

He raised his brows, a casual grin on his face as he asked, "Do you always wear that to bed?"

Seren glanced down. *Shit.*

Well, at least she knew why he was staring. She had opened the door in nothing but her shirt and slips; memories of the previous night played in her head. It had been so dark and she had been so whacked. Her clothes had been filthy from the trip, but her shirt had fared well enough beneath her jacket. So before climbing into Rae's comfortable bed, she had stripped off her muddy clothes and tossed them to the floor.

Standing there now, her cheeks pink, she had two options. First, she could slam the door and be violently embarrassed, or she could embrace the awkward situation with as much confidence as she could muster. "I—uh, I didn't want to ruin your sheets. My clothes were filthy."

Rae pointed into his room, his eyes never leaving her as he answered, "You can grab some of mine. Or come get breakfast wearing just that. I'm sure the others would appreciate it, especially Carr."

Shoving his shoulder, Seren swung the door closed. "I'll be down in a minute."

"Disappointing," Rae said, watching her until the door stood between them.

She waited until the staircase creaked and then walked to the closet. It felt wrong going through his things, but he had said it was okay, more or less.

The closet was as empty as his room. A theme for the enigmatic male.

Seren grabbed the first short-sleeved shirt she found and a pair of cargo shorts she could roll high enough to look sort of normal. It wasn't like anything was going to fit particularly well, anyway. The male was nearly half a foot taller than she, and his —Seren shook her head. Not the time. Luckily, he had a belt with enough holes; otherwise, it would have been a lost cause.

Dressed the best she could manage, Seren followed the scent of maple and cinnamon bread as she descended the stairs. The kitchen was welcoming, its furniture homey and comfortable, and cleaner than she'd expected of five males.

Rae handed her a steaming mug of coffee and whispered in her ear, "You changed... What a shame."

Living in a house with these five was going to take some getting used to. Seren rolled her eyes and brought the warm mug to her lips; the steam carried rich scents of spices, while the taste was sweet and nutty.

"I made breakfast." Rae pointed at the stove. "I would grab some before the others wake up. Or it'll be gone before you get a chance."

"Males are animals," Seren grumbled.

"Was that supposed to be an insult?"

She frowned. That hadn't even been on purpose.

Redirecting Seren to the table, Rae's tone lifted. "Sit. Despite your beliefs, I'll show you we males do in fact have manners...sometimes."

She gave him a curious look, and he pulled the chair from the table, gesturing for her to sit. She watched him glide through the kitchen, and soon enough he held two plates, one piled with eggs and biscuits and meats, another full of fresh fruit and sweet rolls. He placed them in front of her, and her mouth watered; she was grateful for how full he had made them both.

Rae sat across from her with three full plates for himself as Carr strode into the kitchen. Carr asked, "You gonna make me a plate too?" He wore a pair of black exercise shorts, his broad chest on full display as he squeezed her shoulder from behind. "Or is service only provided to the beaut?"

"Morning to you too, Carr." Seren simpered, a small part of her warming up to his zaniness.

"Morning, Seren." He smiled, stepping away to tour the kitchen as Rae dug into his breakfast.

Dax and Izzac entered a few minutes after, and hurried steps pounded down the hall. Tait's voice cracked as he hollered, "Y'all better save some for me!"

By the time everyone sat around the table, their stomachs full and plates stacked irrationally tall, the breakfast that had looked like it could serve a feast was gone. Seren understood why, though; Rae's food was delicious.

It surprised her how natural it felt being with them, participating in their comfortable conversation and ordinary morning routine. Seren's heart swelled at their familial bond—something she'd always yearned to experience.

Dax and Carr spent all morning catching Rae up to speed about what had happened while he was away, Tait interrupting to argue with Carr's exaggerations. A lot had gone down, but nothing that warranted any concern or action on Rae's end. Praising Tait, Rae thanked him for stepping up, and the younger male beamed.

Izzac stuck around long enough to eat, then fled the house, his demeanor unreadable. Something was definitely still off about him, but Seren hadn't worked up the nerve to ask if she was the cause.

Rae cleaned the dishes and his friends finished their rundown. Drying his hands, he turned to her and asked, "You up for a tour?"

Seren shifted her thoughts away from Izzac. "Of what?"

Rae quirked a brow at her aloofness. "The town?"

She blinked slowly, nodding. "Right, yeah that would be great."

Rae led Seren through the lively streets, and familiarity tagged along. Slowly, the pieces of the previous night fell into place as Seren studied the mountain's quaint culture and array of unique homes. She had poorly misjudged the scale of the robust village in the dark. Built into the base of a small summit, the town was bordered by dense woods that overflowed the spaces between buildings with nature. Grassy fields stretched for miles in the distance, which Rae excitedly pointed out were used for training. And miles behind them, the towering ruins jutted above the treetops, their somber history never too far away.

They walked, unhurried, and Seren stopped at anything that caught her attention. Rae fueled their conversation with detailed descriptions of his home and people. The highlights being his favorite restaurant, the best brewhouse to ever exist, according to Carr, the communal school for the young Verti where a few of them had met, the newest weapon shop Dax was obsessed with, and even a dance club Tait was trying to get them all to go to. Rae even answered her frequent questions with minimal complaints, occasionally grunting when she asked too many and he had to answer more than one at a time.

A few Verti waved good morning, while others called out that it was nice to see Rae had made it home okay. He thanked them politely and wished them well as they continued walking. Seren was surprised to see him so laid-back—no hint of the alert warrior that had escorted her through Galaxius.

"This place is wonderful," she said for the fifth time since they had left the house.

Rae smiled gently, and he appeared all the more peaceful, younger even. He nodded, and there was no denying the pride in his tone as he said, "It is."

Seren asked, "Everyone that lives here, are they all Verti?"

"Mostly. The Verti rebuilt here knowing the Fae would erase the truth of what they had done, including their ancient home before the Great Wars. It's safe here because Clarallan has long forgotten that this place even exists beneath the Ruins. We haven't had an external attack in years. But a few citizens who live here come from all over, people with similar stories to yours."

Seren wondered if Rae expected her to stay with the Verti, unsure of whether she even wanted to. She slowed and he matched her pace.

"You can stay here for as long as you wish, Seren."

Gratitude erupted within her, turning into a thankful smile, yet she couldn't help but ponder what she was supposed to do. She didn't want to ask too much of Rae and his friends, but the prospects of safety and friendship were seductive. She smiled at the attractive male, and he beamed, as if her silence implied she would stay. She didn't have the heart to tell him she didn't have a plan yet, and there were a lot of things she needed to handle. She couldn't stay forever, but maybe a little while.

Rae gave her a sideways look. "I think we need to get you some new clothes. Despite how well you pull off mine."

A lie. Seren had seen her reflection in the shop windows. The oversized shirt, the shorts that went past her knees, and the belt strapped as tight as possible—like a child playing dress up in their father's clothes.

"I don't have any money."

"I know a place," Rae said, turning down a new street.

They entered a two-story shop and walked through the lower floor, decorated in a boutique style: dresses and suits, pastel-colored walls, bright floral paintings, and tall plants lining the windows.

She was about to protest that these clothes weren't really her style, when Rae breezed them down a back hall and up a flight of stairs.

The shop owner, a shorter female with copper-brown eyes and a plump, full figure, waved at Rae from across a tall wooden desk. She finished with a customer who gleefully held up a pair of combat leathers and headed on their way.

The woman scuttled around her desk and threw her arms around Rae, her short stature causing her head to barely meet his chest as he returned the embrace. Her voice was kind and mellow. "It's so good to see you, boy."

"I've missed you, Thrina." Rae closed his eyes before pulling away.

"Just not enough to visit more often, I suppose," Thrina mused.

Rae gave her a sheepish look, and his cheeks flushed a faint red. Guilt morphed his face, as if he were a young boy and his mother had caught him stealing too many cookies from the jar. His next words were softer. "I'm sorry, Thrina."

She clicked her tongue, waving him off. "Don't be, boy. Just visit more often, okay? So I don't have to spend so much time worrying about you. It's bad for the health."

Rae simpered and Thrina's wide eyes landed on Seren. Slapping his shoulder, she scolded, "Where are you manners, child? Were you not going to introduce me?"

Thrina's smile beckoned Seren closer and Rae shook his head. "Thrina, this is Seren. She'll be staying with me and the guys for a while. And Seren, this is Thrina. She's like a mother to me."

"It's a pleasure to meet you." Seren smiled, allowing the elated woman to study her. Thrina lifted her hair and grabbed her chin, squeezing her cheeks as she turned Seren's head to get a good look at her. Seren stifled a laugh. Thrina seemed the maternal type, the kind with so much love to give, her compassion spilled from the space most people kept their selfishness.

"You as well, dear," Thrina said, emitting such joy it was contagious. Seren grinned as the woman twisted to Rae and asked, "What brings you guys in?"

"I can't just come and visit?" Rae feigned a hurt expression and humphed, looking Seren up and down as if it was obvious. "Seren is in desperate need of some new clothes."

Seren snorted. "I thought you said I pulled them off?"

He rolled his eyes and Thrina lit up with a childlike giddiness. "Well, dear, what are you looking for?"

"Um—" Seren's eyes explored the second floor. This was much more her style, a surplus of combat leathers, workout clothes, and training gear, but still everything appeared too costly. "Anything casual, I guess."

Thrina waved Rae off and escorted Seren through every aisle, refusing to skip over anything in case Seren happened to love it. They didn't stop until her arms were heavy with clothes, and she was sure there weren't enough days in a year to wear so many outfits. Seren tried to put a few things back, but Thrina refused. By the time they finished, Rae was half-asleep where he lounged on a plush armchair near the window, like a cat curled up to take a nap in the sun.

"I put that there so the males don't pout when us gals take our time to shop." Thrina grinned and Seren's heart clenched. "We're ready," Thrina called out to Rae.

He startled as if he had truly been asleep, and Thrina led Seren to the tall desk. She wrapped and bagged the absurd number of items and Rae jogged over.

"One more thing," he said, placing a set of black leathers on the desk.

"Those are nice." Seren eyed the fine leathers. They were well-made and had a generous amount of weapon attachments, but... "They look a little small for you."

"They're for your training." He gave her a half grin.

"My what?" She raised a brow.

"You heard me. The guys and I talked this morning, and we think you should join us, if you want to, of course. But that way you don't need me to keep saving your life." Satisfaction filled his face and Seren was almost annoyed, but Rae had a point. Plus she loved to train.

Thrina observed their silent exchange and bagged the leathers. "Very well, then."

Seren asked, "How much do we owe you?" She had no idea how she was going to pay Rae back for all this.

Thrina placed a hand over her heart. "Don't trouble yourself." She wagged a finger at them. "Just come see me more often, both of you."

"Understood." Rae bowed his head. "Thank you, Thrina." *She's like a mother to me,* he had said, and it was easy to see how deep his love for her went.

"Thank you." Seren dipped her chin. "It was lovely to meet you."

Thrina walked out from around the desk and pulled Seren into a tight hug, whispering, "Come see me any time, dear." She squeezed her and hollered after Rae as he walked to the stairs. "You be good to her, Rae, and if not—"

"I will," he interjected.

Thrina released Seren and she trailed after him. She had no doubt the woman would have him over her knee in seconds, despite the stark size difference. Rae halted on the first step down, twisting his head to meet Thrina's stare. "I promise."

Rae's words echoed in Seren's mind for the rest of the day, disturbing her theories about him. A switch had flipped from Galaxius to here. He was talkative, kind even, and she didn't have a single idea what his intentions were. Yet despite everything, Seren found herself smiling the entire day.

CHAPTER 15

A week passed, and Seren learned a lot about the Verti, honestly, too much about the five males she shared a house with, especially Carr. The male spoke any thought that came to mind and haggled Seren as if they'd been friends for years. It was irritating, and endearing, and Seren knew he and Mare would get along.

It really felt like she was starting to get to know everyone, except for Izzac. Seren only saw him at meals, and most of the time, he took his to go. She had stopped bringing it up to the guys on the third day when Rae again said Izzac would come around when he was ready.

Rae had given her a week to recover and sleep after how weary her escape had made her. But a week had slipped away, and today marked the first day of her training.

Seren waited at the edge of the vast fields while the guys got a few rounds in so she could watch and learn. She had seen a lot of different sides to the Verti, but watching them spar was incredible. Carr and Rae paired up for a fight, while Dax instructed Tait on a quick fix to his takedown method that would make him less vulnerable. Seren could have spent hours studying them, their methods different from anything she and Mare had practiced.

The afternoon sun was relentless, but a spring breeze waved through the mountain meadow, chilling the sweat that glistened over their skin. Their sculpted bodies moved on instinct, and Seren could barely keep up as their assaults increased. They had cast their weapons aside as Rae wanted to show Seren what real hand-to-hand combat looked like.

It was impossible to tell by looking at them—their steady breathing and stony expressions said nothing about the demanding physical efforts—but they had been at it for over an hour. Seren was winded just watching.

Dax and Tait trotted up beside her, quick to grab two bottles of water. Tait emptied his in an instant and wiped the back of his hand across his mouth. Sweat dripped from his blond curls, and a flush of pink spread over his cheeks. Seren handed him another bottle, and Tait flashed her a toothy grin.

"How long are they going to fight?" she asked.

Tait drained the second water and said, "Probably until one of them pukes or ends up on their ass. Whenever they get like that"—Tait grinned at Carr and Rae, who were mirroring each other's lethal expressions—"it takes a while for them to work it off."

Dax turned to her and asked, "Wanna give it a try?"

Not really. Her muscles ached at just the thought of sparring with them. She had agreed to her training prior to seeing what it entailed. She should've known better than to underestimate Clarallan's ancient warriors.

But Seren trailed after Dax, her eyes on Carr and Rae as they landed blow after blow. Sweat beaded on Carr's sculpted chest, and he wore a pair of thin black shorts, while Rae was fully outfitted in a rust-brown set of combat leathers.

"Don't go too easy on her, Dax," Rae hollered from across the field, his words followed by a distant groan as Carr took advantage of his distraction and landed a hit directly to Rae's chest.

Dax chuckled. "We'll start with the basics until you get the hang of it." Seren nodded, gulping at the powerful predator in front of her. He continued, "The most important principle for anyone to learn in combat—soldier, Verti, or for self-defense—is balance. Without physical balance, your opponent will take every win. And without mental balance, well, you've lost before you've even started." He raised his hands, drawing his left foot into a wider stance, and dipped his chin toward her. "Your feet should be shoulder width apart, and your knees should be aligned in the same direction to minimize instability and risk of injury. When you change positions, regain your balance as quickly as possible."

Seren did as he said, grateful the others were too busy sparring to watch her train. She was uncomfortable enough with only Dax observing her so intensely.

"Mental balance is just as important, if not more. You must fight with technique and strategy, even instinct. The second you let fear or anger control your attacks is the second you sign your own defeat." Dax's thin face was neutral. He gave nothing away, a clear tell for how experienced he was. He looked no older than his early twenties, but he spoke with the wisdom of hundreds of battles.

Keep your emotions in check is basically what he implied—simple enough. Seren had plenty of practice. She'd spent years building mental walls strong enough to protect her from Hellevi. It couldn't be that different using those walls against an opponent.

"When you're balanced and strategic, you have more time to focus on the other principles: timing, distance, and momentum. It's important to understand each of these individually before you can use them to your advantage in a fight. When timing your attack, be aware of your balance versus your opponent's, the distance between the two of you, and how much momentum you can gain to strengthen every hit." Dax turned and gestured to Rae and Carr, the latter reacting quickly to one of Rae's blows. "Too quickly, and your opponent can predict your next move," Dax explained. He was right. As soon as Carr lunged, Rae had anticipated his blow and landed a hit that sent Carr sprawling backward. "Too slow, and you're vulnerable to your opponent's next attack."

As if on cue, Rae acted on Carr's hesitation. He repeated a series of blows, and Carr struggled to regain his balance. Rae didn't give up, but neither did Carr. Carr threw his momentum backward, and instead of falling, he righted himself and gained enough distance to recover.

"Understand?" Dax asked, turning his gaze back to her, his dark brows high.

"I think so." Seren was no stranger to combat, but this—this was a whole level of game that she didn't know how to play.

"One more thing, as a woman and a human, you should never engage in an attack of brute strength. It's exhausting, even for me, and you'll never win that way. But if you learn to be strategic, to give yourself the advantage and use it every time, you can learn to beat even a much larger and much stronger assailant."

Seren knew Dax meant no insult. It was a fact. There was no way she could beat him or any of the Verti guys with strength alone. Just another reason she had to be smarter.

Dax walked her through a series of drills he used to train all the young Verti. Which included balancing her stance, elbows, and knees, then working in punches, strikes, and kicks for a repetition of twenty-five efforts. The basics were similar to what she and Mare had practiced in Stellean, and it didn't take long before Seren could do them with ease. She had kept her limited training experience to herself, not wanting to get the males' hopes up. But what Mare had taught her—countless stances, vital points to hit, and her favorite takedown movement—proved useful sparring with Dax.

The more she sweat, the less embarrassed she was. She focused on how comforting it felt to be strong again, mirroring Dax as he escalated the exercises; his lithe figure a healthy challenge to keep up with. Her body warmed, and instinct took over, fueling her confidence. Dax stopped, but Seren continued.

Punch, strike, kick, repeat. Again, again, and again.

Her body completely took over, throwing out Dax's words along with her insecurities. This time, she didn't care when the others stopped to watch. It felt too good. Somehow better than it ever did in Stellean. She felt stronger, more composed. She didn't stop until she finished twenty-six repetitions—one extra, for good measure.

The high was euphoric. Her heart pounded in her throat and blood rushed in her ears while her system overdosed on endorphins. Seren grinned, jogging back to the guys, feeling better than she ever had in her entire life.

"Either she's a wicked-fast learner, or you're actually that good of a teacher," Tait goaded, bumping Dax with his elbow.

Dax retorted, "You would know, I taught you everything, didn't I?"

Seren grinned wider, staring at them as she allowed the comedown. Their laughter rolled toward her, the males busy bickering about their histories and egos.

Dax's voice snagged her attention with a humble brag. "Remind me again, who was the only Verti of our generation to be awarded ten combat stripes before his eighteenth year?"

Tait shook his soft curls, and shrugged, a serious look on his face. "Doesn't come to mind."

Seren snorted, and her gaze was swept away by Carr's raspy chuckle.

"I, for one, thought that was hot," he declared.

"Yeah, we know, violence turns you on," Seren chided.

Carr barked with laughter and Dax asked, "Where did you learn to fight?"

"I didn't." She paused. "Not really, anyway. My friend and I would practice a bit in Stellean, but it was never anything official, just for fun." And survival.

"That looked like more than 'just for fun' to me," Dax countered. "We can test it out tomorrow, but I think you're ready to train beyond the basics."

Seren beamed at the male's praise, nodding.

"That sounds great and all, but can we be done for today?" Tait asked, clapping his hands on his stomach. "I'm starving."

"Me too," Seren chimed, and the others agreed.

The sun was setting as they left the training fields. Seren couldn't believe how long they had spent out there. Behind them, the cloudless blue sky morphed to swirls of pink and orange as evening light cast their shadows across the grass.

She felt comfortable being with them, watching their abstract shadows bump into each other, long and distorted as they walked to the house. Her words flowed easily and her breathing was calm, her movements relaxed as they joked together. No fear, no anxiety. No king to be afraid of.

Just peace and friendship.

Something Seren hoped she would get the chance to get used to.

After dinner that night, the guys taught Seren how to play Kings in the Courts, a card game from the Great Wars that had been passed through generations. The guys had learned to play while training for their Cere.

Seren was on her fourth win when Carr accused her of cheating.

"There's no way," he groaned, throwing his cards to the ground.

The five of them sat on the floor of the living room, the furniture shoved to the walls. They'd been at it for a few hours.

Dax had won the first two games, Rae won one, then Seren had gotten the hang of it and had been unbeatable.

"Seriously, how are you doing it?" Tait asked, the only other participant besides Carr who had yet to win a round.

Seren shrugged. Twenty years in the Stellean court, and she'd picked up a thing or two—deft strategy being one of them. Yawning, she put her cards down. "I'm calling it a night. Maybe that'll give you two a chance." Carr and Tait didn't laugh, but Seren did.

"I'm out too, guys," Dax said, shuffling the cards into a neat stack.

"Why don't we all get some rest?" Rae stood and everyone followed suit.

Carr pushed the furniture back across the wood floor, adjusting the rug as he reset the cozy living room. Walking to the stairs, he stopped and said to Seren, "I'll get you next time, cheater."

Seren tittered, following him to their rooms. "Good night to you too, Carr." She lifted her hand to the others and added, "Night, guys."

Rae smiled lazily. "Night, Seren."

She walked up the stairs, snorting when she heard Tait complain again, "I still don't get how she did it. It took me weeks to beat any of you when I first learned to play."

"He's not wrong," Carr added, slipping into his room.

Smiling, Seren opened the door to Rae's room. Velvety moonlight glided through the window above the bed, and she lit a candle on his desk and undressed, tossing her training clothes into a pile. She stepped to the dresser, grabbing pajamas from a drawer Rae had cleared out for her after their trip to see Thrina.

Donning a soft pair of sleep shorts and an oversized shirt, she walked to the bathroom down the hall. She brushed her teeth, washed her face, and looked in the mirror. And for the first time in a long time, when she saw her reflection, she knew the girl staring back at her. Life flourished in her green eyes, and her skin was tan and smooth from a week in the sun. She looked like herself, not some servant destined to die. The more she felt like herself, the more certain she was that she had to find a way to stop the king. She glanced at her bright eyes—no one deserved to endure Hellevi's horrors.

She held her chin higher and her shoulders felt light as she left the bathroom and walked to her room, jolting at the guest on her bed.

"Sorry." Rae pressed against the soft quilt. "I didn't mean to scare you, but when I saw the light in the bathroom, I figured I'd wait."

Seren shook her head, her voice light. "It's okay, what's up?"

He turned and grabbed something from the bed. "I picked this up for you today. You said you liked to read, and I knew what material I had around and figured you might like something more entertaining." He pointed at the stack of books near his bed. He wasn't wrong. Seren had already browsed the titles and found nothing but tracking guides and cookbooks.

She stretched her hands and asked, "What is it?"

Rae gave a half-mouthed smile and handed her the book.

"*Wanted By Wolves: Volume One…*" Seren chewed on her bottom lip, one brow high.

"Carr helped me pick it out," he admitted. "Thrina's friend, Katolina, owns a bookshop in town. We could go sometime if you'd like."

That explained the choice of a risqué romance novel. Seren chuckled, smiling at him. "You didn't have to do that, but thank you. And I'd like that."

"It was nothing," Rae dismissed and strolled to the door, stopping halfway out. "Let me know when you're done reading it." He grinned. "I wanna talk about chapter fifteen."

The door closed, and he was gone before Seren could say anything.

She jumped into bed and shoved her legs beneath the covers. Leaning against the headboard, she opened the book, the soft candle offering enough light with the help of the moon for her to see the words. She read the first page, then five more, and eventually flipped to chapter fifteen with a sigh. Skimming the page, her eyes widened near the bottom, and her cheeks grew red as she imagined Carr and Rae picking out such a book.

Giggling, she found her place in chapter one again and continued reading, unable to stop. Somewhere around chapter twenty, she passed out—the book still in her hands and on her chest when she woke up the next morning.

CHAPTER 16

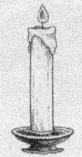

Seren sprinted a short distance behind Dax on the dirt trail bordering the training fields, the brisk morning air fogging around their quick breaths. She and Dax had a new morning routine that mirrored the one she and Mare had in Stellean. They woke up an hour earlier than the others and went for a race around the town before breakfast.

Having a routine again was soothing, relaxing even. With the Verti was the first time Seren had genuinely felt welcomed, felt safe. She appreciated it fully, no matter how short-lived it would be. Because she couldn't stay forever. Not when Hellevi planned to wage a war across the courts.

Dax stopped at the end of the field and Seren slowed. They'd walk the rest of the way to the house to cool down before inhaling whatever Rae had whipped up for breakfast. Dax pulled his damp shirt from his chest and asked, "You sure you never had any official training back in the courts?"

"Yeah." She gazed sideways as they walked next to each other. "Why?"

"You're just in far too good of shape." He paused. "Not to be blunt, but I have no idea how you're keeping up." He shook his head. "I'm not even going easy on you."

Seren grinned—the male looked more out of breath than she did.

Daring him, she poked, "That should teach you to never underestimate a woman, Dax."

He snorted, his mouth shut.

"You're pretty smart," she added, and he gave her a sideways smirk.

"So are you. I still can't believe how quickly you picked up Kings in the Courts. It took all the guys weeks to beat me for the first time, Rae excluded. It only took him one."

She felt Dax's frequent glances, and pride rippled through her. It felt good to have real assurance that she hadn't done too bad a job of raising herself. "Again, you should never underestimate a woman," she reiterated, her high brows drawing her lips into a wide smile.

"I'm starting to figure that out. But fair warning, it'll take the other guys a lot longer than me."

They laughed together and she elbowed him playfully. "So, you're the brains of the group, huh?"

He shrugged. "I guess you could say that."

Seren had spent fifteen days in their home, and she was grateful for every single one. Izzac had yet to come around, but the other four had welcomed her into their lives like a long-lost friend. Her tone was serious, genuine, as she said, "I really appreciate all of you guys. For helping me, and for everything, really. I hope you know that."

Dax wrapped his arm around her shoulder and squeezed as their steps fell in sync. "We're glad you're here. Plus, it's been nice to have a woman in the house." He chuckled. "Everyone's on their best behavior, and Carr doesn't leave his dirty socks all over the living room anymore. It's a win-win."

Glancing at the house, laughter stretched Seren's lips into a smile.

They walked to the front porch and Izzac rushed out the door, a swarm of red hair, anger, and wind. Inside, Rae stood with his back facing them, crumpled sheets of paper in his fists.

Stepping into the house, Dax asked, "Everything okay, man?"

Rae spun, eyes wide. "Oh, yeah." He shook the papers, his gaze searching behind them. "How was the run?"

"It was good," Seren said, giving Dax a curious look.

"You sure everything's good?"

"Yeah," Rae confirmed, closing the front door. "Izzac just came back from an info grab with an old pal. Something about the Fae causing more problems—annoying, but nothing unusual."

Seren's stomach tightened.

From what little she had learned about Izzac, she knew he focused on information collection for the Verti, traveling between the courts to keep an eye on anything that might prove a threat to their hidden territory.

Did he find out about Hellevi's war plans?

The king was capable of a lot, but so were the Verti if they'd survived in secrecy for so long. She couldn't assume anything was off the table.

"Don't let it get to you, man." Dax walked into the kitchen, speaking over his shoulder. "The Fae's problems are not our own."

Seren liked the sound of that. She stared at Rae and waited for him to shake the unease that Izzac had wrapped around him. Heavy footsteps descended the stairs, startling them both, as Carr hurried into the kitchen.

"Mate, what gives, no breakfast?" Carr whined loud enough for everyone to hear.

Rae smiled, smothering the tension in his expression. "Sorry,

Carr, y'all will have to fend for yourself for once. Seren and I have plans."

She perked up. That was news to her. She mouthed "what plans," and Rae waved his hand.

Frowning, Carr stepped out of the kitchen. "And I wasn't invited?"

"Sorry, man, not today. Seren and I have something to do." Rae ushered her out the front door, and Carr walked into the kitchen, sulking.

Seren asked, "What was that all about?"

"Like I said, we have plans." He walked in the town's direction.

"I don't remember making any."

"You didn't." He skipped forward. "But I did."

A warm breeze carrying sweet caramel tones and nutty aromas steered them to a delightful cottage restaurant, a cozy wood building with open square windows and peach shutters, lapped in dark green vines from the surrounding flora, the soft leaves dancing to the whimsical instrumental music coming from inside. A veil of tranquility blanketed every room, every table, even every customer as they mused peacefully through their morning.

A kind-faced, young waitress directed them to a small table in the far corner, away from the early crowd, and placed two painted mugs and a steaming pot of coffee on the table. Letting them know, she'd be back when they were ready.

"This is the best breakfast in town," Rae said, his eyes scanning the other diners.

"Even better than yours?" she asked.

He wrinkled his nose and exhaled. "Yes, even better than mine."

She lifted her brows in surprise. *How humble.* She giggled to herself. He poured their coffee—her cup, then his—and added a few drops of cream to hers, just how she liked it.

"Thank you," she said as he slid the green ceramic mug across the table. The young server came back, and Seren let Rae order as he promised everything would be good.

Their conversation flowed easily—from her thoughts on the town, to how her training had progressed, to Rae's mock attempts at mimicking Carr's incessant flirting from last night, when Carr tried to get Seren to sleep in his room, claiming Rae needed his beauty sleep in his own bed. Seren knew something would have to give soon, since Rae had been sleeping on the couch for two weeks. And if she was going to stay any longer, it wasn't fair to make him sleep like a guest in his own home, even if he never complained.

Talking about Carr, their conversation circled back to her training. The day before, Carr had taken bets on how long it would take Seren to beat one of them in a match. His best guess was two months from now, but she would make it one for spite. She asked, "So, what was your bet?"

Rae answered quickly, "Two more weeks."

That piqued her attention. "Really?" The past two weeks, she'd only landed on her ass a few times sparring with Dax, but even she knew she'd need more time than that.

"I've misjudged you before. If I'm going to do it again, I'd prefer it's because I had too much faith in you, not too little."

She shook her head. "No pressure, huh?"

Rae flashed a genuine smile, and Seren gulped at how disarming it was.

"The food's amazing," she said, searching for a distraction. Rae hadn't been lying when he said everything was good. He'd ordered four different meals and a few sides for them to split, persistent in getting her to try everything. By the time they were halfway through, there was nothing she'd tasted that she didn't love. Every time she claimed something was her favorite, Rae slid over another plate, and she quickly amended her last declaration. At his suggestion, Seren eyed the decadent cherryberry waffle they'd saved for last, topped with a copious amount of caramel-almond syrup. He cut it in half and handed her the larger piece.

"Thanks," she said, taking a big bite.

"You know, that waffle has been my favorite breakfast since I was little," Rae said, still chewing. "My old man was friends with the owner of this place and helped him build it when I was a kid. The waffle was just supposed to be a seasonal special, but I loved it so much my dad got his mate to keep it on the menu year-round, even worked some special import of cherry-berries from the courts to make it happen."

Smiling, Seren wiped the syrup from her chin. "He made an excellent call." She pointed with her fork. "This is fantastic."

A smile tugged at his lips. "I'm glad you think so."

Seren lifted her gaze. "Your father sounds like a good man."

"He was." Rae chewed slowly, then took another bite. "But a good man doesn't mean a good father."

Her bite of waffle turned to rubber, and she focused on cutting her next piece. When Rae said nothing else, she blurted, "What happened to him? I mean...where is he now?"

Rae set his fork down and folded his napkin, his eyes on his plate as he spoke. "My old man loved my mom, more than I've ever seen someone love another. But my mom..." He brushed his fingers through his hair. "She went missing when I was eleven and my dad lost it. He was a decent dad when I was a kid, when he was around. But he loved me because my mother did. I always guessed he never wanted children, or at least not when they had me."

Seren tried her best to comfort him. "I bet he loved you, Rae. He was your dad."

Waving his hand, his curly hair fell over his eyes. "He did love me, but he loved my mother more. I mean, he would have lit Clarallan on fire if it meant he could find her. But the Verti forbade my father from searching for her, worried he was being irrational, that he wasn't thinking clearly. They thought he'd be found out in the courts, and he'd lead trouble back to their sanctuary."

Seren gulped, jarred by Rae's intense eyes.

He continued, "They wouldn't let him look for her, and this drove my father mad. He stopped eating, stopped sleeping. The whole town worried what he would do. They eventually got the Domini involved, afraid my father was gonna snap. The Domini's the leader of the Verti, like your king, but different." Rae's eyes darkened, and he swallowed. "He begged my father to wait it out, but my dad, he wasn't thinking clearly. So the Domini swore in protection of his people that if my father left, he was never allowed to return." Rae paused. "My father left that night."

Seren went still. "That's awful."

Rae shrugged. "I don't blame the Domini. He did what he thought was best for his people. I can't imagine the responsibility of caring for an entire population for centuries. Surviving the Great Wars, and after, keeping his people alive in secrecy. I'll never know what that's like, so I can't be mad at his decision."

Rae was detached, hyper-rational. Searching for something to say, Seren took a sip of her coffee. "Still, you were just a kid, and you'd already lost one parent. He didn't have to make you lose another." Rae dropped his eyes. "Did your father ever find her?"

"I don't know," he said, without looking up. "I haven't heard from him since."

Seren was worried if she asked too many questions, Rae would stop answering. She couldn't believe how much he had shared with her already. Quietly, she asked one more. "What happened to you? If you were only eleven…"

"Thrina took me in. Let me live with her for as long as I needed. I bought the house when I was eighteen." Slight smile lines softened the harshness in his eyes. "I know I said Thrina's like a mom to me, but she is one. For all she had to put up with raising me through my teenage years, she deserves at least the credit that comes with the title."

"I'm glad you had her." Seren's heart swelled, and a pang of envy made it stutter.

"I owe her my life. After my father left, I was hysterical, and it took me a long time to be okay with never knowing the truth. Thrina kept me together, and from hurting myself and others. My anger was my own worst enemy."

Seren's gut churned. She didn't understand how Rae was so okay with never knowing the truth. "How'd you move on? How'd you stop being angry?"

"My Cere changed a lot for me. Seeing what Blaise's anger did to him. It festered in his heart and poisoned his soul. I never wanted to be anything like him, so I had a choice to make. Let my anger steer my story, or siphon it into something positive. I passed the Cere, moved in with the guys, and focused on giving back to my people."

"Wow," Seren praised. She had her own philosophy from years of surviving the king: be careful of what she carried in her mind, because her heart always carried its true weight. But despite her efforts, she was still angry. "I'm happy for you, Rae. And I hope one day, if it's right, you learn the truth."

"Thank you." His jaw ticked. "But I stopped wishing for that a long time ago."

"Oh..." Seren didn't know if she was envious of or sorry for him. Could ignorance be as peaceful as he made it out to be? Or had everyone just beat him down enough to convince him that he didn't deserve the truth?

"Enough about me." Rae's tone lifted. "What was it like back in the courts?"

The change in subject took her by surprise. This was the most they had ever talked about their lives before they met, and he had already shared so much... Seren couldn't believe he asked her something for a change, even if it was just to turn the attention away from him.

She swallowed. "Um... I lived in the Stellean court my entire life, so I don't know much about the other courts." Her eyes scanned the wall behind him, catching on the childish artwork littering the quaint restaurant. *From the Verti school kids,* Rae had explained when they sat down. Her heart strained, but she continued, "Actually, when you found me it was my first time going past the Court Market." Rae tilted his head and his mouth gaped, but Seren didn't give him the chance to interrupt. "Like I said, I worked as a servant for King Hellevi after my mom died when I was four, so there isn't much to say. The wildest things to happen to me basically all happened after I met you."

Rae started and stopped. Seren's palms were damp and her throat stung impatiently.

He asked, "And your dad?"

A shrug. "My mom said he died before I was born."

"I'm sorry—"

"Me too."

"I didn't mean for breakfast to turn so dark."

"It's okay." She looked up, determined. "You didn't have to tell me anything, and you did, and you saved my life, and you're letting me live with you." She took a breath. "The least I can do is tell you about myself."

Even if Seren could think of nothing she hated talking about more.

"You don't have to, Seren."

"I want to, I just—I've never had to talk about it before. I know it's hard to believe, but I didn't have many friends in Stellean."

"That's not hard to believe at all."

Seren glared at his quick response. Then rolled her eyes as he waved his hand and amended, "Sorry, please continue."

"Well, Hellevi basically owned me after she died. And I had

no other family. But it didn't matter, anyway. My mother was a servant too."

"What happened to her?"

Seren steeled her voice. "The king killed her."

Rae's eyes widened. "Your life sounds—"

She looked up through her lashes. "Awful?"

A tight nod. "Why did you wait so long to escape?"

She didn't have a good answer. Maybe because she'd had nowhere to go, no money, or magic, or maybe because it was all she had ever known, and it's impossible to compare darkness to more darkness. So that's what she told him, leaving out the pieces that were too dark to confess. Rae listened intently as she explained the story of her childhood, then her life, all the way to the day she ran from Stellean.

He was a good listener, following along smoothly as his demeanor encouraged her to share things she had never told anyone besides Mare. It was therapeutic to spill the details of her life, and Seren didn't care how vulnerable she sounded—it felt too good to stop.

At the point in the story that involved her hiding in the armoire, Rae asked, "Who was with the king?"

Shushing him, she scolded, "I was getting to that. Anyway, long story short, Prince Evander propositioned Hellevi about a supposed war—"

"War?" Rae whispered angrily.

"The story would go quicker if you let me tell it." She glared. "Hellevi wants to become the High King of Clarallan."

"He what?" Rae's eyes bulged. "Seriously, Seren, when were you going to tell me about this?"

Her brows pinched. She hadn't. Her plan had been to spend a few weeks with the Verti, and then... Well, she didn't know yet. But something that included stopping the king. "I didn't think you would even care to know. Why would the Verti bother themselves with the Fae?" She faintly recalled how upset he had been that morning.

"A war affects everyone. You should have told me sooner."

"Oh, right, my bad. After you found me I should have just been like, hey stranger, thanks for saving my life, but do you want to know why I'm running? A war is coming that'll destroy the entire kingdom."

Rae gave her a pointed look, like he would have preferred exactly that.

Guilt bit at her heart. The Verti deserved to know what was coming, yet she had kept it to herself because she'd been selfish and enjoyed living a normal life for once. She groaned. "I'm sorry. I just—"

"Wait." Rae's eyes narrowed. "You said he wants to become a High King?"

Seren nodded.

"That's impossible."

"Why?"

"How much do you know about Clarallan's magic?"

"Not much."

"Well, the thing about Clarallan is that the kingdom's magic is as alive as you or me. Its magic prevents a High King from being created through war or killing, a fail-safe policy that prevents the wrong people from being in power."

"Whether or not he becomes a true High King"—she threw air quotes around "true"—"he can still terrorize the entire kingdom through bloodshed and violence."

"Hellevi has to know his war is fruitless." Rae clenched his fists and drops of blood pricked his palms beneath his claws. "There is only one way for a High King to be crowned."

"How?"

"I want to show you something." Rae swooped his eyes to the door, then dropped a few copper coins to pay. "Let's go."

CHAPTER 17

Seren eyed Rae's back as he marched toward the Ruins, leaving her trudging behind him.

When they left the restaurant nearly an hour ago, Seren had half a mind to walk in whatever direction was opposite of where Rae wanted to go. This Rae felt like the one she had met in the Galaxius Forest—rigid body language, hasty steps, and that domineering silence of his that set Seren on edge. But she had conceded as he rushed out of the Verti village and dragged her up the small summit.

Fear followed her closely, reminding her of what awaited as they entered the Ruins the same way they once left.

In the daylight, unconcealed by darkness, the Ruins were overwhelming, their nightmares on full display. The ghastly artwork no longer whispered centuries-old stories—it hissed—and the smashed statues lay around her feet, split open for an autopsy of bygone horrors.

Seren's stomach tightened, and she walked over the collapsed remains without a word. Rae's mouth was pulled down, his eyes never staying in one place as he led them through the fallen kingdom. He walked beneath a fractured archway, and Seren trailed close behind.

Rae laced his hands to help Seren climb over the fallen rubble. She towered above him on the cracked stone, then offered her hand, but the Verti male just jumped and landed next to her in seconds. He pointed down a long hall and said, "This way."

A cavernous courtroom loomed before them, steeped in the musk of mold and stiff air. Sunlight filtered in through the decaying ceiling, flashing against towering murals carved into the stone walls; wisps of rainbow bounced across the mosaic tiles, illuminating the entire room.

It was unbelievable and utterly breathtaking. Seren couldn't imagine how something so magnificent had survived such cruel centuries.

The murals blazed with color, so realistic, as if the people might step out of the walls and take a breath.

Seren whispered, "What is this place?"

"The history of Clarallan." Rae pointed to the wall at their left. A brilliant galaxy circled a flaming center, drawing swirls of gold-and-silver ether through the dark sky. "This mural depicts the formation of Clarallan. The solar kingdom was born millennia ago, its magic gifted by the gods from the galaxy." He walked past her, gesturing to the mural on the back wall—an abstract convolution of creatures and humans, light and dark, all encircled by lines of yellow and flames. "This shows the creation of Clarallan's life."

Thick carvings of Fae and shifters jutted from the mosaic tiles, but also beasts that Seren didn't recognize. She pointed, eyeing an intricate avian carving. "What's that?"

Rae stiffened. "A phoenix." He paused. "They went extinct about a century ago."

Seren's heart cracked. The Fae had decimated Clarallan,

leaving a skeleton in place of the glorious kingdom and ghosts of its fantastical creatures.

"I can't believe the Fae..." She shook her head. "I mean I can, but not really. How are they okay with what they did?"

"The Fae are a plague to Clarallan."

Rae's tone sent shivers coursing over Seren's skin, and she sucked in a bracing breath, forcing herself to step after him toward the third mural.

This mural was different from the others. It split into five distinct sections, each labeled near the bottom in bold black words. Seren squinted and read, "Sollian, Lunaan—"

Rae cut her off. "Ocealla, Etiamella, and—"

"Stellean," Seren finished for him. "What do they mean?"

He opened and closed his mouth. "Remember how I said a High King can be crowned just one way?" He gestured with an open palm at the five panels. "This is the way." Seren's eyes narrowed as Rae continued. "The five panels represent the legend of the ancient trials, sometimes called the Lost Trials."

Seren's mouth went dry. She knew nothing about the trials, but at least she had a simple understanding of the history Rae explained. She mumbled, "I guess I should be glad I brushed up on my reading in Stellean."

Rae seemed to consider her past for a moment before turning his attention back to the mural. "The legend goes that when the gods created Clarallan, it was ruled only by magic, lawless and uncontrollable. Many tried to conquer the kingdom, aware that whoever steered its magic would undeniably be the most powerful person in Clarallan. But everyone who tried failed. The gods refused to let their kingdom be conquered through fear, blood, or death. Only someone who could respect, master, and appreciate what the gods had created—someone who could harness the kingdom's magic, not enslave it—could become a High King."

"Like Ares?" Seren asked.

A nod. "Ares discovered this and wanted to protect Clarallan. So the kingdom rewarded him, guiding him to the ancient trials."

Seren had too many questions and not enough coherent words. "How?"

"For decades, the kingdom punished those who tried to kill their way to power. A young Ares, inexperienced and determined, spent years studying Clarallan's magic, until one day, the lands spoke to him. Ares claimed the kingdom whispered its secrets directly to him, showing him what he needed to do to become a High King. The only thing that stood between his pure heart and unimaginable power were five trials intended to test his mastery of Clarallan's magic—to weigh his soul against the wishes of the gods." Rae faced Seren, his expression taut. "The rest, as they say, is history. Ares succeeded and ruled Clarallan for centuries before the Great Wars, and even you know where the story goes from there."

Seren tilted her head. "But it's just a myth?"

"I said 'legend' because no one besides Ares has ever successfully completed the trials, and as you know, Clarallan has only ever had one High King." Rae turned to look at the colorful wall. "Few alive today were around for Ares's rule, the Domini being one of them. But these murals were his design—said to represent the truth, exactly as Clarallan taught it to him."

Seren stood inches away from the wall, gazing at the elaborate art. It didn't surprise her that she had never heard of the trials before, not when she knew so little about the gods. She traced her fingertips over the carvings, confused when heat spread to her palms, warming her entire being.

Curious, Seren pressed her hands flat against the mural—and her entire body flared with heat.

She swore, and Rae whipped his head to watch as cords of light burst from her fingers and twisted around her arm.

All color blanched from his face as he gaped at her. "Seren…"

Yellow light seeped from her skin into the stone, and the stories came to life.

The mural was liquid in motion as Ares's history unfurled before them. Magic simmered across the stone, and Rae stumbled back, swearing as he called her name again. But Seren couldn't tear her eyes away. Her senses were captive, her body beyond her control. Magic seared her thoughts, branding her memory with Ares's journey through the five trials. But when Ares cried out into the darkness, it was her voice she heard instead. And when she saw him trudge through a moonlit forest, her nose filled with the scent of earth and rain. Ares screamed in pain and Seren fell, her hands ripping from the mural as the taste of iron pooled in her mouth.

She gasped, and sand scratched her throat as she tried to speak.

"Bloody, Cere, Seren!" Rae grabbed for her, hauling her from the ground. "Are you okay? What was that?"

Magic crackled as the murals fell motionless, the sentient lives returning to inanimate stone. Seren shook, and Rae kept his hands on her shoulders while he waited for her to regain control over her body. Her senses were fried from the magical experience of living through Ares's eyes.

He asked again, "Are you okay?"

She coughed as words climbed out of her dry mouth. "I think so." But Clarallan's magic still tickled her ears, whispering its pleas. As if the kingdom spoke directly to her—connected to the warmth pooling in her chest.

"What was that? How did you—"

"I don't know." She placed her hands on her knees, her head too light.

"Did you do that?"

"I don't know, Rae." How could she have?

Wind stirred at their feet, picking up strength as it collected the magic that still flickered from the walls.

His jaw tightened. "We should go."

Seren held up a hand, closing her eyes as she willed the magic from her system. "Give me a minute."

He frowned. "We need to leave."

Glaring up at him, Seren huffed. "Talk to me when something like that happens to you. It feels like someone injected fire directly into my veins."

Rae started walking and Seren groaned.

She followed after him, slowly. It felt like she had a fever and the sun was too bright as she drug her trembling body over the rubble. Rae helped her to the trail, and then quickened his pace.

Howling gusts of wind tore through the Ruins behind them, carrying cries of magic that begged for Seren to return. Rae broke into a jog, and Seren could barely keep up as he steered them to town.

Finally, the Ruins were too great a distance for their magic to haunt her. The trials were etched permanently in her mind, but no longer did the eerie whispers drown her ears.

Rae glanced over his shoulder. "Are you okay?"

"I'll be fine."

He slowed to a walk, the house in sight. "How'd you do that?"

"Can you stop asking me that?" Seren snapped. She couldn't make sense of anything herself, let alone explain it to him.

"I'm sorry." He looked down. "But that's never happened before. You had to have done something."

Seren frowned, stopping at the yard as Rae strode ahead. "Where are you going?"

"To see the one person who might be able to explain what the hell just happened."

CHAPTER 18

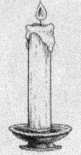

The Domini lived on the far side of the village. His house, settled at the end of a long, tree-lined dirt path, was bigger than any of the others, fit for the leader of the Verti.

"Are you sure this is a good idea?" Seren asked, a step behind Rae.

"It's the only one I have."

Seren searched for any reason to turn around. They could go home, talk it out, and make a different plan for the next day. Anything that didn't involve coming face-to-face with one of Clarallan's oldest citizens. "But what if we're bothering him?"

"The Domini is the leader of the Verti. He needs to know about this." Rae gave her a pointed look and continued, "Like I said, as far as I know, something like that has never happened before. And even if it means nothing, the Domini will want to know."

Seren nodded, defeated.

"You can trust me. The Domini is the oldest Verti alive, and he knew Ares. If anyone can help us, it's him."

"And the Domini..." She peered ahead. She'd never asked

about their shifting before. "He can shift, like the rest of you?" A nod. "And so, what is he?"

"A northern lion, known to rule the highest mountains of Clarallan."

Seren shuddered and made a mental note to learn more about the Verti's magic later; she couldn't handle any more nerves before meeting the Domini.

Fear bobbed in her throat. She wanted to trust him, to exchange her fear for the warm feelings this male stirred within her. But she didn't know how. She'd survived on her own because of her caution and skepticism. It didn't feel right to just let those weapons go because he said she could trust him. She glanced at his kind face and guilt spread through her veins. One corner of his mouth tugged up and his eyes dimmed, a grim hint he could read her doubt.

"I'm not used to working with others," she confessed.

Rae opened his mouth and hesitated. A smirk broke over his lips and he said, "Explains why you don't always play nice."

Seren half smiled. "I'm working on it."

He chuckled. "I'm playing, Seren. I know we already live together and all, but that doesn't mean we didn't skip a few steps. We're still getting to know each other, and trust comes with time. You don't owe me yours."

Seren's smile spread to her eyes. "Thank you…for everything." She was too exhausted to say anything else. She quieted, steeling her energy to face the leader of the Verti while goosebumps soared over her skin. The Domini was centuries old. Seren couldn't imagine what it was like to know so much, to have seen so much. The Fae's history shouted in her memory— she wasn't sure she could endure such horrors for so long.

Silently, they walked to the front door. The trees lining the path cleared, exposing the grand three-story home in the center of a lush meadow, its thick green grass littered with colorful moonbells of yellow, orange, and pink.

Rae braced his hand and asked, "You ready?"

She looked forward and he knocked, bowing his head as they waited for an answer. Seren dipped her own chin, and the door swung open.

A wary voice offered them entry, and the Domini asked softly, "Would you like anything to drink?"

"No thank you," Rae answered for them both. "We just came to talk."

Seren lifted her gaze and followed Rae as the Domini led them down a narrow hall to an open living room. Despite the warm spring weather, soft flames lit the fireplace on the back wall, three leather couches set to face it.

The Domini waved. "Let's sit."

Seren held his gaze as she and Rae claimed the couch across from the Domini, who must have been hundreds of years old, but sitting there, he looked no more than sixty. Sparse wrinkles rutted his skin, laugh lines embedded high in his cheeks, while youthful eyes contrasted any signs of age, their color an unusual mix of crimson and copper.

"Thank you for having us, unannounced," Rae said, his tone pure admiration. He truly appeared to hold no grudge against his leader for playing such a devastating role in his life.

"Anything for my children." The Domini paused, his stare landing on Seren. "But you, I don't think we've met before. What's your name, child?"

Seren's eyes widened, her mouth dry.

Rae answered for her. "This is Seren. She's been staying with me and my friends."

"Very well, Seren." His words were a purr as he slid her name over his rough tongue. "You're not Verti, then." Phrased, but not asked as a question.

"No," Seren confirmed anyway.

"Where are you from?"

"The courts." A hint of fear lathered her respectful tone.

"Stellean, to be exact." Seren swore flames rippled through the Domini's eyes, but they were gone before she could decide if they were a mere reflection of the fire burning at their side.

The Domini dampened his lips, leaning forward and resting his elbows on his knees. "What brings you two here?"

Rae glanced sideways, then stared at the intimidating leader. "We're seeking your wisdom, sir. We visited the murals in the Ruins, the stories of Clarallan's history that you lived through firsthand. But when we were there"—Rae swallowed hard, the only sign he was actually nervous—"something weird happened. The murals moved. Came to life before our very own eyes."

The Domini's eyes narrowed on Seren, and unease crept from her stomach to her throat. He asked, "What happened before the murals moved? Did you do something, trigger anything?"

Rae answered, "Seren touched them."

The Domini's eyes melted to an all-knowing copper. He rose gracefully and stepped toward her, gesturing at her hands with his own. "May I?"

Seren nodded, and he wrapped his aged hands around hers, closing his eyes as he tilted his head back. Confusion surged through her and she looked at Rae. He mouthed a fruitless "It's okay," and Seren looked back to the Domini, not quite as sure as her friend.

The Domini squeezed her hands and opened his eyes. A spark shuddered through her arms and heat pooled in her stomach. Then he let go.

"I see." The Domini hummed.

"See what?" Seren and Rae asked together, eyes wide.

The Domini sat down, his hands shaking slightly as he returned his stare to Seren. "I haven't felt magic like that in a long time. Since before the Great Wars, actually."

"Magic?" Seren blurted.

So it was true.

Her heart was about to tear from her chest when a cord of warmth wrapped around her fear and tied hope to it instead, securing it to her ribs and forcing her breath to steady.

"Seren's human," Rae countered.

"No." The Domini's eyes glowed.

Seren stilled. She didn't understand, but it felt right.

"What do you mean, no?" Rae darted his eyes between her and his leader. For once, he wasn't the calm one, and Seren could tell how much it bothered him.

The Domini's eyes never left her. "Magic runs through your veins, child. An ancient, powerful kind. And although you may not be Verti, you certainly are not human."

She couldn't believe what she asked next, "Fae?"

"I can't be sure."

Seren gulped, not willing to consider what the Domini's uncertainty meant. Part of her wanted to storm from the house, out of the town, and sprint until her legs collapsed; half-heartedly hoping she could outrun the mess that had been made of her unrecognizable life. But an even larger part of her knew she had to stay.

"What do you know, then?" Her tone was cold and sure, and even Rae sat straighter as her confidence grew. She needed answers, ones she'd never find if she ran. The king had shattered her life with one lie—the rest, she would force together until the truth shone through.

"I don't have all your answers, child." The Domini gestured to them both. "But Clarallan does. Listen to its magic. Let it show you its history so that you can save its future."

"How?" Rae asked.

"Why do you think the murals moved?" The Domini quirked his fuzzy brow.

"Clarallan wanted to teach me about the trials." Seren's jaw hung open. "But why?"

The Domini gave her an obvious look.

THE WEIGHT OF WISHES

"No." Seren's stomach churned. Memories flashed in her mind and made her dizzy. She leaned against the couch. Her healing, her strength, the dress, the Seer...the list went on. Prue's words floated above the chaos: *A star's light can end the fight; through trial and test, the kingdom is blessed.* She couldn't remember the rest, but—she turned to Rae and his concerned expression steered her gaze back to the Domini. "What if I can't? What if I don't want to?"

The Domini's face fell. "Clarallan speaks with you, Seren. That is an unimaginable gift. Mustn't you want to know the truth?"

"Yes." She wanted nothing more.

"Tell me, then, what happened when the murals moved?"

Rae jumped in. "I told you, we saw the trials come to life—Ares's story."

The Domini waved his hand. "That is what you saw." He clicked his tongue at Rae. "But, Seren, what did you see? Or should I say, what did you feel?"

Confusion creased Rae's brow.

Seren closed her eyes, and the events of the Ruins flooded her mind. She lifted her hands and traced invisible carvings from memory. "The trials." She paused, and a familiar heat unfurled in her fingertips.

"Seren—" Rae sounded worried.

"Don't," the Domini snapped. "Keep going, child."

"I saw the trials. But I felt them too. It was like I was watching Ares's life through my eyes. Like I was him, or he was me." She was rambling, but she couldn't stop. Warmth spread to her arms, seeping to her core. "It was my body that felt the pain, my mind that was tested, my magic that was unlocked." She trembled as she relived each vivid experience in seconds, her words not entirely her own. She opened her eyes, breathless.

Rae was pale, a frightening look for the golden male. His mouth hung open, but the Domini motioned to her hands.

"See, child..." His eyes glowed. "Magic."

Shakily, she repeated the foreign words, her eyes falling to her hands. "My magic that was unlocked." Thin light flickered across her skin, and she heard the sound of sizzling flames as she brought them closer to her face. She looked up. "How can this be?"

"Clarallan's magic was subdued by the Great Wars, its strength lost over the years, like a curse from the gods. A punishment on the citizens of Clarallan for destroying their greatest creation. But you, child, your magic is pure and primitive. Ethereal even, like theirs. It is what Clarallan has been searching for"—he took a breath—"what the gods have been searching for, for centuries."

The words *I think you have the wrong person* barreled to the tip of her tongue, but the Domini went on. "There is a war coming, one that will destroy the kingdom if it comes to pass. The gods would rather let Clarallan fall than crown Hellevi as their High King."

"You knew?" Rae interjected.

The Domini smiled with the corner of his mouth and chuckled. "Of course, child. But Clarallan walks a dangerous path. The kingdom will fall at the hands of the king. Let Clarallan guide you, or I fear the kingdom will never recover. Clarallan's magic will be lost forever."

A shiver tickled her neck and she shuddered.

The Domini's eyes glassed over. "Your trials and tests will forge a kingdom blessed; by magic and blood, destroy the peace, through five tribulations all is complete."

She'd heard that before. Or at least, Prue had said something similar. Seren had written her off as mad, but... "Why do you say that?"

The Domini shook as a cool sweat clustered on his forehead. When he looked to her again, the eerie crimson-copper color had returned to his eyes. "Those are Clarallan's words."

Seren blinked slowly, and the Domini stared at her as if it was all supposed to make great sense. News flash: her entire life felt like shattered glass. Pieces of her broken by lies, too vague and scattered to put back together. Overwhelmed, Seren stood, turning to Rae. "Are you ready to go?" Rae gawked at her, his eyes bulging. She bowed her head at the Domini, who simply smiled, a lingering sadness in his eyes. "Thank you for your time."

The Domini stood, ushering them to the hall. "Come back soon."

Seren rushed toward the front door, and Rae's boots squeaked against the wood floor as he hurried after her, thanking the Domini relentlessly. The door closed behind him and he leaped toward her, poking her shoulder.

"We didn't have to leave like that," he complained.

"I couldn't be in there any longer. I was going to lose it."

"Are you okay?"

Seren whipped her head to him, exaggerating with her arms as she said, "You should know better than to ask that."

Rae stopped. He'd never seen her angry before. "I'm sorry, I—"

"I, what?" she snapped. She had planned to save the existential crisis for when she was alone—that's why she had rushed out in such a hurry—but she guessed now would have to do. Clenching her fists, she let her words fall. "Did you just find out your entire life has been a lie? No? I didn't think so. Or how about, were you the one who just found out you have magic, like real magic, when you've spent twenty years thinking you were human?" Rae didn't deserve her cruelty, but unfortunately for him, he was the only one around. "Or, what about this one, did you just get told you have to complete five ancient, deadly trials?" Her long-winded assault left her breathless, and Rae stepped back, his eyes dark.

She almost felt guilty about the hurt that flashed across his face, but then she remembered how basically everything that had gone down that day was his fault. She never should have told him about the war.

Look what good being vulnerable had gotten her.

"I'm sorry for caring, Seren." He strode past her. "Next time, remind me not to give a shit."

His voice cracked as he said her name, and Seren knew she'd caused some damage. He'd been vulnerable and caring, and she'd shoved it all in his face. Her heart cracked and pain spread through her chest and she hated every shudder of her body and every gasp of breath—especially every stupid emotion her heart threatened to unleash, as her life threatened to disintegrate before her.

"Rae, wait," she shouted, jogging after him. She reached her hand for his shoulder but he sidestepped her touch. Her lips quivered. "Rae, please."

"What?" He halted, his voice like gravel.

She shook her head, sure he could hear her pounding heart. "I can't do this without you." She willed strength in her eyes as she forced herself to meet his gaze. "I don't know what I'm supposed to do, okay, and I shouldn't take it out on you, but... my life blew up when I left the castle. Everything I have ever known has been a lie, and when I met you, well, you were the first thing in my life to feel real." Seren couldn't believe the vulnerability pouring from her lips. "I need your help, Rae."

Her confession dismantled his anger.

Everything about him softened, and he said nothing as he stepped close to her, wrapping his arms around her. His embrace was warm and safe and she buried her head against his chest. He squeezed tighter and her breathing settled, her heart beat falling in sync with his as his firm chest breathed beneath her cheek. "Then let me in, Seren."

∾

THAT NIGHT, Seren woke up gasping for breath, the dark air cool on her bare skin. She reached for the covers, ready to roll herself under and tuck in for a few more hours of restless sleep, but...

There were no blankets. Not even a bed.

She stood in an endless black void, eight familiar moons whirling above her—dreaming.

"Seren." The cold voice came from everywhere, magic heavy on her name. Even the moons reacted to its strength, its dominance—the full moon spun, and the shadows shook beneath her.

She searched the darkness, but fell still as silver-blue eyes pierced the void. The murky shadows peeled away as the prince strode forward, the moonlight illuminating the intricate lines of dark ink that swirled across his sculpted chest and dipped beneath his loose black shirt, stretching over his shoulders and across his back. Her eyes caught on his collarbones, protruding above tattooed moons, different phases on each side.

Seren mused, "Doesn't a prince have better things to do than sneak around my dreams?"

His eyes softened, and surprise flickered across his face. Shaking his head, he asked, "You still think this is all a dream, huh?" Seren gave him her best obvious look, with one brow raised higher. "Interesting," he said, and the shadows fluttered around his breath as he loosened a low chuckle.

"Why are you here?"

"It's your dream, is it not? You tell me." When she didn't answer, the prince continued, "Maybe it's because you can't stop thinking about me, but I have to say, usually when women dream of me"—he waved at the darkness with a sinful smirk—"it's in a much different setting."

"You sure think highly of yourself," Seren taunted, stepping through the murky shadows. She halted with inches of space between her and the prince, suddenly uneasy with his presence, not because of anything he'd done, but because of how he made her feel when he was so close. "And as fun as that may sound, I'm not interested in having a sex dream with you."

"Who said anything about that?" He faked his most innocent expression. "I prefer not to be used for my body"—his smile grew—"even in the minds of beautiful women."

Seren had a feeling there were a lot of things the prince used his body for, and none of them were as innocent as he was trying to make them seem. She ignored the heat that stirred within her and cursed her cheeks for blushing. Not the time.

She looked up, her eyes never staying in one place too long.

This was the strangest dream she'd ever had. Her mind was probably scrambled after everything she'd learned that day, and maybe this was its way of trying to make sense of everything. With her luck, she was losing it. She could definitely cut herself some slack, even if she still couldn't explain why the Lunaan prince was here.

Casimir's voice interrupted her spiral. "You're not crazy."

Her breath caught as she looked at him, dazed. "How did you —how did you know what I was thinking?"

"Just a guess," he quipped out of the side of his mouth. He leaned forward, inspecting her. "Crazy's all about the eyes."

Seren scoffed. She didn't stop to think about what she did next. If it was just a dream, it didn't matter. She closed her eyes and let her imagination wander. "Tell me what I'm thinking about now."

In her mind she closed the space between them. Her hand graced his tight jaw and his throat bobbed as she brought her chin up. Seren opened her eyes, and Casimir's lips were pressed into a thin smirk as he said, "I can't read minds, Seren." But his voice was thick and his eyes simmered with a cold heat—all the confirmation she needed.

Then it dawned on her.

Of course he could read her mind. This was her dream, and he was quite literally a fragmented piece of her imagination. Her cheeks were warm and she felt silly as he watched her. He tilted his head and exhaled; he was so close she could feel the warmth of his breath. With a bold hand, he reached for a curly piece of hair that fell around her eyes, and his fingertips brushed her cheek as he tucked it behind her ear. His touch was soft and hesitant, and Seren wanted to close her eyes as he traced the lines of her neck. He might have looked like he was carved from marble, but everything about him was alive.

He leaned closer, and despite his warm breath, a chill coursed through her as he asked, "Does this still feel like a dream to you?"

CHAPTER 19

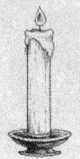

The kitchen was quiet the next morning when Seren took her usual seat across from Rae, the table seized by a glorious breakfast spread—four full pans of savory torte lined the center, with fresh fruit and warm rolls sliced and placed at the end.

Her stomach growled and she lifted her gaze to Rae. "Looks great."

"Thank you," he said, sliding a steaming mug in front of her. "It's Thrina's new recipe."

Seren smiled softly and sipped her coffee, waiting for the rest of the house to rise.

It didn't take long before Carr strode into the kitchen, jumped into his chair, and bumped his shoulder into hers. "Have any sweet dreams about me, sug?"

It took physical effort not to choke on her coffee and spew it across the table. She glared sideways at him. Usually, she was prepared for his taunts, but after her dream last night—

Seren steadied her voice. "Sweet is not the word I would use."

"Sexy?" Carr's brows bounced up and down.

"More like violent."

"Even better." He grinned. "You know how I like it."

Seren rolled her eyes and shoved him. Dax and Tait strolled in as Carr feigned being hurt, and Dax shot her a wink of approval.

Izzac hadn't joined them for breakfast in over a week, so the five of them sat at the table and dug in.

Mouth full, Carr asked, "So, Seren, where were you last night? Were Rae's plans really that disappointing?"

She took another bite and dragged her eyes across Rae, whose calm face was neutral like always—not one hint about how he felt after what happened yesterday. They had walked in silence from the Domini's place, and when they got home, Seren had gone straight to bed, skipping dinner and conversations she wasn't ready for. She needed time alone to think about everything she had learned the past few weeks, and even longer to decide what to do next.

All four males turned to her.

She swallowed hard. "I was just tired, that's all."

Carr waggled his brows. "Tired from what, exactly?"

The front door slammed, and Izzac stormed into the house—perfect timing. But one look at his face, and Seren knew whatever had happened was far from perfect.

"Izzac." Rae stood. "What's wrong?"

"Everything," Izzac shouted, the most emotion Seren had ever seen from the male. He was haunting, his beady eyes, red-rimmed and wild, sunken in against his angular cheekbones, his gaunt expression barely masking the flurry of wind and wings that seemed to live inside of him. He slammed a piece of paper on the table, and her coffee spilled. "The Stellean king made his move." His voice was ragged, shaky. "It's too late, Rae. You were right."

"Right about what?" Seren looked at Rae, but he ignored her and snatched the paper.

"It's a letter," Izzac said. "You failed...my father still lives." Everyone looked at him, and he jerked his chin to Rae. "I intercepted that between the Lunaan and Stellean courts. It's from one of the princes—intended for Hellevi."

Seren stiffened.

Carr threw his napkin on his plate and stood. "What's that mean, 'you failed'?"

Dax crossed his arms. "They planned an assassination."

Here it was. Everything that Seren had been putting off stood before her, screaming in her face that she wasn't ready, that she'd wasted weeks being selfish in her safety. She needed to do something. King Egil lived—but Hellevi never failed. If the Lunaan king was alive it was because Hellevi wanted it that way. But why?

"Egil's death was supposed to mark the start of the war," Izzac said, clenching and unfurling his fists as he paced in the kitchen. Seren swore talons pierced his fingertips.

Her gaze sharpened. "How do you know that?"

Izzac glanced sideways at Rae, his left hand fumbling with his lips.

"I told them." Rae dipped his chin. "Last night at dinner."

"Everything?" Seren stood.

"I had to tell them." He paused, flexing his fingers. "Like I said, a war affects everyone. We have to be prepared."

"We tell each other everything." Carr's eyes were gentle. "You can trust us."

She did, but that didn't absolve the betrayal that lingered in her mind as she looked at Rae. "What happens next?"

Izzac stopped pacing. "The assassination might have failed, but Hellevi still played his first card. A war is coming."

"How do you know all of this?" Seren stared at the hasty male, and he ran his hand through his disheveled red hair, his bright green eyes stark against the dark circles that blotted his pale cheeks.

Rae spoke. "The Verti have been observing the courts for years to ensure our secrecy remains. A few months back, our information channels went silent regarding Stellean. After I told the guys what you said, I asked Izzac to look into it." He glared at Izzac. "I didn't think he would act so quick."

"You should be grateful I did," Izzac countered. "I couldn't sleep after our conversation, so I left to meet up with an old contact. He's been slinking around the Lunaan court, and according to him, the eldest prince has been acting weird, even for the Fae. He started keeping tabs on him after Ardentiella—said something bad happened there."

Evander's wish.

"I also looked into this." Izzac dropped a leather journal on the table and flipped to a page in the middle.

Seren's heart stuttered. "The trials..." Her voice shook and she glared at Rae. "You told them about that too?"

Rae's face was annoyingly neutral—no shame, no guilt, and certainly no apology.

"I understand telling them about the war, but"—she closed her eyes for a breath—"you had no right to tell them about that too."

"I had to."

"Why?"

"You have magic, Seren." Rae threw his hands in the air. "Magic that could restore our kingdom. We have to learn more about the trials." Goosebumps pricked her skin. "You have to complete them, Ser."

"What if I don't want to?" It hadn't even been a day since she learned she had magic; she certainly hadn't made a decision about the trials yet. She'd had little time to think it over last night before sleep welcomed her into its arms and her dreams carried her to sweeter places.

She never wanted to make a decision like this. She'd barely

made any important decisions her entire life—everything dictated by the king.

Of all the males staring at her, she never guessed it would be Izzac looking at her the way he was—with understanding. It was the first kindness he'd ever extended to her.

"You could save Clarallan, and you're saying you don't know if you want to?" Rae's mouth furrowed. "How can that even be a question for you?"

If Rae were in her position, he'd do it in a second. The selfless male would do anything for those he cared about, that righteous hero complex that Seren recognized. She always thought she'd do the same, but her terror rang louder than her confidence.

"Our people need you." Tait's eyes were wide, his voice soft.

Dax cut to the point, straight to her heart. "The Verti won't survive another war."

If anyone had told her a month ago that Clarallan would need her help, she'd have called a healer on them. She still didn't understand her role in any of this. She was a nobody. A servant. A human—she'd thought, anyway—and a girl who had been told her whole life she had nothing to offer.

Now she had magic. And these people were asking for her help. Could she really walk away from the people who had saved her life right when she could save theirs? She had so many questions, the worst being, why her? But in the depths of her soul, she knew one thing.

She never wanted Hellevi to hurt anyone again.

Rae slid the journal toward her. "Read this before you make a decision."

"There is no decision," Izzac said. "If this is our only chance to stop the war, you have to do it."

Seren looked down and grabbed the journal. Their wonderful breakfast now stiff and cold. "I need some time." She didn't look back as she walked out of the kitchen, carrying the journal.

Rae walked after her. "I'll come with—"

"No." Seren felt the heat of his stare as she opened the door, her eyes on the cheerful spring day. "I want to be alone."

She headed away from the house, walking mindlessly through the town, grateful no one followed. It was the first time she'd been without one of the Verti, and surprise caught her off guard as familiar citizens waved and called out their hellos. She'd always thought the Verti only spoke to her because she was with Rae. But there she was, alone, welcomed into the town by people who knew her name and spoke to her with kindness. A rebellious smile puckered her lips as she was appeased by the sense of community.

Eventually she found herself at the edge of the training fields.

She ran for miles, and then a few more, not stopping until she passed the threshold where all pain disappeared and there was only her, the air against her face, and the land beneath her feet. She ran until her body went numb, hoping it would spread to her mind. And when she grew bored, she practiced drill after drill of her combat training. Twenty-five repetitions became fifty, and fifty became uncountable. The physical release was euphoric, and her mind mirrored the sensation. She wanted to feel like this forever—bottle it up and drink it, drown in it until she was drunk.

She cooled down and the feeling faded. The journal watched her, called for her. She trudged to where she'd dropped it and plopped into the grass, the dirt sticking to her sweaty clothes.

She'd known one thing before her workout and two things after: First, she never wanted Hellevi to hurt anyone again. Second, she would do anything to stop the king from hurting anyone the way he had her, even if it meant she had to do the trials.

She clutched the book, steeling her fears. She could still

change her mind, walk away at any moment. But for now, she knew what she needed to do.

Izzac's journal was neatly bound, with sections of handwritten notes, copies of old texts and maps, constellations, and charcoal sketches of places or creatures. Everything was legible and clear, and whatever she didn't understand had a translated footnote at the bottom of the page. Somehow, Izzac had answered every question she wanted to ask.

Seren flipped through the pages of the three main sections: the war, the trials, and magic. She breezed through the first section; Izzac had collected information on King Hellevi and King Dearil's war plan. The two kings had devised an excuse for why Evander would align himself with Stellean—Evander would offer the Lunaan court forces in exchange for Hellevi's aid in avenging Egil's assassination.

After what Seren had heard hiding in the armoire, she'd believed Hellevi was going to deny the prince's request. It appeared Evander's proof had been enough to sway the strategic king after all.

Yet the Lunaan king had lived, meaning Hellevi had failed. But Hellevi was a merciless killer, the type that enjoyed it. If he had wanted Egil dead, he would have taken his last breath.

A chill settled in her core, and she turned to the second section. A warm breeze wrapped around her, whispering thoughts that warmed her core. She was safe, she never had to see the king again if she didn't want to, it was her choice to stop him.

Seren had wished for her freedom her entire life, and this haven of a town had given it to her. The Verti had fought for their lives and gave her back hers—agreeing to do the trials put that at risk, but if she said no... if she walked away, she'd be putting her life above the thousands Hellevi would take by war. Maybe she was being a coward, but she was not a selfish one.

The king would never stop. Not until he killed his way to ruling all of Clarallan.

Doing nothing had just as much risk as doing the trials, and at least the latter gave her a fighting chance. She didn't have to go down as the girl who walked away when everyone needed her. She could fight. Despite the lies and everything she had yet to learn, she knew life was always worth fighting for. She would do anything to save those she cared about.

For the first time, she saw the trials as an opportunity and not a death sentence. For twenty years, all she had wished for was a chance at a better life. And here it was.

Five trials stood between her and the truth, justice and life.

She turned the page.

CHAPTER 20

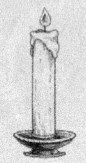

Seren flattened the book against her leg and took a deep breath.

She learned a lot about Izzac studying the journal—for instance, the male's attention to detail and organizational skills were enough to make her a little concerned. The book was divided into three clear sections following the exact same pattern every time. Section two comprised most of the journal, the first page boldly labeled "The Lost Trials" at the top, above a detailed sketch of the Ruins' murals. Following that was a precise map of Clarallan that included Izzac's specific recommendations for traveling between the courts.

She flipped to the first trial, and the page was filled by a close-up map of the Sollian court. Studying the hand-sketched illustration, Seren noted a red circle around the royal gardens and a short note:

The trials test your mastery of the court's magic and your worthiness to the gods. Go to their source.

Izzac didn't know for sure where the trials took place, but

he'd taken a damn good guess for each. Seren continued reading. The back page was blacked out entirely with charcoal, the right littered with neat details. She rubbed the corner of the paper between her fingers and committed the information to memory:

> *The Sollian Fae are healers. They bring light and growth to Clarallan. With their magic, they nurture the kingdom's future and are rewarded with the gift of life.*

Another drawing: a large Fae male standing in a ring of fire —Ares, she presumed. But the next page was blank except for one note:

> *The Sun will grant the first success; by test of life, all will progress.*

Seren rushed to the next page and her brows furrowed. There was nothing else on the Sollian trial.

The Lunaan section began the exact same way. A detailed map of the court and a red circle near the sea's edge behind the castle, but no note. She moved on. The next drawing showed Ares lying down, the space above him colored by a heavy hand.

> *The Lunaan Fae are dreamers. They bring imagination and inspiration to Clarallan. They walk between realms and know your greatest fears.*

Flipping through the drawings, her fingers smudged with charcoal. A vast sketch of a dream realm where Ares stood beneath a cosmic sky. Then two monstrous doors, asymmetrical and covered in moons. The drawings, abstract places and unimaginable objects, went on for ages.

Seren skipped to the last page of the Lunaan trial:

A second win from the Moon will test your mind, conquer dreams and nightmares or forever be lost inside.

She tried to memorize as much as she could, but a dull throbbing sensation bloomed in her temples. Any more riddles and Seren was sure her head would explode.

Studying the Ocealla trial, Seren paused on a sketch of a massive ship, and a chill kissed the nape of her neck. "To surmount the Sea, reach deep into the depths of control; one mistake and a watery grave awaits," she read aloud.

Seren shuddered. Excluding the Stellean trial, she dreaded Ocealla's the most. The ocean was a woman scorned—divine and ruinous. The sea witch's court rivaled her in beauty and cruelty.

Her hands were clammy, and the pages stuck together as she read from the Etiamella section:

A fourth conquest comes from the Comets; through fire and mass, destruction and space.

Seren's anticipation soared, and a cosmic unease washed over her—the Stellean trial was last. One drawing and one sentence concluded the second section. A charcoal sketch of Ares clutching his heart with his chest torn open, red ink dripping from his hands. Few of the drawings had been so morbid. Seren swallowed the trepidation in her throat, but her voice cracked with panic: "The Stars grant the final feat; make a wish and all is complete."

It was the most straightforward line of them all, but that wasn't saying much. Seren still didn't know what to expect of any of the trials.

The third section was the shortest. Izzac had concluded the journal with a few pages dedicated to Clarallan's magic, mostly filled with colored drawings of the kingdom preceding the Great

Wars. About to close the journal, she read: "Clarallan calls for those chosen by the universe, whose blood is blessed by the galaxy, those whose magic can master the stars."

The Seer's words wove with the ink on the page. Maybe there was no connection, but Prue had called her the daughter of the universe. Seren's thoughts were too tangled to unwrap, and she dropped the journal. She'd been at it so long the letters were starting to not even look like real letters anymore.

She fell backward into the grass and sank into the earth. Staring at the sky, she closed her eyes, focusing on the cool soil and the warm sun soaking her skin.

She lay that way for a while, and by the time she shifted upright and stood, the sun had glided to the western horizon and the clouds morphed into swirling hues of soft pinks and oranges. A day outside had served her well. She slid the journal under her arm and again walked alone through the tranquil town. When she ran out of the house that morning, her mind had been chaos. Now, her thoughts were clear, her chin high as she returned the smiles of the lovely citizens.

Seren's steps were sure, and she moved with purpose through the town that had saved her, her mind made up. With every day she spent away from the Stellean castle, she felt more and more like herself. She knew what she would face—the trials, the war, the king—yet her smile stemmed from the peace she had made inside her chest, and it spread from her heart to her face because the truth lay ahead too. As she walked back to the house and the friends she had made, Seren experienced for the first time what it was like to have people waiting for her—to go home.

FRESHLY SHOWERED, Seren stepped into the hall, where she smelled a smoky aroma floating up the stairs.

She walked to the kitchen and was swarmed by rich scents of onions, garlic, and bread. Rae haphazardly removed a hot tray from the oven while stirring a boiling pot on the stove, a strained look on his face as he bit his bottom lip. Seren held back a laugh, watching him stretch his arm and tilt his head as he tried to prevent the rolls from falling off. He danced around the kitchen wearing a tight apron, barely tied around his broad waist—a good look for the tough warrior. Seren barked out the laugh she held when she finally caught a glance of the words across the front: MR. GOOD-LOOKIN' IS COOKIN'.

Rae swiveled his head, a hopeful smile tugging at his lips.

She offered a smile in return and jerked her chin at his apron. "So, whatcha cookin', good-lookin'?"

Rae raised his brows. "You like? It's the best present Carr has ever given me."

Carr's deep laugh rumbled from where he lounged backward in one of the dining chairs, his head resting on top of his muscular arms as he crossed them over the wooden back.

Her smile wrinkled her eyes. "It suits you."

"Hey, Ser," Dax said, standing at the sink as he washed and cut the vegetables, tossing them in a bowl before handing them to Rae.

"Hey guys." She lifted her hand and Tait hummed as he set the dining table.

She placed the journal on the far counter, eyed the elaborate meal, and asked Rae, "Need any help?"

"I'm almost done. But can you hand those plates to Tait, please?"

Stepping around Rae, she set two plates near him and handed the rest to Tait. It was easy moving through the kitchen with them, like they'd practiced it together their entire lives. Love twisted around her heart, and she knew then: this was her reason for fighting.

Rae finished shortly, and everyone helped themselves to large portions. He'd prepared Thrina's version of biscuits and gravy with an abundance of meats and sauces that smelled incredible. It was hearty and delicious and tasted exactly like something a mother would make for her children after a long day playing in the sun.

Their conversation settled casually, and Seren was grateful no one asked about the trials or where she was all day. She didn't know whether or not they were waiting for her to bring it up, but it didn't matter. It was easy being with them again, and when they ultimately asked, she had her answer.

She would complete the trials; knowing that, Seren cherished every second of their meal—maybe one of the last normal ones they would get for a while. The only feeling of discomfort radiated from the empty chair at the end of the table. Apparently, Izzac had left shortly after Seren and had yet to return. His absence was somehow more disconcerting than his presence, and Seren couldn't help but wonder where he was. He'd been a ghost in their house ever since she had arrived and a not so small part of her believed it was her fault.

They ate unhurriedly, the males all going back for seconds and thirds. Rae was a remarkable cook and Seren knew Thrina was to credit. As they finished, Seren collected the empty plates and went to the sink. She plugged the left basin and filled it with warm water.

Rae stepped beside her as the others continued their drinks and conversation. "I can clean up."

"You cooked." Seren grinned, lopsided. "At least let someone else do the dishes."

Rae gave her an insistent look, and instead of joining his friends, he grabbed a rag and a bar of goat-milk soap. Seren gave him some room and Rae scrubbed the dishes, passing them to her to rinse and dry.

The others moved to the couches in the living room, their clinking drinks and rolling laughter echoing through the house.

Rae handed her the final soapy plate and dried his hands. "How was your day?"

"Productive," she said, her back to him as she stacked the plates in the cupboard. His steps were light as he approached, and his sudden nearness sent a shiver of shock through her. A plate in hand, he reached over her shoulder and started a pile on the top shelf. His empty hand brushed her arm as he let it fall back to his side, but he didn't step away.

The smell of earth and fire swarmed her senses as he lowered his head and spoke near her ear. But she didn't hear what he said, her feelings fried.

He stepped back and the space between them chilled. "Seren?"

She could hear then, her senses resuming their function without his overwhelming presence. Shaking her head, she turned and met his stare. "Yeah?"

"I asked you a question." Rae's grin was telling. He leaned against the counter, his arms flexed.

She looked at his eyes, bemused. "Did you?"

His laugh was soft, but his voice was low and thick. "Are you not going to ask how my day was?"

Seren's mind sharpened and she rolled her eyes. "Seriously?" Rae stared at her, and she scoffed. "Fine, how was your day, Rae?"

"Terrible."

Whatever she expected him to say, it certainly wasn't that. "I —" She spoke with no plan as to where her words were going, a terrible habit.

Rae stepped toward her, his hand extended. "Come with me?"

Taking his hand, a shrill of nerves shot up her arm. Rae's face gave nothing away as he led them out the back door and eased into the darkness; Seren's eyes taking longer to adjust.

"Where are we going?" she asked, and he pointed up. Her eyes widened and she shook her head. Rae ignored her and tugged her around the side of the two-story home. He halted and she gulped, looking up. "How are we even going to get up there?"

Rae said nothing and instead wrapped his arms around her waist. She wasted seconds freaking out about the way he grabbed her, so she didn't have time to ask what he was doing before he bent his knees and jumped.

Cold night air tampered with her gasp and her breath caught as Rae landed them gracefully on the highest point of the roof. She used her free arm to shove him, but his grip tightened, and he jerked his chin at the ground.

Her eyes couldn't pierce the darkness, but she knew how tall the house was. She grasped at his loose shirt, and he let out an amused chuckle.

"Seriously, Rae!"

He loosened his grip on her waist enough to have her scrambling toward him, and his chuckle morphed into a bark of laughter.

She glared and he pulled her closer. They sat with their backs against the steep slope, their feet far from the edge. "How'd you do that?"

He quirked a brow. "Verti, remember?"

"You could've at least given me a warning."

"If I'd done that, you would've run away before I had the chance to jump."

Seren nodded. He was right about that.

Rae leaned his head against the roof and stared at the stars. The weight of his arm drew her closer to him, and she adjusted her nervous body until she was comfortable, the scratchy roof irritating her skin. Rae spoke softly, "This has been my favorite place for years, especially at night."

"It's amazing," Seren whispered. She'd always loved the sky, all its phases equally. But at night, it was everything, beautiful and infinite, all-knowing yet mysterious. In Stellean, she would sneak onto the balconies and stare at the stars, usually after one of Hellevi's lessons. She'd talk to them as if they could answer, telling them the stories of her dreams, wishing they'd guide her to a better life. The stars twinkled and blinked, a silent witness to her pain, but at least they were the best listeners. Seren turned her head to the side. Rae remained staring upward and the moonlight cast shadows over his serious profile. "I used to talk to the stars back at the castle. For years, they were my only friends, the only ones who would listen."

"I've never brought anyone up here." He closed his eyes for a few breaths. "I love the guys, but growing up, I spent a lot of time alone."

"Why'd you bring me?"

He laid his cheek against the roof, his eyes meeting hers, ignoring her question. "You didn't ask why my day was terrible."

"You didn't give me the chance." Seren pointed at the sky with her free hand.

"Right," he huffed. "Well, all day I couldn't stop thinking about you and the trials. What we're asking you to do, the danger we're putting you in." He paused, his gaze scanning her face for something she didn't understand, his eyes burning darker than she'd ever seen them. "If you'd asked why, I would've told you I felt awful about this morning. Yesterday too. We threw you into this and didn't even stop to ask how you feel about everything. This morning I didn't mean to make you feel like you didn't have a choice." Rae brushed a strand of hair from her eyes, his fingers gracing her cheek. "I know what we're asking is a lot. It's risky and dangerous, and we don't know nearly enough about anything. And you, you're just now learning about all of this and your magic…" His eyes drifted to where he twirled her hair between his fingers.

She opened her mouth, but he shushed her.

"I want you to know this is your decision…and whatever you decide, I'll understand. We all will."

Seren's heart swelled at his admission. She hadn't realized

she'd been waiting to hear that. But even if he and the others could understand her decision either way, she didn't feel the same. Deep in the center of who she was and who she wanted to be—she knew she would never forgive herself if she walked away from the kingdom when it needed her most. "It's okay, Rae, really." Her words were steady. "I'm going to do them. The trials, I mean."

"Really?" The corners of his mouth curved up, but his eyes told a different story—a flash of pain or regret that he blinked away before Seren could understand.

"I have to—"

"You don't have to do anything you don't want to."

Seren closed her eyes and shook her head. It was a choice that made her future clutch its chest—with the power to change her life for good—but she knew what she had to do. "I do...and not because you're making me or even because of Clarallan— but for myself. Because if I don't do the trials and Hellevi destroys this kingdom, then saving my life and walking away will have been for nothing. All I've ever wished for is a chance at a better life, and at this point, I'm not surprised that the chance I've been given is a difficult one." Rae's face was full of admiration and she had to glance away. "Nothing in life is easy, Rae. And sometimes it takes a little blood and magic to make wishes come true."

Rae wrapped his palm around her chin, rubbing his thumb in circles on her cheek. "Then let's go make a wish, Ser."

CHAPTER 21

Seren watched four Verti children play in the streets as she waited for Carr to exit the meat shop. Each carried a wood-crafted practice sword, dull at the tips, as they swung and missed and jabbed and stumbled through a game of two-on-two. Their laughter ricocheted between the shop fronts and down the cobblestone street toward her, exaggerated when one boy tripped over his feet and fell into a trash barrel. Seren laughed too, not at the poor child but because of the joy she felt watching them laugh and play, knowing they lived in a haven where they would grow up and become everything they could ever wish to be. It was the childhood she had wished for herself, the kind every child deserved.

A sense of purpose stirred inside her. Here was the reason she was fighting. She could use what she'd been through to create something better, and she would risk her life for the sake of protecting others from sharing the same type of pain—her strength not determined by her past but because she still wished for something better, despite her pain.

Carr placed a heavy hand on Seren's shoulder, and she startled. He asked, "Ready?"

She smiled, at peace with her choice. There was nothing that could stop her from doing what she had to do. "Yeah, let's find Dax."

It had been three long days since she'd told Rae she would do the trials. She had demanded they go immediately, part of her worrying that if they didn't act fast, she would lose her confidence. But Rae, always the leader and sense of reason, had insisted against her impulsivity and suggested they take a few days to prepare.

Since then, they'd spent the past few days gathering information, which didn't end up being a lot more than what they already knew. All they had was everything Izzac included in the journal—a good start, but their journey would not be easy. They hit a dead end that morning, and Seren argued spending any more time in town was a waste. Rae had disagreed, of course, his reason being they still weren't ready. But eventually he compromised.

They would leave tomorrow morning.

Therefore, any final preparations had to be finished by nightfall. The group divided and conquered; Dax, Carr, and Seren hit the shops to collect rations and anything Rae put on their detailed lists. Rae stayed behind to pack, and Tait was somewhere running around, telling whoever needed to know that a few of them would be gone for a while.

In town, Carr oversaw buying food, Dax handled cleaning and buying new weapons, and Seren was responsible for collecting the miscellaneous items Rae had requested. She finished first and found Carr, and the two of them walked to Dax's favorite weapon dealer.

"Did you get everything we need?" she asked him.

"I got enough to last the trip to Sollian and some nonperishables we can save for worst-case scenarios, but we'll need to buy as we go." Izzac had told them to pack light, since there was no point weighing everyone down with things they could buy later. He asked, "What about you?"

Seren rustled her two totes—full of random things, including but not limited to flint, medicinal creams, a sewing needle, and an oily bug repellent. "Everything Rae asked for."

"How you feeling about the trials?" Carr glanced sideways, the blond in his tied-back dreads lighter from the consistent spring sun.

Seren hesitated, gathering her feelings into something coherent. "I know I'm going to do them, that I have to, and I want to, but I still don't understand why." He cocked his head and she elaborated. "Like, why me, you know? Until a few days ago I thought I was human, and now everyone is telling me Clarallan needs me to restore its magic. I don't get it. What do I have to do with anything?"

Carr gave her a sympathetic look. "I don't think we're always lucky enough to understand our purpose before we're forced to face it, or at least start it. But that's what filters out the real leaders, the heroes even, because only they are the ones that can walk into the uncertain and leave as its master."

Seren had never heard Carr be so serious. She bumped his shoulder and giggled. "That was pretty deep."

He chuckled. "I'm serious, though, Seren. Sometimes we're faced with a decision without knowing all the facts, and it's up to us to rely on our gut—what our heart is telling us to do."

"Thank you." She smiled.

Their conversation carried them to the storefront of the weapon shop, where Dax was still inside.

Carr jerked his chin at the door. "We'll probably have to drag him out of here." He laughed and opened the door for her. "Dax loves this place. I'm pretty sure he'd live here if he could."

"Sure would," Dax hollered from the back of the shop.

Seren laughed, and they found their friend near a clear case of daggers, taking his time to admire the beautiful weaponry lining the walls. Swords of all lengths and metals covered one far side, shields of all sizes the other, and the back wall was warmed by a large firing pit, where a short, wide male worked on a new piece.

Dax leaned over the case and Seren studied the blades. Each dagger was a different length, metal, weight, and design. One caught her eye, a short, curved blade with a hilt painted a shiny gold. But her favorite was a long, engraved silver blade that met a jet-black hilt, its edge decorated with stars.

It reminded her of her dagger, but the one in the case was breathtaking. The owner noticed her daze, and in a voice deeper than Seren expected, he asked, "Do you want to see it? I can get it out for you."

Seren waved her hand, but Dax answered with a grin. "Yes, she does."

The round male walked behind the counter, and a few loose strands of his braided wiry gray hair fell across his dark brown eyes as he peered into the case. He used a ring full of keys to unlock the vitrine and lifted the dagger from its velvet box, handing it to her.

Seren used both hands to hold its light weight comfortably in her grasp as she flexed her arm, testing the weapon. Satisfied, she brought it to her face to admire the craftsmanship. Up close, the engraved details became an array of unique stars, their swirls and patterns never repeating. She unfurled her palm and traced her fingers over the dynamic hilt.

"We can engrave it if you'd like," the shop owner said, his large eyes patient and generous.

"Oh, no, I—"

"She'll take it." Carr winked. "On me. You'll need a nice weapon for the trip anyway."

Seren agreed to the engraving and the owner led her to the fire pit. Placing the dagger on the worktable, he grabbed a few tools and asked, "What would you like it to say?"

She paused. What was important enough to want to remember forever?

She and her dagger shared something in common: both of them would find their purpose through the trials. They would be at each other's sides amidst the danger, so what words did she want to bond them?

There was one quote she had read and saved in her soul, something that meant enough to her she had used it to make her decision to fight.

Seren repeated the words from memory and watched as the male took his time adding something special at the base of the blade at her late request. She thanked him when he was finished and joined her friends outside.

"Let's see it," the guys said together.

The shiny intricate stars reflected against the bright sun, and she unfurled her grasp so the guys could get a good look.

"Sanguis et magicea sumus?" Dax asked.

Seren beamed and interpreted the words that grounded her to what she had been through and who she wanted to be: "We are but blood and magic."

Four of them left town the next morning. Rae wanted someone to stay behind and keep an eye on home, especially in case Izzac found any new intel.

Dax was an obvious choice to come along because of his extensive combat experience, and Carr would never let his best friend go alone. Seren was thankful for Carr's comforting presence, but that left Tait with little choice beyond holding down the house. The younger male resented missing out on the adventure, but ultimately agreed it was for the best. And Rae boosted his feelings with praise for being mature enough to be put in charge of their home, which left the golden boy smiling the entire time as he watched them walk away.

They left the Verti village behind with their packs, weapons, the journal, and a plan, incomplete as it was. The Sollian court was their first destination, and fortunately, it was the closest to the Ruins. Rae expected the journey to take only a few days, but the unfortunate catch was at least one of those days would be spent traveling through the Galaxius Forest.

A place Seren had no interest in seeing again.

Izzac had mapped their entire trek, providing alternative routes for situations that could arise. From the first trial, they would travel to Lunaan, then Ocealla, Etiamella, and last, Seren would be forced to return to the Stellean court. A fearful voice in her head tried to argue that the benefit of Stellean being last was that she might not even live long enough to return—four deadly trials stood between her and the place that haunted her soul.

She shook away her dark thoughts and picked up her pace at Rae's side. Dax and Carr walked a few yards ahead, both dressed in their respective black and brown combat leathers, their packs and weapons strapped on their backs. The cut of Dax's leathers left his complex tattoos visible over his arms, dark ink sprawled in unique lines over his olive skin, mesmerizing as they shifted over his muscles with each step.

Rae's leathers closely matched Carr's, their dark shade of brown soothing against his tan skin and golden hair. Rae glimmered beneath the sun, his toned arm muscles left free of restraint as his leathers covered only what needed the most protection.

Seren was slightly self-conscious wearing her leathers. She had tried and failed to convince Rae to let her wear her usual clothes, but he refused until she adorned the striking black set he'd bought her weeks earlier. She rarely trained in them, but Rae insisted she wear them on their trip, ultimately explaining his insistence with a Verti legend.

He informed her the Verti created all their war equipment using an ancient ritual, a liquid cast to dip all their leathers and metals in, which was intertwined with ancient spells of healing and protection.

Mostly believing his tale, Seren conceded, eventually deciding she needed as much help as she could get. Her gear was most like Dax's—black and elegant, yet comfortable and protective. But a far cry from the casual clothes she preferred. The leather was tight on her skin and shaped perfectly to her every curve. There was nothing loose or covering that could get caught or hung up in a fight. Which meant every part of her was on display.

But, hey, if it saved her life, she could find her confidence.

Rae offered her a folded map and when she opened it, he pointed to where they were and where they planned to stop for the night. His fingers landed on a marker near the edge of Galaxius. "This is where we'll stop. It's not as far as I would like, but any farther and we'd have to go into Galaxius. And I'm not trying to spend the night in the forest again."

Seren loosened a breath, thankful that, for at least today, they would not be entering the deadly forest.

Rae noticed her trepidation and smoothed his neutral face into a thin smile. "It'll be okay, Ser. The guys and I have traveled through Galaxius hundreds of times." He bumped his shoulder into hers without missing a beat. "It's how we met, remember?"

"How could I forget?" She smiled, grateful Clarallan had brought her to Rae.

THE REST of the day was uneventful, and they made it to their stopping point before sundown. Carr had been the only one on her side when she'd brought up taking a moment to rest or eat, the other two sharing an annoyed look every time she mentioned needing a break.

The spot they chose for the night was far enough away from the edge of the Galaxius Forest that Seren knew they were safe, yet she still had trouble falling asleep. The stars watched her twist and turn on her mat as she wrestled between consciousness and unconsciousness.

Carr and Rae passed out as soon as they cleared the area and their bodies hit the cool ground. Dax, it seemed, was the only one who shared her struggle. *Is he also worried about tomorrow? Or is he keeping watch, and if so, for what?* Seren didn't want to risk waking the others to ask, and honestly, she didn't want to hear his answer anyway.

She was pretty sure she had just drifted off when morning light warmed her face.

Unsurprisingly, as she rolled out from beneath her blanket, all three males were already up and ready to go.

Seren swept her knotted hair behind her ears and rubbed the sleep from the corners of her eyes. Rae walked up to where she sat on the ground and jokingly poked her leg with his boot.

"You're kinda an ugly sleeper, you know."

Seren slapped his foot. "Good morning to you too, ass."

"Someone's feisty this morning." Carr grinned. "Did you not get enough beauty rest?"

Seren responded with a vulgar hand gesture and gathered her things, brushed her hair, and rinsed her teeth. Once she was up, she stepped past Rae and called over her shoulder, "Just so you know, you snore loud enough to wake all the courts, even from here."

Carr barked out a laugh and even Dax and Rae joined. The three of them fell into step behind her as they all marched toward the edge of the forest, until Carr picked up his pace to walk at her side.

Rae was the first to reach the tree line, though, a knife in both hands as he slashed at the thick vines and foliage keeping them out—or rather, keeping its monsters in. He made some progress, and the darkness of the forest seeped across the sun-covered land. Seren stood yards away yet still felt the temperature drop, her blood chilling as the writhing shadows raced toward her.

Galaxius was a land of death, its darkness hunting for any source of life to steal.

The guys worked, and Seren watched the sky above the trees. A flutter of beating wings crashed through the canopy, drawing her attention as a red bird shot up with unnatural force, too big for a hawk, or even an eagle. She'd never seen an animal like it before, and she swore the creature looked directly at her before flying away—its expression vulpine as it swiveled its head in her direction before soaring higher into the sky. The guys were too focused to notice, but she watched until its powerful wings carried it out of sight.

Rae called out that it was time to move from where he crouched beneath the fighting vines and branches, barely holding open the hole he had created.

"Did you see the bird?" Seren asked as she approached the others, a creeping sensation crawling up her limbs. They gave her a quizzical look. *I'll take that as a no*, she said silently and shook her head. "Not important. Are we ready?"

"Are you?" Rae asked.

Seren stepped forward. Ready as she'd ever be.

Dax boldly entered first, wielding a short sword at his front. Carr was at her side, his dagger in one hand, holding her hand in the other as they entered together. Rae was last.

The forest was deathly still.

Seren didn't know how it was possible to have forgotten how dark and eerie the woods were. Maybe it was her mind's response to the horror of her last experience to erase as much of her fear as it could.

As they trekked, it was difficult to leave behind the terrifying memories that consumed her. The all-encompassing darkness surrounded them in a shadowy fog, thick with earthy smells of mud and decay. It was impossible to see in front of her as the mist bit at her face and the damp fog dissolved any sound. The silence was utterly unnerving.

Rae appeared at her side, and Seren flinched, tripping. Carr's grip tightened around her arm, holding her up.

"I almost forgot how much I hate this place," Seren said, her words barely audible above the absorbing shadows.

"I still can't believe you ran in here alone," Carr said.

"Neither can I." But her desperation had sworn to her one thing: she had to get away from Stellean, no matter the cost.

"Maybe we can make it in and out unnoticed," Carr added, but his strong jaw was rigid, and his throat bobbed.

Seren and Rae shared a glance.

If she learned anything from her first trip through Galaxius—their fear was their worst enemy. The thing that attacked her, called a Khaous, as Rae eventually explained, was a monster that fed on fear. It preyed on the vulnerable and amplified its victim's pain until there was enough fear to scrape from their minds to feast on.

Seren's every nerve lit up as she remembered the feeling of claws in her brain. Scraping, scraping, scraping. Misery had slashed through every piece of who she was, lacerating her mind until there was nothing left inside of her.

Shaking her head, she shoved her thoughts from the Khaous—thinking about it only increased her fear. She wasn't even sure the Khaous was the worst monster in the forest, but she prayed they wouldn't put that to the test. It was foolish to deny what lived in these woods, even if those things remained unseen. A healthy dose of respect was needed to survive unscathed.

Dax led them through the forest, following some path only the Verti could see. Seren resorted to counting her steps to busy her mind and keep a sense of the time. She guessed they'd been walking for a few hours, based on how loudly her stomach growled. She hoped lunch would come soon.

If it was up to Rae, they wouldn't stop at all. He wanted to get out of Galaxius before nightfall, but even the relentless warrior needed food.

Her stomach rolled and nausea threatened her throat. She swallowed. "Can we stop soon? I need to eat."

Ahead of them, Rae grunted.

"It's a good idea," Carr added, bumping her hip.

"There's a clearing up ahead," Dax said over his shoulder. "We can stop there."

"Thank you," Seren said, shooting a glare at Rae's back.

Dax stopped in a mossy clearing, and he and Carr dragged two fallen trunks to the side. Seren sat down, the damp wood uncomfortable against her leathers as she swung her pack to her chest. Rae had prepared three days' worth of meals on top of everything Carr had bought. For once, Seren was thankful for how many servings the guys preferred, their second and third helpings giving her a little extra time to rest her aching feet.

"Maybe save some for the rest of the trip," Rae chided as Carr unwrapped his fourth sandwich. Carr frowned and took a bite anyway.

Giggling, Seren stood. "I'm going to the bathroom. Come find me if I'm not back in a few minutes."

"I can come with," Carr said, his mouth full.

"I'm good." Seren gulped, squinting into the darkness. She walked as far as she could without getting lost and hated knowing that the Verti could hear every move she made. But with her luck, if she went any farther, she'd lose them in an attempt to relieve herself, and she couldn't think of anything more pathetic.

Content, Seren hurried back to the clearing, where all three males were ready to go. Dax took the lead again while the others walked on either side of her.

"If we keep pushing, I think we can make it to Sollian by the end of day," Rae said. And for everyone's sake, Seren hoped he was right.

"I really don't want to spend the night here." Seren shuddered. The last time she'd fallen asleep in Galaxius she'd nearly been Cariper food.

"Me neither," Rae admitted.

Seren resumed counting her steps. She needed a distraction from her rebellious imagination as it ran wild, creating nightmares in the darkness. She counted to a thousand and then repeated. Somewhere near her fourth repetition, Dax halted, raising his right hand above his shoulder.

Rae and Carr stilled, and Seren followed their lead. She couldn't see or hear anything that would have made them stop. "What is it?" she asked.

Rae held a finger to his lips and positioned his back to hers, his stance tense and ready, bracing his blades against the shadows. Carr mirrored his movements, covering her on both sides.

The shadows moved, withering and stretching as the darkness pressed in. Gray-and-black shadows coiled and sprang, creeping toward them—an ebb and flow of inky darkness that felt them out.

Seren froze in terror as the smoke flicked against her legs and ascended her body, her shallow breathing forcing the shadows to pulse in front of her lips. The guys tensed, and she clutched her dagger with sweaty palms, pointing it away from her chest.

The darkness eased, cleaving a path between the dense trees as an uncanny voice flew toward them. Seren lifted her blade, but suddenly the voice came from behind her. She whirled—darkness. The voice was somehow steps ahead.

"Who's there?" Rae boomed, and Seren spun again.

She took a breath. At least she wasn't hearing things this time. They could face the monster together.

"Who are you?" Seren asked.

"Do you not recognize me, child?"

Fallen branches crunched deep in the trees, and a figure stalked toward them.

Carr leaned his head over his shoulder. "Who's it talking to?"

Seren's grip tightened on her weapon, her feet pressed into the ground, her heartbeat in her ears. A short woman stood before them, long black hair covering her face, her chin held low. Then the woman lifted her chin, and Seren's shoulders relaxed. "Me."

The Seer's frigid violet eyes sparkled with pride, her moonstone skin harsh against the shadows. "Yesss, my child." Prue's melodic voice tickled Seren's ears, and she shuddered as goosebumps consumed her arms and warmth stirred in her core. The Seer's words stroked Seren's face, and darkness wrapped around her legs. "The stars have been watching you, dear, one of their own. They whisper to me."

Dax stepped closer and Rae tightened his jaw, which made his words clipped. "What's she talking about?"

"Who are you?" Dax and Carr's questions collided.

The Seer tickled a gentle finger along Seren's cheek. Rae tensed.

Seren placed a hand on his shoulder. "It's okay." At least she hoped it was. "I know her, sort of."

"Who are you?" Carr repeated.

Prue's voice lifted. "Oh, forgive me. My name is Prue, I'm a Seer of Clarallan."

"What do you want?" Rae stepped forward, and Seren's hand fell.

Prue crooned, a high-pitched tone, "To see the war complete and the king to face defeat. A star to face denial and a kingdom to see revival."

Carr lowered his voice to Seren's ear. "Does she always speak in riddles?"

"Unfortunately."

Rae cut in. "We should go."

"Wait." Seren pushed past the towering males, holding Prue's stare. "I didn't want to listen before, but I'm ready. Please, what do you know?"

Prue lifted her thin hands and closed her eyes, a smirk thinning her pink lips. "Let me show you."

A familiar veil of darkness returned, and the guys fell back, Rae with an irritated expression. The Seer's hands swirled through the mist, orchestrating the shadows as they morphed from gray and black to flashes of greens and blues, pinks and reds. Prue's eyes glossed over as the colors merged, and she placed a hand on Seren's forehead. Seren's grip loosened—her dagger fell—and her body went limp. Rae and Carr caught her sides, supporting her as the Seer continued.

"Close your eyes," Prue instructed.

Seren obeyed, and Prue's fingertips graced her eyelids. The Seer trailed her hand over Seren's skin, and when she pressed her forehead, Seren opened her eyes, gasping.

The Seer had used her magic to create a liquid painting of the shadows—castles soared through clouds, courts and territories appeared and grew, waves crashed and thunder cracked, and a battlefield went up in flames.

Seren's temples throbbed, and her skin felt warm where Prue touched her. The last thing she saw before Prue dropped her hand was a galaxy—a night sky encrusted with stars and constellations, painted in deep colors of navy and gold, silver and black. Their connection lost, Seren regained control of her body, her breathing ragged as the magic dissolved. The guys dropped their hands, and Seren took a step.

Rae leaned forward, his breath hot on the back of her ear. "You okay?"

A nod. If she could stand on her own, she would. She asked Prue, "What was that?"

Prue smiled. "Everything I've seen of the trials, revealed to me a few days ago by the kingdom. Apparently, Clarallan believes you are ready. I came to find you immediately."

Seren closed her eyes, and the colors were still there, magic transforming behind her eyelids, guiding her where she and the Verti needed to go. She swallowed, her throat thick. It felt like the shadows had been shoved right into her. "What did you do to me?"

"My magic has grown stronger the past few weeks. Now, it's strong enough that I could use my power and convey a glimpse of my gift."

"So that was"—Seren paused, it sounded impossible—"the future?"

"No, child." Prue giggled, an unsettling childish sound. "I can't see the future, because it is always changing—nothing is permanent, especially not the future. One decision and everything is different. My magic is powered by time, and I've shared a glimpse of my sight—snippets of what may or may not come to pass. But given the sight, it can guide you. Use what you've learned, and let what you do not yet understand bring you to the truth. Clarallan chose you, let it."

"How?" Seren was desperate for anything that wasn't a convoluted riddle or rhyme about her fate and time.

Prue twirled her frail fingers. "Clarallan speaks with all who carry its magic. But you, dear, Clarallan sings to you. Open yourself up to what's inside—your magic knows what to do."

The shadows thickened, pouncing on the group as Prue retreated and disappeared, her words dissolving into the air.

Seren's mouth gaped, and she lunged, her hands clutching nothing but mist. She swung to face the guys and swore, clenching her fists as heat spread from her hands to her core.

"Seren…" Rae's eyes widened as he met her gaze. Dax paled and Carr's jaw cracked. "Your eyes—"

"What?" Seren held her face, darting her eyes between her friends. "What's wrong?" All three stepped closer, baffled.

"Seriously, guys, can someone tell me what's going on before I freak out?"

"Stars…" Rae trailed off.

"What?" Seren demanded.

"There are stars in your eyes, Seren. Like, they look like real stars."

"This is some crazy shit." Carr cracked his knuckles in front of his chest.

"Tell me more." She blinked fiercely, but her sight was no different. She could see perfectly fine, better even. Rubbing her fingers over her eyelids, Seren saw specks of white as she removed her hands, but only from the pressure. Still no sign of the stars the guys saw in her eyes.

Eventually, Seren wrangled a description out of the bewildered males: silver stars shone in her pupils, and her normally hazel irises reflected a dark navy, nearly black. Like a night sky, Carr said.

A hazy memory sparked—what Prue showed her in the market. Unease claimed residence in her gut as they resumed their trek, desperate to catch up on lost time. As they traveled over the uneven ground, Seren could see farther and farther ahead, the darkness less devastating. Whatever the Seer had done to her proved to enhance her senses. She could finally see a trail through the woods, possibly what the Verti had been following all along.

An overwhelming feeling spread from her core, and as the path unfurled before her, she knew where she was going—the steady warmth in her middle tugged her forward. When she turned to check the darkness at her sides, the heat would dim. At one point she stopped, pivoted, and took a few steps in the opposite direction. Her middle chilled instantly.

Seren gulped, walking the correct way once more. She tested it a few more times before Carr noticed.

"Did the Seer scramble your mind more than you've let on?"

The concern coating his tone diminished his attempt at a joke. He swiveled his head between her and the others. "You know Sollian's this way, right?"

Seren ignored his mockery. "I think whatever the Seer did to me messed with my magic."

Rae looked over his shoulder. "What do you mean?"

"I can feel something, like a tug in my core that keeps pulling me toward wherever we're going. It wasn't there before, and now"—Seren stopped and turned—"every time I turn around, it's gone."

"So the mad woman in the forest turned you into a compass?" Carr's head bounced. "Nice."

Seren raised a brow, a curl in her lips. Carr *would* take something serious and say it like that. "I guess."

"Maybe it'll help with the trials," Dax said, yards ahead.

That could be what Prue meant by looking inside of her—letting her magic be her guide. She needed more answers, and maybe this new gift would help her find them.

The warmth in her center blanketed her in comfort against the bitter forest, and the rest of their walk went a lot faster.

Dax pointed to a soaring tree line maybe a mile ahead, its dense foliage the sentient bars of their beastly cage. Everyone picked up the pace, and their hope grew as they raced to the edge of the forest. All four wielded a blade, slicing at the thick branches that grew again and knotted against their efforts.

Seren's arms ached from their relentless exertion, and luckily, the guys had better results than she did.

She never would have made it out alone.

CHAPTER 22

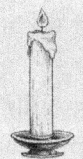

Night fell across the Sollian court, the sky an unusually bright dusk as Seren and the group crawled through the trees and left the Galaxius Forest behind. Miles ahead, Seren gasped at the striking castle built into the foothills—a mosaic of lush green forest and gold architecture embedded into the mountainside. Its tallest points soared above the rolling mountain range, cutting through the violet night sky.

They marched forward, and Seren could hear the rushing water of giant waterfalls flooding around the castle into a river below. Grass fields stretched for miles across the border before meeting a cavernous cliff side. The Sollian castle connected to it by a large stone bridge that extended across the nothingness.

It was magnificent even in the darkness.

The vivid coloring of the grand city beckoned them, and it was impossible to resist the lovely feeling that radiated through the warm air, like reminiscing about idealized childhood summers. The royal castle was centered against a cliff slope, surrounded by overflowing flora and towering trees, descending to a valley below—to the heart of Sollian. Momentous towers sprouted from the city, topped with giant stone observatories, connected by towering bridges that soared from the castle across the entire territory.

Exhaustion weighed on the guys, but Seren's bewilderment fueled her steps. She'd never seen any of the other courts before, and seeing Sollian was even better than she'd imagined. But her anger nipped at her astonishment, her bitterness rising as thoughts of Hellevi knocked on her peace, until she realized something...

He'd denied her everything, dug her a grave in Stellean and buried her alive beneath his punishments. She'd escaped with a drained soul, but ever since she'd left Stellean, everything she'd seen had brought life to her emptiness.

Hellevi couldn't control who she was anymore.

She followed Rae with light steps while the others scoped the court's border up ahead. Dax estimated they had at least six hours before sunrise, which meant they could get some sleep before entering Sollian.

They needed rest, but it would be hard to fight off the excitement and anxiety that danced along her nerves and released butterflies in her stomach. She'd be lucky if she even fell asleep before morning.

Seren and Rae found Dax and Carr in a small cove of trees on the side of the cliff overlooking the Sollian city, a safe distance from the edge. Everyone rolled out their mats and got comfortable, and Seren took it as a good sign that none of the guys stayed up to keep watch.

The sounds of waterfalls lured them to sleep, but uncertainty circled her thoughts, infecting her dreams. Seren woke up in a sweat, the lingering flashes of her stressed imagination haunting her mind. She'd dreamed they'd been caught sneaking into the royal gardens and the guys were exposed as Verti.

Sunlight warmed her skin, and she lifted her head from her pack to watch her friends. For once, all the guys were asleep, their chests rising and falling together. She was thankful they were with her, but guilt weighed on her heart. She hated that they were putting themselves at risk by helping her, but she hated even more that it put their entire community at risk too.

Without the Verti community, Seren wasn't sure she'd have made it, and she certainly wouldn't have felt supported enough to challenge Hellevi. She needed them all, but a certain five in particular. She knew it was their choice to be there, but she couldn't shake an overwhelming sense of pressure. If she failed—

No.

She couldn't think like that. Not with the first trial hours away.

Easing her sleep-ridden limbs upward, she crept over to Rae. She was never awake before him. She stirred his shoulder and waited for his eyes to crack before saying, "Has anyone ever told you you're really an ugly sleeper? Oh, and you snore."

Rae rubbed his knuckles over his eyes and grumbled, "Sounds familiar."

Seren smirked, grabbing her pack to get ready.

"Did you get any sleep?" he asked, his voice gruff.

Seren turned and saw the rising sun reflecting against his tan skin and wild eyes.

"Yes." No need to tell him most of it was soured by stress dreams about the first trial.

Rae's lips pulled down. "You need to be prepared for what we face today. It won't be easy."

He didn't have to remind her how important today was. "I know."

He gave her a look.

"You guys ready?" Carr hollered a few yards away.

"Yeah," they said together. Seren grabbed her pack and strolled toward Carr and Dax, Rae trailing behind as he read Izzac's journal.

Carr asked, "You eat anything?" Seren shook her head, and he tossed her an apple. "I have more."

"Thanks."

Dax looked at her sideways. "Your eyes are back to normal too."

"Y'all weren't just playing a trick on me, were you?"

They chuckled. "Not this time."

Seren shrugged. She knew what the guys had seen was real. That the Seer had done something…or maybe just revealed something. She just didn't know what yet.

The morning was unusually warm as they walked down the hill toward the bridge. Everything glistened: the golden architecture, the sparkling water, even the thousands of trees appeared speckled with glitter. Her surprise grew as she got her first good look at the city beneath the cliffs. It was larger than she'd expected, a grand display of white-and-cream homes and shops, lathered in lights and lush flora.

The royal castle rose high above the town, the power of the court mirroring the sun as it soared through the bright blue sky. Seren studied the lively city, its design an abstract intersection of a spiraling sun and beaming rays. Large streets curved in a circular pattern, smaller near the center, where it wrapped around the royal garden, expanding as the streets swept toward the city's borders. Smaller cobblestone alleys cut directly through the swirling streets in various lengths between the unique buildings.

Gold swirls and carved designs decorated the town's culture, and lush vines littered with flowers filled any open space, tangling around the stone arches and swaying peacefully in a warm breeze.

Seren focused on the garden, directly in the center. It was Sollian's most beloved treasure and represented their magic. If Seren had to prove she was worthy of Sollian's gifts, the garden would be the best place to start.

Rae caught up to her and she asked, "How are we going to get to the garden?"

He opened the journal and flipped to a map. Izzac had suggested the quickest path to the garden from three different entry points. Rae pointed to the sketched cliffs. "We're here, so we're going to take this route once we get into the city."

"Speaking of"—Seren looked across the vast valley as they approached the stone bridge—"how are we going to get to the city? We're not just going to waltz into the castle, are we?"

"Come on, Ser, don't you think we're smarter than that?" Carr asked as he dropped his pack.

"Do you want me to answer honestly?"

He slapped a hand across his heart. "You wound me, Ser."

She laughed despite herself. "But really, guys, what's our plan?"

"Get to the garden." Carr spoke as if it were really that obvious, and even Dax rolled his eyes.

"What happens if anyone realizes you're not Fae?"

Rae answered, "Seren, how poorly do you think of us? The Verti have been considered extinct for centuries, and yet we travel to the courts all the time. Don't you think we know how to keep our secret?"

Seren sharpened her gaze. Of course Rae's logic made sense, but the closer the trial became, the more her anxiety grew and the more paranoid she became. "But how?"

"Just watch."

All three males stood in front of her, yet despite looking exactly the same, something was different, or just off.

"What did you do?" She couldn't physically see a single difference, yet a cold, distant feeling washed over her, telling her something wasn't right. She examined the males she'd spent so much time with and yet still couldn't put her finger on what was different.

Rae smirked. "We look human."

"Uh—" She studied them, tilting her head as she stepped closer. "I suppose you do." She snorted. "How?"

"It's our eyes," Rae explained. She studied his eyes, now an unusually dull brown. That warm familiar feeling she got from being around the male knocked on her memory as his eyes brightened, glowing gold. She turned to Dax, and his pale eyes grew into a bold green while Carr's melted to a dark brown.

"I—" She was at a loss.

Rae's eyes gleamed. "As Verti, our magic stems from our ability to shift, an ancient power. Our magic is strong enough that it can be felt by those around us. But with practice, the Verti can dampen their power, cutting the tie between themselves and others, a survival technique. All of us know how to harness our magic—the result is that our eyes dull, allowing us to appear human."

Rae dimmed his eyes again, and a chill brushed Seren's skin. "With calm control, we can stay like this for as long as we need without anyone suspecting anything."

"What happens if you lose control?"

He swayed his head. "Control is a spectrum. Say we get a little distracted, our eyes may return to their Verti state. But a full loss of control—well, I hope you're never around to witness that."

Seren shuddered, dragging her attention away from the predators that hid in her friends. She needed to learn more about their magic, but so far, she'd been too nervous to ask. "How are we getting to the garden from here?"

The bridge stretched directly to the Sollian castle, but Seren saw no other way into the city.

"There's a different entrance into the city, but it's at least another day's hike. And since we can't just go the normal way"—Dax gestured at the bridge, his expression bored—"we'll be taking a less traditional way in."

A grin captured Carr's lips, and Seren's stomach dropped.

She latched onto her composure as Dax swung his pack off his shoulder and reached for something inside. Carr and Rae did the same, and Seren knew she wasn't going to like whatever the guys did next.

"Here." Rae handed her a thick metal clasp. "It'll attach to your leathers."

Seren gulped, her eyes racing to the cliff's edge. She barely kept her voice from choking as she glared at her friends, taking a few steps back. "Absolutely not."

"Would you rather try our luck going through the castle?" Dax pursed his mouth, and he threw a long wrapped rope over his shoulder.

"One more day's walk sounds just fine to me."

Rae held his hand out to her. "We don't have the time, Ser. You know that. Hellevi would never waste a day."

Seren cocked her head, her gaze sharp. She couldn't argue, but—she shook her head and grabbed Rae's hand. There was no winning three to one anyway. Carr stood watch while Rae and Dax attached the rope beneath the stone bridge. Seren paced a few yards back, her hands wrapped in the ends of her hair. It wasn't a fear of heights that worried her, or even the falling, because at least that would be quick, but the chance they'd be caught...

There was no easy way to explain their way out of what they were doing—three shifters and a fugitive sneaking into Sollian's most holy ground was not a good look. She prayed Clarallan was looking out for them, and then she approached Rae.

"It's going to be okay," he said, but his words were of little comfort as they crouched near the edge. Rae pointed his chin. "Carr will go first, then you and I, and Dax will be last. You don't even have to go alone."

"You're sure it'll hold?"

"Positive."

His face was smooth, no signs of worry or fear, just a slight crease above the curve of his mouth as he smiled. "It's a long way down, that's why you and I will go together. So I can help you if you get too tired."

"Sure you don't wanna switch, Rae?" Carr hollered as he strolled toward them. "I'd gladly carry our girl down the entire way while you go first." He winked.

"Hey, someone's gotta test the rope, and it's not gonna be me." Rae smirked with a flippant attitude and Seren shoved his shoulder.

"I thought you said it was safe?"

"Just a joke." Rae waved his hand. "We'll be fine."

"Can we get on with it, then?" Seren curled and loosened her fists, airing her sweaty palms.

Chuckling, Carr swung his arm and pointed at the rope. "Ladies first?"

"You guys are not as funny as you think you are." Seren held her breath, and Carr wrapped one large hand around the rope and used the other to balance as he eased his tall body over the edge. He crossed his ankles, and his forearm flexed as he used one hand to hold the entirety of his weight until the other clasped the rope. Loose stones plummeted around him, the drop too far for Seren to hear them crash.

"See y'all at the bottom," Carr hollered, replacing one hand after the other as he descended into the city.

Rae waited for Carr to be at least a hundred feet down before he lowered his body over the rocky side and helped Seren join him. Everything in her begged to throw herself onto solid ground, her heart stopping when her fingers slipped on torn grass and rocks cascaded around them. Rae clipped her leathers to a metal ring and did the same with his own. Then he secured one arm around her waist, sliding his hands down the rope with her body tucked between his firm bicep and chest.

Closing her eyes, Seren took her first deep breath since Carr had gone over the edge. She knew better than to look at the ground before she was ready.

She latched onto the stiff rope.

Rae asked, "Good?" His voice wasn't easy to hear over her pulse drumming in her ears, pounding hard enough she could feel it in her palms as she clenched the gruff rope. Seren gave a slight confirmation, and Rae lowered one hand, then another, the rope swaying between their legs as Carr continued beneath them.

About the time Rae said they were halfway there, every muscle in Seren's body ached with fear. She clenched her jaw and kept her core tight, and a tension headache blossomed in her temples. It had been a good call going with Rae; she was exhausted.

She risked peering at Carr a few times, and the ground never appeared any closer. It felt like they'd been descending for hours. She preferred to look up at Dax, the sky's company more comforting than the ground's. Dax was careful not to get too close, despite the fact he moved much quicker than she and Rae, leaving him suspended, waiting.

Seren kept every thought she had to herself—too afraid to even risk distracting Rae, since by now, he was doing most of the work. She busied herself thinking about the trials. What would they find in the garden? What would she have to do? There was still more that they didn't know about the trials than what they did. One pesky question begged her heart for an answer, but her mind refused to ask it—she couldn't doubt whether she was worthy of the trials; she had to believe she was.

Even if no one knew what to expect. They could be making the worst decision of their lives, and they would all be ignorant to the fact. Seren begged her anxiety to go away, but it was more than just a waste of breath, it was impossible. The more she pleaded with her worries, the more voraciously they told her she was in over her head.

Rae's voice broke through her distress. "Carr hit the bottom. We're getting close."

That was the best news she'd heard all day. The time it took for them to reach solid ground felt like the longest test of patience in her life.

Then Rae's boots crunched on hard gravel, and his arms wrapped around her as she released the rope. Her legs wobbled from what felt like a year at sea, and her swaying pulled Rae close as she fought to gain her bearings. She leaned on Rae's chest as they waited for Dax, her feet tingling.

In minutes, the four of them were walking. Their descent down the cliff had spit them out at the mouth of a river leading into the city. They followed the calm water and Rae wrestled with his pack to grab the journal.

Seren rubbed the back of her neck, glancing behind them. "I can't believe we did that."

"I told you we'd be fine." Rae flipped to the Sollian map and pointed. "This river leads right to the gardens. Should take about an hour."

Her eyes chased the bouncy ripples that spread across the babbling blue surface, and Rae tucked the journal beneath his arm. Izzac had included all sorts of calculations and estimations; there was a time and note for everything they did.

"Have you ever been to Sollian before?" Seren asked, her gaze flickering between the tall willow trees up ahead and the orange poppies lining the trail.

"Quite a few times. It's the closest court to the village, and the easiest to get any goods we can't otherwise make ourselves."

Seren glanced at the pink-and-blue flowerbeds kissing the river shore. "It's beautiful."

"It's my favorite court…if I had to pick."

"This is the first court I've seen besides Stellean." Seren shrugged. "I guess one good thing about doing the trials is getting to see all of them."

Rae opened and closed his mouth.

"What?" she asked.

He glanced sideways. "Just… When this is all over, let's plan a proper trip. Something you can actually enjoy."

Seren's heart swelled, and the contraction made her queasy. *When this is all over* implied that she would succeed. She swallowed. "I'd like that."

The guys dulled their powers as they neared the city, and without the warmth of the Verti's magic, a chill buried itself deep within her.

Studying the court from above didn't even come close to walking within the walls of the heart of the golden city. Seren had never seen color so bright, felt life so rich. The citizens were pleasant and warm and strolled carelessly through the streets, where horses pulled carts and vendors sold homemade treats.

A summer breeze carried scents of honey and orange blossoms, and the warm air radiated a welcoming kindness as they wandered the bubbly streets. A familiar pull tugged on her core and sweat swelled on her forehead. She followed her magic, her steps light as she hurried over the cobblestone roads.

Her magic hummed, growing louder with each step she took toward the gardens.

She stilled, her eyes wide, her neck tilted back as she gazed at the golden arches opening to the most magnificent garden she had ever seen.

She had no idea what they would find in the garden, on the other side of the towering gilded rampart. Magic itched her sun kissed skin, and she sucked in a smooth breath.

For the first time since Seren had escaped her cage, she felt the possibilities of magic fuel her life with purpose.

CHAPTER 23

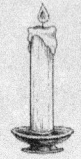

The golden arches were two halves of a circle—or half of a sun.

The entrance to the Sollian garden was what Seren imagined paradise looked like. The curved columns were grandiose, warm, and engulfed by green vines interlaced with wisteria flowers in purples, blues, and yellows. A high afternoon sun cast warm rays of light over the entrance, reflecting a gleaming trail that beckoned them across the grass.

Seren gazed at the rolling fields ahead and the sharp hedges lining the dirt paths scattered through the meadow of astonishingly large buttercups and bluebells. She glanced at her friends, their wondrous faces captured by the garden.

Together they crept over the sacred lands, entertaining a guard search as they reveled in the garden's vitality. With the all clear, Rae suggested the group split up to cover more ground.

Everyone agreed, and Seren followed the faint chirp of a stream somewhere ahead while distant flurries of wings whispered through the hundred-foot-tall willow trees. The sun beat down on the canopies, and magic surged through the air, raising the hair on the back of her neck. Her magic lived inside of her, growing for twenty years—wrapped around her ribs and tied to her heart. She reached for it, begged it to spread. But her chest locked her out, and her magic fizzled long before it could offer her any guidance. In Galaxius, Prue had disappeared before Seren could ask her more about it. She still had no idea how to call on her magic intentionally, and it couldn't help her when it only appeared by accident.

Seren kept trying as she wandered through the garden, but nothing happened. She waved her fingers over the tall grass, accidentally disturbing a cluster of sprites basking in the sun. They flew from the petals, their tiny glowing bodies breezing around her as they tangled her hair and chirped in her ears.

She smiled and their translucent wings tickled her skin.

"Hi there." A thin sprite with emerald eyes and blue-tinted wings hummed above Seren's nose. "What's your name?"

Seren flinched, her eyes wide. "Seren, what's yours?"

"Ziaa," she chirped, and three sprites flocked to Seren's face. "I've never seen you before."

Seren smiled, her movements slow. "It's my first time in Sollian."

A swift green sprite asked, "Are you supposed to be here?"

Seren's eyes were jittery and bright. "I'm looking for something...something important."

"What is it?" Ziaa asked.

"I don't know just yet."

Ziaa's sparkle dulled and the green sprite darted through Seren's loosely tied back hair. "How are you supposed to find it if you don't know what you're looking for?"

Seren pursed her lips. "That's a good question, but my friends and I are searching together."

A yellow sprite asked, "Where are you from?" Her Lilliputian stature and translucent wings were nearly impossible to see.

Seren swayed her head. "Somewhere far away."

Two sprites asked in unison, "Is it nice there?"

"Not like this." Seren motioned at the garden and Ziaa landed in her hand.

"Let us help." Ziaa's tiny blue wings tickled her palm.

"Can you?"

Ziaa nodded, and her friends buzzed excitedly around Seren's head, lifting her hair as they cheered. "We've lived in these gardens for decades. If anyone knows anything, it's us." Ziaa raised her hand in a playful salute and Seren beamed.

Seren looked back in the direction she'd come and said, "Come on, let's go meet my friends."

Ziaa curled in Seren's palm as she walked, warming her skin, while at least ten more sprites bounced over her shoulders and stirred her hair. Seren turned her head from side to side and asked, "What are the rest of your names?" They all spoke at once, so Seren only caught a few: Sol, Tansy, Pipi, and Bloom. "It's nice to meet all of you, and thanks for the help. We really need it."

"Soo, what are we looking for?" Ziaa leaned against Seren's palm, curling beneath her fingers, away from the sun.

Seren lowered her voice. "Have any of you heard of the Lost Trials?"

Sol gasped, the smallest yellow sprite that had asked about her home.

"Are you..." Ziaa's high-pitched voice trembled. "Are you doing them?"

Seren offered her best comforting smile. "I have to—to save Clarallan." Sol gasped again, and Seren felt a little guilty for disturbing their peaceful home. "How do you guys know about the trials? Do you know anything that might take me to the first one?"

Ziaa pinched her palm, and Seren lifted her hand close to her face.

The other sprites buzzed among themselves, and Seren asked Ziaa, "What was that for?"

"The trials are no secret to us." Ziaa's tiny beryl eyes scurried nervously across Seren's face. "But I can't help you until it's time."

"What does that mean?"

"You'll know soon. But for now..." Ziaa flew to Seren's ear and whispered something that made little sense.

Seren strode out from beneath the trees and kept her voice soft. "I still don't understand."

"Seren," Rae shouted from across the meadow, and Seren scanned the garden for her friend. Ziaa nestled back in Seren's palm as Rae walked toward her, his boots quiet across the soft grass, his expression warped. Seren knew with his Verti eyesight he could see the sprites even a mile away.

"That's Rae," Seren said to the sprites. She turned, pointing at Dax as he crouched over a fallen marble statue with broken wings. It was the only sign of destruction Seren had seen since Hellevi had restored the garden during Ardentiella. "And that's Dax."

Tansy, the feisty green sprite, slapped her hands on her cheeks and squeaked in Seren's ear, "He's beautiful." The others agreed and Seren chuckled.

"Seren—" Rae stiffened, his brows high. "Care to introduce me to your new friends?"

Seren let the sprites introduce themselves, and Rae's shoulders tensed as they went one by one. She smirked when they were done and said, "Ladies, this is Rae. He can be a bit bossy sometimes, but he's a pretty good guy."

The sprites beamed and whizzed around his head as they studied him. Rae couldn't hide his displeased glare, and Seren bit back her laughter as Carr sprinted toward them.

"Guys!" he shouted, and the sprites squeaked, shielding themselves within Seren's hair. "I think I found something."

Rae lifted a hand and made a sibilant sound with his lips. Carr didn't say anything else until he slammed to a halt, grass flying as he skidded onto the dirt path. The commotion stirred Dax's attention, and he hurried over, his eyes on his best friend as he asked, "What's going on?" The sprites poking between strands of Seren's tangled hair caught his gaze. He cocked his head, but said nothing, returning his eyes to Carr.

Tansy climbed through Seren's hair and swooned. "He's even prettier up close."

Seren's lips twitched to hide a smile, and Rae turned to Carr, his eyes imploring and expectant. "What'd you find?"

"A fountain." He pointed to the trees. "Like a mile or two that way, there's an alcove and a small meadow, and a huge fountain in the center." He reached his hands above his head. "It's gold and taller than me, and it has these carvings that sort of look like the murals."

"Anyone else find anything?" Rae asked.

Dax shrugged, and Seren gestured to the sprites sitting on her shoulders.

"Take us," Seren and Rae said in unison.

Carr's discovery revived the group, and Seren had to hold herself back from sprinting as Carr led them to the fountain. Ziaa still rested in Seren's palm, and she lifted her hand to ask, "Do you know anything about the fountain? Are we on the right track?"

Ziaa stretched her delicate arms and flew to Seren's hair. Latching her fingers in the wispy flyaways, she whispered, "The fountain belonged to Ares. He ruled Clarallan from Sollian's territory—well, before it was the Sollian court. This fountain is one of Ares's only treasures that survived the Great Wars. Queen Hamara declared the fountain a sacred artifact a few weeks ago, and its location in the garden is permanently written in their formal laws to preserve Clarallan's history."

Seren gulped. *Carr did it.* "That sounds exactly like what we're looking for."

Ziaa squeaked and flew around Seren's head, chirping with her friends.

After hiking a little less than two miles, Carr hurried into an opening, a perfect circle imprinted within the dense willow trees. The high sun cast a spotlight over the blinding fountain in the center as it towered at least two feet taller than the six-foot-something males with her, its three thick tiers of circular gold overflowing with crystalline water. Each level was adorned with fine carvings, and the top two had curved lips decorated with miniature sculptures of humans and creatures, the people kneeling as they drank from their hands.

Seren inhaled, and for the first time since she'd entered the garden, a faint heat spread through her limbs, burning hotter as she exhaled. By the time she approached the fountain, a layer of sweat covered her from head to toe and her magic hummed in her chest. She tried to focus on what it felt like when her magic spread, but her power was too overwhelming; she was still out of control.

The sprites leaped from Seren and floated around the fountain, splashing in the clear water as the group studied the art. The top bowl was the smallest of the three-tier design, its sides carved with suns and stars and moons. Sculptures of young children and elders topped the rim, their expressions stolen by wide smiles and laughter.

The next level down was much larger, with carvings of mature Fae and creatures sitting around the thick gold sides covered with delicate carvings of swirling suns and sharp rays. Gilded flower petals floated on top of the blue surface, sinking and rising as water trickled over the edge of the top bowl.

The fountain radiated an ancient magic, imbued with the sun's warmth and the sound of children's laughter. It was as if

Clarallan's magic lay dormant beneath the layers of gold, just waiting to be called upon.

Life flourished over the first two levels, but as Seren lowered her gaze, the warmth inside her chest twisted into something discomforting. Her breath caught—the third bowl was covered in untamable flames made by deep, jagged cuts in the gold. Magic bubbled in her veins, and she took a step back, holding her sweaty palms to her chest as if she could pull the fire from her heart.

Rae was the first to notice her distress. He placed a hand on her shoulder, but she shook him off, her skin tingling where he touched her. His eyes narrowed. "Ser, you okay?"

She coughed and waved her hand. Ziaa paused midsplash and shook out her wings, then bounced to Seren.

"What's wrong?" Ziaa asked. Seren staggered, bracing herself against her knees. She opened her mouth to speak when Carr called for everyone to come look at something, but nothing came out. Then she stood, her head a little too light. Faces a mirror of concern, Rae and Ziaa stared at her.

"I'm okay guys." She took a step. "Just got a little hot, that's all."

Rae held out an arm, but she took a breath to regain her strength and strode past him, staring at Carr.

She asked, "What'd you find this time?"

"Look at this." Carr pointed at the lip of the bottom bowl. At the largest level, the sides were thickest, but flattened at the top, while the others were smooth and curved. Carr trailed his finger over the thin engraved lines, a spiraling, loopy print that was difficult to read.

Seren followed along as Dax read the words out loud, "Sacred flame of fiery Sun, take us to the eternal kingdom."

Everyone shared a silent glance.

Dax stepped around her and circled the fountain, continuing

to read as he found more scripture: "The Sun will grant the first success, by test of life all will progress."

Seren pivoted to Rae and her head spun. "Do you have the journal?"

Rae swung his pack and unlatched the leather strap, handing her the journal from the top. "What do you know?"

Seren ignored his question, flipping to the last page of the Sollian section. She pointed. "Here. Those words"—she lifted her gaze to Rae—"they're exactly the same." She handed Rae the journal and stepped to read the quotes, Ziaa's wings tickling her neck.

"Good memory, Ser," Carr added, stepping back to let her see.

The guys huddled close and brainstormed behind her, and she heard Dax try to put something together. "The Sollian Fae are healers, right? Maybe 'by test of life' means she has to save someone?"

Seren shuddered—she was going into the trials completely blind. She traced her fingers over the first few words. The stone was warm against her tingling skin as a prickling sensation crawled through her arms, over her shoulders, and down her spine. Her hands flickered with magic, and thin tendrils of bright light kissed the hot air between her fingers and the fountain.

Seren read the quotes out loud and opened her heart to Clarallan. "Sacred flame of fiery Sun, take us to the eternal kingdom. The Sun will grant the first success, by test of life, all will progress."

Her vision went dark at the edges, and a faint voice whispered in her ear—from Ziaa or Clarallan, Seren couldn't tell. Her magic burst, and as her mind slipped to nothingness, she repeated three words over and over:

You are worthy.
You are worthy.
You are worthy.

CHAPTER 24

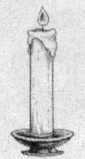

One minute, Seren held onto the sacred water fountain, a sense of worthiness fueling the fire in her soul.

The next, she woke up staring at the canopy-scattered sky, her backside flat against the cool grass as Ziaa bounced on her cheek, asking Seren repeatedly if she was okay. Blinking slowly, Seren stood and rubbed the back of her head. "I think so."

"You had me worried." Ziaa's eyes flared—the same color as the surrounding forest—as she flew around Seren's head. "You passed out for quite a while."

Squinting, Seren scanned the garden. The clearing was much larger and the fountain was gone—replaced by the biggest tree Seren had ever seen. Its wide furrowed trunk twisted hundreds of feet in the air, its weeping branches cascading infinitely around them. "Where are we?" Panic kissed her neck. "Where are the guys?"

Ziaa twirled in front her eyes. "Welcome to the first trial." Seren wrinkled her nose and Ziaa continued, "Come on, Shaya's waiting for you."

"You—" Seren gaped, scrambling after Ziaa as she flew

toward the tree. *Shaya?* Seren glanced at a large gold door consuming the base of the trunk and swallowed. "Ziaa... Wait up!"

Ziaa bounced a few yards short of the ancient tree. "What's the hold up? We've been waiting for you."

Seren's gaze climbed the spiraling trunk. Her voice trembled as she asked, "Did you say Shaya?"

Ziaa beamed.

"Like—like the Goddess of the Sun?" Seren was going to be sick.

Shaya, the ancient Goddess of the Sun was one of the eight gods responsible for the birth of Clarallan—the kingdom the complete culmination of the eight gods' unique solar magic. There were hundreds of stories about the gods in the Stellean king's library, but nothing past the Great Wars. Many were in ancient languages Seren couldn't understand, so she'd read the ones she could, but after the Fae wreaked havoc on Clarallan, the gods were never seen again.

Not once did Seren think she would have to meet the gods. Not even the Seer or the Domini had proposed the idea. The gods were believed to have abandoned Clarallan after the Great Wars, returning their attention to the other four planets that claimed their corner of the universe.

Ziaa clapped her hands together. "Isn't it so exciting?"

Seren shook her head and Ziaa pounced, too quick to catch.

"Ouch!" Seren flinched, rubbing her nose. "Why'd you do that?"

"Why do you think?" Ziaa threw her curly hair over her tiny shoulders.

Seren's gaze fell. "I'm not ready."

Someone really should have told her she had to meet the gods of Clarallan to complete the trials. She had only prepared to prove herself worthy, not to stare into the face of life itself. Seren had hoped ignorantly the gods would observe her from afar.

She gulped, hard.

Ziaa flew to the door. "Come on."

Seren reined in her emotions, smoothed her expression, and trailed reluctantly after the pesky sprite. Standing at the golden door, Seren's magic coiled inside her. In seconds she was going to meet a goddess. She worked her throat against her fear and asked, "Is there anything I should know before I go in there? Like how to get Shaya to like me?"

Ziaa's smile was an accelerant to Seren's weak confidence. "Everything you need is already inside you, Seren." She paused, then giggled. "But don't look directly into her eyes."

Seren asked, "What happens if I do?"

The sprite didn't give Seren an extra second. Ziaa knocked on the colossal door, an impossible sound, and yet the golden hinges cracked and the door swung inward. Ziaa beamed. "Just don't." She gestured down the stairs. "Now go save Clarallan."

SEREN DESCENDED A SWIRLING STAIRCASE, lit by floating orbs of sunlight. Water dripped from the roots hanging around her.

She followed the hundreds of stone stairs to the mouth of a cave, her hands wrapped around the rails as she entered a cavernous kingdom deep below the garden. A damp smell clung to her skin, and an intoxicating voice slithered toward her. Seren lifted her gaze between the rows of benches facing the dais and stared at the Goddess of the Sun.

Shaya—a beautiful woman with gilded snakes for hair—sat in the towering black throne with her legs crossed, her piercing green eyes narrowing on Seren. Silence fell over the large crowd. Seren lowered her gaze and Shaya stood, her golden dress falling to her ankles, emphasizing her warm skin. A thin smile curled the ends of her red lips, and the crowd turned as one.

Hundreds of spirits sneered at Seren's side, and her knees buckled.

"Come," Shaya beckoned.

Magic cracked in the goddess's voice like a summer thunderstorm. Seren obeyed without hesitation, her magic tugging her forward as it reconnected with the master of its power.

Keeping her eyes on the damp ground, she walked beneath the crumbling stone, approaching the jagged boulders that sat at the base of the dais. *You are worthy*, she reminded herself. The crowd leaned in, studying her as she presented herself before the goddess. She took small steps up the black stairs and approached the deity, unable to tear her eyes from the golden snakes that coiled and sprang in her direction.

"Seren." Shaya waved for her to stand in the center. "We've been waiting for you."

Seren stilled, silent, her fear an impossible-to-swallow knot in her throat.

Shaya commanded, "Tell us, Seren—why are you here?"

The crowd studied Seren with an intensity similar to Hellevi's right before one of his punishments. She willed herself not to flinch away, a near impossible feat as the crowd gaped at her. She turned to look at the hopeless spirits—Fae, Verti, human, and creature. Their eyes were dim, and the hair on the back of her neck stood as she met their hollow faces. A light haze misted through the rows of benches dominating the sacred courtroom, casting a damp chill over the cave.

Seren knew one thing. This wasn't Clarallan.

At least not the land of those alive.

She inhaled, and her traitorous voice cracked. "I'm here to complete the Lost Trials of Clarallan."

The crowd gasped and Shaya grinned, gesturing to her side. Eight Fae males strode from the shadows carrying a long wooden table, while a ninth followed behind with a single chair. All nine kept their chins tucked, their eyes unusually dull for the Fae.

Shaya pointed her thin chin to the chair in the center. "Sit."

Seren obeyed, her eyes landing on a spirit near the back. He was just a big Fae male with his head down until she recognized his armor. Her anger flared—the emblem on his chest was a crown of stars above two crossed swords. Hellevi's personal design.

Shaya waved at the eager spirits, and her haunting voice echoed against the cracked stone, stealing Seren's attention. "Tonight, we bear witness to history in the flesh. Decades have passed since the last time anyone attempted our trials." The goddess peered over her shoulder, and Seren looked away. "And never has a woman dared to consider them."

Seren stiffened and her gut twisted, her eyes fixed on the crowd of gaunt and hollow faces.

"It makes me wonder," Shaya mused, lifting her hands as her snakes wrapped around her fingers. "I see you know not to stare into my eyes, but do you know why?"

Seren shook her head, her dark hair shielding her face.

"Do you want to find out?"

Seren shook her head again.

"That rarely works," Shaya mused, walking to her throne. Sitting, she continued, "As the Goddess of the Sun I have accepted the role as the judge of sin. Stare into my eyes long enough, and you'll confess the worst pieces of your soul, unable to stop."

Seren closed her eyes, willed her breathing to calm. Honestly, she had expected something much worse, like a fiery death in the flames of the sun. She didn't even know what her worst sin was, so it couldn't be that bad. Shaya asked another question, and Seren jolted.

"Does anyone know how many Fae have attempted the Lost Trials?"

Spirits shouted answers from the crowd, their anticipation soaring with Seren's fear.

The goddess clarified, "Seren is the one hundred and eleventh." Shaya's silky voice wrapped around Seren's neck and squeezed, the gravity of her words settling as doubt in her woozy gut. Going into the trials, Seren had known the odds were stacked against her, but she hadn't expected them to be that bad. But it didn't matter. Seren would complete the trials either way, pay whatever the cost.

Shaya's voice drew Seren's attention to her snakes as she avoided the goddess's hungry eyes. "Seren, do you consider yourself a moral person?"

Confused, she gulped. "Yes…"

Shaya's lips pursed. "Do you believe all life is precious?"

"Yes."

"And do you believe sins to be forgivable?"

Seren hesitated.

"Yes or no?" Shaya demanded.

She hadn't said all, right? Seren answered, snapping her teeth together. "Yes."

Shaya's snakes hissed and their yellow eyes glowed as the goddess cocked her head, clicking her tongue. "And finally, do you believe anyone has the right to decide who lives and who dies?"

Seren swallowed. "No."

"And you wish to complete the solar trials…" Shaya tilted her head. "Why? To be like Ares?"

Seren steadied her voice. "The Stellean king is waging a war against the courts." She gazed upon the recoiling crowd. "He wants to become a High King."

Shaya snorted. "That's why the trials are set in place, girl. To prevent the wrong people from being in power. Why are you really here?"

Seren focused on the goddess, eyeing her silk dress. "I lived beneath the king's torture for twenty years." Her mouth felt like cotton. "This war that's coming…I know what Hellevi will do to

Clarallan. And if there's any chance for me to save our people from the pain I have felt, I have to try."

"Much better," Shaya cooed, her smile warming Seren's core. "Had to get that out of the way. No point in wasting my breath on someone I can easily tell will fail my test." Shaya flicked her sharp tongue, a smooth split down the center, over her thin lips. "My siblings and I created this universe, the planets, and the stars. This planet was our favorite, the perfect home for Clarallan, the complete culmination of all the gods' magic. We pulled on our unique powers: from the suns, moons, stars, comets, and the sea. Our combined energies created the perfect kingdom. But my sisters and I feared our own creation. Clarallan was such a powerful kingdom we worried, without proper limits, its magic would fall victim to devastating rulers—those who took our creation for granted."

Seren's blood chilled, her thoughts flashing glimpses of what Clarallan would look like after Hellevi's war—something from her nightmares.

The goddess's voice lifted, her tone a pinch kinder after Seren's admission. "My sisters and I convinced our brothers to believe our fear, and together we created the five trials. So only those who proved themselves worthy might unlock mastery of Clarallan's magic."

The crowd leaned back, a unanimous yawn across the sea of faces. As if they'd heard Shaya's speech a hundred times. Which, Seren realized, they had: one hundred and eleven to be exact.

"The Sun Trial has two phases." Shaya lifted a finger. "First, we hear the confessions of the worst sins committed by those present tonight." Something sinister slid over the goddess. "And don't worry, I handpicked those lucky enough to be here. And you, Seren"—she gestured to the table—"you will feast on the spoiled parts of them, get to taste how much this kingdom has valued the gift my siblings and I have given you all. Then, after hearing the best of what your peers have to offer and gorging on the rotten fruits of their morals, phase two will begin." Seren squeezed her eyes shut and Shaya continued, "Then I'll test the depth of your morality, and only then will we know if you are worthy of the Sun's gift."

Blood pounded in Seren's ears, and she opened her eyes. "Phase two…can you tell me what my test will be?"

A *tsk*. "That must remain a secret. I can't risk swaying any bias." Shaya's voice lifted with desire. "So, Seren, with the chance to stop your king, do you accept my conditions?"

"He's not my king." Seren choked, her mouth dry as she braved the crowd. "But I accept."

An unnerving clatter of haunted screams erupted, the cries rattling the fractured cave.

Shaya hissed, "Let the Sun Trial begin."

SHAYA SUMMONED twenty spirits from the crowd, instructing them one by one to stare into her eyes and divulge their worst sin.

After the first five, Seren knew Shaya had not invited just any spirits to attend the sacred trial. Rather, she had selected Clarallan's worst. The kind with no shame, who betrayed those they loved with pleasure and hurt the others for fun. Most were thieves, killers, and wannabe kings, while a few were just hateful and numb to their own cruelty.

A plate slid in front of Seren with each confession, a rotten food of Shaya's creation that symbolized each spirit's failure to respect the gift of life. Seren choked on each bite, fighting the assault of verbal confessions that competed to inflict the worst of her nausea.

Her face turned yellow, and Shaya ordered her men to get a bucket. "Puking counts as cheating," Shaya said. "To pass phase one and understand the meaning of life, you must consume the full extent of their sins."

Her stomach roiled.

Consume, or be consumed.

Seren shook with disgust despite the sweat that dampened her skin and swallowed the tenth confession: a rotten apple, sour and moldy, for the spirit's life of lies. She felt feverish, and she wondered how quickly food poisoning could set in. By the thirteenth confession, Seren stopped tasting the foul food, her attention solely focused on keeping it all down.

Her mind numbed, resorting to the hours of practice she had surviving similar horrors—just at the hands of a king, not a god. But where Hellevi craved pain, Shaya desired justice.

"You," Shaya beckoned, jarring Seren from her daze as a tall male—the twentieth to go—marched toward the goddess. It was the Stellean soldier she had seen near the back of the crowd. Seren knew Shaya had saved the best for last; a Stellean sin could make even a devil repent. He trembled, and the sound of his silver armor rattled against the hollow caves. His fear taunted the snakes and they lunged, liquid gold dripping from their fangs as they hissed. The goddess asked, "What is your name?"

He lowered his eyes. "Harbin Akross."

Shaya leaned back in her throne and crossed one tan leg over the other, motioning with an open palm. "What is it you wish to confess?"

Seren scolded her gaze for hunting Shaya's engrossing eyes. Her voice was daring, sweet like forgiveness—a cruel joke.

Seren focused her attention on the soldier. He stumbled to his knees, unable to rip his eyes from the goddess. His heavy armor cracked against the stone. "I've killed a lot of people over the years and never thought twice about it. Not until the last one."

Seren shook as she sipped from a cool glass of water that Shaya was kind enough to provide, waiting for the goddess to strike her verdict of the deceased's sin. Despite how it felt, Seren knew this wasn't about Shaya punishing her—it was about her gaining the goddess's favor, proving she was worthy of sharing a pinch of her power.

"Go on," Shaya demanded.

"What else do you need to know? She was innocent, and I killed her. That's my worst evil."

Shaya's snakes coiled. "Why did you do it?"

"It was on the job." His voice deepened. "I was one of the king's soldiers and this older woman... She was protecting someone we needed to find. She was lying, and we knew she was lying and I—" He shook his head, clenching his fists. "There was this rage. It was blinding and I couldn't control it. I just wanted her to stop lying to us." He pressed his palms to the ground as he lowered himself before the goddess. "I never thought about who I killed before her...all the lives I ruined. She haunts me more than any awful thing I ever did, and I don't know if it's because she was innocent or because of the last thing she said: 'There are simply some things worth dying for.'"

A heavy silence fell across the crowd, and even Shaya's snakes stilled.

Shaya clicked her split pink tongue and steepled her fingers above her crossed legs. "And how did you end up here? Did someone take your life in return for your wrath?"

Here. Seren's blood chilled as she considered Shaya's words. She still had no idea where here was, but it wasn't the Clarallan she knew.

"No. Hellevi killed me... But not because I killed her. Because she lied to us, and I didn't get her to stop lying to us. He didn't care that she was dead. I went back empty-handed." Regret swelled in his eyes. "I never should've gone back empty-handed."

Seren lurched at the king's name, a regrettable reaction as her stomach coiled and heat flushed her face.

The goddess asked, "And what was her name?"

His shoulders fell. "I don't know."

Shaya's jaw clenched and her pupils dilated to thin slits. "Her name was Rosella May, and she didn't deserve to die."

Seren didn't know she could feel the way she did—gutted. Tears threatened her lashes, and Shaya's men dropped a silver platter in front of her.

The goddess hissed. "A dragon's heart—for the life of an innocent."

Seren gulped, tears pouring down her cheeks as she stared at the bloody plate, guilt lathering her tongue as she opened her cracked lips.

One more plate.

A heart for a heart.

SEREN'S HEARTBREAK WAS RAW.

And bitter and chewy.

Bile surged her throat and she forced herself to swallow the taste of spoiled iron. She squeezed her eyelids together as tears burned her cheeks, and she pawed at the revolting feeling of guilt dripping from her chin, down her neck.

She shook.

Her worst fear lived outside of her, snapping jagged teeth, its gaze like claws across her skin, tearing at her heart. It whispered in her ear, *Their blood is on your hands, Seren.*

Something traitorous flared within her. A thought. Defiance maybe. Something primitive, divine, and dominating. Seren grasped at the strands of hope her magic poured into her veins, blinking away her useless tears.

Shaya stood, and her gold gown cascaded to the floor, trailing her as she walked to the middle of the dais. Her red heels clicked against the stone, the shoes' laces coiling up her tan legs in bands of scaled gold. She waved slowly and the crowd leaned in, their breath caught, and their hollow eyes widened as she said, "Phase one is complete."

Seren straightened, snuffling a little—the trial wasn't over.

The saying "everything happens for a reason" had never made much sense before. After all, she'd spent twenty years in hell believing she'd waste her entire life there. But her punishment was fit to a cosmic scale, fated for something much larger than herself. It wasn't about what she did or didn't do to deserve her trauma. It was about who she was—in the purest part of her soul—and how the universe knew she could survive.

Her pain had a reason. It encouraged her to fight, because despite everything, her heart still beat to a lighter rhythm.

If she passed these trials, she could save everyone, her friends, Clarallan.

No one had to die.

Things didn't have to be this way.

Rosella had said some things were worth dying for, but Seren was greedy—no one else would die. The real triumph would be to live. To survive against all odds and come out a person to be proud of.

It made sense—why Shaya had designed the Sun Trial the way she did. To find the souls not just strong enough to stare evil in the face, but those capable of leading them toward the light. But even Shaya had not been strong enough to escape blemish free: her soul had chilled, stealing from her gift of life, warping her heart.

"I'm impressed," the goddess sneered. "I didn't expect an encore of entertainment tonight... I was grateful for just a slap of excitement." Shaya giggled, a sweet sound that rose above her mockery. "It's been decades since anyone was foolish enough to believe they could be worthy of the gods. But you...what did you think of my surprise at the end?"

A shiver crawled up Seren's spine. Shaya had guessed her fatal flaw.

The crowd was a hiss of snorting spirits, fueling the parts of Seren that begged for revenge, threw her morality to the wind, and demanded she welcome the darkness inside of her.

Seren didn't believe in coincidences that extreme. Shaya's grand finale was supposed to have been what bled Seren dry, her virtue drained until only her evil remained. The Goddess of the Sun had orchestrated a performance. *Entertainment,* as she'd regarded Seren's suffering.

But Seren saw right through it—the story of her own pain reflected through the details of her trial.

Shaya's words echoed in Seren's mind, dampening her rage. *The perfect kingdom,* she had said. Listening to her speech, Seren knew she and the other gods had great dreams for Clarallan, molded it after their greatest wishes and what their hearts most desired. But what Shaya and her siblings had failed to account for was the overwhelming sin that infiltrated the inhabitants of Clarallan. Their superiority limited them from experiencing what the pressure of living in such a magical hot spot would do to the minds and morals of those who were not a god.

After the Fae took control of the courts in the Great Wars, to live in Clarallan was to sin. Its citizens lived in the blurred line between good and evil—a perpetual fog that warped their perspectives and twisted their virtues. The Fae fought against Clarallan's values, ensured the darkness never cleared. The kingdom had its rules, but the Fae believed everyone was meant to be broken.

Shaya had been charged with the weight of Clarallan's sin for centuries, her soul bearing the heartbreak of what the Fae had done to the gods' perfect creation.

The goddess had given Seren just a taste, and it had almost been too much; any more and Seren was sure her soul would shatter beneath the weight of such evil. Shaya had designed the Sun Trial to prove that her pain was justified, and over one hundred souls had testified that her darkened heart was not her fault, that it was impossible to have witnessed such horrors and still see the good.

But if Seren was to pass, she had to see the light.

The crowd cheered and chanted. "Phase two, phase two—"

Shaya's men cleared the dais, removing the table and chair. Seren stood at the center of the crowd and rolled her shoulders, daring the goddess. "I'm ready."

Shaya smirked. "Seren, do you remember the questions I asked you before the trial began?" A nod. "Do you remember your answers?"

"Yes."

"After phase one of the Sun Trial, have any of your answers changed?"

Seren weighed her morals in her mind and held her chin high. Seren was certain if Harbin Akross was still alive after killing Rosella, she would have killed him. But Hellevi had kept the blood off her hands. Phase one had been designed to steal her light, her ability to see the good. But Seren's magic filled her heart with warmth and reminded her of her strength—her ability to see the good, to wish better for herself and the kingdom. Her answers were the same. "No."

"Is that the truth?" Shaya raised her brows. Again, a nod. "The Sun's gifts offer you the power to create life, to help it grow and heal, to flourish. But it is a great responsibility to bear the weight of the Sun." The goddess strode to the back of the dais, far away from the crowd. With a flick of her wrist, she split the air, and her magic built a wall of fire that hovered above the stone. Seren stepped toward the crackling wall of flames. It stretched at least ten feet tall, and she welcomed how its warmth fought the chill of the spirits.

Shaya's snakes relished the fire, dancing around her face as they absorbed the increasing heat. The goddess waved one hand through the spitting flames and beckoned Seren closer with the other. "To pass phase two, all you must do is walk through the fire. If your answers are as true as you say, you will walk through the flame and return to your friends, having earned the gifts of the Sun. But the Sun will judge your heart, even the darkest of corners you don't like to think about, and if the Sun doesn't find you worthy, well..." She flicked the flames and they leaped and crackled, spitting liquid heat across Seren's skin. Seren flinched but she didn't step back, her eyes wide as she gazed into the wall of fire.

Shaya was numb to the heat, her skin cast in an impenetrable gold after centuries of being cut down by everyone's sins. Seren saw her cruelty for what it was: a shield that protected the last remnants of her broken heart. The king had helped Seren forge one just like it. Shaya clicked her split tongue. "One last thing. Seren, look into my eyes."

Her heart raced. She could handle whatever she confessed. She was doing this for a reason. She was worthy. Curling and uncurling her fingers, Seren turned to face the goddess. Goosebumps raced the length of her left arm, which was cold as the fire burned at her right side. Seren lifted her chin and her gaze crawled over Shaya's torso, up her neck, and over her pink lips—blinking once—before her gaze sparked at the intensity of Shaya's eyes, entire forests of gleaming emeralds that stole her breath away.

Shaya lifted a corner of her mouth, barring her white fangs. "What is it you wish to confess?"

Seren felt nothing. Shaya repeated her question, and still Seren casually returned her stare. She glanced at the fire, then back to the goddess. "I see your pain," Seren said, and Shaya narrowed her sparkling eyes. "I see you, and I understand because I've felt pain like that before. That's why I'm going to walk through the fire now. So I can save my friends"—Seren's heart clenched—"and our kingdom from knowing hurt like we do. Just because you and I have suffered doesn't mean others have to. It's not fair, but there's no pressure like pain. And it's what you decide to do with it that matters."

Seren inhaled, closing her eyes as she invited her magic to grow.

She had no idea why she was immune to Shaya's gift, and she really had no idea if this was going to work, but...

She jumped, diving headfirst into the engulfing sea of liquid orange. She fell. And kept falling. The pressure in her chest built, and a searing pain burned the top of her sternum as cosmic voices drowned her ears with whispers of light and life.

Falling.

And falling.

CHAPTER 25

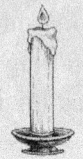

Everything was dark.

Seren's magic did compressions on her heart and her mind stirred. An unnerving warmth crept over her limbs, and she regained feeling in her body. Damp grass pressed against her skin...

She was lying down.

A steady rhythm pounded on her chest, and a sharp pain pierced her heart, her entire body flooded by a wave of untapped magic. Someone was speaking to her. But it was nearly impossible to hear over the drumming of her heart and the crackling of her magic.

"Come on, Seren," a familiar voice shouted, so desperate it clouded the tough male's identity. "Open your eyes, dammit."

Her eyes were closed. That's why everything was dark.

Pain flashed through her temples, and she peeled her crusty lashes apart. She stared at the sky, certain the sun was brighter than it ever had been before.

"Thank the gods." That was Carr's deep voice above her.

She coughed, choking on her words. "Don't thank the gods." Her mouth was dry and her lips were cracked. It felt like someone had poured melted iron down her throat, or maybe it was just raw from screaming as she fell through time and space. She pressed her palms against the cool ground and lifted her sore limbs into a sitting position. Her body resisted, but Rae was there, his muscular arms against her back, holding her up.

Sweat rolled down the center of her chest and her sternum burned. She hissed and all three of her friends gaped at her, their expressions mixed with fear, confusion, and relief. She pawed at her leathers, peeling the sticky material from her skin, nearly exposing her bare chest. Desperate to find the source of pain.

Carr's words were rushed. "Don't get me wrong, I'm all for seeing you without clothes, but what are you doing?"

"Something burns," she said through clenched teeth, getting a clear view of her pain. A fine-lined sun sprawled in abstract spirals in the middle of her sternum, right between her breasts, rays of light drawn over her skin in short, crisp lines of black.

"Woah. When'd you get a tattoo?" Carr asked.

Seren would have slapped him if she could. Did she look like she had any idea what was going on? Her skin stung, and she rubbed her fingers around the irritated red, dissipating the prickling sensation. Her fingertip brushed the ink, and it glowed, a pale yellow center with reds and oranges fading through the swirling lines.

"What the—" Seren's eyes widened, gaze glued to her chest. Her heart raced, and she was seconds away from freaking out when Dax leaned close and took a second look.

"Guys...I think we've seen that before." His voice quickened and he turned. "Rae, where's the journal?"

Rae swung his pack off his shoulder, never taking his eyes off Seren. He let it fall into Dax's hands and asked her, "Are you okay?"

The Sun Trial blazed through her mind, and she stifled a shudder. She was alive. They could talk about her feelings later. First, she needed answers.

She stood, shaking clumps of grass and soil from her clothes. Her limbs tingled and she wobbled, as if she were taking her first steps. Rae offered her a hand but she shook her head. The faintness in her head and body didn't last long, and besides her skin, which fought to reject the foreign ink, she felt okay. Better than okay, actually.

Dax undid the pack's leather straps, grabbed the journal, and flipped to the Sollian section. His dominant hand scanned the detailed pages, his eyes moving quicker than his fingertips. He stopped, tapping at the bottom of the page. "Here." Seren took a step. He tapped again. "Look there." Dax pointed at a sketch of Ares standing in front of a towering fire. His loose shirt was torn, and down the center of his spine was a tattoo.

"It's the same," Seren whispered. "The exact same."

Carr bumped elbows with Dax. "Matching tattoos with Ares. Sweet."

"What happened, Ser?" Rae asked, his eyes full of concern. "One second, everything was fine, and the next—" He snapped his teeth together. "We thought we'd lost you."

"Seriously, girl, you scared the hell outta us." Carr wrapped his arm around her and squeezed. "When you fell, you…you stopped breathing. We thought you were gone."

She shuddered. *She* had stopped breathing. During the Sun Trial, Seren had guessed she wasn't in Clarallan. And all the spirits— But where had she been?

The guys jumped to explain what happened, restarting a few times as their words blended together. Something cracked inside her, and her heart broke listening to her friends, the pain in their voices: how they begged her to get up, to breathe, to open her eyes. They apologized for failing to protect her—and Seren hated crying—but the fear that radiated between her and her friends was overwhelming. Tears swelled in her lashes, and Carr pulled her into a full embrace. "I'm so sorry, guys," she said, snuffling against his chest.

"Don't be, Seren." Dax raised the journal. "You did it. You really did it."

Carr released her and she stepped back, nodding. She lifted her chin and mumbled, "I know."

Rae lifted his brows. "The Sun Trial?" More nods. "How?" Rae asked.

"You guys seriously aren't going to believe this." Seren wiped the back of her hand against her cheeks and straightened her spine. "But you know Shaya, the Goddess of the Sun? Well, I met her." Seren steepled her fingers and paced. "Like she was really here. Or—" Seren stared at the shredded grass where her body had lain. Where she had stopped breathing. Where the guys had thought she'd died. "I was really there."

"The gods haven't been seen in centuries, Seren," Rae rebutted.

Carr cocked his head at Dax. "Sure we still don't need to call a healer?" Rae looked about to agree when Dax interrupted.

Seren halted.

"She's telling the truth." Dax flipped the journal pages and pointed at a second sketch of Ares. Directly below the sun tattoo she shared with him was a tilted crescent moon. Dax skipped to the last trial and lifted the journal to show the three of them the final sketch. Ares's spine was filled with ink: five individual but connected tattoos. "Each one symbolizes the completion of the Lost Trials. Izzac's notes mention going to a place of worship or connection to Clarallan's gods. That's why we're in the garden. It's Sollian's place of honor to Shaya."

"You did it." Rae beamed, excitedly placing his large hands on her shoulders. "You passed the first trial." He shook her and she grinned. "And you're really okay?"

She stretched her smile to her eyes. "I'm good, Rae."

"So…what was it like?" Dax asked.

"Yeah, are you, like, bloody powerful now?" Carr laughed.

"I don't know." Seren's giggle fell away and guilt flashed

through her mind. She had completed the first trial, but at what cost? Rosella was dead, and her heart had been exposed to such evil... Yet, she'd still found the light, held on to just enough, that the Sun had found her worthy. She glanced at her friends. "Can we get out of here? It's a long story, and I can explain on the way."

Dax mercifully tapped his finger on one of Izzac's maps, drawing everyone's attention. "Izzac knows a guy, a trader that travels between the courts. We talked about it back home. Izzac said he can take us to Lunaan."

"Let's go," Rae said, grabbing his pack.

Grateful for the extra time to gather her words, Seren mouthed a silent thank-you to Dax, and he simpered in return.

SEREN JOSTLED awake when the cart they caught a ride out of Sollian in went over a particularly rough patch of road. Izzac's guy, North, had followed through on his word and offered them a fair rate for a safe ride to the Lunaan court.

Her head bounced and Rae groaned. She'd rested it in his lap while sleeping, and now she looked up at him and gave a coy half smile. "Sorry." She sat up, stretched her legs, and leaned against a wooden crate.

Izzac had written the address for his connection in the journal. North, with his horse-drawn cart, ran an import service for the most expensive goods found in Sollian; and *horse-drawn* really meant North was a centaur—both the product and the salesman.

Seren barely remembered meeting him, just that North had taken one good look at her and said "Gods to bones, get in". She'd been too exhausted to resist and let the guys handle the rest of the talking. The Sun Trial had drained her more than she thought. After her adrenaline wore off, her body ached as if she'd caught the winter fever. Her magic—like a jar in the center of her core—was drained to just a few droplets after Shaya drank her fill.

The back of North's cart was tight and crowded, with barely enough room for the stacks of locked boxes and crates, let alone the four of them. She and Rae sat along one side, while Dax slumped across a short bench on the other, and Carr sprawled out on the cluttered floor.

Seren was thankful getting out of the Sollian Court had been easier than getting in, with a more reasonable amount of deadly cliffs to scale—and by "reasonable" she meant there were none. If it were up to her, she never wanted to do that again.

"How long have I been out?" Seren whispered. After they'd found North, they decided to keep their conversations light and airy, excluding anything that mentioned the trials. Izzac may have said North was trustworthy, but they could never be too careful.

"Most of the night. We should be well out of Sollian by now, but it'll take the rest of tomorrow to reach the Lunaan court. We should get there sometime in the evening. And from there we can go straight to…work."

Right. Izzac had recommended that she attempt the Lunaan trial at night, when the moons would be at their greatest power.

"You should get some rest," Seren said, glancing at the others. Dax might have been awake, but his eyes were closed, and Carr's snores vibrating against the wood were a sure sign he was out.

"I will," Rae said, his eyes dark.

"I'm serious."

He rubbed the back of his neck. "I know."

"How far will North take us?"

"We paid for passage directly into Lunaan, but I think we'll part ways with him sooner. We don't want to draw any attention by getting out of the cart in the heart of the city," Rae explained. A natural leader, he was the moth, and strategy the flame. He scanned her face and continued, "I also want to send a letter to the house. Let Izzac and Tait know that Sollian was a success and we're continuing our trip." He chuckled under his breath. "And, you know, to assure them everyone is still alive."

The last thing Izzac had said to her was try not to die. She hadn't been sure if it was because the trials were truly that dangerous, or he didn't have that much faith in her. But after meeting Shaya, she guessed both were true. The goddess had done everything to break Seren, to prove that her light could not withstand the taint of evil that infested Clarallan. That the kingdom and the Fae were a lost cause.

But Seren had passed.

Hope tickled her ears, whispering its awe and encouragement. Despite everything, she'd really done it.

She leaned against the rough wood and Rae shifted his legs, just enough that they touched hers. He didn't even seem aware of the gesture, his neutral features smoothed into a tentative expression while he looked over their friends. Pink heat blushed in her cheeks, and she closed her eyes, easing her throbbing temples.

Fear settled as lactic in her stiff muscles, and she kneaded her neck. Beneath the garden, she'd been too overwhelmed after surviving the Sun Trial that she had yet to think about what came next—four more.

And seven more gods.

Seren wanted to ask Rae what he knew about Clarallan's gods, specifically the Gods of the Moons, but they'd all agreed to save any trial talk for later, with wandering ears and all. She asked instead, "Have you ever been to the Lunaan court?"

"Quite a bit," Rae answered. "Both Sollian and Lunaan are pretty safe for travelers, meaning guests and traders come and go as they please. And they both treat their citizens kindly. Even the humans."

Seren cracked her eyes open. "It should be like that

everywhere." Even if she wasn't human, she'd spent twenty years suffering as one. The Stellean and Etiamella courts had the worst reputations: all their humans were servants, their status on the same level as the livestock. Rae seemed to agree, and she asked, "What about the other courts, have you been to them all?"

"Dax, Izzac, and I have been to all five, mainly for scout work for the Verti. Carr's been to Sollian and Lunaan. And Tait hasn't left the village."

Seren's face tugged down. "I hope he can one day." She slipped her eyes to the head of the cart, through a small window where a thin red curtain bounced in the wind. "Maybe when this is all over, we can go on a real trip. Like, all of us, Tait, even Izzac. I want to see all the courts for real, when, you know…" Seren caught a glimpse around the red curtain, where North strode ahead, his hooves a pleasant rhythm against the hard ground. She swallowed her words in exchange for something more vague. "Things are different."

Rae paused, and his hesitation drew her attention. She met his dark gaze, his golden hair skimming his stern brow. Finally, he said, "I'd like that too."

Seren tilted her head. "I know how you feel about the courts…but you said Sollian is your favorite. Why?"

Rae weighed her question. "Because of the royals. Of all the courts' rulers, Daryn and Hamara are the only two I respect."

Seren nodded, not surprised. Rae had always reminded her of the Sollian court, and he had a point. King Hellevi was a monster, and King Dearil and the sea witch chased at his heels in their competition of cruelty. And King Egil…

Sorrow surrounded Seren's thoughts about the Lunaan royals: the death of Queen Quinlan and the illness that had fallen upon King Egil. As far as rumors went, Prince Casimir's nightmare was becoming king, while Seren knew it was Evander's dream.

A dream he would kill for.

She leaned closer to Rae, her eyes flickering between her friend and North. She hated keeping secrets. In Stellean, anything she knew Mare knew, and it went both ways, always. Every time Casimir appeared in her dreams, guilt festered in her heart. She wanted to warn him about Evander's allegiance to King Hellevi, but it was only ever a dream. She whispered, "Come here."

Rae shifted toward her, angling his ear close. "What's up?"

"There's something I haven't told you about the war—"

"Seriously, Seren." Rae shushed her, wrapping his palm over her mouth. "Not here."

She stuck out her tongue and Rae dropped his hand. Glancing toward North, she said, "He can't hear us."

"You don't know that." Rae hastily wiped his palm across his thigh. "And you're gross."

She looked at Rae with doe eyes. "Please...I need to tell someone."

Nettled, Rae clenched his jaw. "Fine, make it quiet."

Seren softened her whisper and brought her lips to Rae's ear. "You know Prince Evander—he's the one who wanted his father killed, and he bartered with Hellevi for it." She pulled away, quiet and quick.

Rae's brow narrowed, and his eyes did the same while his mouth gaped and closed. Seren jutted out her chin, brows high. Rae swept his hand through his hair, his eyes glued ahead. "You knew it was him all along?" She gave a nod, and he asked, "Why didn't you tell me sooner?"

She looked down. She'd wanted to tell Casimir before her friends, figured he deserved to know first. But after how dangerous the Sun Trial had been, and with how little she knew what to expect once they arrived in the Lunaan court—Seren wanted them to know.

Just in case.

She stifled a yawn, but it was a losing battle.

"It's okay." Rae's eyes were softer. "You should get some more rest."

"So should you." She gave him a pointed look, but her exhaustion stole the vigor from her tone. "Have you even slept at all?"

He returned her frown with a glare, tangled his fingers and stretched his arms above his head, as he leaned against a tower of crates at his side, each with tens of labels: FRAGILE, PROPERTY OF SOLLIAN, CAUTION, and so on. "I will," he said. "I promise."

He dipped his chin, and Seren gave him one last glare before lying down. She rested her head on his thighs and tucked her hands beneath her cheek, mumbling her thanks.

Rae huffed, his left hand running through the ends of her hair.

Seren whispered, her voice heavy as sleep drew her in, "I'm glad you're here, Rae."

"Me too."

His calloused hands brushed her skin, and a shiver coursed through her when he spoke again. But exhaustion fogged her thoughts, and she slipped into sleep before she could hear what he said next.

CHAPTER 26

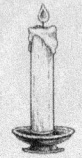

Seren jumped from the back of the wooden cart, her hand in Rae's for balance, as North dropped them off at the last trading post before the Lunaan court. Carr and Dax jumped out after and closed the rear door. Swaying from almost two full days on the road, she waved at North. "Thanks again."

"Anytime."

She watched as the centaur trotted on his way, breaking into a gallop with a racket of clacking hooves and rumbling wood as the large cart bounced along the gravely road. A violet dusk fell across the small trading town, and Seren donned a sweater from her pack. Shouldering her bag, she scanned the humble outpost. One of the few to exist beyond court borders, created for traders and travelers venturing across the vast kingdom, providing necessary shelter and services between the long days.

Rae pointed at a rickety sign ahead. "That's where we can send a letter to the house." He dropped his pack into the grass and untied the leather straps. "You guys can wait here. I already wrote it up, so I'll be quick." Rae grabbed two folded letters and handed his bag to Carr. "Will you hold this please? I don't want to walk in there with *those*." He eyed the multitude of weapons strapped along the canvas.

Carr shouldered the bag. "Sure thing, mate."

"Who's the second letter for?" Seren asked, one brow high.

"Thrina." Rae shuffled the two letters. "So she doesn't spend too much time worrying about us... Remember?"

"Good idea." Seren giggled, remembering meeting Thrina for the first time, how she'd scolded Rae for making her miss him so often. In just the few weeks Seren had spent with the Verti, she and Rae had started a tradition of dinner at Thrina's place at the end of the week. It made Rae feel good and the kind woman smile, and let Seren experience something she thought was impossible—a mother's care. Seren beamed at Rae. "I hope you told her I miss her."

"Sure did." Rae grinned, walking toward the town. "I'll just be a minute."

The three of them stepped out of the road, waiting on the edge of the grass with their backs to a forest of dense pines. Rae was halfway to the post service when Dax said, "I forgot to tell him something, I'll be right back."

"Can't it wait?" Carr asked. But Dax had already sprinted after their friend. "That was weird."

Seren tilted her head. "What do you think it was about?"

Carr shrugged, a lazy look on his face. "Beats me."

She pressed her lips together and watched both Verti disappear around the corner of the building up ahead. "Maybe something he forgot to tell Izzac."

"Sounds right to me." Carr chuckled. "I've never met bigger control freaks than those two."

"I know a few who are worse," Seren said, listing them silently: Hellevi, Izara, Hubort. But Carr knew. By now, Seren had told the guys almost everything—minus Hellevi's torture. Seren believed some things were so dark just talking about them stole the light from others. She stifled a wince. "At least those two just care to be in control; the ones in Stellean hurt for it."

Carr offered a half smile. "Not for long."

Seren smirked, echoing her friend. "Not for long."

"So..." Carr tried to give her a serious look, but curiosity rebelled in his dark brown eyes. "When do we finally get to hear it? You know"—his gaze slipped through the trees and he leaned closer—"the Sun Trial."

After two days of holding everything in—lots of spiraling, some compartmentalizing, and too much overthinking—Seren had almost forgotten she'd yet to tell the Verti the whole story. In the garden, she'd given just enough to muzzle their infinite questions, too tired and overstimulated to say much more. Physically, she was fine. Her magic felt stronger. And yes, she *seriously* met the Sun Goddess, Shaya. Even saying the last part out loud had sounded absurd, but after repeating it plenty of times, Seren had finally convinced herself it really happened.

Dax and Rae appeared around the corner, and she asked, "How about I fill y'all in on the road?"

"Deal."

"I'M SO SORRY, SER," Rae said, glancing over his shoulder as he walked ahead with Dax toward the Lunaan court.

Pain constricted her throat and she swallowed hard. Telling the Verti what happened to Rosella felt like confessing a crime. Deep down, she knew it wasn't her fault, but that didn't stop her heart from sinking in guilt.

In stride, Carr wrapped his arm around her shoulders. "Bloody hell, girl."

It had taken almost an hour for Seren to explain just phase one of the Sun Trial. She had tried to skip over the details of the spirits' confessions, but the guys had insisted on knowing everything. With each confession she'd echoed, her stomach lurched in remembrance, nauseous from the taste of their sins on her tongue.

"Shaya saved Rosella's killer for the end?" Dax looked back. "Seems personal."

"It was." Seren shuddered. "After I passed phase one, Shaya asked how I felt about her surprise. She did it on purpose. To ensure I'd fail."

"So the trials aren't a one-size-fits-all," Rae noted.

Seren shook her head. "Shaya explained the Sun Trial as how it was every time. I think the gods just throw in a few curveballs to increase the stakes. She was jaded, like, seriously. Shaya and her siblings were scorned by the Fae, just like the Verti. It's not just about me proving worthy of the gods anymore. I have to prove Clarallan is worth saving. That despite the pain the wrong Fae have caused, their once-glorious creation is still redeemable."

"Intense." Carr squeezed her shoulder, then dropped his arm. "Do you think all the gods will be that way?"

She shrugged and Rae jumped in. "Considering the gods haven't been around in centuries, I think it's impossible to predict anything."

"I guess." Seren peered at the ground. "But isn't it sad? What we've done to Clarallan—"

"Not us," Rae interrupted.

Seren looked up and waved her hand. "You know what I mean. Like, what happened in just our ancestors' times that caused the gods to just..." She locked eyes with Rae. "Give up."

"But look what we're doing, what you're doing," Rae countered.

"It's what they say, isn't it?" Dax glanced back, and his green eyes seemed extra bright against his olive skin, which was a few shades darker since the start of their journey. "If you believe in something—you fight for it, even if you're fighting completely alone."

And she wasn't alone. Glancing at the three males, Seren's heart swelled, the feeling a key to unlocking something she had never fully understood before—hope. For twenty years, hope had been something she observed from afar. She knew what it was, sure, even longed for it, but hope was more like bone than muscle, more difficult to break at first and required longer to heal.

"I know what you're going to say." Carr elbowed her playfully. "You're glad we're here."

Seren rolled her eyes, but a smile stole her face. "I am."

"So, then what happened?" Rae asked. "What was phase two?"

"Shaya created a wall of fire on the dais, and remember the questions she asked me at the beginning?" Seren waited for all three guys to agree. "Well, then she asked if my answers had changed."

"To see if your morals had changed?" Carr asked.

"I think so." She swayed her head back and forth. "But that wasn't it. She wanted me to confess my greatest sin. Forced me to look at her eyes—"

Rae cut her off. "You don't have to tell us."

Seren shook her head. "No, it's okay. Get this, when I looked into her eyes...nothing happened."

"Seriously?" Rae halted and the others stopped just after. "You're telling us, you looked into the eyes of the Sun Goddess and didn't confess a sin? How?" Rae's eyes bulged. Earlier, when she admitted she hadn't known about Shaya's power, the Verti males had all shared the same expression: their sharp jaws on the ground. Apparently, the Verti's education was heavy on the Clarallan gods. Pretty useful, as it turned out.

"I don't know. But I didn't question it." Seren resumed walking, her eyes on the dense trees lining the gravel path, their leaves waving in a salty, cool breeze. By now, they had to be close to the Lunaan court, and the plan was to immediately search for the second trial. Her blood itched with anticipation, and she had to keep moving to curb her nerves. "Then I walked through the fire for the Sun to have its turn. Or as Shaya put it, for the Sun to judge my heart—to decide if I was worthy of the magic it and Shaya share. Then I was falling, from and through somewhere I don't know." She exhaled. "And, well, you all were there for the rest."

"What was it like walking through the fire?" Rae asked, catching up to her side as Carr and Dax hung behind them.

"Like warm water, wading through a curtain of flame that licked comfort across my skin instead of burning it. I don't remember anything except falling, but I wasn't afraid. And when I landed in my body, my magic felt different. When I learned I had magic, I still couldn't really feel it. And when I did, it was always in control. But after I passed…" Seren peeked sideways at Rae, shaking her head. "It's almost like it opened a channel between me and my magic. Does that make sense? Like, now I can feel it, almost communicate with it."

"I get it," Rae said.

"Us too," Carr added, and he and Dax picked up their pace.

"The reason the Verti train so much is to learn about our magic," Dax explained in his training voice. "To understand it, respect it. That way instead of raw explosions of blunt force, our Verti warriors fight with skill and intent."

Rae added, "Magic and power are art, things to craft not control, and properly used, to change the world for good. That's what the Cere teaches the Verti."

Seren asked, "So the trials are sort of like my Cere?"

Rae swayed his head. "Pretty much."

Except if Seren failed, she wouldn't be the only one to lose, the entire kingdom of Clarallan would pay.

But luckily, she wasn't fighting alone.

EIGHT MOONS, each a different phase of the lunar cycle, illuminated the velvety black sky.

Seren studied them quietly, their light a clear guide into the Lunaan court. The guys had fallen silent after learning the details of the Sun Trial. She guessed her friends' thoughts were heavy with each step, walking in her shoes, weighing their hearts against Shaya's tests: Did they consider themselves moral? Did they think they could succeed?

Up ahead, the Lunaan court stretched into sight—a coastal city built into miles of terraced cliffs, replacing the northern mountain peaks and pine forests. Seren's magic flared, and an irresistible feeling wrapped around her racing heart. She quickened her steps and the others followed.

Charging ahead, the Verti dimmed their magic, and the group descended upon the Lunaan court. The city comprised hundreds of cliffside houses and shops, all stacked on top of each other, while the Lunaan castle perched at the end of a rocky promontory, its front watching the city, its back overlooking the eastern sea. The ancient castle was built of white-and-silver stone, its array of endless towers and columns cutting through the night.

Following Dax's lead, Seren fell a casual distance behind Rae. Dax knew the court best, had studied Izzac's maps for hours, and already had a plan to get to the second trial: Lunaan's holy Temple of the Full Moon. Izzac had suggested it specifically as the trial's location since it was Lunaan's house of worship for their two deities—the Gods of the Moons, each representing one-half of a full.

As they wove through the bustling coastal city, Seren stuck close to Carr, her senses a blur of color and sound. Lunaan citizens filtered through the narrow streets, enjoying a night out. A chilled breeze kissed her skin with goosebumps, carrying hints of salt and rain and mesmerizing sounds of live music.

She had praised Sollian beneath the Sun, its warmth and

softness. But Lunaan was at its peak beauty, sharp and dramatic, when caressed by the touch of night. The two courts couldn't have been more different—their energies entirely incomparable. Seeing Lunaan for the first time was like stepping into a dream: so much emotion, imagination, so much life. A kind of overwhelming beauty that captivated as much as it disturbed.

Hundreds of Fae and humans alike gathered outside of pubs and restaurants, creating a spirited nightlife, reveling in their laughter and clinks of sloshing glasses. An array of small fires flickered throughout the streets, their light reflecting against the moons', creating an enthralling interplay of flame and shadow.

Silently, Dax guided them along the frays of the festivities. Leaving the city, they passed the castle plateau and descended a steep hill toward the Temple of the Full Moon, at the shore base of a terraced cliffside jutted with gaping caves. Dax was sure no one had noticed them, but as they climbed down the steep descent, Seren was certain they were being followed; someone was watching them from above, maybe peering over the edge. But when she looked up, the dark shadows gave nothing away. She had only a gut feeling. Anxiety coursed through her veins, and she clenched her sweaty palms between grasps for balance every time her boots caught spots of slick gravel.

The closer they got to the temple, the stronger her magic beat in her chest. She called on it, and it expanded, beckoning her forward as hope replaced her fear.

Clearing the precarious descent, Seren and the Verti charged forward, abandoning craft and opting for quickness. Seren's heart sang as she pressed her sprint quicker.

The temple was breathtaking—something seen only in art.

Constructed of towering arches and columns, capped with open ceilings, the night sky on full display between the stone openings. Nearly every inch of stone was engraved with intricate designs, eerily similar to the carvings on the fountain. Magic pulsed in the air, wrapped with an intoxicating scent of saltwater and summer thunderstorms.

Seren took soft steps toward the grand archway cutting through the center. It was different from the rest of the temple, not built of the same white stone. Rather, one side appeared sculpted of ivory and the other carved from horns. Seren looked up, studying the sculpture that decorated the top of the large archway: a carved full moon held in the center of two open hands.

Seren gulped, and the sweet taste of magic laced her throat, dousing the doubt that crept around her gut. Glancing at her friends, she stepped into Lunaan's sacred Temple of the Full Moon.

"Seren," Rae whispered, catching up to her side. She halted, and he asked, "Are you ready?"

She looked at him sideways. They'd walked into Sollian blind; at least this time, she had a vague idea of what to expect. She nodded, thin-lipped determination on her face. "I have to be."

Seren could have said something more reassuring like yes, of course I'm ready. But honestly, it didn't matter how prepared she felt. Either way, she was throwing herself into deep water. All she could do was give it her all. The rest was out of her control.

Rae insisted, "You've got this, Ser." But his words didn't match his twisted expression, and something that looked like regret sharpened the lines of face, drawing attention to the harsh scar across his eye.

She gave her thanks with a half smile, and Carr and Dax added their comforts.

"Maybe the Sun Trial was the hardest," Dax reasoned. "The gods could have made the first one so difficult that everyone just fails right away." She tilted her head back and forth. "Even if that's not true, you're stronger now."

"Yeah, and each time you pass another trial, you'll just keep leveling up," Carr added. Her gaze slid to him, and he flashed his big, toothy comfort smile and squeezed her shoulder. "Go show those Moon Gods who the real goddess is, you beauty."

"Sure thing, Carr." She snorted and heat blushed her cheeks. Turning away, she walked forward, her friends just behind.

The grand archway stretched into a straight path, widening in the center of the temple. They walked into a ceremonious auditorium with a capacity for hundreds, empty save for a long, horizontal pedestal that resembled a smooth closed coffin, flat across the top.

"Woah..." Carr exhaled.

They hurried forward. Seren wasn't sure she was breathing as she approached the pedestal. In Sollian, the fountain had been the trigger. Whatever this was, it had to be what they were looking for. It radiated magic more intensely than anything else in the temple.

Seren looked up when they neared the pedestal. Through an intricate design in the ceiling, a full moon gleamed directly above the sacred sculpture, casting its light through a large, circular gap—a spotlight for her second stage.

She stopped short of touching the stone, and her hands trembled. She wouldn't touch it until she was ready, not after what happened in the garden. From far away it had been impossible to see every detail carved along the sides, across the top, covering the entire surface. Everyone studied the carvings closely, their eyes struggling to look at everything all at once as they whispered their amazement and offered theories about the meanings of the designs.

This time, Seren found the quotes. She pointed. "Guys, over here."

Just like in Sollian, the first inscription matched what Izzac had written in the journal. Since they hadn't been able to talk much in North's cart, everyone had taken turns studying Izzac's guides, and Seren had given extra attention to memorizing the last notes he'd emphasized for each trial. She read the words engraved in the stone, the same words sketched in her mind: *A second win from the Moon will test your mind, conquer dreams and nightmares or forever be lost inside.*

The Verti hurried to join her and leaned close as she read the next quote in silence: *To be asleep in the arms of fate, let dreams lead the way or deceit awaits.*

Seren spoke first. "The first one matches the journal, just like in the garden."

"That's good, isn't it?" Carr asked. She nodded.

"Lunaan magic heavily revolves around dreams and nightmares. The first quote makes sense—your test will involve some challenge between the two." Dax knelt down, his finger skimming the words. "But the second…" His voice teetered off.

Seren turned to Rae. "What do you think it means?"

He ran his hands through his hair. "To let fate lead the way?"

"Truly insightful." Carr chuckled.

"Do you have a better idea?" Rae grumbled.

"Dreams could mean goodness," Dax said under his breath, staring at Seren as he stood. She urged him on, and he spoke boldly. "You know, like, let light lead the way or fall victim to darkness. Since Shaya was so hung up on sin, the fight between good and evil doesn't seem like too big a jump."

"But is it ever just a fight between good and evil?" Seren asked, convinced nothing was that black and white. "Even Shaya, the Goddess of the Sun and Life herself, wasn't all good…" Her words hung in silence and Dax's eyes dipped. "I think you're right about the dreams and nightmares, light and dark, I just think it's a little more complicated."

The Verti nodded.

"So, now what?" Carr asked. "Do you have to be asleep?"

Seren followed Carr's train of thought: *To be asleep in the arms of fate.* She shook her head and said, "Maybe I have to lie down? In Sollian, all I did was touch the fountain and say the quotes out loud."

"Yeah, and your body was launched halfway across the garden." Rae gave her a pointed look.

Seren giggled, remembering Carr's reenactment of the garden's series of events from the Verti's perspective. The large male had hurled his body away from the fountain, emphasizing the drama with a little help from his Verti strength as he flung himself impossibly far.

"Lying down is probably smart," she said coyly, looking up at Rae. She took another glance at the quotes, memorizing the second, and placed her jittery hands on the pedestal. Her magic flared through her fingertips, sparking with light. Rae knit his fingers together and gave her a step up as she climbed onto the tall box.

Three intense sets of eyes watched her as she got comfortable. Sitting up, she met her friends' glances, forcing bravery into her eyes. "I wish you guys could be there with me."

"Us too," Carr said, taking a step away from the pedestal as Rae and Dax did the same.

"Remember, you're the one doing this, not any of us." Rae gestured at his friends. "You're already worthy, Ser, you just have to let the gods see."

Her smile was involuntary, and courage steadied her racing heart. Prue's words echoed Rae's in her head as she lay down: *A star's light to end the fight; through trial and test, the kingdom is blessed.*

Everything she needed was already inside of her. If her magic could shine through every heartache she had experienced, then maybe her light could be worthy of the gods.

Lacing her fingers, she crossed her arms over her chest. Before gazing at the full moon, she glanced at the darkness at her sides. Movement in the shadows drew her attention, and the beat of her magic thrummed wildly in her chest.

"What is it?" Rae asked.

She shook her head. "Nothing," she said, staring at the moon. Whatever she thought she saw was gone and only a shiver of a chill kissed her spine, the one sign she had seen anything at all.

Carr spoke one last time, his voice low. "Sweet dreams, Ser."

Seren repeated the words from memory. "A second win from the Moon will test your mind, conquer dreams and nightmares or be forever lost inside. To be asleep in the arms of fate, let dreams lead the way or deceit awaits."

Her magic sparked.

CHAPTER 27

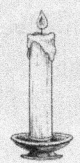

Seren stared at the sky. Or at least, what should have been the sky.

She eased her tingling limbs into a sitting position, still on the stone pedestal from the Lunaan court, but no longer in the temple.

Flashes of color burst through the night air, changing quicker than her eyes could follow: blue, green, red, purple, and so on. The chaotic land transformed hastily. Snow-covered mountains dominated the horizons, lurching into buzzing green jungles, morphing into waves that crashed against a sandy shore.

Studying the dream realm, Seren felt as if she'd been smacked upside the head and everything before her was a nasty consequence of severely rattling her brain. She closed her eyes, rubbed her forehead for a moment with one hand, and called on her magic as her other hand slid through her hair.

Her powers felt stronger in the dream realm, the same as when she had first seen Shaya. A primal feeling that reconnected with something much larger than herself. Taking long, centered breaths, she waited until she felt in control, and opened her eyes.

The scent of rain washed over her, and a prickling sensation crawled through her limbs. She waited for the dream realm to change again, for the madness to return, but the world remained still. She braced her hands against the cool stone and jumped from the tall pedestal, her knees wobbling as she landed on the firm ground.

Fixed in a scene of dark night, eight moons hung suspended in the bold sky encrusted with silver-and-gold stars, their bright light a harsh contrast to the blanket of swirling blues and blacks.

Familiarity steeped within her, brewing over as she recognized her dream realm. Swiveling, Seren stared across the vast expanse of magic, and her gaze landed on something in the distance. Something large, cosmic. Her heart sputtered.

She charged forward, nearly floating as she sprinted through the darkness. Her power sang in her chest, flushed with desire, urging her faster. Her hair flew around her face and magic kissed her cheeks, like saltwater in a cool breeze.

Magic cracked behind her, and a voice raced toward her.

"Seren—"

She froze involuntarily as her magic responded to such raw power. The voice spoke again, now directly behind her.

"Did you miss me?"

That voice—she jumped, and her mouth gaped.

The Prince of the Moon strode forward, halting inches away from her.

"What the—" Her voice was weak, breathless. "Casimir?"

Of all the ludicrous scenarios Seren had imagined preparing for the Moon Trial, one thing she had not expected was the Lunaan prince's participation, even in dream form.

He tilted his head, his brows pulled together. "What's going on?"

Now that she'd seen the Lunaan court for the first time, Seren realized the prince was the physical embodiment of his people's magic. His sharp features and fair skin. Dark hair and eyes the color of the Lunaan emblem. He radiated what it felt like to be in the moon court—enticing and untamed, a lethal combination. His silver-blue eyes scanned the dream realm, returning to hers with a glacial expression. "We shouldn't be here."

Shaking off her disbelief, Seren asked, "Why do you keep showing up in my dreams?" She waved her hands. "And do you even know where here is?"

Casimir crossed his arms, his voice low. "Your dream realm, but something's different." He reached for her, but Seren stepped away. "We should go."

"I have to be here." She started walking. "But you can leave whenever." She wasn't even sure how she'd dreamed him up in the first place, but if he wasn't going to help, he could take his distractions and go.

He huffed, trailing after her.

She didn't look back. "Why are—how are you even here? This isn't a normal dream." This was serious, unlike the other times the prince randomly ambushed her sleep. Heat flushed her cheeks remembering how the last dream had ended. How real it had felt when their skin touched. How, after, he'd asked in a voice that made her weak in the knees if it still felt like a dream to her. Looking forward, she said, "I had no idea I could even imagine you in a place like this."

Casimir ignored her first set of questions. "What do you mean a place like this?"

Seren stared at her destination, slowly coming into focus the farther they walked. An ancient door stood alone in the distance, attached to nothing. "I mean…" Could she tell him everything? He was just a dream after all. "I'm here to complete the Lost Trials." She glanced at him for a heartbeat, and asked, "Heard of them?"

"You can't be serious."

So, yes. "More than ever," she said.

"Why? How did someone like you get wrapped up in

something like that?" Casimir's tone set her on edge, his voice as dark as the night sky. He shook his head, his black hair curtaining his face. "Do you realize how insane that sounds?"

Seren stiffened. Clenching her fists, she marched ahead, panic and anger pulsing in her veins. But honestly, she would have the same reaction in his position—if anything, hers was worse the first time she learned what she was expected to do.

Her magic warmed her core, a beacon of comfort in her tense chest. Seren considered the prince's words. "I know how it sounds, but I'm telling the truth. And to be honest, I'm still working on the why me part too. Something to do with my magic, I guess."

"The trials are dangerous, Seren." Casimir's eyes drifted to the moons, then to her. "And I'm not just saying that. I mean, really dangerous. Do you know how many Fae have died trying?"

"One hundred and nine," she said without skipping a beat.

He frowned, confusion lifting his brow. "And you're still delusional enough to be here?" Seren half smiled, and he asked, "Why?"

"Like I said"—she peered at the towering door ahead—"I have to."

SEREN WONDERED how many times she was going to repeat herself before Casimir finally believed her—she was already near her limit. One more scoff from the prince, and her anger would boil past its threshold.

"You *seriously* met Shaya?" Casimir asked again.

Seren nodded, her lips thin.

"You actually did it… You completed the first trial—"

"I did." Seren halted, glancing at the door. Pulling on her leathers, she tugged the stiff material away from her chest. "Look." Casimir leaned close, and the hair on the back of her neck stood. Seren gulped, silently cursing herself for being so on edge.

"I've seen that before," he said.

"Where?" Seren let go, taking a step back.

"I had a royal education," he said flatly. "Evander and I had the best tutors in Clarallan. I doubt there's much my father didn't insist on us learning."

She tilted her chin, blinking slowly. Of all the dreams she'd had of the prince, this was the first time he'd revealed anything even remotely personal. "It sounds like you know a lot about the gods."

Casimir nodded. "Raising us, my parents honored the gods heavily, tried to get my brother and I to be the same. But I haven't thought about them since my mother…" He looked away and started walking.

For a moment, Seren lagged behind. Her magic flared and her chest tightened. It felt as if her power had been caught, tied, and involuntarily hauled forward. She followed the prince with the distinct feeling this dream, for reasons beyond the trial, was unlike any before—as if a foggy night had been cleared in her mind by moonlight, revealing the stars. Her heart raced as she caught up to the prince. "Casimir—"

He gazed sideways, his bold features sharpened by the emotion in his eyes.

Her voice wavered. "You—you're really here, aren't you?"

Casimir tilted his head back with snort. "I'd nearly given up."

"On what?"

"Thinking you were ever going to believe me. It's not like I haven't tried to tell you all along."

Seren considered the dreams they'd shared. Her cheeks flushed and she looked away—all the things she had done, the things she had said when she'd believed he was just a fragment of her imagination. She swallowed her embarrassment. "Can you blame me? I just found out I had magic. I didn't even know it was possible for you to be real."

He chuckled, a strangely soft sound. "It's called dream-walking. Most Fae can do it, but those from Lunaan have a few advantages, especially the royals."

"Like what?"

"Dream and nightmare manipulation are the big ones, but that's in a normal dream realm." He scanned the sky slowly. "Like I was saying earlier, something's different here."

"Because of the trial?"

"That's the obvious reason, but still...there's something else."

Something bothered her too, but she knew it wasn't what Casimir was worried about. She sharpened her tone. "You know what I still don't get? If it wasn't all just a dream, why would a prince continuously harass me? We don't even know each other."

Now that she knew about dream-walking, that sounded a lot more like a lie than she intended. Over the past few weeks, Casimir hadn't shared much, but Seren... she had told him everything. To be fair, she'd believed she had been talking to herself—a way for her subconscious to work out the mess her life had become.

Miffed, Casimir crossed his arms. "You really believe I was bothered enough to seek out your dreams?"

Seren nearly flinched at his tone. "It was me?" A nod. "How?" The dawn of her realization weighed on her chest.

He taunted, "Magic."

Irritation spoiled on her tongue, and she snapped, "Why are you even here?"

"Shouldn't you be asking yourself that? Your magic called, and I simply answered."

Every time it felt like Seren was grasping the threads of her understanding, a gust of wind swept in, scattering what she knew with thousands of new facts, questions, and doubts. She guessed her magic was more powerful than she had imagined, even before she completed the first trial.

She thought to apologize but quickened her pace instead; the colossal door loomed yards ahead. She asked briskly, "Do you know anything else about the Moon Trial?"

"There isn't much to know. Since Ares was the only one to survive the trials, his record is pretty much all we have. From what I remember, the trials are based on the courts' unique magic, gifted by the gods of Clarallan. For Lunaan, that suggests the Gods of the Moons test your mind. To earn their respect, you must conquer your fears—basically from what I was told, you must live through your worst nightmare."

Seren had been doing that her entire life beneath Hellevi's reign. She had only started to have real dreams after she escaped the Stellean court. Simultaneously wanting and terrified of his answer, she asked, "What happens if I fail?"

He shook his head. "I don't know."

She couldn't tell if she believed him. "It's probably not the best to think about right now anyway," she said, coming face-to-face with the most incredible architecture she had ever seen, unlike anything before.

A beautiful stone archway bordered a set of double doors, one side made from what looked like ivory, the other from what appeared to be horn, and hanging in the center of both doors was a sculpted face. Each face was a crescent moon made of ivory and horn, both looking toward one another similar to the archway leading into the Temple of the Full Moon.

The doors radiated an intoxicating power, and Seren's magic thrummed wildly in her chest, begging to get closer.

Casimir walked a quick circle, scouting the illogical architecture. Back at her side, he said, "I recognize this, or at least sort of. Lunaan's temples are similar. They all use ivory and horn to honor the Gods of the Moons."

She glanced at him and back to the door. "What does it mean—the ivory and horn?"

"The future versus falsehoods, or simply, dreams and nightmares."

"Which is which?" she asked.

"Horn for fulfillment, or dreams, and ivory for deception, nightmares."

Casimir's words triggered her memory—the inscriptions in the temple. She repeated the words with ease under her breath. "A second win from the Moon will test your mind, conquer dreams and nightmares or be forever lost inside. To be asleep in the arms of fate, let dreams lead the way or deceit awaits."

Casimir stiffened. "Where did you hear that?"

"I saw it in the temple; it's about the trial, I think." She met the prince's cold eyes. "What do you know?"

"That second line, those are the gods' words." Casimir's throat bobbed. "The Gods of the Moons to be exact, Kaelu and Larir."

As if on cue, the faces came to life, blinking slowly as emotion flooded the eyes of the inanimate sculptures. Seren startled and jumped back, accidentally bumping into the prince. She tripped and he gripped her arm, saving her just in time.

Letting her go, he asked, "You alright?"

She met his eyes, shaking off the unnerving heat that danced across her skin in the form of the phantom touch he left behind.

The faces spoke, and it took everything Seren had to not jump away again. If things had been weird before, they were off the charts now. The faces stretched and wrinkled with every word, every breath, life hiding just beneath their impossibly hard exteriors.

The face to her left asked, "Can you believe it, brother? Dreams really do come true."

"Oh, Kaelu, you know what comes next is nothing like a

dream." The ivory face loosed a low chuckle. "A nightmare suits it much proper."

Seren gulped. "The Gods of the Moons?"

"It can't be." Casimir took a step closer to her. "The gods haven't been seen in centuries."

"If this is anything like the first trial"—Seren shuddered—"I don't think the same rules apply."

"She's right," Kaelu said, and Seren's gaze met his eerily mortal eyes. "Something to know about the gods, nothing is ever the same when we're around... Isn't that right, Larir?"

Larir chuckled. His ivory face lit up, and mischief tinted his dark eyes. "Especially with us, you know."

"Especially with us," Kaelu mimicked.

Seren leaned close to the prince and lifted her chin. "What are they going on about?"

"They're the gods of dreams and nightmares, pleasure and madness, chaos and manipulation." Casimir lowered his voice. "They're tricksters. You can't believe just anything."

"Oh." Seren's heart thundered. At least with Shaya, the goddess had been demanding of the truth, of justice. But with these two, anything was possible.

"Come closer," Kaelu commanded, his voice unusually comforting, the likes of being wrapped in a warm embrace. She stepped forward, Casimir at her back, and Kaelu continued, "We weren't expecting you to bring a guest, Seren."

She flinched and Larir cut in, "Let alone one so special."

She could feel the prince's reaction on her skin, his rage vibrating between them.

"Sereennn..." Kaelu stretched her name, his brows sculpted in curiosity. "What *are* you doing with our dear Child of the Moon?"

She looked at Cas; a flicker of hatred flashed across his face. "We're here to complete the Trial of the Moons." She swallowed. "Or at least I am."

"That's not what I asked," Larir protested, staring at the prince with eyes so dark Seren feared what she would see if she looked at them too closely. He asked the prince, "Why are you here?"

Casimir rolled his shoulders, lifted his chin. "I'm here because I can be." He spoke in a tone that reminded Seren who he really was—not a dream or her imagination, maybe not even a friend. But a prince, and an intimidating one at that. Someone who most of the kingdom believed could be one of the most powerful kings Clarallan's courts had ever seen.

Larir scoffed but didn't argue, turning his attention back to her. "You think you have what it takes, then? To face your fears? To survive your worst nightmare?"

"I do."

Larir released an unearthly laugh.

Kaelu asked, "What do you think, brother? Shall we let her try?"

"It has been awfully long since we've had any entertainment. It might be worth the mess..." Larir drawled, a confession that he would find great pleasure in her torment.

"I already passed the first trial," Seren cut in, willing her magic to give her strength. "I can do it."

Larir sneered, revealing his serrated ivory teeth. "But can you survive *our* test?"

Fear slickened Seren's palms, and she regretted not asking anyone if the trials got more difficult as she progressed—too late now.

"You wish to be worthy of our magic..." Kaelu said, and Seren wasn't sure if he expected an answer. He continued, his face light despite the gravity of his words, "Very well. But first, you must understand the stakes." He paused. "If you fail to prove yourself worthy, you'll be lost to us forever—destined to live through your worst nightmare, over and over—with nothing anyone can do to save you."

Seren asked, "So I won't die?"

"No." Larir scoffed. "You will only wish that you had."

She swallowed and fear burned her throat.

"Do you wish to continue?" Kaelu asked, and for a second, Seren thought guilt dampened his deep blue eyes.

Casimir spoke softly, "You don't have to do this, Seren."

She mustered her courage. "Yes." She stepped forward. "I do."

"Then just walk through the door." Kaelu spoke as if it were really that easy.

She nodded to Cas, then the gods. "I'm ready."

"Me too." The prince stepped closer and Seren's power surged.

"You don't have to come." Seren looked down. "And it's probably best if you don't."

Casimir bit back a laugh, wrapped his hand around hers. A tingling sensation spread from the place where their skin touched, and she wondered if he could feel it too, but as usual, his harsh face gave nothing away. "Show them who you are, Seren."

The doors swung inward, stirring together the creaks of desuetude and the gods' dark laughter. She walked into the darkness, and the doors slammed shut behind them, punctuating Kaelu's last words.

"Remember, child, nightmares are dreams too."

THE SIGHT WAS WORSE than anything Seren could have imagined.

Her eyes adjusted slowly as her nightmare came into light. An overpowering stench flooded her senses: blood, sweat, and fear, a rotting smell that told the haunting story of death and decay.

Of torture.

And punishment.

Seren forced herself to look around, to breathe. On the far wall hung two thick chains she recognized immediately. To their left sat King Hellevi's favorite chair, its cracked leather seat indented from the hundreds of times Hellevi had sat and watched, whiskey in hand, as Seren fought to hold onto what felt like her last breath.

Releasing Casimir's hand, she stepped forward. Her boots squelched in thick pools of red, while copious amounts of sprayed blood made long, distorted patterns across the stone walls. A sickly feeling stabbed in her gut, begged her to turn around, to run while she maybe still had the chance.

She couldn't be here. Not again.

Even if it was just a nightmare, if she failed—a phantom pain flashed the length of her spine—she'd be trapped forever.

Larir had suggested the weight of her failure would be enough to make her wish for death. Little did he know this nightmare already had. In the Stellean castle, every time Hellevi demanded blood for her *sins*. If what she'd done could even be called that, they were merely excuses and miserable ones, at that.

Casimir lifted his hand, covering his nose and mouth as he inhaled. "Where are we?" he asked, his voice nearly inaudible above Seren's hammering heart.

My worst nightmare, she wanted to say, but that was redundant. "In Stellean."

"Where?"

She lifted her eyes. "The castle."

Casimir pried, irritated. "And this room is?"

Seren hesitated. The truth tasted an awful lot like shame. Admitting what Hellevi had done to her felt like telling the prince she was worthless—that she didn't deserve to even attempt the trial because who was she to believe she could save Clarallan, when she hadn't even been able to save herself?

"Seren?" Casimir took a step.

She shook her head. At least he was with her. "It's one of

Hellevi's private rooms, his favorite to be specific." Her voice wavered more than she had intended. "For his pleasure...and everyone else's torture."

Seren turned, staring at the chains. How many times had she hung there, bleeding, while the king exacted his worst? A hundred? Two? Maybe more... The first time had been one too many, and she had lost track of the countless others over the years.

She lowered her gaze and shuddered. Within easy reach were the king's favorite leathers: a pair of handcrafted whips, placed on top of a small silver cart.

Every time she had managed to walk away from his carnage, she wanted to believe it a miracle. But to do that she would have had to believe in a higher anything—a reason for her suffering. And when the gods left Clarallan centuries ago, they left behind countless citizens to suffer at the hands of monsters like the Stellean king.

Escaping Hellevi's unyielding darkness had been the only way to see the light—like a rose, she couldn't grow in the soil that had poisoned her. Her magic buzzed, and its strength banished the fear from her heart and warmed her core.

She could do this.

Movement twisted in the darkness at their side, stirring the thick shadows as heavy footsteps smacked against the blood-soaked floor, a sickening sound that sent Seren's stomach lurching for what felt like the tenth time in minutes.

She couldn't move, couldn't even close her eyes as the nightmare took control. Screaming erupted from everywhere, and her chest constricted. Those screams—they were hers...but she wasn't the one screaming. Not exactly.

Anything goes, she reminded herself, but that stole more than it offered to her courage. Darkness spread across the room, crawled up her legs. She clenched sweaty palms and spun, begged her gaze to pierce the thick murk that rolled over them.

A crack of magic and the nightmare shifted again.

Where the chains had been empty a second ago now hung Hellevi's next victim: a muscular female with long black hair, her bare back exposed, laden with scars—just how the king preferred it.

Preferred her.

Seren's trauma lived outside her body then, its powerful hands wrapped around her throat, squeezing. She couldn't breathe, couldn't think. Magic electrified the air, and the room felt impossibly small, as if she were buried underground and her oxygen was running out with each second.

King Hellevi strode from the shadows—a monster designed by darkness. He sneered, his yellow eyes locked on his prey. Taking his time, he wrapped his hands around the whips, balanced his stance, and brought his right arm behind his head.

Seren watched her nightmare play out like it always did.

Her every instinct screamed to run.

A *crack* split the air.

Split skin.

Seren fell to her knees. She hadn't been hit, but her body seized, and Casimir dropped beside her. Pain exploded across her back—the permanent memory of ripped skin, a feeling she could never forget. Tears welled in her eyes, and she forced herself to watch as Hellevi reeled back his arm—*crack*.

Her ears rang, and this time, Seren screamed alongside her dream-self. The sound was overwhelming, and it felt like her eardrums would burst any second.

The king turned and stared at Seren and Casimir, his eyes burning a deep gold. "Like what you see?"

Casimir stood, staring at the king.

Hellevi's sharp face contorted with pleasure as he slashed his whip again.

Seren closed her eyes. The torment was unbearable.

She had to do something, but—

Casimir was yelling, his hands on her shoulders, shaking her. She couldn't hear what he said over the sound of her own screams. The madness dug into her mind, consuming her control. It was too much. She couldn't do anything.

Hellevi's manic laughter broke through her agony.

"GET CONTROL," Casimir shouted, and it was the first time Seren had ever heard the prince sound afraid.

She opened her eyes and pressed herself up from her knees, the sickly, warm feeling of blood on her hands, saturating her leathers. The room changed again, and this time what she saw was worse than anything she had ever experienced.

Her worst nightmare, something yet to happen, but what she begged the stars against every night.

The ground was littered with bodies, covered in blood, their unnaturally bent limbs twisted in ways only death was capable of.

When Seren looked at the nearest face, she didn't know it was possible for her heart to hurt that much.

Mare.

Dead.

Seren stopped breathing, and her heart pummeled against her chest.

Her friend's body had been mangled, her face disfigured, but Seren knew it was her. Her once brilliant blue eyes left unseeing by a glossy gray film. Ripping her gaze away, Seren looked to the next body, unable to stop the tears that flooded her cheeks.

Rae.

Dax. Carr. Tait. Rosella. Thrina.

The bodies kept coming, and she cried and her lungs burned.

Every person she had ever loved—gone. Discarded like garbage at Hellevi's feet.

It was her fault. Or it would be.

She had never voiced her fear, afraid her confession would somehow breathe it to life. But somehow, the gods had known.

She jerked her gaze to the king, his pale skin spotted with red.

"This is what will happen, you know." He flicked blood from his short gray hair. "That is, of course, if it hasn't happened already."

Seren cried out, "NO."

Casimir was yelling too, everyone was. "It's *your* nightmare, Seren. Stop it. You're the only one who can."

She looked at the prince, the king, her friends.

She saw red.

Felt red.

She slammed at the fear that ravaged her mind. It felt stronger than her, but that didn't mean it was.

All those years the king had tortured her, haunted her, nearly killed her. Now her memories held her under and guilt drowned her lungs.

Casimir pleaded, right behind her. "Come on, Seren." He placed a hand on her shoulder, grounding her.

She focused on his words, his nearness, felt her magic strengthen with his touch.

The king would never get to hurt her or anyone else again. He would never control her.

No one would.

That's why she was doing this—risking her life to stop the king.

So that she would never feel that powerless again.

Seren felt the walls of her fear shatter as her magic exploded against their defense, pumping her veins with cold, sharp strength.

Her breathing steadied, as did her stance, and Casimir was there to catch her if she fell again.

But she never would.

A crack of pure, raw power burned through her limbs, so hot it nearly felt cold.

No.

No more.

She charged Hellevi and darkness greeted her.

S‌EREN STOOD where the king had been, vengeance pumping in her veins as she raised her arm above her head. The whip felt light, ready to be used.

Hellevi's body hung from the chains, his suit ripped across his back.

Casimir lunged, but Seren held him back with her magic. It was her nightmare. She was in control.

"Seren, no," Casimir yelled, the muscles in his neck straining as he lurched against her power. "Don't do this."

The drumming in her head drowned out the prince's words. She never took her eyes off the king.

Casimir begged, "This isn't the way. You have to get control."

What was he yelling about control for? This was more control than Seren had ever had her entire life. She felt stronger, powerful, malefic…

Unrecognizable.

The nightmare rallied Seren's magic, pulled on her hands to strike, her mind completely at the will of such chaos. She heard her own voice, a vengeful sound—how it demanded she do to the king what he'd so enjoyed doing to her.

Something begged her to give in—she the tinder, her trauma the match. One wrong decision and she would go up in flames. The whole room would and everything inside.

The king would pay.

Hellevi twisted his neck and his eyes bulged. But there was no fear, as if he believed she was too weak to do anything. "Do it," he spat. "I know you want to."

She tightened her grip, the leather handle warm in her palm.

She did. She wanted nothing more than for Hellevi to experience a taste of his own tribulations.

"Seren—" Casimir's voice trembled.

For the first time since she'd held it, the whip faltered in her hands.

The king laughed. "You can't do it. A coward like your mother."

Her anger boiled, bubbled near its threshold. "You don't get to talk about her." Seren gritted her teeth hard enough her jaw ached. "Not after what you did."

"You mean since I killed her?" Hellevi sneered. "No need to talk like it's a secret, I'm not ashamed." He paused, his eyes pits of yellow that reminded her of sickness. "It was her fault anyway."

Seren's eyes narrowed. Just because it wasn't a lie didn't mean she believed the king. If that was truly how he felt, he could say anything with ease. Despite that, Seren asked, "What are you talking about?"

"Wouldn't you like to know—"

"Tell me," Seren demanded, her tone calm, unnerving.

Hellevi's weight strained against the chains. "Your mother was a thief, thought she could steal from me and get away with it. She deserved to die." He bared a cruel sneer, exposing his sickly, pale gums.

She raised the whip again, its weight suddenly heavy. Something cracked in her chest—this wasn't her. Her voice softened. "No one deserves what you've done to them."

Even when Seren thought she had mastered her nightmare, she wasn't the one in control. Hellevi still had power over her.

"Seren, please." Casimir thrashed against her magic and she released him. He rushed forward, and the scent of rain washed over her, cooling the embers in her chest.

The whip hit the floor with a wet *smack* and blood splashed against her boots.

She closed her eyes, slammed a mental wall between her and the monster that Hellevi lured from her darkest parts. Casimir was there, his hands on hers, her fire easing with his touch.

When she opened her eyes, everything was gone.

Just an empty room and a door made of ivory and horn.

"Cas?" Her voice was raw. She spun.

Nothing.

Seren stared. And stared. Too drained to move, to cry.

Maybe she failed. Or she was dead. The gods had assured her that wouldn't happen, but she didn't have any other way to describe how she felt.

Empty.

The doors heaved and moonlight cleared the darkness. *Too bad it can't do the same to the void inside me.*

She squinted against the blinding light, blinking quickly. It called to her, not with words, but with magic, a cool tendril of power that wrapped around her shattered soul and tried to stitch the pieces back together.

It was soothing.

She stepped forward, hesitant. She had no idea what waited on the other side, but there was no better option. She quickened her steps, pressed her eyes shut.

Then walked through the door.

CHAPTER 28

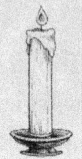

Back in the Lunaan temple, Seren stood surrounded by friends, unable to match their excitement, her eyes locked on the cold stone pedestal.

Her heart hung up by the guilt of her worst nightmare.

"You did it," Rae exclaimed.

"Way to go, Ser." Carr clapped a gentle hand on her shoulder and offered his other for balance. "We all knew you could."

She hadn't failed, but it didn't feel like a win either. She raised her chin, mustering a thin-lipped smile that stretched to just one side.

Rae lowered his voice. "What's wrong?"

She didn't look at him, couldn't. How was she supposed to confess what she'd done? Granted, she hadn't gone through with it, but she almost did. And somehow, that made her feel equally as miserable.

"It's okay, Ser. You can tell us when you're ready." Dax, too aware for his own good. "The important thing is you're alive."

The Verti nodded in unison, and their kindness, their unconditional support, made her feel even worse. She felt their stares, how they looked at her as if she were a miracle, when they should have been disgusted.

She certainly was.

And she wasn't sure that disgust would ever go away—that she would ever be ready to admit such darkness rotted deep inside her. Seren had told the Verti even the smallest details of the first trial, but after this nightmare, there was nothing she wanted to share.

She didn't want to burden them with her worst fear. Or see the hurt on their faces when she described how Hellevi had made her imagine their deaths. Or their shame after she confessed what she had wanted to do in return. And Casimir—was she expected to tell the Verti about him too? Or the dreams they had shared?

It was too much.

Everything was.

And what about after her nightmare—when she had seen that bright light, had walked through the ancient door, and knelt at the mercy of the Moons?

They had found her worthy, and she had a new tattoo to prove it: a dark full moon between two crescent phases, just below her swirling sun. So maybe it *had* been a miracle, because if it had been up to her, she would have let herself burn.

Shouting came from outside the temple, and the clanking of metal on metal echoed through the hollow walls. The sounds were nearly a distracting relief, until her heart raced as she realized they were in danger of being caught.

Dax spoke under his breath. "We need to leave." His head jerked, his Verti eyesight piercing the midnight. "Right now."

Rae grabbed Seren's hand, squeezing as he tugged her arm.

They ran, their steps too loud. It would draw too much attention.

Seren whispered, "They're going to catch us."

Rae hushed her with his hand. "Not if you're quiet."

Too tired to even roll her eyes, Seren halted. "We need a distraction, something to draw them in the opposite direction."

All three Verti stopped, annoyed.

"I'll go," Carr said from behind her, clenching his fists. "I'll lead them away so you guys can escape, then I'll meet back up with you."

"No, it's too risky," Seren argued.

Rae squeezed her hand. "It's our best chance."

"Our only chance..." Carr countered.

No, no, no. There had to be a better idea. She asked, "What if they catch you?"

"Then you'll come save me." Carr smiled over his shoulder, and it wasn't nearly as comforting as he had likely intended.

He turned back in the direction from which they'd just run, and Seren begged, "Please, let me go instead."

Rae pulled her closer. "That's not happening. We need you, Clarallan needs you, and you're exhausted." His golden eyes seemed dim, but maybe she was just that tired. Rae added, "Trust me, Carr has a plan. He always does."

A plan that could get him killed. Or worse.

"Seren"—Carr grabbed her hand and pressed a quick kiss to her skin—"if for some reason this goes south, I want you to be the one to save me." He didn't give her any chance to respond.

Seren watched with fear in her heart as the brave, or reckless, male disappeared into the shadows, seeing just a shimmer of magic before the darkness consumed him.

"Come on." Rae tugged her arm again, his words barely audible above the deafening growls not that far behind, loud enough to shake the temple walls.

Seren ran, and for once, it was one of the hardest things she had ever made herself do. She was exhausted, yes, but it was the hope that Carr would emerge at any second that held her back. She flickered her eyes between their path and the emptiness they left behind, but there was no sign of him.

THE WEIGHT OF WISHES

He still hadn't found them by the time they fled the holy temple into the darkness. They raced up the cliffside, exposed, not stopping until Dax found a small cave and directed everyone to hide.

Seren dared to speak, "He should be here by now." She looked at Dax, at Rae. "We have to go back."

Rae blocked the entrance. "He'll be here."

"When?" Seren wanted to yell. She couldn't believe she had let them convince her to leave Carr alone. "What happens if he uses magic? What happens if he gets caught?" She flicked her eyes between her friends. "Rae, you told me the stories…" Her fear flashed images of Carr captured by the Fae—what it would mean for the entire Verti village if he was discovered. "We have to go back for him."

"That would only put the Verti more at risk." Dax's eyes softened with shame. "We can't go back."

Rae ran a hand through his hair. "It'll be okay. Carr's smart. He knows what to do."

Dax cut in, "He'll be fine, Seren. He always is."

"Yeah, I always am." Carr's deep voice wrapped around her, freezing her in place as the smiling male descended through the mouth of the cave, as casual as if he had simply gone for a bite to eat.

Relief replaced her anger and Seren rushed her friend.

Carr hauled her into the tightest hug of her life. She squeezed her arms around him, his stature too wide to reach all the way. He tilted his head back, glanced at his friends, and looked down at her, a toothy grin on his face. "You know, it hurts that you didn't think I could handle myself, Ser, but I'll take your worry as a compliment that my life means so much to you."

Seren pressed her cheek against his chest, landing a playful punch to his arm when she finally pulled away. "You scared me, you ass."

"Ouch," Carr teased, rubbing circles where she had hit him.

"You deserved that."

"That's what I get for saving our lives?" Carr scrunched his nose. Seren couldn't deny him that. They certainly would've been caught if he hadn't risked himself, even if he was Verti. "I thought for sure I would have earned at least a kiss for my efforts." He winked, always his goofy self, even in the face of death.

"Thank you," Seren said. "But no kissing. I'm still mad at you."

Carr fleered. "I guess anger is better than you not caring at all."

Rae interrupted their bickering. "You okay, man?"

He smirked. "Not even a scratch on me."

That was a lie. Although nothing looked too serious, Carr's skin was littered with bloody cuts and purple bruises. But luckily, everything appeared to already be healing. Seren watched in shock as his skin stretched intricately over itself, lacing his wounds together as if they had never even been there.

"Is this the point where you tell us we ought to see the other guy?" Seren asked.

Carr chuckled. "I'm fine, really, but there is some—"

Seren didn't catch what Carr said next. Rae talked over him, emphasizing that they could talk about everything on the road. But she couldn't focus. Her magic buzzed, and then Carr's voice brought her back to the present.

"There is one more thing." Carr let his words hang in the tense air. His eyes pounced from Seren to Rae to Dax, then back to her before pointing to the mouth of the cave. "Everyone, meet the other guy."

A strong silhouette cut through the darkness as a tall male descended into the cave, moonlight at his back.

Seren's heart stalled.

"Who the hell is this?" Rae demanded, his every muscle on the defense.

"Casimir…" The name fell from Seren's lips before Carr had the chance to introduce the Lunaan prince.

"You know him?" Rae's mouth gaped.

Ignoring his question, Seren took a step, only to be met with Rae's hand on her shoulder. She shook off his grasp, the hum of her magic irrationally loud, like a heartbeat in her ears.

"Seren—" Casimir stared at her, and the sound of her name on the prince's lips transformed her magic's hum to a song.

He looked exactly as he appeared in her dreams, every inch of him intricately sculpted into lethal beauty. There wasn't a scratch on him: no bruises, no cuts, no blood. If he'd been the one Carr fought, he walked away undefeated.

"Why are you here?" she asked.

"You two know each other?" Rae stepped closer.

Seren glanced over her shoulder. "Sort of."

"Yes," Casimir cut in, straight to the point. "We do."

"How?" Rae asked.

Seren studied the prince, couldn't believe he was really there. "It's kind of a long story."

"One we can talk about on the road," Casimir said a little too nonchalantly. "We need to get going."

"We?" Rae nearly spit.

"Wait." Seren gaped at the prince. "You're coming with?"

"No, he's not," Rae answered for him.

Seren glared, she didn't understand why Rae was acting this way—this tough-guy-alpha attitude was already getting old, and it had just begun. Sure Casimir was Fae and the guys were Verti, but didn't they need all the help they could get? She looked to the prince and waited for the only answer that mattered.

"I want to help," Casimir said, and Seren couldn't hold back her smile.

"Thanks, but no thanks." Rae stiffened, looking at a point beyond the cave.

Irritated, Seren pushed the conversation forward with Casimir. "Help with what?"

He stared only at her. "The rest of the trials."

Seren's mouth went dry. Sure, now she knew about dreamwalking and had finally put all the pieces together, but after the second trial, a small part of her believed she had made it all up. But seeing the prince now, knowing for certain that everything had been real...

She fumbled over weighted words. "You were really there," she said, but it sounded more like a question.

One nod from the prince, and it felt like the weight of everything Seren didn't know came crashing down on her chest.

"We can talk about it later." Casimir glanced toward the jagged opening, and moonlight danced over his fair skin. Then, turning back to her, his eyes darkened with what looked like regret.

Shocked and exhausted, Seren nodded; she would hold him to that. And later meant he still wanted to come despite the Verti's less than warm welcome.

"You told him?" Carr nearly choked.

Seren shrugged coyly.

"Seriously?" Dax asked, rubbing a hand over his head.

Seren waited for Rae's reaction, but he said nothing, which honestly was worse than anything he could have said. Waiting for the awkward standoff to end, Seren had enough. "Did everyone forget their manners? What happened to introductions?" She glanced at Casimir and gestured to her friends. "Everyone, this is Casimir, Prince of the Lunaan Court. And Casimir, these are my friends."

Seren pointed at Carr, who grinned at her attitude. "As you know," she spoke to the prince, "the one whose ass you handed to him, that's Carr."

"That's not how it happened," Carr denied, but her mockery didn't dim his smile even a bit.

She groaned, deciding she would get the details out of them both later. Shaking her head, she continued, "And this is Dax."

"Nice to meet you." His tone was as neutral as his expression, but he got points for effort. At least one of them could be civil.

"And finally, that's Rae." She smiled smugly at her friend.

Casimir dipped his chin. "It's a pleasure to meet all of you."

"Now"—Seren looked at her friends, each wearing a different expression: Carr, confused; Dax, worried; and Rae, resentful—"I suggest we get going, unless anyone else wants to turn out like Carr."

"THIS WAS YOUR GREAT PLAN?" Rae frowned. "A river?"

If Casimir noticed Rae's snark, he ignored it. He approached the riverbed, his eyes closed as he waved a hand through the empty space above the water. The air split at his command, as if he were drawing the curtains at the theater. Where seconds ago there had been nothing but calm, clear blue, now there idled a sturdy wooden boat close to the shore. The proud male said nothing and stared at Rae, his actions proving better than words.

"How?" Seren gasped, stepping close to the prince. "How did you do that?"

"Seriously?" A glimmer caught Casimir's eyes before a half smile split his lips. "Magic."

Obviously. Seren rolled her eyes, then turned her attention to the river. Crystal water stretched hundreds of yards wide and veered around a bend that obstructed their view of where it led.

"This boat can take us out of my court and close to Ocealla," Casimir went on.

Rae scowled. "We're going straight to Ocealla? Shouldn't Seren rest?"

"No. I know of a quiet place to stop for the night. We can

walk to Ocealla from there. Tomorrow." Casimir met Seren's gaze. "But we don't have much time to waste."

"He's right." Seren glanced at the boat, her friends. "I can do it."

"How long will it take us?" Dax asked. "To reach Ocealla?"

"About a day's journey on the boat and a few hours' walk tomorrow."

Rae crossed his arms. "Wouldn't it be safer to make our way on foot? We're vulnerable on the water, too exposed."

"I can cover us with my magic, just like how you couldn't see the boat before I unveiled it—no one will see us on the water." Casimir spoke like it was a matter of fact. "It's the safest way."

It sounded good to Seren. No scaling cliffsides or running from guards, sign her up. She knew the Verti were far less eager to jump at the stranger's idea, but she trusted Casimir. For some reason she didn't quite understand. Waiting until the others agreed was pointless. Seren brushed past Casimir and eased her tired body into the boat. It rocked back and forth under her weight, settling when she took a seat at the front. "You guys coming, or what?"

Casimir gestured with an open palm. "I'll go last to close the veil."

No one made a move to follow her lead—enough was enough. This egotistical-male standoff was past being ridiculous. Seren plastered on her most innocent expression, complimented by a shameless grin. "Anyone have a ruler, because at this point it might be quicker if y'all just whip it out and see who's bigger so we can get on with it."

"Can always count on you being such a lady, Seren." Carr barked with laughter so strong the boat rocked from the water's vibrations. Even Dax couldn't hold back a grin as he watched his wheezing friend try to control himself.

Casimir's lips curved upward, and he glanced at Seren too

quickly for her to fully register the heated look in his eyes. Turning back to the others, he said, "There's really no need to embarrass you all, so I suggest we get going."

Rae said nothing.

But her plan worked.

Carr caught his breath by the time he plopped down beside her with the grace of a boulder falling off a cliff, and Dax followed quickly after. Eventually, Rae crawled into the boat, still silent as he took the empty seat at Seren's other side.

Casimir was the last to board, and again, Seren watched in awe as he wielded his magic and sealed the air around them. Nothing looked different. She could still see the forest they'd walked through, the ground their feet had just stood on. Could still hear the chirps of birds and bristles of branches, and the hiss of the breeze skimming over the water's surface as the boat floated down the river.

If she didn't trust that Casimir had done what he said, she wouldn't have been able to tell the difference.

They spent the first half of their trip digging through their packs for food and water. Seren offered to share hers with the prince, but he declined every time. Eventually she moved on to asking him more about his magic, but he hid every truth behind vague answers and promised to tell her later.

When they both tired of her failed interrogation, Seren resigned to rest. Carr happily allowed her to lean against him, and she closed her eyes, ignoring Rae's stare. She focused on the smooth sways of the boat coursing down the gentle river, its motion like rocking a weary child to bed. Her thoughts were on the prince as she drifted off, grateful he had been in her nightmare. That he had helped her find the strength to see the light.

"What are you doing here?" Seren asked the prince as they both stood in her dream realm.

"I wanted us to talk"—Casimir's voice was low and daring—"in private."

"About?"

"The trial."

Seren stiffened; she didn't want to think about that right now. And anyway, she was supposed to be resting. "Why?"

"Because"—he paused—"I thought you died."

Her gaze fell, unable to look at the guilt cast across his face. "I'm sorry." She didn't know what else to say.

"Don't." Casimir closed the space between them. "Just tell me what happened. One second I was with you, and the next you were gone. Or I guess I was. It felt like I was ripped from your nightmare. I've never experienced anything like it."

Her hands trembled. She couldn't explain what happened either. Her voice wavered. "When you disappeared, I thought I failed." She stared at the ground; she hadn't told anyone yet. "But then something happened, the doors opened and there was this bright light. It was so intense and it felt like it called to me. I didn't know what else to do, so I walked into it." She squeezed her eyes shut and tears slipped through her lashes.

"Then what happened?"

"I don't really know." But that wasn't entirely true. It was like when she had walked through Shaya's fire—overwhelming. A cosmic experience too difficult to put into words. What she had felt was easier to describe than what had happened: afraid, guilty, unworthy. She hadn't expected for the Moons to find her redeemable, had waited for them to strike her down and destine her to an eternity of madness. Her worst fear brought to life when she'd believed she'd failed her friends. That she would never see any of them ever again.

But the gods had seen something in her, something worth saving.

"Can I tell you something?"

Seren nodded.

Casimir started, "From what I—"

But she didn't get the chance to hear what he said next, pulled awake as she fought to hold onto the prince's voice, his silver-blue eyes the last thing she saw before soft sunlight cascaded over her warm face.

SEREN STIRRED AWAKE, her face smashed against Carr's muscular legs. She lifted her head, rubbed the sleep from her eyes, and glanced at the peaceful prince. *What did he want to tell me?*

Her body cracked in time with the rickety sounds of the boat as she sat up and got comfortable. Casimir sat opposite her, his eyes closed, and Seren searched his face. He opened his eyes to catch her staring, and a half smile formed on his lips. *Caught you.*

Seren looked away, her thoughts on her dream. Their conversation wasn't over, she would make sure of that. She asked everyone, "Are we close?"

"We'll dock soon. If everyone is on board with the plan, it's just a short walk from the inn." Casimir's voice was authoritative, not demanding. He simply offered his opinion.

"We'd all benefit from a good night's sleep." Carr's yawn punctuated his words. At least he and Dax seemed to be coming around.

Everyone nodded besides Rae. Seren ignored his stare and asked the others, "Is everyone good with that?"

A thick pause. Casimir's eyes jumped between the Verti, giving them the chance to speak first. Seren noticed the keen self-awareness, the desire to not irritate her already tense friends. When no one jumped to answer, Casimir said, "It's a small town where we'll be safe. I know the owner of the inn. If he has the rooms, he'll let us stay."

"Count me in. I'd do anything for a real bed right about now." Carr offered one of his typical, all-defense-lowering smiles and waited for the others to agree.

Seren stifled a yawn. "Me too."

Dax elbowed his best friend playfully. "Anything, huh?"

"Anything," Carr reiterated with a wink.

The two of them laughed quietly, Dax joking about what he could convince Carr to do, while Casimir brought the boat to the shore. Seren watched intently as he opened and closed the protective veil, his magic just as intriguing as the times before.

Casimir disembarked first, then held the boat steady for everyone else. Seren was thankful to connect with solid ground, her body swaying slightly as they walked, remembering the motion of the river.

Their ride out of Lunaan had taken the entire day, leaving them to walk to the inn under the soft light of sunset. By the time they reached the small town, the only light left beamed from the moon.

Town was maybe too strong a word to describe the place that Casimir had brought them to; just a pub, a stable, and the inn the prince had mentioned.

That was it. A road stop more than a town.

Everything was quiet in the dark. Only faint conversation drifted from the pub, the likes of others searching for a safe place to rest. Casimir led the group to the inn, which looked more like a barn: a small wooden room for check-ins and roughly ten guest rooms outside, with X-crossed windows and barn doors that reminded Seren of stalls for livestock.

"You guys can wait here if you want. I'll go find the owner." Casimir glanced inside, speaking over his shoulder as he opened the front door. "It shouldn't take long. I'll be right back."

With the prince out of earshot, Seren turned to Rae. "What's your deal?"

Rae tilted his head. "What do you mean?"

Seren glared. "Seriously, you're just gonna act like you don't know what I'm talking about?" Rae shrugged, and it made Seren want to stab him. "You're being an ass."

"It's fine."

"No, actually"—Seren turned away—"it's not."

"What do you want me to say, Seren?" Rae reached for her but missed.

She spun. "The truth maybe?"

"We shouldn't be traveling with him. Even you must know the stories."

"They're just rumors, Rae."

"Do you really believe that?" He paused, his face red. But he cut her off before she could answer. "He's hurt people, Seren. Killed, even. He's more trouble than he's worth, and I don't want to be a part of it."

"Rae—" Seren started on her defense, but stopped when Carr pointed at the inn right as the front door creaked open.

Casimir approached, his brows raised. But all he said was, "There's two open rooms. He said they're ours if we want them."

"That's perfect," Seren agreed before anyone could argue. "Tell him we'll take them, please."

The prince disappeared once more and returned seconds later with two keys. "Numbers nine and ten." He pointed down the length of the inn. "At the very end."

Seren wasted no time, and the others trailed behind. As far as rumors went, Casimir was everything from short-tempered, to truculent, to exactly what Rae claimed. But Seren couldn't shake the feeling there was more to the prince than being the talk of the town. She stopped in front of the first door, and Casimir passed a key to Carr. Carr opened the second door, his hand braced against the frame, his eyes bouncing from Seren to Rae and hesitantly to the prince. "Come on, brother."

Rae didn't take his eyes off Seren, his mouth slightly agape.

Seren spoke before he had the chance, "I'll room with Casimir, so no one is alone if something bad happens." That sounded like as good of an excuse as any, but Seren knew the Verti saw through it. Everyone knew the prince was one of the most powerful Fae in Clarallan. He could handle himself.

"Fine with me." Casimir opened the door to room number nine and held it ajar.

"Good night, guys." The words felt sour on her tongue. A line had been drawn and crossed with one decision. Seren cleared her throat, and before she could change her mind, slipped past Cas and into the room.

The prince let the door close—Rae still standing there.

Seren refused to move until she heard him walk away, jolting when the neighboring door slammed.

CHAPTER 29

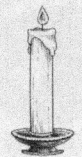

"That was only slightly awkward," Seren said, unlacing her boots and leaving them near the door.

"Slightly?" Casimir's deep chuckle rumbled through the darkness.

Seren turned to face him, a faint smile teasing her mouth. Moonlight flickered through the high window and cast shadows across his sharp features from behind. At least one rumor was true: he really was stunning. "Yeah, there's no need to downplay it, huh? If there was ever a definition of awkward, it would've been that."

Casimir's laughter grew. "I don't think your friends like me very much."

"I wouldn't take you as the kind of person to care about that sort of thing." Seren searched the dark room. This was as good of a time as any to test out her new magic. She focused on the rhythm in her core and willed it to spread to her fingers. A few seconds, and light sparked at the tips, faint tendrils of yellows and golds that licked the air. Casimir stepped forward. The closer he got, the louder her magic hummed and the stronger her light burned.

"Sollian?" he asked.

She nodded. Together they combed the room, found a fireplace, and soon enough, the air was lit with warmth and light.

Seren circled back to the conversation. "Don't blame them. My friends, I mean. It's not that they don't like you—I guess it could be, but...I think it's more that they don't know you. They're wary of strangers."

"And you're not?"

Casimir's question caught her off guard. It wasn't that he didn't scare her. He most definitely did. His status and life and magic, and the stories...

"I know we don't know each other. But it kinda feels like we do..." She glanced around the room. And they did know each other, at least, sort of. He knew everything she had confessed in her dreams, and she hadn't held back. "I'm sorry, that probably sounded super weird."

Casimir let her words linger, then asked, "Does it matter? Us not knowing each other?"

"It should, I think. But for some reason, it doesn't."

His lips curled. "I know a lot about you."

"What?"

"Your dreams."

Her embarrassment flared. She hated that he knew so much when she knew so little. It made her vulnerable. She asked, "How does it work, dream-walking?"

"Usually by invitation, sometimes by force. All Fae can experience it, as in someone entering their dreams, but only Fae with magic from the Moons can dream-walk themselves, and only those with the strongest of magic can manipulate the dreams of others. Every time I appeared in your dreams, you initiated the connection. It's like a pull on my magic coming directly from yours."

Seren had felt something like that before. When her magic guided her to the trials and when it flared in the presence of the gods. Or when it tethered her to the prince, like a pull at her core, or a hum whenever he was near. The first few times it happened, she thought she'd made it up. But then it kept happening. And it never stopped.

A flicker of amusement crossed his face. "I only ever followed the tug. Except on the boat. That time, I wanted to talk to you."

Ignoring that invasion of privacy, Seren asked, "Can I do that? Dream-walk into other dreams?"

Casimir nodded. "Passing the Moon Trial should mean your magic is as strong as mine or any member of the royal family's, or even stronger than."

Her stomach lurched. She knew her magic was powerful, but to be stronger than the prince—someone had taken her entire world and flipped it upside down like it was nothing. "How?"

"Practice, probably, if you don't think you can do it right now."

An idea flared and her mind raced. "Can you help me dream-walk? There's someone I need to talk to."

"Who?"

"Someone I need to apologize to—explain why I left." When he didn't answer, Seren added, "She's a friend."

His expression lifted. "You have friends?"

She glared. "Please, Casimir."

The prince considered, holding her gaze for a long moment. "Some other time. You need to rest before the next trial."

She groaned. "Will you do it for me, then? I need to know that she's okay."

He blinked at her persistence. "This is important to you?" A nod. "Okay"—he sighed—"tell me who she is."

Mare's face flashed in her mind and guilt soured her throat. "Her name is Mare. She's from Ocealla...but now she's one of the queen's servants in Stellean. I just want to know that she's okay, and I don't want her to worry about me, so don't tell her about the trials. Just tell her I'm sorry and that when I can, I'll come find her."

His face softened. "Is she Fae?"

"Yes. But Hellevi tampers with the Fae servants' magic—makes them wear these iron bracelets so they can't escape. Is that a problem?"

"I don't know," he said quietly. "I've never tried something like that before."

"But you will?" She chewed on her lip. "Try, I mean."

"Tonight." He hesitated. "After you're asleep so I know you're prepared for tomorrow."

"Okay," she agreed, her eyes gleaming. "Thank you, Cas." A corner of his mouth turned up and she asked, "What else can my magic do?"

He looked at her funny, but his expression was unreadable. "What do you know about Lunaan magic?"

"Not much."

"Sometimes I seriously can't believe you've made it this far," he gibed. "In your shoes, knowing as little as you do, anyone else would be dead."

Seren couldn't tell if that was an insult or a compliment. She looked away, stepped in front of the fire, and sat, facing the heat.

Casimir sat next to her, his legs stretched out; one breath out of place and their bodies would touch. "Can I tell you something?"

Her head jerked. "You asked that on the boat, but I didn't get to hear what you said next." She urged him on. "What is it?"

Casimir leaned back and stared into the fire, hesitating long enough for Seren to study him. Besides her dreams, she hadn't seen the prince since that dark night in the alley. He looked different now, a hint of life returned to his intense eyes. Still, he wore an all-black outfit, tight enough around his arms that Seren's gaze caught on his taunt muscles and tattooed chest. She snapped her eyes to his face when his low voice cracked against the growing fire. "I wasn't completely truthful earlier. There was one other time I walked into your dreams, the first actually."

Leave it to the prince to find loopholes around the Fae's limitations.

He asked, "Do you remember?"

How could she forget—the first time Seren ever shared a dream with the prince, coincidentally, was the first time she almost died in the Galaxius Forest. Right before Rae saved her from being torn apart by Caripers. She shuddered at the thought, and Casimir took that as a yes.

"Another of the Moons' gifts is something the Lunaan Fae call *lunaas*, or moon-sight. Like glimpses of insight or time, future and present." Casimir ran a hand through his hair, his eyes searching hers. "It's an incredibly rare power, comparable to wish-granting for the Stellean Fae."

Seren knew that gift too well; Jassin had made sure of it. "And you can do that? See the future?"

With a tight jaw, he said, "Ever since I was a kid. The gift hadn't been present in our family for generations before me. That's half the reason why the old man called me the golden son, destined to become the next Lunaan king." He looked down. "But that's not the point. I saw something after that night I saved you in the alley. You were in danger, and I could see it, feel it. But after I left you, I spent the rest of that night so drunk, I honestly thought I'd hallucinated it."

Seren breathed, "It's okay—"

"It's not." He sat up, and the intensity of his stare burned hotter than the flames at their side. "Sometime the next day, I was passed out and hungover when I felt it again. You were in danger, but this time I felt your magic too, that tug. I followed it, and that's what led me to dream-walk to you the first time."

"That's why you were yelling at me to wake up?" Seren had forgotten that detail, between the attack she couldn't remember and waking up tied and being dragged across the forest floor.

Casimir exhaled. "I could've prevented it."

"How?"

His eyes were darker than Seren thought blue was capable of. "I saw the attack hours before it happened, but I was too fucked up to care if it was real or not. Just like all the other times I was too gone to care who got hurt, or even worse, when I enjoyed it."

A chill kissed her spine. *So the rumors are true.*

Every part of her screamed to look away, but that was what he wanted. For her to cower in fear or shake with disgust so that he could just be a monster, in hopes the guilt he seemingly didn't want to face would simply walk away.

But true monsters did not contend with conscience. And that was why she couldn't.

Seren asked, "Why?" He twisted his head and she clarified, "Why were you doing that to yourself?"

"To forget." His throat bulged and he looked away. "To escape."

"What?"

"It doesn't matter."

Seren didn't believe that for a second, but who was she to force his hand? "Look, I can't speak on everything else, but what happened with me wasn't your fault. And I'm here, right? Which means everything worked out okay."

"This time," he said through clenched teeth.

Her heart raced. She hesitated. "Why are you telling me all this?"

"Because it's why I'm here. A few days ago, I saw something again, but this time I knew it was real." He swallowed, cracked his knuckles.

It felt like the prince was serving her crumbs while his own guilt feasted. She guessed there was so much he wasn't telling her. "What did you see?"

"Another vision, like when I saw you in the forest. But this time, you and your friends were in the Lunaan temple, and there was this overwhelming magic, this fear, and all I could hear was you."

"What was I saying?"

"Nothing." He shook his head. "You were screaming. The type that only comes out when someone thinks they're dying, or wishes they would. I couldn't see what was happening, but I knew it was bad..." Casimir fell quiet.

Seren inhaled, her lips sealed by the silence he left, her thoughts on the one person who could make her scream like that.

Minutes passed before Casimir found his words. "Then I saw you last night in the Lunaan court. I couldn't believe it. I followed you all the way to the Temple of the Full Moon."

Seren snapped her eyes to his. "That was you?"

"Yeah." His dark hair curtained his eyes. "I wanted to talk to you, but I never got the chance. Then the trial started so I stuck around, waiting. I sat down and I think I nodded off for a minute...and that's when I felt it, the tug."

"And that led you to me? The trial?"

He nodded.

"How?" Seren spoke with her hands. "I mean I don't know everything about the trials, but from what I've learned so far, they're sort of a big deal. Shouldn't there be, like...I don't know, something in place to keep people out? What if you had tried to sabotage me? Or gotten hurt?"

"More rules, less stakes." Casimir shrugged, arrogance tainting his tone. "And I wouldn't have gotten hurt."

Seren flinched. He'd gotten a front-row seat, a glimpse at the horror, yet he still underestimated the gods and their consequences. "If you're going to join us on the last trials, you have to understand what we're up against." Her friends' faces flashed in her memory—how they had looked on the bloody floor. "I don't want anyone else getting hurt because of me, Cas."

His mouth opened, then closed. He glanced down, his sharp face framed by soft black curls, dark as the shadows. "Okay."

"Okay?"

"I'm here to help, not argue."

She angled her head. "You keep saying that you're here to help...but I still don't understand why. Yeah, you have these visions, but they're not your responsibility. And with the war coming, doesn't the Lunaan court need you?"

"I haven't been there for my court in years," he admitted. "Even if I had, I'm not sure it would've mattered. Evander has been working against my father for years, and now that he's aligned himself with Hellevi, it's too late. There's only one way to stop my brother, and it's by stopping the Stellean king's war."

"How?" Seren asked.

His gaze met hers. "You."

She knew this already, and still his words were a punch to the gut. It really was up to just them. Up to her.

His eyes softened, roamed her face. "Now that you know why I'm doing this, what about you, why are you risking so much?"

Seren stared into the fire, mollified by the rhythmic flutter of spitting flames. For the first time in her life, she had something to lose besides just her own. How ironic—what made her life worth living appeared to also be her greatest fear.

Love.

"When I left Stellean, I had nothing to lose," she said. "I was alone, empty-handed, and honestly, I thought I was losing it. It wasn't until the guys saved me that I started living. It was like I was shown what life could be, then told it would all be taken away again by the same monster, but this time it'd be worse."

"So you chose to fight?"

"Mmm."

"I don't get it."

"What?"

"Despite everything you've been through, you haven't let your heart turn cold. I don't understand how." He shook his head. "How can you still see the good when all life has shown you is bad?"

"What you saw in my nightmare...that was my life before I escaped—pain, lies. I didn't know the truth, and when I got a taste, I couldn't stop." Seren couldn't believe she was saying this. "And it hasn't all been bad. There are my friends—the guys...you." She chuckled. "Even in Stellean, I had Mare and Greyson." She took a breath. "Then there's Clarallan, its magic and life and every new thing I see is somehow better than the last. And yeah, there's a lot of bad and I'm tired of it. Tired of the evil and the greed and the lies. But when it's night and the darkness looks infinite, that doesn't stop the sun from rising again the next day. It doesn't have to be this way forever. Or at least, I hope not."

A lazy smile curved his lips, softened his harsh jaw.

"What?" Seren asked.

"Nothing."

"Tell me."

He lifted his hands. "Maybe later."

Seren gave him a look with no zest. She covered a yawn and stretched her legs, bumping him as she stood. She walked to the bed and looked over her shoulder. "Maybe I'll look forward to hearing it."

"You will." Casimir smirked, and his low voice sent goosebumps over her skin as she crawled beneath the sheets. He stood and checked the locked door. "Get some rest. I'll sleep on the floor."

"You don't have to," she said, not sure where she got the confidence.

A pause.

Her breath hitched when he looked at her, his slow gaze

sliding from her to the bed. His lips curved to the side. "Get some rest."

She leaned her head on the pillows, tugged on the covers. "Good night, Cas."

"Good night, Seren."

CHAPTER 30

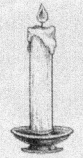

"Seren!" Carr pounded on the door to room number nine. "Get up, will you?"

She lifted her head, groggily rubbed her cheeks with her palms. Carr yelled her name again, her heart picked up, and this time, Casimir woke too.

"Seren, open up already." The door shook.

"One sec," she groused, kicking her legs free of the warm sheets. She pressed bare feet to the wooden floor, scattering goosebumps across her skin.

The prince sat up, ran a hand through his messy hair, and stared at her with sleep-ridden eyes. "Who is it?"

"Just Carr." She opened the door, squinting at the early sun.

Her friend barged in, and the prince jumped up.

"We have a problem."

"Good morning to you too," Seren said, closing the door.

"What's going on?" Casimir asked, his voice thick.

"It's worse than we thought." Carr shifted his eyes between Seren and the prince, the bed and the floor. "The war has progressed. Rae got a letter back from the house this morning.

Izzac got word that Hellevi sent his troops to Sollian right after we left."

Casimir tensed.

Seren didn't want to know, but she had to. "What happened?"

"Troops descended into the city just days after us; luckily, they terrorized the court more than ravaged it. Izzac thinks Hellevi's goal was fear, not death, parading his war so publicly like that." Carr rubbed the back of his neck. "He also said they were looking for something."

Seren looked down. "Me," she said, her voice weak with guilt. "He's looking for me."

"You don't know that. Maybe it was the king's plan all along."

Smirking, Seren blew air from her nose. "You don't really believe that, do you?"

"Why would he be looking for you?" Casimir asked. "You were his *servant*." The way he said the word made her stomach roil. "I think he has bigger things in mind."

Carr added, "Yeah, like wanting to become a bloody High King."

"What if he found out about the trials?" Seren asked. "That we're trying to stop him?"

"But we've been alone at both trials. How could he have known?" Carr crossed his arms. "It's not like they're a real regular occurrence, you know?"

"I know," Seren groaned. "But he said he was going to kill me. And just days after?" She paced. "That's too much chance, right... It has to mean something."

Carr merely said, "The war isn't about you, though. It could be a coincidence."

"No such thing as coincidence in war," Casimir answered, his eyes following her. "Say the king is looking for you—how did he know where you were?"

"He's a king." Seren used her hands. "Don't you think he has his ways?"

"He has a point," Carr cut in and his eyes glowed. "You've been with us...and we've been careful."

"Still—" There had to be something they were missing, but this was going nowhere. She stopped pacing, took a breath. "What else did Izzac say?" She glanced at Cas. "Did he say anything about Lunaan?"

"Nothing specific." Carr's eyes flickered between them. "But Izzac's informants last reported Hellevi's troops were seen leaving Sollian, traveling in the direction of the Lunaan court after exhausting a few days search."

Seren stepped to Casimir. "You should go home. Your court... your father, needs you."

Casimir asked, his jaw clenched, "Do you know anything else?"

"Izzac mentioned Hellevi's soldiers were chanting—that a new High King had come to reclaim his rightful place as Clarallan's true leader. Izzac's guy said it was terrifying. That Hellevi's following praised him like a god."

Seren shook with fear, Casimir with anger.

"We have to do something," she insisted. To Cas, "You should go back."

"It's likely Hellevi has already made it to Lunaan." Casimir's dark hair covered his eyes. "By the time I got back..." He clenched his fists, his shoulders taut. "I can help more here, now, with you."

Seren sucked in a cold breath and her heart hurt. They had to go before Hellevi caught up to them. She whirled. "Where are the others?"

"Rae went to send a letter to Izzac, and Dax is scouting a few miles around us. Both should be back soon."

"Then we need to leave." She glanced at the door and began

gathering her things. "We have to get to Ocealla as fast as we can."

"Do you know where the third trial is?" Casimir asked.

"Mostly." She spoke again before he could question her, "How far away are we?"

"About a two-hour walk."

"Good." She stared at them both. "Let's make it one."

THE SUN WAS warm on Seren's back as they left the wooded trail behind.

The trees grew farther apart, and the moist soil slowly turned to deep sand. They walked to Ocealla in silence, the only sound the howling wind that whipped saltwater across their skin. Seren's mind was a mess as she charged on, her eyes locked on the sweeping expanse of a picturesque sea just ahead.

She couldn't get Mare out of her head as she took in her friend's home court for the first time. That morning, after Carr had gone back to his room to gather his things, she'd questioned the prince about his task, and his reaction had since left her in a constant state of worry. He hadn't been able to reach Mare and tried over and over to convince Seren that it was because of the tempers Hellevi placed on the Fae's magic. But Seren couldn't bring herself to believe his comforts, his tense shoulders and sealed expression filling her mind with doubt even as the prince promised to try again after the third trial.

Reining in her worries, Seren focused on Ocealla. Remembering all the stories her friend had shared, it was easy to see why Mare loved her home. Infinite beaches stretched at their sides as far as they could see up and down the magnificent coast. For miles, there was nothing but empty sand and endless shore, cloudy blue skies, and that relentless wind.

Casimir caught up to her and pointed at the horizon. "There."

Seren's eyes widened and magic pumped from her heart. "Is

that"—the wind whipped her voice around—"is that the Ocealla court?"

He nodded, staring at the colossal island erupting from the dark sea, its mountain peaks soaring through the misty clouds. An array of idyllic castles sprouted in the center, a swirl of stone and gold and green. Ocealla was a court of jungles and waterfalls above, but something even more incredible below.

Seren bent down, plunged her hands in the sand, and let it fall through her fingers. Her magic sparked at the tips, and she closed her eyes, focused on the salt that stung her face. A childish part of her wanted to kick off her shoes and run splashing through the water—instead, she swallowed the thought, shook the sand from her hands, and looked at Casimir.

They caught up to the others, and Rae led them along the shore, the journal in hand. Fortunately, Izzac marked a dock on the beach he guessed was the best place to start. Unfortunately, Izzac said the trial happened somewhere on the water. Seren hated the idea even more than returning to her nightmare—she didn't know if she could swim, and she really didn't want her first time to be in the trial.

The longer they walked, the easier it was to hear her magic, how it searched for its source. It was a similar feeling to when she stood before the gods, like a flared tether sizzling at the ends, begging to connect with something big.

The stronger she felt, the louder the wind howled. A misty fog rolled over the sounds of crashing waves, and a dark storm dominated the sky. Seren ran blindly, the temperature dropping with each step, the thick sand dragging her back.

On the water up ahead, she could just make out the eerie silhouette of a massive ship. It started to rain and they ran faster. Eventually, an ivory dock stretched across the sand and protruded into the sea, its sturdy legs built directly into the water, decorated with gothic sculptures of sea creatures, their macabre faces frightening as lightning flashed close by.

Seren dashed up the slick stone steps, slowing down as she waded through the frigid mist. Her teeth chattered and her clothes stuck nauseatingly to her skin. She pulled on her magic, her sight almost completely obstructed, and willed her power to spread. Reaching for the railings, her hands met warmth, not stone.

Casimir laced his fingers through hers and wrapped her arm around his. His nearness was a breath of relief, and she felt her magic pool beneath her skin at his touch. Warmth spread through her limbs, and she blinked slowly, the veil of thick gray dissolving from her vision.

She looked down the dock and saw the water—not clearly, but better than seconds before, when she could barely see a foot in front of her.

"Guys, come look at this," Dax yelled.

Her head jerked and Casimir pulled her to a halt.

"Your eyes." His throat bulged.

"What?"

"There's something in your eyes." He leaned closer. "It looks like—"

"Stars?"

A nod.

She gulped, her pulse in her ears. "It's—"

"Incredible."

"Guys," Dax shouted again.

"Let's go." He tugged her hand.

A ghastly wooden ship cut above the violent water, tied to the colorless columns of the ancient dock. Seren cranked her neck and studied the boat, its size greater than most civilian homes. A steep wooden drawbridge descended from the port side for at least twenty feet between the stone and ship.

Tall sails whipped above the ship as the storm intensified and an unforgiving rain poured down. Seren raised her hands over her eyes and looked up. There was no crew, no flags or emblems, no sign of life beyond the sea crashing beneath the haunting vessel.

"Hello?" Rae's voice barely broke through the sounds of the storm. He yelled again, louder. "Anyone there?"

The brazen male walked forward and ascended the narrow drawbridge, the half-rotted wood creaking beneath his weight. When Rae took his last step, Carr followed, his eyes on his feet as he climbed the soaked plank.

Seren and the others stayed on the dock as the two Verti disappeared, then emerged what felt like hours later. Carr shouted, "All clear."

"There's no one else here," Rae added.

Seren walked forward, Casimir at her back, as Dax studied something on the side of the ship. One foot after the other, she ascended the bridge, then Casimir, and Dax a few minutes behind. Fear nagged at her mind, threatening what would happen if she fell overboard. She shook water from her face and said, "I really hoped we wouldn't have to do this."

Rae shot her a sympathetic look. "It's going to be okay."

"Yeah," she sighed, glancing at the sea—they all knew how to swim.

Rae asked, "Now what?"

"Look around?" Carr suggested and everyone agreed.

Seren walked slowly, her steps splashing in water as waves poured over the deck from both sides. The ship swayed and she slipped, her balance stolen as the boat tipped toward the bow. *Smack*—her knees cracked against the wet wood. She grimaced, and splinters split her hands as she crawled over the slick floor.

Lightning flashed through the dark sky—*one, two*—thunder roared.

She hurried to the front of the ship, her hands wrapped around the slick beams as she fought the rain, searching for any signs of the trial.

Nothing.

The rain beat down on her like hail, stinging any skin her leathers left exposed.

"Seren?" Dax's voice cracked at her side. "I think I have something."

It took her a minute to find him, the others too. When everyone was together near the prow of the ship, Dax pointed at the writing along the sides. The wood was engraved with thick lettering in a bold hand and endless constellations.

"This is it," Seren said, reading the inscriptions. "We're in the right place."

"What are you waiting for?" Rae asked, his arms crossed above his head, his hair flat to his face.

"Give her a minute, man." Carr stepped closer, his body shielding her from the rain.

Seren stared at Rae. "He's right, we don't have any time to waste." Not when Hellevi was breathing down their necks. She glanced between her friends, then overboard at the raging sea. "Y'all might want to hold on to something."

Taking a deep breath, she read the quotes out loud. "To surmount the Sea, reach deep in the depths of control; one mistake and a watery grave awaits. Listen to who sings for thee, sweet songs of promises, life and mystery."

The ship lurched and the floorboards shook, hurling Seren and the others through the air as lightning lit the dark sky. She braced herself as she slipped, but before she hit the hard wood, two large hands swept beneath her arms. The force of her fall collided with Casimir and sent the two of them crashing into the floorboards.

The boat steadied and she scrambled off him, rubbing the back of her neck as her nerves fried with whiplash. Casimir muffled a groan and stood, offering Seren a hand.

"Thanks." She winced.

"You guys okay?" "What the hell just happened?" Carr and Dax shouted, running over to them.

Her legs strained against the rocking boat, and she swayed against Casimir.

Carr spoke first, "That must have been one hell of a wave."

"Guys," Rae said, catching up after the crash. He braced his hands on the railing and peered across the riled water. "I don't think that was just any wave."

Everyone rushed to look.

The navy sea crashed against the hull of the ship, capped with frothy waves that splashed their skin as they looked down.

Rae's realization came with an overwhelming sense of dread.

The waves no longer swayed back and forth. Now they dragged the ship to sea. The boat moved across the water like a blade, cutting through the violent waves with ease—advancing quickly, farther and farther away from land.

With no crew in sight.

Seren gazed back to where the ivory dock should have been, but the ship was already too far away.

Sailing on—no crew, no captain.

"What do we do?" Seren stammered through cold lips, teeth chattering.

The Verti shared a look, and Rae said, "I don't think there *is* anything we can do."

Seren shivered.

The third trial had begun, and they were at the mercy of the sea and its goddesses.

There wasn't anything they could do.

Her magic flared, and she looked around in panic.

Then the music came.

CHAPTER 31

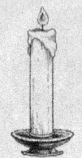

There was nothing but water as far as Seren could see.

A mellifluous melody all she could hear.

The ship broke through the eye of the storm, and the warm sun reflected against the calm, deep water. In the distance, the storm raged on, and lightning split the dark horizon.

Taking slow breaths, Seren tried to ease her seasickness, her stomach in her throat as fear rooted in her core. She glanced at her friends—somehow, all five of them were still together—then back to the still water, entranced by the approaching feminine song.

Seren was the first to see them: the Goddesses of the Sea.

Their soft melody floated above the ship, sweet notes of desire and pleasure. Seren leaned into their alluring song, her chest pressed against the soaked wood as the guys involuntarily did the same.

The three goddesses were flawless, their beautiful faces wrapped in lavishly long hair that fanned out in the water. Sharp scales lined what should have been bare skin, in blues, purples, golds, and greens, each woman sparkling beneath different hues. Their approach sped up in time with the tempo of their intensifying song, and Seren's heart raced. She tried to focus on the words, but the music changed.

A raucous sound assaulted her ears, replacing the magnetic melody from moments ago. Seren stepped back, braced her arms against the wood, and stared at her friends—caught in a trance, their eyes locked on the nearing goddesses, their mouths agape just slightly.

Seren slid to Rae, never taking her eyes from the water. She nudged his shoulder. "Rae…Rae, snap out of it."

But his golden eyes remained glued to the goddesses.

She tried the others. Carr. Dax. Even the prince was under some sort of spell. She shook her friends, desperate as the horrendous song grew overwhelming.

The goddesses stopped just waves from the ship. Peering overboard, Seren scrambled away upon seeing them up close.

Looking from face to face, she couldn't believe her eyes. One-half of each was rotted, cheekbones exposed beneath peeling skin. Their eyes small black pits that echoed the death ravaging their bodies.

Seren clasped her hands to her ears and forced herself to brave the Goddesses of the Sea. It felt like their song had grown claws and slashed at her eardrums. She begged her magic to do something, anything.

"Ssseren," the goddesses sang together.

Her cheeks warmed and their song dulled—a slight reprieve that left Seren's ears ringing.

The goddess in the middle swam forward, her scales a royal shade of blue that blurred with the color of the sea. "We're glad you're here."

"Are you?" Seren asked, stopping just before she could say, *If that was true, you would shut the hell up*. Her eyes scurried to her friends, their mesmerized faces hopelessly entranced. If Seren couldn't get them to snap out of it, she at least hoped none were foolish enough to fall overboard while she completed the third trial.

"Very." The goddess flashed her teeth in a serpentine smile that stretched across the mangled side of her face. Seren couldn't tear her eyes away, watching the bones contract without the limits of flesh. It was unnerving, an asymmetrical snarl of decomposing muscle and skin. "It's been a long time since anyone has made it this far—to the Sea Trial."

"Shaya has all the fun," said the goddess to the right, her scales a dark shade of green that covered her entire chest. "She's entertained every time, unlike the rest of us girls, who have to wait for the right one to come along."

The goddess on the left giggled. "A girl could only wish to be that lucky."

"Are you lucky, Seren?" The blue-scaled goddess smiled and clicked her tongue as Seren watched through her decaying cheek. "Is that how you've made it this far?"

Seren didn't move, but she wasn't sure it was even a choice.

The green goddess asked, "How else could she?" She swam forward and her golden hair swirled around her. "There's no other way *she* has done what so many others could not. Look at her. Does she look like she deserves to be here?" The goddess scrunched her nose and tilted her chin away.

"I think our sister is right, Nephein." The one to the left laughed again and squinted at Seren. "She does look kind of sad, doesn't she?"

Seren stiffened, studying the insulting goddess; her long black hair and fair skin the perfect contrast to her vibrant purple scales. Of all the sisters, Seren expected she would be the prettiest, if half her face wasn't falling off. Turning her attention to the goddess up front, the one her giggly sister called Nephein, Seren said, "I'm here because I deserve to be—"

All three cut her off with a fit of laughter, their powerful tails splashing behind them. Seren gritted her teeth. She didn't think any of the gods could be more infuriating than the brothers of the moon, but that was before she met the sisters of the sea.

"Quiet, sisters." Nephein raised her hand, and Seren's gaze caught where black skin met dark blue scales seamlessly, her wrist deluged with gleaming, gold bangles. "Like I was saying, it's been a long time since anyone has dared the Trial of the Sea...and even longer since anyone has passed. But the same goes for all the gods' trials, and if you're standing here—well, then, there must be something to you, something our siblings found worthy."

"Have you met our brothers? That's not saying much," the green goddess jeered, and even Seren wanted to laugh.

"But Shaya blessed her too," said the purple goddess.

Nephein said to her jaded sister, "Yara's right. And Shaya is one of the hardest to please. That's why her trial is first, after all."

Seren's eyes widened, and before she could decide if she liked knowing that information, Wren swam forward, her emerald scales reflective beneath the water's surface.

"Don't let that get your hopes up. Shaya might be tough to crack, but inside, she's still soft." Wren laughed, and Seren had to look away as her torn skin flapped up and down and black blood dribbled into the sea. "We, however, cannot say the same."

"Ugly inside and out," Seren said under her breath.

Big mistake.

"What did you say?" Wren's face was a gnarled mess of muscle and rage. She swam to her sister. "Did you hear that, Yara?"

Yara gasped, her hands on her chest. "I can't believe it."

Nephein splashed the sea. "That is no way to speak to us."

Seren flinched, and even her magic seemed to quiver like a scolded child at Nephein's tone.

"Do you really believe insulting us is the way to pass our tests?" Nephein asked.

Staring ahead, Seren rode her wavering confidence while she still had it. "It was nothing worse than what you've all said to me."

Wren strangled her fists in the air, her long nails the color of her scales. "We're goddesses—"

"Let it go, sssisterss." Nephein smiled. "I think it's finally time for some *real* entertainment. But this won't do." She clicked her split tongue, splashed her hands through the waves, and sneered at Seren, "Do you still wish to see if you're worthy?"

"Yes." Seren steadied her voice. "I've earned my way here."

The waves reflected in Nephein's gaze, her dark eyes lit with excitement. It felt like Seren had made a grave mistake. Terror ripped through her and the goddess nearly sang, "Let the Sea Trial begin."

AIR SWOOSHED in Seren's ears, an unbearable pressure as she plummeted toward the raging darkness, hurled from the ship by the goddesses.

Panic gripped her throat and she flailed. The wind whipped her hair, and she choked and she screamed, and at the last second, she took the biggest breath she could and held it.

Crashing through the water, she froze, her eyes slammed shut and her lungs cried. Breaking through the ocean's surface was like tearing through glass. Her skin burned from the force and speed of her icy plunge, and she couldn't do anything.

Move, dammit.

Swim, she begged.

But it was like the connection between her mind and body had been severed. Her magic buzzed, but she couldn't reach it, frozen in her chest just like the rest of her.

Down.

She was still going down, falling closer and closer to her watery grave.

Pressure came from her side, and a current dragged her limp body up as something sharp brushed her legs. She kicked, gasped in pain, and opened her eyes, clamping her mouth shut as saltwater burned her throat and bubbles gushed from her lips. The goddesses circled her quickly, their powerful tails spinning her through the water. Their scales glowed, and they shackled Seren to their magical current, like a leaf caught in the wind.

Stifling another scream, she thrashed her arms and kicked her feet.

Swim, swim, swim.

But she didn't know how.

And it was so cold.

She couldn't move, couldn't breathe, could barely think.

She twisted, and she wasn't sure her lungs could hold another scream. The goddesses' laughter vibrated through the freezing water as Seren struggled. She tried to look up, but the currents were too strong, the surface too far away. Darkness clouded her vision and pressure beat on the inside of her skull. She kicked as hard as she could, but—

She wasn't going to make it.

Her friends' faces tore through her mind as her lungs begged to inhale. Just a few more seconds and Seren was sure her heart would explode.

One. Two.

She couldn't take it anymore…

She took a breath.

If SEREN HAD TO GUESS, she thought she was dead.

She coughed and water spilled from her raw lungs. Shivering, she sat up and looked around, her drenched leathers sticking to her pale skin. She ran her hands over her arms, hair raised with goosebumps.

She stood, legs weak. "Where *am* I?" she asked the darkness.

It kind of looked like a castle, if one could be underwater, weakly lit by sporadic lanterns along the cave walls. Clear arched ceilings soared high above the gothic courtroom, the dark ocean on full display. Creatures of all kinds swam just above the glass, their vibrant colors and lights illuminating the macabre castle beneath.

Seren turned and studied the cavern. She had never seen anything like it, not even in Hellevi's books. A stone staircase descended from the barren dais, reaching beneath the calm water that filled the courtroom.

A voice rang behind her. "You made it."

Seren whirled and her blood chilled. Nephein giggled, baring her pointed teeth, but her face—it was beautiful: smooth dark skin, full lips, and bright smile. "We weren't sure you'd survive the trip."

Not with your help. Seren loured, and Wren strode from the shadows, an emerald dress floating behind her long, feminine legs. "*I* was hoping you wouldn't."

Seren's knees buckled. All three goddesses stood before her, their faces as perfect as when she had first seen them from the ship. No sign of the death Seren knew lurked just beneath their flawless skin.

"Where are we?" Seren's voice cracked, her throat dry with salt.

Nephein answered, "Our old home."

Yara clasped her hands together and her eyes gleamed. Seren tried not to stare, but she had been right. The dark-haired sister was stunning, with thick brows, a straight jaw, and a button nose, lips the color of roses. "It's just like I remember."

This time, Seren kept her opinions to herself. She asked, "Why did you bring me here?"

"Silly girl, did you really believe our trial would happen up there?" Nephein looked up, her blue eyes reflecting the pattern of the waves. She stepped toward Seren, dressed in a satin navy gown so dark it seemed to consume any color or light.

I guess, Seren shook her head. "Now what?"

"Why the hurry?" Nephein twirled her thick hair between thin fingers.

Seren had a list of reasons she wanted the hell out of wherever here was. One, they had nearly killed her. Two, she needed to know if her friends were alive. Three, Hellevi was right on their heels up above.

And, oh right, did she mention they had nearly killed her?

When Seren said nothing, Nephein continued, "Very well. Let's get on with it then, shall we?" Nephein raised her hands, curled her fingers, and released a wave of magic that threw open the stone doors. The temperature plunged, and Seren spun, her eyes on the water that poured into the courtroom.

Not again, Seren took a breath. *No more swimming.* "What are you doing?" Her voice shook.

Yara giggled. "You'll see."

Seren wasn't sure she wanted to, but her eyes remained fixed on the rising water. Hundreds of creatures flooded the once-empty waves, all worse than anything Seren could have imagined lived in the deepest parts of the sea. Heads bobbed above the currents, their every stare on Seren as they swam toward the dais.

Stumbling back, Seren slipped on the slick stone. *Smack.* Her backside slapped the cold dais, and she flailed, trying to stand, stammering nonsense. "Wha—what the—"

"My children." Nephein's melodic voice rose above the crashing water. "How wonderful it is to see you all again."

The creatures cheered, splashing as they clapped, a cacophony of scales and fins.

"Now," Nephein's voice fell, barring all kindness, "who's ready for some fun?"

Again, screeching erupted from the water, and Seren blinked

rapidly, her eyes darting between the goddesses and their creatures—Kelpies, mermaids, a whole lot of terrifying faces on creatures Seren had never even heard of.

Nephein was well into what felt like a never-ending, ceremonious monologue by the time Seren wrangled her thoughts and emotions enough to focus. "My siblings and I had such high hopes for Clarallan. But we knew the risks of creating such a powerful kingdom, especially my sisters and me. Our brothers didn't care at first, even encouraged the upheaval among the Fae." Nephein's speech mirrored Shaya's, but where rage controlled her sister's words, sorrow carried Nephein's.

Something cracked in Seren's chest—her heart or magic, she wasn't sure. What the Fae had done to the gods' creation was villainous, and what Hellevi planned to do—

Nephein's change in tone jarred Seren. "The Sea is a glorious yet dangerous place, and us, it's protectors." She gestured between her sisters. "We created the Sea Trial in honor of our magic's greatest strengths: control and wisdom." Seren listened intently, focused on any potential points of deception. "To earn our gifts, my sisters and I will each ask you a question. To pass, you must answer all three correctly."

Seren asked, without thinking, "What happens if I don't?"

"Then you stay here. Forever."

Wren gazed up at the sea overhead, her face wrinkled with pleasure. "And those lovely friends of yours, well, let's just hope they can swim better than you."

Her breath hitched. "You wouldn't."

Nephein looked up through her long, dark lashes. "Oh, dear, we certainly would."

"And we'd enjoy it," Wren cut in.

She swallowed, hard.

Nephein's dark skin seemed to sparkle with water. She asked, "Is it a deal, then?"

Seren froze. Deals that involved magic were never a good

idea. And she trusted the goddesses about as much as she thought she could outswim them, and since she still didn't know how to swim—despite her trip to the bottom of the ocean—she didn't trust them at all.

Nephein looked Seren up and down. "Is that a yes?"

Seren didn't have any other choice.

She stared and stared, then finally nodded.

"Very good." Nephein pursed her plump lips and stepped back. "There are two rules: you must answer the questions by yourself, and you must do so in the time given. If you get them all correct, then the Waters will be your final judge, to see if you're truly worthy. Any questions?"

Seren shook her head, a lie, her anxious thoughts a mess.

Yara squealed and skipped over, her steps light as she twirled her lissome body at the front of the dais. She inclined her head to Seren, her eyes a vibrant tourmaline. "I'll go first."

"Okay." Seren took a step, just one. "I'm ready."

Yara giggled and a sweet smile stretched her fair skin, dimpling her cheeks. "You'll have three minutes to think of an answer, and if you need, I can repeat the question once. Understand?"

"Yes." Seren cleared her mind, readied herself the best she could, and listened to Yara's entrancing voice:

"Some find me through violence,
For others, I come naturally,
At times, I seem to favor thy rich,
But my blessing is for all who dare.
I may be used to conquer,
To bring life,
And to kill,
I am fought for and worshiped,
wished upon, and dreamt of
But despite great efforts and beliefs

I cannot be taken,
Nor given.
And only you may decide if you have me."

Yara flashed an innocent smile. "So, Seren, what am I?"

Seren stared, wide-eyed, and doubt pounded in her ears. She hadn't been prepared for a riddle, just a simple question. She asked Yara to repeat herself, and luckily, the riddle was easier to follow the second time.

As Seren replayed her words silently, her gaze caught on Nephein. The goddess lifted her palm, flipped it up and down, and with a spark of blue light there appeared a crystal sandglass, already counting down her fleeting time. But unlike the hourglasses Seren had seen before, when this sand spiraled through the twisted center, it disappeared completely.

Fear kissed her skin and she trembled. Her mind fought against her, her every idea slipping through her head like the sand in Nephein's palm. She racked her brain: Was the answer some kind of wealth? Silver coins or gold? That made sense until the end, because riches could be both taken and given.

She flicked her eyes between Yara and the sandglass. Her heart raced. It was almost half-empty. Her eyes skimmed over the other two sisters. Wren crossed her arms and laughed, but Nephein appeared the opposite of amused, her expression bored, or maybe disappointed.

It had been foolish to believe she could outsmart a goddess, or even be on the same level. She clenched her fists and focused, her mind a blank slate where her thoughts should have been.

If the answer couldn't be wealth, Seren needed other ideas, but every time she thought she had something, she got caught at the end.

Only you may decide if you have me...

Running out of time, she debated between luck and success, but neither fit the riddle well enough.

It felt hopeless.

She had less than a minute to come up with an answer, but at this rate, it appeared she had already lost.

Yara and Wren snickered, and a wave of laughter rolled across the water, carrying all the creatures' mockery as the final grains of sand raced downward.

Nephein stayed silent and her blue eyes seemed to glow.

That's it—Seren squeezed her eyes shut and listened to her magic.

To earn the gods' gifts, she needed to be worthy—her and her magic. But the trials didn't teach Seren about her magic—no, they taught her about herself. Her morality had been tested in Sollian, her bravery beneath the Moons. And if she wanted to prove herself to the goddesses, she had to understand what it meant to master *their* magic.

Their unyielding control.

Their ultimate wisdom.

Her power drummed in her core, and this time when she called, her magic answered. She allowed it to strengthen, to spread, to guide her soul. Then Seren realized that only after she had accepted her magic, had she begun to understand.

Only you may decide if you have me. Magic, courage, strength of heart...

Seren locked eyes with Yara. Her expression flushed with greed, as if starving for just a taste of—

"Power." The word fell from Seren's lips and Yara's face twisted with devastation. Wren whispered something urgently in Nephein's ear, and the crowd gasped. Seren lifted her chin. "I know my answer is right."

"Do you?" Wren snapped.

Nephein lifted a hand and glared at her sister. "She is. Looks like you're up, Wren."

Wren scoffed and said to Seren, "This time, you won't be so lucky."

Nephein rolled her eyes, stepped back, and ushered her sister forward. "Go on."

Wren narrowed her jaded eyes and snarled, "Unlike my sister, I will *not* repeat my question. Got it?" Her voice was arrogant, predatory—like a black widow aching to trap Seren in her impossible web.

Seren forced confidence into her voice. "Got it."

"Very well." Wren wrinkled her thin nose and said to Nephein, "Give her three minutes." Nephein agreed with a wave of her hand, and the sandglass was full once again. Wren sang:

"I indulge in war and thrive in thy,
If you see green, you'll find me,
Get too close and stay forever,
Oh, you'll see, none do it better,
But if you run, I must chase,
Craving more than just a taste.
I want your heart to beat for me,
And your life to waste my enemy...
What am I?"

With Yara's question, Seren had wasted too much time telling herself she wasn't smart enough, that she wasn't worthy.

She wouldn't make the same mistake twice.

This time, she had a plan.

Replaying Wren's sinister song, Seren broke the riddle into four pieces, focusing on the words that caught her attention in the first two lines: indulge, war, and green.

She snorted. Of course, Wren would make it a point to include something about herself. The wicked goddess was full of it, her insuperable ego incomparable to her sisters'.

Then it clicked: *Oh, you'll see, none do it better.*

"Than me," Seren said under her breath and glanced at

Nephein's hand. The glass was still more than half full. She continued, struggling to remember the riddle word for word.

Seren had expected Wren's riddle to be trickier than Yara's, but what she hadn't expected was her biggest problem: there were too many potential answers. Each line seemed to point her in a whole new direction, and it was nearly impossible to understand the riddle all together.

By the time she got to the fourth and final piece, she thought maybe she'd narrowed it down, until the last line: *And your life to waste my enemy.* Now, she had even more questions.

Most importantly, what was the answer's biggest enemy?

She knew if she could figure that out, the answer would be clear. But of all her potential ideas, she had no clue where to start.

Wren flashed Seren a vulpine smile, her head tilted back as she looked down at her.

Seren swallowed. She had to pick an answer and quick. Otherwise—she peeked up and her heart lurched—she wasn't the only one who would face the consequences of her failure.

Quickly, she ran through her list of potentials: green made her think envy, while chase brought her attention to lust, and that's when she realized...

"I know my answer," Seren said, and her confidence caught everyone's attention. The room fell silent, almost unbearably so —the only sound that of her thundering heart. Seren believed she was right, but until she said it out loud, her fear would not let go. There was still a chance she had it all wrong.

Wren tapped a finger against her lips and shook her head, her eyes a sickly shade of green. "So, what am I, Seren?"

Doubt sealed her cracked lips, and she paused, her eyes on the nearly empty glass. The sand raced quicker than her heart, and finally, Seren answered, "You're sin."

"You," Wren snarled. She lunged, her hands raised. "Who do you think you are?"

Seren didn't back down. She had her answer and with it, the courage to face the vulgar goddess with her chin high.

Wren charged her like a starving predator, shut down just before her claws could rip Seren to shreds. Yara gasped, and Nephein demanded, "Enough." There was so much magic in her voice, she cast waves across the crowd.

Nephein walked to the front of the dais, her cold eyes glued to Wren as she waited for her sister to get control. Satisfied Wren would let Seren live for now, Nephein addressed the crowd. "It's been a long time since anyone has made it this far." She tapped a finger against her lips, and asked, "How's tonight been for entertainment?" The water erupted with cheers as the creatures pounded their limbs and wallowed through the waves. "One right answer is luck. Two, maybe chance. But three? That *just* might be worthiness." Nephein pointed a finger at Seren and curled it toward herself.

Seren took a breath—success just one test away.

And she believed she could do it.

Nephein angled her head. "My question is a bit different from my sisters', simpler even." Seren didn't believe that for a second. "Are you ready?" Nephein asked with a half smile.

"How long do I have to answer?"

"One minute." Nephein's eyes softened despite her response.

A nod.

Something unreadable crossed the goddess's face, but it left as quickly as it came. "My question is this: What is the one secret of yours that you have never told, and otherwise would never wish to tell, another living soul?"

Seren blinked slowly, her mouth agape. Sure, Nephein's question was the easiest to understand, but easiest to answer?

Quite the opposite.

Seren bit her lip and darted her eyes nervously to Nephein, the sandglass. It wasn't that she didn't have any secrets, she had plenty, just none that she wanted to confess to the goddesses. She thought about making something up, that if what she was supposed to admit was a secret, then how would they know if her answer was right—but the sisters dealt in wisdom and deception. And there was no chance she could trick a god.

Shameful and embarrassing memories flooded her mind, and half the sand was already gone before Seren started thinking instead of freaking out. The problem was, she told Mare almost everything. Had to. Secrets and problems were never mutually exclusive.

But there was one thing no one knew anything about. Even Mare, since it happened just before they met.

Something Seren had whispered only to the stars, that they were the only witness to.

She closed her eyes and tears welled in her lashes.

"Five seconds," Nephein said, while her sisters muttered their mockery.

Seren blurted, "Okay." Shaking, her words crawled up her throat with a bitter taste. "There is something I've never told anyone." Her gaze fell and she forced herself to look again. She inhaled, crying real tears. "When I was sixteen...I couldn't take it anymore. Anything. Not the king and his punishments, the pain and the loneliness." Her voice trembled but she pushed through. "It felt like I had nobody, and the truth was, I didn't. I was completely alone and given a life that felt created with the sole purpose of destroying me."

Yara wiped her cheeks and even Wren tensed. But Nephein simply watched, her eyes cold.

"Keep going," Nephein said.

"Please—" Seren didn't know if she could bear to say more. She choked, shaking again. "I spent a lot of time crying to the stars, but one night, I'd had enough." The world went silent, and the only thing Seren could hear was the regret in her voice. She whispered, "I picked the king's balcony because it was the highest. I thought I'd feel something standing that high up:

terror, panic, a change of heart. But I just felt empty. And the truth is, I shouldn't be here, but I'm glad I am." Something had saved her that night, and for years she didn't know who to thank. But knowing what Seren knew now, she owed her life to Clarallan.

To her magic.

She fell to her knees under the weight of her realization and started to speak again, but Nephein cut her off.

"That's enough." Nephein took a step and offered her hand. "Stand, sister."

Seren couldn't hold back the sobs that racked her body as she let Nephein wrap her hand in hers and pull. Seren stood and swallowed her shame, patting her cheeks with the back of her hand. Vision blurry, Seren glanced between the goddesses and the crowd, then tilted her head back and closed her eyes.

Disbelief floated through the air, carried by the not-so-quiet murmurs of the sea creatures. But Seren didn't care, too emotionally drained to worry about their opinions of her. Her magic warmed her chest, and she clung to it, willing it to fill the empty space left behind without her secret.

And to her surprise, it did.

She opened her eyes and stared at the goddesses. Despite how she'd expected to feel after her confession, Seren was okay. Better, even. Like the pain she'd let rot her soul had been cleansed. She couldn't believe it.

"A deal is a deal," Nephein hummed.

"I passed?" Seren gasped.

"You did," Nephein said. "What's left is up to the Waters." Seren tilted her head and she clarified, "Just like the trials before, it is not up to only the gods to find your worth." Seren nodded, beginning to understand how everything worked. "The last step to earning your gifts is easy—simply swim to your friends."

Seren's eyes bulged. *Easy? That sounds impossible.*

Before Seren could argue, Nephein waved her hands,

softened a smile, and snapped her fingers. "Good luck, sister. Until we meet again."

Then they were gone. The goddesses. The crowd. Everything besides Seren.

All there was left to do was jump.

CHAPTER 32

Seren gripped the slick railing of the haunting Ocealla ship, retching saltwater from her lungs after telling her friends what happened with the Goddesses of the Sea: the drowning, the riddles, and even the things she couldn't explain when she had leaped from the dais and into the freezing water—only excluding the confession Nephein required to prove her worth, the real reason Seren had been bent over the ship's side for the past ten minutes.

Maybe she would tell them one day, but for now, she couldn't bring herself to say those words again. Even if saying them out loud had cleansed a dark part of her; something she hadn't thought was possible. But she couldn't risk her friends looking at her differently. Not now. Not when they needed her to be strong.

Because there were still two more trials.

And she was still their only hope—a fact that had terrified her, that she hadn't understood. And although she was still as scared as ever, Seren was finally beginning to get it. She tugged on her damp leathers and ran her fingers gingerly over her new burning tattoo: two untamed waves on the verge of crashing, creating a circular pattern that looked almost like two open hands reaching for an embrace. She looked back across the water. *Only you may decide if you have me*, Yara had said in her riddle, the missing piece Seren couldn't find before. For weeks she had been asking why it had to be her, begging others to tell her what only she could answer. Now she realized it was a choice. And with her past and her power, the only choice she had was to fight.

Casimir took slow steps and walked to her side, a damp cloth in his outstretched hand. "Here, this should help."

"Thank you." Seren grabbed the cool cloth without meeting his concerned gaze.

"How're you feeling?"

"Better." Seren dabbed her forehead and watched the water speed beneath them as the ship cut seamlessly across the vast ocean. "Just ready to be on solid ground."

A soft chuckle. "We still have a while."

She glanced sideways, and his tormented gaze forced her to look away. "How long?"

"About a day at this speed," he said, and Seren groaned. "But we're lucky. If we were on a regular ship, it'd take three times that."

Seren winced. She felt cursed with more bad luck than good. But she was alive and had somehow passed another trial, which had to count for something.

When she didn't answer, Casimir offered an open hand. "Come on."

Seren hesitated, then wrapped her clammy hand in his and allowed the prince to lead her across the slippery floorboards toward the Verti. Earlier, she had been too concentrated on trying not to cry or hurl after her ascent from the bottom of the ocean to focus on whatever the guys had tried to tell her. She asked, "Can you tell me again what happened? After I fell overboard."

The guys had explained that when under the goddesses' spell, they could still hear everything that was going on, could feel Seren's panic as she shook and begged them for help. But there had been nothing they could do. It was like they were trapped inside their own bodies, unable to move. It was the goddesses' rarest magic at play, Casimir had explained. The strongest of Ocealla powers were some of the most dangerous in Clarallan: their ability to control water in any form, even that inside someone's body. Luckily, the prince clarified that power hadn't been seen in nearly a century, and for everyone's sake, Seren hoped they never encountered it again.

The prince spoke with a tight jaw, his every muscle tense. "Their spell didn't release us right away, probably to keep us from coming after you." He squeezed her hand and studied her face. "I would've, you know." He glanced at the Verti up ahead. "We all would have."

"I know." Her voice was weak. Maybe she was lucky, because if her friends had been with her, she might not have been able to spill the shattered pieces of her soul to Nephein—fearing how they would look at her after, as if she was truly as broken as she had felt that night on the king's balcony. She swallowed and asked, "Then what happened?"

Casimir led them toward the dry cabin where the Verti waited. "I don't know how much time passed, but I don't think it was long. When the goddesses released us from their spell, you were still gone, but they had returned—promising if you survived the rest of the trial, they'd give us safe passage to Etiamella." The cabin door swung open, and Seren gave a half smile to the Verti. Casimir continued, jerking his chin at Carr. "He tried to jump overboard, and Dax and Rae had to hold him back, because the goddesses threatened if we interfered with the trial at all, you would fail. So again, there was nothing we could do except wait and hope you made it back to us."

"I knew you would," Carr said and patted the seat next to him. "You always do."

Seren's smile grew, and the prince dropped her hand so she could sit with her friend. Over her shoulder she mouthed a thank-you as Cas walked across the small room. It wasn't much, but at least it was dry and not seeing the water made Seren feel a little better. After they got out of Ocealla, if she never saw the sea again, it would still be too soon.

Carr wrapped a heavy arm around her shoulders, and she leaned against his side, thankful for his warmth. She said to everyone, "I'm glad you guys are okay."

Dax shook his head. "I don't think we were ever in real danger. The goddesses didn't come for us."

A shiver prickled her skin remembering what the sisters had implied would happen if she failed their tests, and Carr rubbed his calloused hand up and down her arm. "So, you really bested three goddesses." Carr perked up, and Seren was grateful for the slight change in conversation. "I've said it before, and I'll say it again"—he chuckled—"beauty and brains."

Exhausted, Seren let her cheek rest against his chest, comforted by the steady rhythm of his heart. "You know it," she said, barring her usual attitude.

"You should get some rest." Rae spoke for the first time since they'd entered the cabin, his golden hair a mess. "The ship will take us directly to Etiamella. It won't be long before the next trial."

Seren's stomach churned, and she squeezed her eyes shut. "That's probably a good idea."

"There's a cot over there." Rae pointed to the corner. "I'll see if I can find a blanket."

"Thank you," Seren murmured, too tired to look, her breath caught in Carr's shirt.

"SEREN." Casimir's voice brushed the dark corners of her mind.

"Cas?" she answered, searching her barren dream realm as his voice grew clearer. The prince drifted closer. "What are you doing here?"

"To make sure you're okay." His throat bulged.

"And the real reason is?"

He looked past her, paused, and ran a hand through his curled hair. "I have to tell you something...and I wasn't sure you'd want the others to hear."

Her chest tightened. "What is it?"

Staring down, his expression softened, sincere. "This isn't going to be easy to hear, okay, but I want to tell you, not because I pity you. Quite the opposite, actually."

"Just tell me, Cas." The longer he skipped around whatever he came to say, the more her heart felt like it was going to burst. "Whatever it is, you can tell me."

"Okay." He swallowed. "I didn't tell you everything earlier—about you completing the Sea Trial. Something else happened, and I can't really explain it. That's partially why I didn't tell you, and because I wanted to do it in private."

"Spit it out, Cas."

"You know how I told you about *lunaas*? What it is?"

"Moon-sight." Seren shifted her weight, nervous about where he was going with this.

"Yeah. And you remember how I saw you in the Galaxius, when you were—"

"Dying," she cut him off, and he gave a grim nod.

"Well, it happened again when the goddesses hauled you overboard. I could see you in the water, could feel what you were feeling when you thought you weren't going to make it."

She spoke quietly, "I thought I was going to die."

"Me too." His voice was guttural.

"I'm sorry—"

"Don't apologize." He shook his head. "But that isn't what I came to tell you. Well, it's part of it, I guess. But something else happened, something I've never experienced before. I didn't even know it was possible."

Seren really didn't like the sound of that.

He stretched a hand to her, a question. She took it, and a thrill of energy coursed through her veins. He continued, "Usually the gift of *lunaas* offers just a quick vision, it never lasts long. But this time, something strange happened. It didn't stop, maybe because of the goddesses' spell. I don't know. But I saw everything, right until you jumped back into the ocean."

"Oh." She was going to be sick again. She pulled on his hand, tried to retreat, but the prince held on.

"Seren, it's okay."

She tugged harder, and he released her, tears in her eyes as embarrassment spoiled her insides. "Get out."

"Seren, wait."

She tried again. "Leave." A cry and a plea.

"No," he said, his voice heavy with demand, conviction.

She risked looking at his face and regretted it instantly. His eyes stormed a dark blue, his intense gaze freezing her in place as her vulnerability made her stomach churn. Her throat burned as she fought the violent cries that threatened to escape, and her voice cracked. "How the hell is any of this okay, Cas?"

"Because you're strong—"

"Stop." She wanted to scream. "Please." In that moment, Seren felt anything but strong. Her heart felt like splintered glass, on the verge of cracking beyond repair. Her knees buckled, and she wanted to fall to the ground, for the darkness to consume her and never spit her out. "You don't get it." Her hands were shaky, and she was seconds away from not being able to hold back her sobs.

"But I do." His voice was softer than she thought the unnerving prince capable of. He took a step, watching her carefully as she wrapped her trembling arms around herself.

She forced herself to look up. He took another step, now just a breath away. She blinked quickly, and tears dripped from her lashes, dampened her cheeks, and poured down her neck. "How?"

Darkness sharpened his face, yet sorrow carried his voice. "After I lost my mother and my father got hurt, I wasn't strong enough. I was bitter and angry, and when I hit rock bottom, I was uncontrollable. And with my magic, how powerful it is, I let it consume me, afraid of what I would do to myself if I didn't."

Seren didn't know why he was telling her all of this, but she didn't want him to stop. Afraid that he would, she stayed quiet.

"It was either darkness or pain, and I was done with pain. I never wanted to feel it again, but it's impossible not to hurt unless you feel nothing at all."

Her heart twisted as the prince's words found their home there. She knew what that felt like—to hurt so badly that feeling nothing was the only better option. "Cas—"

He shook his head, his dark hair curtaining his dolorous eyes. "For years, darkness was all I knew. I shut out the light and let wickedness walk at my side. It was easier for a while, freeing, even. I didn't care what I did or what happened to me. It was addicting—the feeling of pure pleasure without fear of consequence."

Seren couldn't stay quiet any longer. "What changed?"

"You," he answered, so quickly the rawness of his confession threatened her balance.

Her words nearly failed her, but she managed to ask, "Why?"

"Because before you, I had never seen anyone faced with so much darkness and still choose the light."

She looked down, and Casimir extended a tentative hand, cupped her chin gently and lifted. What he was saying didn't feel true at all. Not after what she had almost done four years ago, or what she had wanted to do to the king in her nightmare. She wanted to argue, to tell him about the darkest parts of her and help him see how truly broken she was. But she couldn't, because she had already shown him the worst parts of her. First in the Lunaan trial, and then, without even knowing, at the bottom of the sea.

And still, the way he was looking at her, as if she had personally hung all the stars in the sky—with so much emotion in his eyes, it was like she could feel it herself.

He stroked his thumb mindlessly over her teary skin, and her cheeks tingled beneath his touch. "You are so strong, Seren. Despite everything you've been through—or maybe because—you still haven't let your heart turn cold." She leaned into his touch, her magic flaring as he wrapped both arms around her and said, "It's the most beautiful thing I have ever seen."

And despite the fear rallying in her mind, Seren let herself believe him.

CHAPTER 33

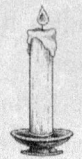

After too many days at sea, Seren could have kissed the ground as she and the others disembarked the Ocealla ship at the Etiamella border, leaving behind the gleaming blue water and salty breeze for blistering heat and a barren wasteland.

Unlike Sollian's warmth, which had brought bliss and life, Etiamella's neared uninhabitable: a desert, dry and parched, its temperatures boiling, and its lands stricken with drought. Only the Etiamella Fae preferred to live in Clarallan's most arid climate, alongside any of the kingdom's most cold-blooded creatures.

"We'll have to walk from here," Rae said, pulling Izzac's journal out of his pack.

Seren wiped sweat from her brow. "How far?"

He flipped to the Etiamella section and angled the map for everyone to see. "It's hard to tell with nothing but sand, but hopefully not too long."

"Yeah, it's already hotter than when Seren kicks your ass." Carr smirked at him. "And that's hot."

Everyone laughed, even Rae. He asked, "Ready?" A few

nods and he marched on, quickening his steps despite the deep sand.

Seren walked with Dax, while Carr and the prince followed up the back, talking quietly, with fits of laughter in between, about something Seren couldn't hear. Smiling, she looked ahead. Over the past few days and after a few near-death experiences, the Verti had slowly begun to accept Casimir. Well, at least Dax and Carr. Rae had yet to drop the tough-guy act completely and avoided the prince as best he could, which Seren figured was at least better than before. But it also meant she hadn't talked to him much the past few days, and it was starting to get old. She missed her friend—the one before they were fighting for their lives.

"How are you doing with all this?" Dax asked after a while.

Seren shrugged. "I'm alive, aren't I?"

Glancing sideways, he gave a half smile. "That's better than the alternative... But seriously, Ser, if you need to slow down, we can. You've been pushing yourself since we left home. No one would judge if you needed a break."

"You know we can't risk waiting." Seren stared ahead, nothing but a tan expanse as far as she could see, blurring on the horizon where the cloudless sky met sandy hills.

"We also can't risk you being exhausted. You have to be at your best for the last two trials. Otherwise—"

"I know, Dax." She softened her voice to make it as comforting as she could. "And thank you, but I'm good, really."

He nodded reluctantly. "But if you're ever not, promise you'll tell me?"

She bumped his shoulder with hers. "I promise."

"Good." He glanced back when Carr's thunderous laughter rumbled across the sand, then asked Seren, "What do you think those two bogans are talking about?"

She snorted, then halted. "Let's ask." Dax shrugged,

following her lead. Seren hollered over her shoulder, "What's so funny back there, guys?"

A devilish smile split Casimir's sunburned lips, and Carr chuckled. "Just guy talk," Carr said. "Trying to get to know the prince and all that."

Seren's eyes narrowed. "Care to let us in on it?"

Casimir shook his head. "Not really."

"Whatever." Seren carped and turned to see Rae quite a bit ahead. She spoke quietly to Dax. "Is he okay?"

Dax cracked his knuckles and his forearms flexed, his vascular olive skin already darker from walking beneath the relentless sun. "I wish I knew."

"What do you know?"

"Not much. I know he's not happy about you know who, but something else is going on. He hasn't said anything, but I've known the guy for years. I can tell when something's up."

"I think we can all tell." She frowned at the sand stirring around her boots. "He's not exactly hiding it awfully well."

"He'll get over it, Ser. He always does."

"I just wish we knew what *it* is, you know? If he talked to us, maybe we could help."

"He will when he's ready. But Rae—he likes to do things on his own."

Seren understood that. She'd spent twenty years saving her own skin. But the Verti had taught her how much easier problems were to carry with friends at her side. They had already saved her more times than she cared to admit, and all she wanted to do was return the favor. "I hate that he's struggling alone."

"He's not alone…and when he's ready to realize that, we'll still be here, ready to help."

Seren exhaled, and a rebellious smile tainted her distressed expression. "How's it feel to always be right?"

Chuckling, he knocked her shoulder playfully. "Goes straight to the head every once in a while." He glanced back and forth between his friends. "But someone's gotta do it, and it isn't going to be either of them."

"You're not wrong about that."

A FEW HOURS had passed by the time the merciless sun reached its peak in the center of the pale blue sky. Seren wiped relentlessly at the sweat beading at her temples and the damp hair on the back of her neck, only for it to return as soon as she removed her hand.

The longer they walked, the quieter they were—saving their mouths' moisture with silence—like someone short on oxygen, too afraid to speak—their tireless perspiration draining enough as they trudged on.

Rae had been right about one thing: it was impossible to tell where they were. Etiamella's deserted landscape appeared infinite, and each sandy hill they summited revealed a horizon identical to the last.

Seren never thought she would want to see the ocean again, but her sandpaper throat and near heatstroke were enough to make her yearn for the cool sea. Holding her hand above her eyes, she scoured the sand and tugged on her magic, but nothing happened. She wasn't sure she could handle walking much longer—something had to budge.

Casimir quickened his pace and brushed past her and Dax, catching up to Rae, while Carr appeared at Seren's side.

Seren licked her cracked lips and asked Carr, "What's going on?"

"I don't know." Carr cleared his hoarse throat. "He didn't say anything, but it must be important."

"I hope so. I can't take this much longer."

"Me neither," Carr groaned.

Seren glanced ahead, her eyes landing on the horizon. She tensed, and the Verti at her sides stiffened too, alert. Flashes of color and movement blurred along the sandy hills, too far away to make out against the haze. She thought she was hallucinating—not too far of a stretch since her brain felt like melted goo.

She pointed. "Do you guys see that?"

Dax and Carr shared a nod.

"What is it?" she asked, ignorantly hoping for a desert oasis with plenty of shade and water.

Carr unsheathed a wide silver sword from the back of his pack. "Nothing good."

Seren's eyes widened, and a shiver twitched at the back of her neck despite the heat.

"Come on," Dax said under his breath, arming himself with a set of sharp knives. Exposed in the desert, it wasn't smart for the Verti to use their shifter magic if they were attacked. Not when they were supposed to be extinct.

Seren grabbed her dagger from her thigh, the hilt hot in her palm after baking in the sun, and hurried after them. "What's going on?" she asked Casimir when the group was together.

"Fall back," Casimir demanded through clenched teeth. "Everyone. Now."

For once, Seren didn't argue, her eyes on the fast-approaching sandstorm carrying sounds of metal and riot. Rae grabbed her hand and tugged, and she followed the Verti's lead, retreating through the thick sand.

It wasn't a hallucination. And it sure wasn't some sort of desert paradise.

Seren's stomach crawled up her scratchy throat, her heart hammering in her chest.

Quickly, everything came into focus. A unit of soldiers, maybe fifty, all dressed in the reddish-brown war leathers of Etiamella, cascaded over the desert hills. Metal swords drummed against handheld shields, the harsh clanks and clangs echoing against their war cries as others raised weapons Seren hadn't even known existed.

An ambush.

Clutching her dagger, her eyes ricocheted between her friends and the enemy troops. "What do we do?" Her voice cracked, a mixture of fear and sand in her throat. "Do we run for it?"

"No." Casimir rushed over, glancing over his shoulder at the soldiers. "We fight."

Seren stared ahead. They were outnumbered and underprepared.

A few daggers and swords. A girl, three Verti males, and a fallen prince.

It was all they had.

"And try not to die," Carr added, a grim joke in the face of real life or death.

In a matter of seconds, the Etiamella troops swarmed the desert before them, creating a battlefield of their homeland. Screams of excitement and violence tore through the dry air, and their feet stirred the sand into chaos.

Casimir separated himself from the group, Dax and Carr following his lead as they put a safe distance between everyone. Too close to each other and they'd be surrounded instantly.

They would never stand a chance.

The warriors cleaved through the deep hills like they were nothing. Seren held her ground, prepared for the first blow. Years of training had made her agile, even in the sand as she spun and hit and spun again. But quickly, her lack of real combat experience became evident through her faulty technique.

There was no time to remember all the drills the Verti had taught her. No time for relief as the soldiers relentlessly rushed their small group.

She reeled, narrowly avoiding a swipe of a blade that would have torn right through her leathers and skin. The soldier rushed her again, his weapon pointed straight at her chest, his snapping yellow teeth barred. Seren jerked to the side and steadied her dagger in her palm, and when the soldier missed his mark again, she lunged, dragging her blade across his neck.

Dark, warm blood spewed across her face as the soldier dropped to the ground. Her stomach lurched as she zeroed in on the next assailant.

She had never killed anything before.

A crack of bone jerked her head to the right. She could fret about the morals of it all later.

Right now, she had to focus. Had to do anything to stay alive.

Her eyes hurt as she stared through the sandstorm. A soldier fell backward, his head twisted at an angle only death could create, with Carr standing above him. Three more soldiers charged, and a lethal grin took over her friend's face.

Seren was certain they didn't stand a chance, but—

Carr dodged, and two soldiers slammed into each other, the force of their attack enough to send them both toppling over. Carr wasted no time, grabbed a third soldier, and wrapped his hands around his neck.

Crack.

Seren shuddered, distracted, as she watched Carr drop the soldier's lifeless body. A blow to her backside sent her staggering forward, and her knees drove into the thick sand as her neck whipped to the side. The taste of iron pooled in her mouth. She rolled onto her back and scrambled to stand, but another hit forced her down again.

Sand burned her eyes as she fought to get away from the soldier, catching sight of his face as she hurled herself back. He laughed at her, his skin slick with blood as he charged, swinging his sword over his shoulder, about to slam the point in her chest—

His head whipped back, sending his body tumbling through the sand. Seren jumped up and scanned the chaos for what saved her life. From a deadly throw, a dagger lodged itself directly into the soldier's skull. Seren gripped the weapon, yanked it from the torn flesh, and turned to see Rae smiling as he gripped another soldier by the shoulders and sent his own sword through his chest.

Seren spit a mouthful of blood. Before she could think about anything, another soldier charged her side.

She lost herself to the killing, each body that dropped easier to bear than the last.

At this point, they were holding their own, but the soldiers kept coming.

And coming.

At least twenty more raced across the open battlefield, the sand littered with blood and gore as the fight worsened.

There were too many left.

Her gaze landed on Casimir, and she shouted a warning, but the prince was already prepared. Unlike the Verti, the Fae prince could use his magic. With a wicked grin and a twist of his wrist, Casimir took down four barreling soldiers, leaving them thrashing and screaming as they clawed at their temples.

Seren steadied her stance as three more soldiers locked onto her, and she focused her eyes on the one in front, different from the rest and not dressed in Etiamella war leathers. Her stomach churned as she recognized his silver armor, her eyes narrowing on the fiery star emblem. He didn't hold a weapon, but his rage was terrifying enough, and her dagger would be useless against his thick metal suit.

Seren whirled, tried to run, but stumbled when her feet dragged through a rough patch of sand that threatened to pull her down. She yelped, struggling for balance, and then the soldier was on her.

He kicked and she fell forward, her back crying in pain. Grabbing her hair, the soldier yanked her head back and threw her to the ground, sending her dagger flying out of reach and the air whooshing from her lungs.

He slammed his fist into her jaw and sharp pain exploded

across her cheek. Blood pounded in her temples, and she heard a crack as her head rolled back, but she forced herself to look through the agony.

Her breath seized as she recognized the soldier.

Standing above her, Prince Evander's cruel face contorted into a sinister smile. "You've been very hard to find, Seren."

"Evander," she spit, her jaw cracking to form the word as blood dripped from her lips.

"The king has been looking for you." His eyes were colorless, the male nearly unrecognizable from the charming prince she had met at Ardentiella. "It's time for you to come with me."

"Never." She ground her teeth, the physical pain enough to shock her back to action. She launched herself at the eldest prince, and her attack caught him by surprise, giving her blow the opportunity to send him scrambling back. She didn't waste any time and threw herself at him again, fighting with everything she had. They struggled in the sand, body on top of body, fists cracking against bone and armor.

With a second to breathe, Seren coughed up a fit of sand and blood, and for the briefest of heartbeats, she searched the battlefield for Casimir. The younger prince stared directly at her, lifeless soldiers at his feet, others launching themselves in his direction. He was faring better than the rest, but her distraction cost him. From the left, a sword tore through the exposed skin of his abdomen, and her blood froze at the sound of sliced flesh.

Seren screamed and fell to her knees, grasping at her side as warm liquid poured over her palms.

"SEREN," Casimir yelled, and the magic in his voice was overwhelming.

Her vision darkened at the edges, and she felt a wave of the prince's anguish crash through her. Her magic surged in response, burning through every limb as an intense, unwavering force ripped through her chest, spreading to every muscle, every nerve as her eyes stayed locked on the prince.

She tried to stand, but Evander wrapped his large hands around her neck from behind and hauled her to her feet, lifting her from the ground. Seren thrashed and fought to send air into her inflamed lungs, but his hold was too tight.

No, no, no.

She couldn't breathe. Could barely see.

Her limbs tingled, and panic gripped her heart tighter than Evander's hands around her neck.

This is it.

She watched Casimir, blood smeared across his tragic face as his gaze landed on his brother. Recognition fueled by a lifetime of hatred distorted his expression, and the sound that exploded as he charged Evander—it would have sent Seren to her knees if she had been standing.

She struggled against the eldest prince, twisting and kicking against his armor, but her blows only caused her more pain.

If she didn't do something—anything—she was going to die.

She was going to fail, and her friends would face the consequences—alone.

It was now or never.

Seren's magic rallied in her chest, stronger than ever as it fought for her life. She had no idea what would happen if she tried to use it, but she knew that if she didn't—

They were all going to die.

Her power burned right beneath her skin, feeling as desperate as she did. She summoned everything she had and let the force of her magic slam against Evander.

He screamed, releasing her. A high-pitched, unnatural sound escaped his lips, and she fell, gasping for air as her vision cleared. Her joints rattled, but she ignored the pain and forced herself to stand, to face him.

Everything was hot. Her magic boiled, and she wasn't sure

she was the one in control. It felt like someone had injected the sun directly into her veins and she was overdosing. She looked down as Evander clutched his hands together, the skin of his palms burned, the smell of fried flesh worse than everything else. Then her gaze caught on her own hands as power surged through her arms.

Red-and-orange flames erupted from her fingertips, and fire coursed over every inch of her exposed skin.

Never had Seren imagined her power could be that strong. The feeling was unlike anything she had ever experienced.

Terrifying. Intoxicating.

Addicting.

She lifted her hands, palms open, ready to blast Evander if he charged again. The male stayed down, fear flashing in his eyes, hands scrambling to drag himself away.

She aimed at his chest, her power demanding to be released.

She could kill him. Wanted to, even.

Her body trembled with raw power; its pure strength swelled around her heart and stole her breath away, constricting her laboring lungs.

A wounded cry whipped her head to the side before she could blast Evander to nothing.

Rae fell to the ground and dark, inky blood gushed from his head, his entire face caked in gore, twisted with agony. A soldier pummeled him relentlessly, then lifted Rae's chin with his sword while its point drew blood from his neck.

Her vision blurred, and a sizzling sensation swirled around her head, picking up a cloud of sand and wind. She closed her eyes and held her balance against her power's momentum.

The battlefield faded away, and her vision went white behind her eyelids.

In seconds, the soldier's sword was in her hands, and as she lifted it higher and higher, the blade glowed a molten orange. Seren plunged its melting tip straight through the soldier's sternum with a burst of smoke. Flesh sizzled, and the sulfurous smell burned her senses as the soldier's body went up in flames. Blood spewed across her face and ashes lathered her skin.

She knelt over Rae.

"Seren," Rae started.

She interrupted. "Are you okay?"

He shrugged, his deft fingers covered in blood as he rubbed his head.

Finally, the surrounding battle lessened. There were too many bodies to count, thrown one on top of the other like waste. Seren blasted away a horde of soldiers that chased Casimir—temporary, but effective—and those left standing all stared at her in terror.

Dax and Carr kept fighting, their backs to one another. Whatever hits they took, they amplified tenfold at the soldiers attacking them. Bodies crumpled to the ground, dead before they even hit the sand. Alone, the two Verti males were weapons. But together, they brought death itself.

The Etiamella soldiers tried to retreat, their weapons clanking as they dropped the extra weight and made a run for it. An uneasy grin stole her face, and she let her magic take over again.

If she was going to put an end to the battle, she would have to give herself over completely.

Grainy whispers floated from the sand, and power itched in her veins. *A fourth conquest comes from the Comets; through fire and mass, destruction and space. A choice to fight, to kill and scar; with passion and suffering, can strength be found.*

Her actions not entirely her own, Seren lifted her hands to the battlefield, power bubbling at her fingertips. Then she just—

Let go.

The sand collapsed beneath the escaping soldiers' feet, and they fell into a cyclone of dust and cries. Screams erupted from the cavernous hole as darkness stole the land's grainy surface.

The remaining soldiers hurried away from the disintegrating expanse as others clung to nothing when sand slipped between their fingers and their lives slipped away.

Wind and sand and magic whirled around Seren's head, ravaging her mind.

Carr whooped triumphantly from afar, pumping his fist in the air as he cheered before throwing another soldier into the pit.

Seren's eyes caught Casimir and her smile jerked away.

The younger prince charged his brother, fists clenched and eyes lit, glowing a ravenous blue.

"CASIMIR," she screamed.

Evander jolted, eyes wide as he tried to run, but Casimir was faster. Seren had never seen the prince like that. His skin prickled with raw silver power, his exposed teeth drowned in blood as he smiled at his brother, like he was going to rip his throat out. Seren took a sharp breath. Given the chance, Casimir would kill him.

She yelled again and her vision went white. "CAS." Her voice was lost to a whirl of wind that pressed against her chest. Her steps staggered, but she caught herself in time.

Looking up, she now stood directly between Casimir and his brother—she would have to freak out over that later—as the former continued to charge. "Stop," she yelled, flames rolling over her skin, and she lifted her hands in case Casimir refused to listen. But he stalled, and Seren said, "We need him."

"Dead." Casimir's voice shook the sand at his feet.

Seren rolled her shoulders and sheathed her magic. The flames sputtered out, as did the heat lathering her skin. Casimir took a step, and she placed a hand on his chest. "We need him alive."

Casimir's face was tragic, heartbreak and rage swirling in his eyes. He stared, unblinking, beautiful even beneath the layers of carnage. Her heart raced and magic pooled in her palm as she held him back.

"He's working with Hellevi. He tried to have my father killed." Casimir snapped his teeth. "He almost killed—"

"I know." Seren stopped him. There were so many things she wanted to say to him, but it would all have to wait. She let her magic out just a little, enough to warm his skin beneath her fingertips. Her magic drummed wildly at the contact, and Casimir stared down at where she touched him, his expression bewildered. "But we need him."

When Seren believed Casimir would no longer launch himself at his brother, she turned, one hand still on his chest as she glared at Evander. "I have a message for the king."

Evander sneered through bloody teeth. "Tell him yourself."

Seren assumed a bored expression. "Very well." She looked away, to her friends watching from afar, the remaining soldiers either dead or retreating, and back to the deadly male at her side. "Have at it, Cas"

Seren released her grip from the prince's chest and Casimir took an imposing step forward.

"Wait," Evander yelled, the stench of fear heavy on his breath.

Seren hesitated, staring at the Verti long enough for Evander's panic to build and Casimir to take another step. She pretended as if she would walk away, to allow Casimir to do his worst.

"Seren." Evander tried again, and she conceded, shrugging over her shoulder as she looked down at the arrogant soldier. She raised her brows and waited. He wasn't worth wasting another breath. "What's the message?" Evander asked, his tone more afraid than he would ever have admitted to.

She spit her words like venom. "You can tell the king to stop chasing me. Because I am coming for him."

CHAPTER 34

Seren toed the sand over the cliff's edge and stared into the pit—the one she had created with a desperate act of magic. She couldn't see the bottom but knew what was down there. The darkness shattered the light-colored land; a void so deep that the soldiers who fell to their deaths now rested in an eternal grave within the kingdom's fiery core.

"Seren." Rae's voice was barely a whisper, careful not to surprise her so close to the edge.

She turned and retreated, her gaze slow to reach his as she looked him over. His bloody face had been wiped clean, but his golden-brown hair still stuck against his forehead in little red curls. Seren had tried cleaning herself off too, but her blood-soaked leathers and stained hands had only smeared the drying gore further across her skin. She couldn't imagine how she looked from his perspective.

"Are you..." It felt silly to ask after everything. "Are you okay?"

"Because of you." His reply was quick and his expression genuine, like he had found her to say exactly that.

Seren looked away, to the carnage, then the pit, the dry sand eagerly soaking up the sickening amounts of blood as life returned to the starving lands. "Because of all of us."

He started to argue, "But you—"

"*Seren...*"

Her head jerked to Rae, her eyebrows tangled as suspicion creased her forehead. "Did you hear that?"

He tilted his chin.

Taking that as a no, she walked closer to the sandy edge.

"What are you doing?" he asked.

She hesitated, shaking her head slightly. "I thought I heard something, but—"

"*Seren.*"

She jolted. "There it was again. You seriously didn't hear that?"

He offered his most obvious look and stepped toward her. "What did you hear?"

"My name."

"Is that all?"

Seren nodded.

"What do you think it is?"

"I don't know." She knelt down and leaned over the pit as far as she could without slipping in the sand. "I think something's down there."

"Do you think a soldier survived?"

Seren shook her head. "I don't think anyone could survive that."

"What's going on?" Carr asked, walking side by side with Dax.

Rae answered first. "Seren's hearing things."

"Oh?" Dax raised a brow. "What kind of things?"

"Voices," Rae said.

"Maybe we should get out of here," Dax suggested. "So you can get some rest."

Carr rubbed the back of his neck. "Yeah, we could all use some of that."

Seren waited to hear the whisper again, but when nothing happened, she pressed her palms to the sunbaked sand and stood, her shoulders drooped. "Maybe you guys are right."

"Always." Dax chuckled. "You said it yourself."

Studying her friends, Seren asked, "Where's Cas?"

Dax pointed at the hazy horizon, where the sun neared its descent. From their distance, Seren never would have guessed the dark figure slumped against the sea of tan was the prince. He faced away from them, his back hunched as he stared in the direction they had sent his brother running.

She had let Evander live for one reason: to give the king a message. She couldn't be sure he would do as told, but it didn't matter. Seren was coming for Hellevi either way. It would be his downfall to underestimate her again.

She took a step and Rae braced a hand across her chest. "Not yet." His eyes softened, but not for the prince. "He needs space. He'll come when he's ready."

"If he's ever ready," Seren muttered, forcing herself to look away. She wanted to go to him, to say something—but what was there to say?

I'm sorry your brother tried to kill us just didn't have the right ring to it. She shook her head, and her eyes caught on something jutting from the sand: a glimmering silver dagger. Taking quick steps, she paused next to a lifeless soldier, his glazed eyes still open, unseeing. She knelt, and her breath hitched as she folded his eyelids closed, his skin warmed by the sun despite the passage of death. Reaching for the familiar weapon, she squinted through tears as her abdomen strained in agony. The smooth hilt was comforting as she wrapped her stiff hands around her dagger and yanked it from the ground, thankful to have found it. Her breath steadied as the weapon fit perfectly in her palm.

THE WEIGHT OF WISHES

Blood pounded in her ears as she stood, stifling the urge to clutch her left side.

"Seren, you better get over here." Rae stared wide-eyed into the void. "Now."

She winced, hurrying back. "What's going on?"

He tipped his chin down, jaw clenched. "Take a look."

Ascending from the bottom of the magical void, from what Seren had imagined was only shadows and death, was an infinite staircase, ashen and cracked. Mouth agape, Seren stuttered. "What the—"

"Hell is that?" Carr finished for her.

Seren trembled, tightening her grip on the dagger. "Where did it come from? And how?"

Rae lifted his hands. "Don't look at us. We didn't do anything."

"Neither did I."

Carr clenched his fists, his skin unusually pale. "Well, you did create *that*."

"The pit, yeah, but not those." Seren looked down. She still had no idea how she had created the pit in the first place.

The wide staircase plunged into the shadows, and small lights floated in the murky darkness, but it was impossible to tell how far down they went.

With cautious steps, she walked to the edge, her magic thrumming in her veins—the same intense beat from when she stood before the gods. "I think it has something to do with the trial."

"Really?" Rae perked up. "How do you know?"

"My magic," Seren said, bending down to study the stairs. "It always feels the same and stronger than ever, as if it's searching for something."

Upon a closer look, what Seren had thought was ancient

stone appeared to be bone. The bones of what, she really didn't want to know. She reached for the top stair, her hands tingling, when Casimir spoke. She jerked, her heart racing as she nearly lost her balance.

"I wouldn't touch that if I were you."

Too late.

Her fingers brushed the rough bone and gold light sparked at the tips. "Why?" she asked, sand in her leathers as she pushed away from the edge, panicked, and stared at the prince. She scrambled to stand. "Do you know where it leads?"

"If I had to guess, Vulkan's fallen kingdom."

The God of Comets, better known as the God of Fire and Death.

Before Seren could say anything else, a voice flew from the ancient darkness, grating and immoral, followed by the thunderous echoes of heavy steps. "Death has brought me a gift today."

Seren's chest ached against her pounding heart and tight breath.

Rae reached for her. "We should run."

"No." She forced her breathing to calm and stepped in front of her friends. "I have to do this."

"What if it's not Vulkan?" Casimir asked.

"Oh, but it is."

Despite her gaping mouth, it wasn't Seren who answered, her tongue tied in knots of fear as her eyes landed on the god. His tall, pointed ears, like those of a fox, sat atop an unusually long face split by a sinister sneer that made him appear all the more bestial.

"Vulkan…" Casimir blinked slowly. Seren had never seen the prince so surprised.

At least a head taller than the tense males at her sides, the god stepped forward, his power stirring the sand as he struck the bottom of his skeletal spear into the ground. "It's been ages since I've been impressed."

Seren held her ground, too afraid to look anywhere besides at Vulkan, his dark eyes as red as the richest of faerie wine.

"But you..." He pointed the tip of his spear at her chest and shook his head. "I didn't believe my siblings at first, always so sensitive. But it appears this time, they were right."

"Right about what?" Casimir asked when Seren couldn't find her words.

Vulkan stared only at her, his breath hot on her skin. "Centuries have gone since anyone has passed the Etiamella trial, or even attempted it. My dear sisters of the sea love to steal the show, rigging their tests near impossible with their asinine riddles and siren tricks. I always argued that my trial should be first." Vulkan grinned, revealing jagged gold canines. "After all, power means nothing if those who hold it are not strong enough to fight for it."

Seren paled. "You mean the ambush—that was you?"

"The king's troops were already on your heels." His eyes flashed. "I just used the situation to my advantage."

A shiver of fear slickened her skin, and she clenched damp palms into fists. "Why?" Her anger bubbled. "It almost killed us."

Vulkan cracked out a harsh laugh. "Oh, dear, that was the point. The Comet's gifts are too dangerous for just anyone to earn, and my siblings warned me about you—how strong you already are. It appears Clarallan has gifted you a great deal of power. And, well, I couldn't throw any test your way. My trial had to ensure that you were strong enough to truly deserve them."

Seren didn't really mean to ask, "And did it?" Between Izzac's research and Casimir's studies, she knew how dangerous Etiamella magic could be—the ability to control land, fire, and so much else she didn't yet understand. But that was why, decades ago, Hellevi had allied himself with King Dearil—wanted his warriors' strength on his side when waging a war.

Vulkan paused, tapped clawed fingertips along the edge of his ancient weapon, then finally—when Seren thought she couldn't take the silence any longer—a nod. "Yes, child. You passed."

"How?" She risked a glance at her friends, their expressions fixed with disbelief.

Vulkan explained, his rough voice like sand, "Anyone can fight, and anyone who makes it to the fourth trial is clearly strong, at least of mind. But not many can or will fight when their chances are as good as none. And you did."

Seren paled. "I don't understand."

"I couldn't risk walking you into the trial, not when I needed to know the truth about your power—how deep it already runs—and what is truly in your heart. Explaining my test would have prevented all that. I needed to see what you were capable of when you didn't know you were being tested."

"Why?" Seren asked, her thoughts a mess of triumph and angst.

Wrapping a hand around his spear, Vulkan lifted the weapon. "Because true strength comes from those who do the right thing, even when they believe no one is watching." His eyes burned, and before he struck his spear into the sand and disappeared into the pit, he said, "And you, Seren, you just might be strong enough to save us all."

CHAPTER 35

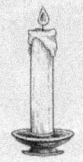

"Seren, this is fucking nuts." Carr frowned, placing his large, shaky hands on her waist. "There's no way this will work."

"It already did." She rolled her eyes. "Now just hold on and stop complaining." Wrapping herself around Carr's wide chest, Seren tugged on her magic and warmth spread from her core to her fingertips. Then she closed her eyes and envisioned the Lunaan castle—the one place safe enough to rest before traveling to Stellean.

Carr had suggested going back to the inn, but considering how far it was, it would waste too much time, and no one had a better idea than Casimir's offer of his home. Rae had been the only one to argue, opposed to staying in the home of the prince who had just tried to kill them. *It's not his home anymore,* Casimir had said, assuring everyone that Evander would never be welcomed back to the Lunaan court. Not just because of the attack, but because of the attempt on their father's life.

When Casimir swore there was nothing he wouldn't do to stop his brother, Seren had believed him—and that confirmed their decision to travel to his home.

She steeled her confidence and spoke to herself. *Just like before.*

The familiar whirl of air spun around their heads as Seren's vision went white at the edges. It felt like their bodies turned to smoke as they watched the desolate land of Etiamella fade into a blur.

It had all made sense after Vulkan declared Seren passed the fourth trial.

The fire. The pit. Her ability to *levis*, as Casimir had explained after the fact—Etiamella's rarest power: to have such control over land and mass, to be capable of traveling through air. In the battle for their lives, it had been the only reason Seren had been able to save her friends. And now, Seren used the same magic to take everyone back to the Lunaan court.

Her power called to the swirling galaxies as they flew through time and space before landing abruptly on the hard ground with a thud.

That's going to take a lot of practice.

Wincing, Seren pulled herself from the pile of shaking limbs belonging to her and Carr; the male's weight too much for Seren to hold up alone. She stood, groaning, while Carr still squeezed his eyes tightly together. She chuckled, using her booted foot to toe the dramatic male's shoulder. "Carr, you can open your eyes. We made it."

Carr cracked one eye open at a time and asked, "It worked?" A nod, and the arms he'd wrapped around himself sprang to his sides as he jumped up—a hint of embarrassment tainting his flushed face. "It actually worked," Carr said again.

Seren bristled playfully at his disbelief as Carr's gaze barreled around the castle room. "Told you it would."

"Are you sure we're in the right place?"

Seren shook her head, amused, and the prince appeared as if on cue.

Casimir leaned against the doorway and said with a tight-lipped smile, "Welcome to my court."

Seren responded with a smile of her own, and her eyes bounced between Casimir and Carr. "I'll be right back with the others."

"You're tired, Ser." Casimir's gaze devoured her from head to toe, pausing just long enough on her side that Seren worried he knew the truth. But when his gaze met hers again, all the prince added was, "Be careful, okay?"

"Always," she said, drawing on her power once more, which waned dangerously low from the number of times she had already magically traveled between the two courts. Not helped by the fact that a few of her injuries from the battle refused to heal. But she couldn't worry about that yet and wrote it off as exhaustion. She knew she was expending more magic than she probably should, but she had to keep pushing, even as her body struggled to keep up.

Only one trial remained between her and stopping the king for good.

SEREN LANDED in a flurry of sand and aches, her body taking the toll of her heart's relentless fight to keep going, despite the pain that exploded at her side. She stood, shaking her limbs to empty the buckets of sand trapped beneath her leathers, and looked to Dax and Rae. "Who's next?"

"You're up." Rae urged Dax forward, then asked, "You doing okay, Ser?"

"I'll be better when I know we're all safe."

"Good luck," Rae answered slowly, his fingers twitching.

"Thank you." She smiled and wrapped her throbbing arms around Dax's leaner figure. Her magic grew easier and easier to understand, but her well was running dry. She desperately needed to get everyone to the Lunaan court before it drained completely.

Unfortunately, the time Seren had to spend resting between the two courts grew; she needed longer breaks to ensure that she was strong enough to travel, especially with someone else.

Landing in Etiamella for the last time, Seren poorly estimated the location with her magic. She tumbled through the rough sand, exhaustion hauling her sore body down the deep hill. Reoriented, she searched the vast desert for Rae; he was just a few hundred yards off and already walking toward her.

Her every muscle cried out by the time she landed in the Lunaan court with Rae. She braced her hand against his shoulder for balance, grateful she had gotten everyone safely to the court before her magic ran out. She was certain another trip would not end well. The spinning in her head lessened slightly, but her vision remained dark around the edges. She rolled her stiff shoulders, then pulled on and cracked her joints until her achy limbs felt loose enough to use. "Is everyone okay?" Her attention flickered between the four males.

Everyone exchanged quick glances, and Casimir said, "We're on my personal floor of the Lunaan castle, and I sent the guards away. The whole place should be empty, save for us."

Seren exhaled, relieved.

"And are you okay?" Rae asked, his hand placed gently on her arm.

Her lips curved upward in a tight smile as she clutched her hand against her left side. "Just tired."

The chance they believed her was small, but it was still worth a shot.

Casimir's jaw ticked. "I can show you all to your rooms. Everyone should get some rest before dinner."

"Do we really have time for any of this?" Seren kept her voice neutral despite the frustration budding in her throat. Yeah, they needed to rest, but she needed to complete the final trial more.

"You have to be at your best for the fifth trial. Our only chance of stopping the war is if we go in prepared." Dax, always so logical. "And right now..." He gave her a sorry look and shook his head. "Let's just say we could all use a few days to catch up."

Even Rae nodded in agreement, and for him to be willing to stay in Lunaan meant it was the right thing to do. Seren could only hope that nothing got too bad while they played pretend in the castle.

As if Hellevi wasn't a step away, breathing down their necks. Seren flinched, remembering the king's last words: *"I'm going to kill you, Seren."*

Casimir's voice caught her attention. "There's nothing we can do right now, anyway. We still need to eat, to sleep. Might as well do it here, where we know we're safe." He walked to the door, his sure steps telling her that he would not take no for an answer.

She glanced between her friends. One by one, everyone turned to follow the prince, Seren the last out the door, a slight hitch in her step as she tried to cover the urge to limp.

The entire hall was well lit, with crescent chandeliers illuminating the rich colors and elegant artwork. But really, everything was art. The murals covering the walls depicted such abstract realms, Seren wondered if they were even real, while floating lights bounced between the silver chandeliers, each a different phase of the moon. Even the stone floors were littered with carvings of a glorious night sky.

"These two rooms are open." Casimir pointed at the first two doors on the left, both nearly ten feet tall, made from a deep mahogany wood, and accented with hints of navy and silver. He led them quickly to the other end of his chambers, over the silver floors, and gestured to two more rooms on the right. "These are free as well."

The prince said little else, his tour limited to only the rooms they would stay in. But Seren wondered what was behind the other doors, wishing they could linger a while longer to fully appreciate the pure grandiosity of the Lunaan Castle.

At the end of the hall, they faced a wide set of double doors with two silver handles that met in the center: each side half of a moon that, when closed, joined to create one in full. Casimir stared numbly for a moment, and Seren wondered how long it had been since he'd called the castle home. He blinked softly. "This is my room if any of you need me. You're welcome to pick and choose where you all stay."

"Thank you," Seren murmured, lost in her own thoughts as she tried to understand his.

"Let's meet here in a couple hours. We can go to town for dinner." Casimir nodded a brief command, disappearing behind the colossal doors before anyone could say another word.

She caught a glimpse of the prince's private room right before the doors clicked shut, and her heart raced.

"Town?" Rae asked.

Carr slapped a tired hand across his friend's back. "Sounds good to me. I could eat just about anything right now. And I've heard Lunaan has some of the best food in Clarallan—everything caught fresh from the eastern sea."

Seren agreed, her stomach growling at Carr's words. It had been too long since they had been lucky enough to get a full meal, and weeks on the road made her miss Rae's cooking, maybe more than anything else. Plus, an innocent part of her couldn't turn down the chance to explore more of the Lunaan court.

The four of them spoke quietly before going their separate ways, too exhausted to say much. Eventually, Seren and Rae chose the two rooms closest to them, while Carr and Dax took the first two at the far end. As the others slipped into their rooms, Seren and Rae stood in silence, each pretending to look at the gorgeous art.

Seren rocked back and forth on stiff legs, her eyes darting to the nearest door handle. Tension was a knot in her throat that kept the words she wanted to say silent. "I guess I'll see you soon." Her voice was quieter than she expected.

Rae's gaze lifted, his mouth slightly agape, unmoving, his expression distorted with whatever he wanted to say. But he only shook his head, eyes following hers as she reached for the door. "Get some rest, Ser."

"You too, Rae." Quickly, she slipped inside her room, and the temperature cooled her flushed skin. A welcome reprieve from the awkwardness of being with the Verti in an enemy's home.

With wide eyes, Seren studied the decadent guest room, larger even than the entire first floor of Rae's home. It held a bed that could have fit ten people if needed, and a plush white rug that led to the silver bed frame. And above, the ceiling was painted with a rich mural of a dark night sky against a ravenous cliff side, cascading to a stormy ocean. A crescent moon hung delicately against the dark background, illuminating a strong figure leaning precariously over the rocky edge, one breath away from falling.

It was at once one of the most beautiful and tragic pieces of art Seren had ever seen, and she made a mental note to ask Casimir about it, given the chance—where it came from and who the artist was. Maybe even what it meant to him. Granted, it was a guest room, so it was possible he just liked it. He might not have even decorated his chambers himself.

Seren studied the intricacies of the mural for a while, unable to make out the male's identity, until her burning side demanded her attention. Casting one last glance at the shadows, her breath caught at the sight of two whimsical silhouettes stretched across the cliff's surface.

Wings.

Feathered and alluring, and jaw-dropping in size, their tips reached yards away from the silhouette of the vehement figure. The awe they inspired within her transformed into something harrowing, her mind cast in a blanket of questions and doubts as she walked away from the gripping art.

As she searched for the washroom, her attention caught on the far side of the room, where clear glass doors covered the wall from floor to the ceiling; they slid open to reveal a narrow balcony that looked out on the breathtaking court, at least ten stories below. A cool breeze floated upward, carrying the sounds of the city's teeming nightlife and casting her skin in goosebumps.

Clutching her hand to her side, Seren checked the two other doors. The closest led to an empty walk-in closet, while the second opened to a striking bathing chamber, the entire far side dominated by a marble tub meant for more than just one body. She washed her filthy hands before touching anything and avoided glancing at the spotless mirror; she waited until the water in the sink was no longer a pool of mud and red before reaching for the tub's golden faucet.

While the water warmed, she pulled off her filthy leathers—entirely saturated by a nauseating amount of dry blood—careful as the stiff material clung to her tender flesh and stretched her open wounds. Steam quickly filled the bathroom, and Seren was grateful for the warm fog that hid her grim reflection. She glanced down at her battered body instead, thankful that most of her injuries had begun to heal as her magic slowly replenished itself. Her skin was littered with blue-and-yellow bruises that gradually replaced her open wounds.

Seren lowered herself into the hot tub, and her body tensed as scalding water met her tender skin. Cursing, she lifted her abdomen out quickly and darted her gaze to her left side.

A bloody gash, showing no signs of healing, exposed split

muscle and torn skin from the bottom of her ribs to the top of her stomach. "Dammit," she swore again, pushing her body beneath the water once more, allowing the heat to numb the pain.

Her body screamed in agony as she gently scrubbed her skin, careful to avoid contact with her side. When she was as clean as she was going to get, she hauled her resistant body from the tub and dried off slowly, then she found the courage to clear the steam from the full-length mirror. Holding her breath, she glanced down, hoping her side had started to heal like the rest of her, when her gaze caught on the glowing ink of her newest tattoo: a fiery comet centered directly on her sternum, beneath the waves.

Bracing herself to look at the mess of blood and wounds that graced her skin, she forced her gaze to her side. "That can't be good," Seren whispered, despite being alone. The wound no longer festered, but her frayed skin still hung open, red with agitation and dribbling blood. With a desperate idea, she hovered shaky hands above her side and closed her eyes, drawing on her Sollian magic. Warmth pooled in her palms, and she urged the Sun's gift to speed up the healing process. Her fingertips tingled as she felt her magic blossom, and she tried to imagine her skin stitching itself back together. But the harder she tried, the stronger her magic resisted, its warmth dissipating in her palms as she squeezed her side. Cracking her eyes open, Seren bit down on her bottom lip and stared at her reflection.

Her chin dipped, and she fought back tears of disappointment.

It didn't work.

"But why?" Seren asked no one and reached for a small hand towel, placing it delicately over the gash before grabbing the soft robe that hung nearby. If her magic was as strong as everyone said, she should have been able to heal herself, unless there was something she still didn't understand. Vulkan said she might be worthy of saving Clarallan, but given how she felt in this moment, his words sounded like nothing but false promises.

Exhausted, she took slow steps to the welcoming bed, tucked herself beneath the weighted blankets, and as tears dampened her cheeks, fell asleep hoping a quick rest would help her body heal. Seren didn't remember when her unconscious took over, easing her worried mind. It was the kind of sleep that resembled death: no tosses or turns, and certainly no dreams. And when the time came, she was surprised to wake up at all. Rubbing the sleep from her eyes, Seren panicked first at the sight of the unfamiliar room, then inhaled slowly.

The Lunaan court.

When her nerves finally calmed, she noticed something that hadn't been there when she fell asleep. Draped along the edge of the bed was a fresh set of simple clothes, placed next to a new set of leathers that looked exactly like her old ones. Seren didn't care as much that someone had come into her room. What really bothered her was that it hadn't woken her up.

Hauling her aching body into the cold air, Seren decided to don the set of simple clothes to hide her stubborn wound: a silky pair of warm black pants, perfect for the cool Lunaan night, topped with a creamy golden sweater that was so soft it was likely intended for sleep, but was the only thing that didn't rub against her tender skin.

By the time she got dressed, the view outside her balcony displayed the brilliant night sky hanging above the lively city. Soft music filtered through the open glass doors, harmonizing with cracks of laughter as citizens filled the bright streets below.

Before leaving, Seren threw on the dark blue coat to combat the breeze, then slipped into the empty hall, grateful that at least some of her pain had subsided. A few minutes passed before the others eventually joined her; Casimir was the last to emerge, but by his flawless appearance, Seren understood why.

The tall, intense male was dressed in firmly pressed navy

pants and a carelessly unbuttoned white top, exposing his fair, tattooed chest—leaving little to the imagination. Seren had to drag her eyes away from his decorated bare skin and check to make sure her jaw wasn't on the floor for everyone to see. His eyes sparkled when she finally met his gaze; he'd definitely noticed the amount of time it took for her eyes to reach his face.

Flustered, Seren resorted to her typical humor—insults. With one brow raised, she asked, "You all really took longer than a girl to get ready, huh? And only to appear looking like that?"

Everyone chuckled, including Rae, and Seren smiled watching them all get along.

"Come on, Ser, you never know when you'll bump into a pretty lady." Carr winked. "Always have to be prepared."

Rolling her eyes, Seren feigned disappointment, then glanced again at the prince. His expression was hungry as he watched her and Carr throw insults back and forth—and if she was right, it wasn't because they were heading to dinner.

"This way." Casimir motioned down the hall, allowing everyone to take the lead. He waited until Seren was the last to step forward before following, his breath warm on the back of her neck as he leaned close to her ear, and whispered so only she could hear. "You're a terrible liar."

"What did I lie about?"

Casimir's voice made the hair on the back of her neck bristle. "I saw how you looked at me. There's no point in denying it."

Over her shoulder, Seren narrowed her eyes. "And how exactly did I look at you?"

He shrugged, a slight smirk tilting his pink lips. "Your words might say one thing, but your eyes another."

Asshole.

Seren quickened her pace, catching up to the Verti to escape the arrogant prince, with the intensity of his stare warm on her back, wandering slowly down her backside, as she walked away.

The dark blue coat she wore was suddenly way too hot, its

cinched waist nearly claustrophobic against the rapid beat of her heart. Seren stopped herself from glaring back at him, from mouthing the vulgar names she thought suited him perfectly in that moment, refusing to give the prince the satisfaction of knowing how he got under her skin.

Even if he already knew.

He brushed past her, and goosebumps took off on Seren's skin at Casimir's touch as he directed the group down the seemingly endless hallways toward a set of steep stone stairs that eventually opened to the vibrant and wide city street beyond.

Pale moonlight illuminated the lustrous and alive town center, bordered on both sides by pubs and restaurants and shops. The clean street was overwhelmingly full of Lunaan citizens seeking company and pleasure. Laughter littered the streets from all angles, the clanks of glasses in tune with the genuine delight of the city. Carelessly, Fae of various statuses pressed by, unhurried as they bumped into the prince and the Verti. Some were dressed in suits and poofy skirts, their flamboyance glistening beneath the soft moonlight, while some wore fighting leathers and others simple garb designed for work and service. A casual air floated through the streets as everyone meandered by, too caught up in their conversations and nights out to worry about the time or people they passed. Delicate live music played somewhere in the distance, the hum of handcrafted instruments floating through the patter of drunken steps against cobblestone streets.

At once, Seren felt both overwhelmed and excited to be submerged in the city's culture, to laugh and enjoy herself with her friends. Holding back her guilt, Seren reminded herself there was nothing they could do about the war tonight. The only thing required of her was to rest and experience the glorious court.

The colorful city was located directly in the heart of the court, its revelrous center beaming beneath the towering silver castle, bordered by cliffsides and forests as water snaked between the illogical architecture, racing toward the salty sea.

Seren stuck close to Casimir as he followed a bend in the narrow street; the turn revealed more dancing and laughter, the cobblestones filled with patios of well-fed and drunken citizens, unconcerned despite the war that brewed beyond their borders and the attack just days before. But based on appearance, the city had fared well regardless of the descent of Hellevi's troops. *It's about fear, not violence*, was what Izzac had written in his letter, and from the looks of the court, he had fortunately been right. Its citizens bereft of fear, despair, or grievance was a good sign.

When they left Etiamella, the attack was the main reason she had taken Casimir to Lunaan first. He had wanted to check on his father and witness firsthand the destruction of his people. She waited over an hour before returning with the Verti males, giving Casimir enough time to handle things before adding guests to his plate. But from what little Casimir had said, most of the damage had been washed from the streets before the prince even returned home.

If Seren hadn't known better, she never would have guessed that Lunaan had suffered an attack at all.

Seren watched Casimir as he beheld his city, his people. He normally wore an ignorant expression to support his reputation as the rebellious, uncaring prince, but Seren could see through it. She didn't claim to know how he felt, but a hint of relief seemed to wash over the guilt that clawed at the ashamed prince since he had first learned about Hellevi's troops. Guilt that Seren guessed had taken root long before the attack.

Casimir would never admit to it…

But he was a pretty bad liar too.

The prince glanced back and Seren looked away, then he guided the group to the front doors of a cozy stone building with open windows and a patio decorated with fire pits, flickering lights twisted through the waist-high, metal fence—both quaint and comfortable, and not the place Seren thought a prince would favor. But she figured maybe that was the exact reason why he picked it.

Casimir smiled and the gesture made Seren's heart warm. "After you," he said, opening the front door.

A beautiful Fae host welcomed Casimir and directed their group to a room in the back corner, far away from the other guests' frivolous conversations, and out of earshot of potential eavesdroppers and gossips. The golden room was empty save for the long wooden table set with five comfortable chairs. The host beamed a wide smile, bright against her tan skin and fiery hair, then grabbed the prince by his shoulders and pecked a joyful kiss on his cheek before seating them, with not even a greeting or recognition for Seren and the others. "It's good to see you again," she said.

Casimir half-smiled before she flitted away. "You as well, Kirra."

"See, Ser, I told you." Carr waggled his brows, then said to Cas, "She's a real beaut."

Seren shoved his shoulder a bit harder than she planned, then took a seat across from the prince next to her vexing friend. "Have I ever told you not every thought needs to be shared?"

Carr laughed. "I always speak my mind. It's what you love about me, isn't it?"

"Sure," Seren groused, glancing across the long oak table.

"Don't worry, Ser. You're still the prettiest in my mind."

"Uh-huh." Seren forced herself to look up and chuckled. "Too little, too late, Carr."

Carr flashed puppy-dog eyes, and worn by such an intimidating warrior, the expression was almost comical. "Does that mean I can't stay in your room tonight?"

Seren's laughter grew, and she couldn't help but smile. "Never gonna happen, pal."

Frowning, Carr started again but was interrupted as Kirra

neared the table, hands full of trays with colorful drinks and tasters. She didn't offer anyone the chance to order, simply discussed with Casimir how she would bring out nothing but the best for him and his friends.

Carr lifted his second glass, having downed the first before Seren could even reach for her water, and cheered. "A toast—to making it out alive."

Rae lifted his drink. "To stopping a war."

Taking turns clinking their glasses and echoing "cheers," Dax added, "To one last trial."

Casimir turned last, his sculpted face soft as he spoke quietly. "To Seren."

"To Seren," the Verti said in unison.

Seren bit back a grimace, lifted her glass, and clinked her drink against Casimir's. His lips curved upward in a genuine smile, and her heart swelled as the darkness disappeared from his eyes. "Cheers, Cas."

CHAPTER 36

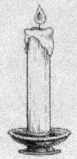

"Maybe you should slow down," Seren said to Carr as he rubbed his stomach and took a few deep breaths. The dining table was overflowing with empty plates, stacked precariously near the edge, waiting to be replaced by not seconds or thirds, but fourths, and even fifths for the insatiable males. For over an hour, their conversations had been limited to grumbles and moans and the occasional comment about how incredible the Lunaan dishes were. Seren wondered how the guys could put away so much food, and how it seemingly went directly to their biceps and somehow still-chiseled abs.

Chuckling, Carr slid another plate in front of her.

It was delicious, all of it was. But Seren couldn't handle stuffing herself any further, queasy just at the thought of more food after so many days of eating small snacks on the road; anymore of the royal meal, and Seren was sure it would put her to sleep for days.

She folded her napkin, propped her elbows on the table, and smiled, sliding the plate back to him.

"More for me, then," Carr said, tossing another honey-baked biscuit into his mouth.

"Do you ever get full?" she asked.

He shrugged, washing down the full bite with a swig of aged faerie wine, and Dax answered for him with a snort, "Not since I've known him."

"Seems about right." Seren giggled. Their conversation continued as Casimir explained why the restaurant was his favorite. Carr gave Casimir's words ample support by adding that the food was some of the best he'd ever had, foolishly taunting Rae when he said Rae could learn a thing or two about cooking from the Lunaan court.

Seren stifled a wince. *Not his smartest move.* Her thought proved right by Rae's uncomfortable silence as they cleared their plates and Kirra returned to ask about dessert. After the prince ordered for the table, Seren knew she was running out of time to talk over what she'd been worrying about all night.

Her full meal turned to lead in her stomach.

She didn't want to ruin their fun, but ever since the battle in Etiamella, Seren had known what she had to do. Waiting for a pause in conversation, her voice wavered as she drew her friends' attention and blurted, "I think it's time for everyone to go home."

Smooth, Ser, way to ease into it.

"There's no need to rush, it's not that late," Casimir said, leaning back in his chair.

Carr stopped mid-chew, his fork raised halfway to his mouth. "Plus, we haven't even had dessert yet. I bet it's incredible."

Casimir lifted his glass of water. "It is."

She hadn't been very clear. "No, no…" she started, unable to spit it out before her courage faltered. "I'm not talking about right now, I mean…before we go to Stellean." She let her voice die off as her friends' confused expressions stole her words.

Rae angled his chin to the side. "We can't give up just yet,

Ser, not when we're so close. Why would you even suggest that?"

Shaking her head, her thoughts and emotions tumbled. "What I mean is...I'm not giving up." She lowered her eyes to the table. "I want to go alone. The battle in Etiamella nearly killed us." She continued, forcing her nervous gaze up to give the guys—her best friends—the respect they deserved. "I can't risk that happening again. Not with you guys. It's too dangerous for everyone to go."

Silence.

So heavy, Seren could hear the audible gulp as Carr swallowed his last bite and the clinks of metal as the others dropped their silverware on their half-eaten plates, their appetites rotten.

"Have you completely lost it?" Carr asked.

"Let's think this through," Dax cut in. "You say it's too dangerous for us to come with, but imagine how dangerous that makes it for you to go alone."

"I know, but—"

Rae interrupted, his tone a mixture of confusion and demand. "Seren, we're not letting you go alone."

"It's not up to you to *let* me do anything," she said, regretting the bite in her voice as she watched hurt flash across Rae's face. "I'm sorry... But it's my choice." Rae prepared to argue, but Seren continued, pointing at him. "You're the one who told me that, remember? Before we even started. Don't take that away now."

She wanted—no, needed to go alone to face the king. It was something she had to do for herself and for the entire kingdom of Clarallan. Her friends were her biggest weakness, a dangerous distraction. The thought of them in danger, especially against Hellevi... The Lunaan trial seared her mind, and Seren flinched at the thought of what the king was capable of.

Caring about them made her vulnerable, because if it came

down to it, she would give anything to save them, and Clarallan needed her more than she wanted them at her side.

"And it's our choice to stay," Rae said, his voice void of the emotion that stirred in his eyes.

"Yeah, Ser." Carr managed a thin smile. "We want to help."

"I know." She closed her eyes and rubbed her face against her resting hands. "But if I'm too late, if I fail and I can't stop the king...then you guys have to be prepared for what happens after. Your people will need you to keep fighting, to save them from the horrors of the war."

"Don't talk like that." Casimir clenched his glass and Seren thought she heard a crack. "You're..." He shook his head. "We're not going to fail."

Seren spoke with her hands. "But what if I do?" She had yet to voice her fears before, hadn't given them the power to exist outside of her mind. But now that she had breathed them to life—her emotions were overwhelming. "You can't swear that I'll succeed. And you can't promise all of you will be safe, and everything will be okay."

"Seren..." Carr tried wrapping an arm around her shoulder, but she shook him away.

"I can't lose any of you." Her voice cracked as she held back angry tears. "I can't."

"She's right," Casimir said, and Seren swore she saw claws as Rae clenched and loosened his fists before shoving his hands beneath the table. "We're fighting a war. There are no promises. No guarantees."

Seren stared at the prince and in return felt the intensity of the Vertis' eyes as Casimir continued, "We would be foolish to only consider the outcome we want, to not be prepared if we lose." Casimir looked at the others. "As warriors, I thought you all would know that."

Rae bristled, but ignored the prince's jab and spoke only to her. "We're not leaving you."

"You have to," Seren pleaded. "The Verti need you." She waved her hand among her friends. "The entire kingdom will need you to keep fighting if I fail. We can't let Hellevi win."

"We won't." Carr puffed up, and her heart broke at the unwavering faith of her best friends.

But she needed them to understand—begged them to face reality.

"I'll go." Dax leaned back, arms crossed. "I'll warn our people so the rest of you can stay."

Carr's head snapped to his best friend, his brother, and something flashed across the warrior's face that Seren had never seen so prominent there before.

Fear.

"I won't let you go alone." Carr shook his head, his dreads curtaining his molten eyes and tight jaw. "I'll come with you."

Dax nodded, his expression taut with a grim smile.

Rae demanded, "It's settled, then."

"No." Seren stared at Rae, her haunted eyes begging him to understand. "Go with them… Please."

"I have to go with you." Rae's scarred arms flexed as he clenched his fists tighter. "You'd have to lock me up and throw away the key to even try to get me to not come with you."

"Don't give her any ideas," Carr said, the only one capable of making a joke out of such a dire situation. Seren's face lifted envisioning the scenario, and he added, "She's a wicked one, you know. She might just do exactly that."

Rae shook his head slowly. "Please, Seren."

"Fine," she forced out. At least Dax and Carr would return home. With them, the Verti would still have a fighting chance, and Rae—she figured locking him up was always an option if it came down to it. "But I swear, Rae—"

"It'll be okay."

"You better hope so."

THE WEIGHT OF WISHES

AFTER SEREN'S ANNOUNCEMENT, they didn't stay long enough to enjoy dessert. The prince paid for their meals and thanked Kirra when she wrapped a few sweets for them to go, then led the group in silence to the castle. What was supposed to be a relaxing night, was now ruined by her betrayal.

Deep down, she knew it was the right thing to do. But somehow, a small part of her still questioned whether she had made the right call.

Walking through the radiant city, Seren couldn't bring herself to enjoy Lunaan's magic, the life it had represented now just a dismal reminder of how quickly it could all disappear.

No one said a word as they entered the castle. Even when they reached their rooms—nothing but awkward silence.

Seren hesitated in front of her door, opened her mouth to say something, but the males all kept their heads low, their eyes lost as they closed their own doors without looking back. Alone, she stood outside her room for longer than she planned, her forehead pressed against the cool wood as she waited to catch her breath over her rising panic.

She hadn't meant for their night to end like this.

Her words hurt them more than she thought possible.

Her decision more powerful than she ever imagined it would be.

When she finally went inside her room, she threw her jacket on the floor and kicked off her boots; the metal lock latching shut was the only other sound besides her strained heartbeat. Dropping her exhausted body into the massive bed, she rolled herself beneath the covers and let their heavy weight drown her beneath false comfort, her chest tight as she stifled the urge to cry.

Sleep evaded her as she lay on her side, staring at the pool of white moonlight that flooded the silver floor. Her body was slick with sweat, shaking despite the unbearable heat and stress, even as a gust of cool wind blew through the open glass doors. She squeezed her eyes shut, blood pounding in her ears, and raked her hands through her tangled hair, pulling hard to try and relieve the pain that coursed through her temples.

Nothing worked.

She sat up, sucked in a burning breath, and peeled herself from beneath the damp blankets, her sticky sweater clinging to her still-unhealed wound stinging at her side. Her breath caught as she stood, and lightheadedness filled her mind.

That needs to heal. And soon.

Shoving away her body's pleas to crawl back under the covers, she walked on bare feet over the cool stone tiles to the door, moonlight her guide through the darkness as her thoughts wandered rebelliously.

She stood, unmoving, then wrapped her hand around the silver crescent handle and paused.

Would he be upset if she bothered him so late? Would he even be awake? It was the middle of the night after all, and with how they left things after dinner…

Doubt froze her in place until eventually her desire to talk to him, or even just see him, took control.

The lock clicked, and Seren did her best to open the door quietly. Her hands flew to cover her mouth, stopping a surprised yelp from escaping as she lifted her eyes to the hallway.

The hallway she had expected to be empty.

CHAPTER 37

Seren's heart lurched at the sight of Rae, standing with his head down, wearing only a soft pair of black sweats that hung perilously low. His dirty blond hair curled carelessly over his eyes, covering a hint of purple circles that blossomed above his sharp cheekbones and emphasized his old red scar. Her gaze crawled over his bare skin, noting the frantic rhythm of his tanned chest as it rose and fell in time with her racing heart.

Lifting his gaze, his golden-brown eyes glittered against the darkness.

How long has he been standing there? And why *is he standing there?*

"Rae?" Seren gulped, forcing air into her tight chest, her expression molded into surprise as she tried to hide the hint of disappointment that stung her heart. "What are you doing?"

Equally shocked to see her, Rae's voice was coarse, heavy with sleep. "Seren, I…I wanted to talk to you." He pushed his fists into his pockets. "I don't like how we left things at dinner."

Blinking slowly, her breath steadied with her easing heartbeat, and she angled her gaze away from his intensity. "I'm sorry about that. It was my fault. I didn't mean for it to go that way."

"I know you didn't." Rae looked past her. "Can I come in?"

"Yeah, of course." She took a step back and held her breath as he slipped through the narrow space between her and the door, then she eased it shut, closing her eyes for a heartbeat before turning to face him. But when she looked again, Rae had already walked through the room and onto the open balcony. Trailing after him, she forced her mind to focus on the quiet patter of her bare feet instead of her faltering heart, beating with disappointment.

The brisk night air spread goosebumps over her slick skin as she leaned her crossed arms against the thin metal railing and peered across the court, her long hair twirling around her red face in the salty breeze.

They stood far above the city, watching the spirited sea collide with the cliffs, and vulnerability crashed over her, her thoughts on how beautiful the view was with a little risk.

A stiff, full silence enveloped them. So much had happened since the last time the two of them were alone together. Too many words, both spoken and left inside.

She didn't even know where to start.

Slowly, she turned her head, her cheek resting on the back of her hand. "I'm sorry, Rae."

"I'm sorry," he blurted at the same time.

She chuckled. "I guess we both have things to apologize for."

"Indeed." Rae looked away, his forearms taut as he rested against the rail, close enough that Seren could feel the heat of his torment against her bare skin.

Time passed over them in silence, each reflecting on the tragic events that led them to this point. Seren wasn't sure how long they sat like that, but it was long enough that when Rae spoke again, she jolted.

"Things have been weird between us," he said quietly.

That's an understatement. But Seren kept that to herself.

He continued, "Ever since Lunaan, maybe before, even. And I know you probably think it's just some stupid, jealous male thing about me not liking the prince, but it's more than that." His voice lowered. "So much more than that."

"What is it then?"

"I'm afraid." He stumbled over his confession. "If you can believe it." But Seren knew the tough male didn't say those words often, especially when he didn't mean it.

There were infinite reasons to be terrified, but Seren asked anyway, "Why? What are you so afraid of?"

He raised his hand and drew back the pieces of curly hair that had fallen across his eyes. "My people have lived in fear for centuries because of the Fae and their senseless violence. To ask us to work alongside one of their kind to stop a war of their making? It's hard, Seren. And it's nothing personal, but I don't trust the prince… And I'm not sure that I ever will."

"Casimir's different. He's not like the others."

"I knew you would say that. But how can you trust him?" Rae's voice sharpened with a lifetime of hate. "You don't even know him."

"He's on our side, Rae. You know I wouldn't trust him unless I truly believed that." Seren tried to soften Rae's rage, to direct the conversation away from the prince and back toward them and the reason they were doing all of this. "Plus, we need all the help we can get."

Rae derided her excuses. "And yet you wanted to send us all home? Despite everything we have done for you, with you—you wanted to pack us up and ship us off under some sorry excuse of safety."

"I need you guys to be safe. Don't you know how badly I need that?"

"But you never said that he couldn't go with." Rae's eyes

were as wild as his wind-blown hair. "You don't know how much that hurt."

But his words hurt too. More than he would ever know. The only reason she wanted them to go home was for everyone to be safe, because she cared about them too much. "I don't want anyone to get hurt because of me," Seren said breathlessly, focused on the night sky and constant, blinking stars intertwined with the shadows of the many moons while she caught her breath. "Can't you see that?"

"People get hurt all the time. You can't control that."

Seren stepped back. "But I can." It felt like she was pounding her emotions against an immovable wall. "If all of you went home, you'd be safe. Even if I failed. It's the safest choice."

"Is there not more to life than playing it safe?" Frustration spilled from his lips. "And even if there's not, it's a stupid choice. Because for how long?" He paused. "Say you do fail—how long until Hellevi destroys every last court in his war? How long until he finds my people and destroys them too? You might think you're protecting us, but it's only temporary. And if you failed because you were alone, when maybe I could have done something… That would hurt more than anything."

Seren couldn't bear to look at him. The intensity of his words, his pain—begging her to agree.

He added, "The only way to keep anyone from getting hurt is to stop this war before it truly starts."

She tore her eyes from the calm night sky and sucked in a sharp breath as she looked at him and the untamable emotion that ravaged his face. The night breeze suddenly cool against her cheeks. She rubbed her hands against her skin and found it damp as tears of frustration and fear that threatened her lashes won. Her voice choked, and she closed her eyes before admitting, "I'm scared too."

"I know." His words sounded at once like understanding and an apology.

Then they were silent again, studying the stars, while Seren let her tears fall.

She asked, her tone unsure, "Why are you doing all this?"

"Why are you?"

"You know why, Rae. To stop Hellevi from hurting anyone else." There was more to it, but he knew that already. That Seren never wanted anyone to hurt the way she had. "But seriously, why?"

"I've spent years fighting against the Fae's cruelty. I think, after spending my entire life trying to protect my people from the bad, that it has become all that I know."

Seren understood. Her life had been one tragedy after another until she met the Verti and they showed her what life could really be.

"But there's a comfort in that, when darkness is all you know. Because when more bad things happen, it's easier to adjust to more darkness, because there isn't any light left to lose."

They stared at each other, sharing breath within the close space between them.

"That's why I'm scared," he said, stepping closer. "But it's also why I'm risking everything for this. Because for the first time in a while, I have something I don't want to lose." His fingers grazed hers, and Seren instantly forgot about the cool night air whispering against her now burning skin.

Seren wanted to hear him say it. "And what's that?"

He traced his fingers over her arms to the delicate skin of her face, his eyes tracking the movement as he stalled. His voice was low, warm and genuine as he whispered after an uncertain pause. "You." His touch was patient, asking, as his hands glided to cup her chin. But for what was happening between them, Seren didn't have the answer. He stared at her, the pad of his thumb drawing gentle circles against her red cheek, his face thoughtful and almost entirely too honest.

For weeks, Seren had thought about this moment. What it

would be like to cross the line of their friendship with daring touch.

With his lips on hers.

But now that it was happening? Rae leaned in and captured her mouth with his—right as she decided.

His lips were soft as they moved hungrily over hers, his free hand tangled in her wavy hair. For a second, Seren nearly convinced herself it was what she wanted. Because she had, for weeks, she had wanted to know what it would be like to kiss the first male that made her feel good about herself. That had grown to be so important to her, that cared for her in ways no one ever had before.

But as his lips pressed deeper, she knew it wasn't right.

She stepped back quickly, her feet tangling together as she jerked her head away. New tears flooded her cheeks and she shook her head, her dark hair graciously hiding her face as she muttered over and over, "I'm sorry."

"Seren, I—"

She risked glancing up and instantly regretted it. The look on his face could have brought her to her knees if her body wasn't trembling so severely. She opened and closed her mouth, searching for a better answer. But there was nothing she could say to fix this.

Rae's face twisted, his tone sharp as he asked, "When you opened the door, before you saw me, where were you going?" His change in conversation forced her back.

"What do you mean?" she asked, Rae's expression deluged with an emotion she couldn't place.

"Where were you going?" His words dripped with a threatening tone that chilled Seren to her core. "Who were you going to find?"

She couldn't lie, but she didn't want to speak the truth.

"Tell me, Seren. You owe me that." She trembled, and he accused, "You were going to him, weren't you?"

Seren hesitated long enough that Rae took it as proof he was right.

"I can't believe that," he said in disgust and stepped toward the metal railing. "I can't believe *you*."

"Rae..." Seren kept her voice soft, low, as if she were cornered by a predator.

"Don't," he bit out through clenched teeth as a muscle ticked in his jaw, his sadness transformed to anger. His golden-brown eyes boiled a dark brown before he whipped his head to the side, half-hysterical, his arms flexing as he gripped the thin metal.

Seren wiped her eyes with open palms and took a step forward.

Crack.

The dark metal bent beneath Rae's hands, his Verti strength exploding from the raw emotion that surged through him.

Seren's blood froze at the sight. She stood still, torn between sorrow and fear, unable to move. She wanted to run—to him and apologize, but also as far away as she could from the friend who was now completely unrecognizable.

His head jerked, his stare piercing.

"Leave," Seren choked, her voice not entirely her own.

"Seren—"

She jolted at the sharpness of his tone.

Rae's eyes simmered and he blinked slowly, their golden-brown cracking through his dark torment as his voice softened. "Please, Ser. I'm sorry."

She took a step back. She couldn't stand to face the hurt and regret on his face, not when her own threatened her wavering heart.

"Let's talk about this."

Holding her ground, she forced a trembling arm to point to

the door, her voice more demanding this time. "Leave." When Rae didn't move, she wanted to shout. "Get out. Now."

Her words fell into the tense silence. Rae took another step as he tried to catch her gaze, his eyes returned to normal, and he lifted an arm toward her, then stopped. His hand fell to his side, and his fists slackened as he looked down. Then, keeping his eyes on the floor, he walked back into the room.

Seren stood on the balcony until she heard the slide and click of the heavy front door. And even then, she remained still.

The night air dropped dramatically in temperature and she couldn't control the shaking that ravaged her limbs—from the cold, but more from the pain—her red skin raised as she stood alone. She reached for the railing, needing something sturdy amidst the upside-down world into which she'd just been tossed. Tracing her fingers over the splintered metal, tears threatened to spill once more.

But this time, she shut them down.

No more crying.

No more wasted tears.

The urge to scream was an excruciating sensation that stirred in her chest and climbed up her throat, scratchy against her dry mouth, an overwhelming feeling that she couldn't ignore.

All her pent-up sadness, rage, and fear spilled out, released in such an animalistic sound that even the balcony shook beneath her cries. Never had she let herself scream like that—even when Hellevi exacted his worst—too afraid of how weak it would make her feel.

It was cathartic.

At any second, she expected Rae to rush back, ready to fight whoever made her cry out, to kill the monster that forced such a tortured scream out of her.

But unless he cut his own fists on the glass of his shattered reflection, there was no one else for him to fight.

She was alone.

No Rae. No monster.

Surrounded only by her own heart-shaking emotions that had grown so strong, it felt like they could live outside of her body. She kicked and punched and clawed at the empty air, her body overtaken by every nasty thing that needed to escape her system.

But the weight of her soul remained unbearable. So many appalling memories stitched into the sensitive muscles of her heart. She didn't know how anyone believed in her. Not when her sadness was sewn so deeply into her skin, exposed for everyone to see. She didn't believe there was any way her friends could look at her and not see the mess she was.

Shaking and slick with sweat, she slumped her drained body against the cool railing, pressed her head into her hands, and rested them firmly against her propped knees as she willed herself not to fall apart.

A hazy amount of time passed while she pulled herself together. Seconds, minutes, hours. The stars watched over her the whole time, their sparkling comfort the only witness to her breakdown.

Her eyes were nearly crusted shut from the dried remnants of her sobs when she finally gazed at the night sky—the pieces of her just strong enough to face souls beyond her own.

"I know it's been awhile..." Her voice scratched against her raw throat, void of moisture after she had rung every last bit out with her screams. "But this is really hard. Harder than I ever could've imagined."

Seren let her voice float toward the silent night sky. For as long as she could remember, the blinking stars were the best listeners. The only souls she could always talk to. The only ones that would never leave.

"I don't know if you heard all that." Seren shook her head, a hint of embarrassment tainting her tone despite being alone. "Though you probably see everything." She paused. "Well, I could really use some help. And I know it's mad to ask, and honestly, I'm not even sure anyone is listening, but if someone is...Clarallan, if you are, now would be the time to let me know."

She knew, if anyone could see her then, how broken she looked. The crying and screaming. The fighting. Talking to herself.

"Because I'm lost. And I thought I knew what I was doing, but I don't. So, if something could just give me a sign, I'd really appreciate it."

She didn't know what she expected to happen, but ultimately, nothing did.

She stood staring at the stars, the beautiful city, refusing to lose sight of why she was fighting so hard—why she was risking so much—when a golden flame flashed through the darkness: a shooting star with so much light she could almost feel its warmth in her chest as she took a deep breath.

She waited until the heat dulled, unable to stop herself from shivering as her magic dimmed to a low spark and she gave in to her begging mind. She needed sleep, to rest and to heal. She couldn't face anyone this way—not the final trial, and especially not the king.

It would take everything she had to succeed.

And sometimes, standing on the edge was the only way to live.

CHAPTER 38

The next day, Casimir stalked quietly toward Seren's room, focused on his mother's artwork lining the long halls, glancing at each painting. His guilt lowered his eyes, remembering how much of it he had destroyed after her death. Back then, everything had been too painful of a reminder, and his rage had bested him—too young, impulsive, and angry to realize the regret he would create for himself years later.

"Seren. You up?" He knocked on the door. Then again. And again. His impatience growing with each raised fist. "Come on. Open up already."

It wasn't like her to sleep in so late, especially considering she had made him swear at dinner to meet early that morning to go over the plan for the final trial. At first, the prince didn't know whether he should bother her—he was grateful she was finally getting some rest. But after a few hours had passed, he couldn't shake the urge to go check on her.

Rapping his knuckles against the door once more, he exclaimed, "I hope you're decent because I'm coming in." He twisted the cool handle and pushed the door open. "You know, I was being polite by knocking, princely even, but it's time to get up. We were supposed to meet hours ago."

Still no answer. Not even a chuckle.

Casimir loudly closed the door and marched to the bed, his eyes adjusting slowly to the dark room. Every light was off, and the curtains were drawn across the glass doors, blocking out the bright spring day. He glanced at the bathroom, but that too was dark and empty.

"I think sometimes you forget who I am," he grumbled under his breath and pulled the thick curtains away, muttering a bit more about oversleeping and annoying inconveniences. "Really, Seren, this is getting ridiculous." He ran his fingers through the tangled ends of his hair—that desperately needed some attention soon—and stared at the bed.

A mess of heavy blankets were piled and wrapped suffocatingly around a small, unmoving lump in the center. He gripped the corner of the largest quilt, and without hiding even a sliver of his irritation, he asked, "Are you actually going to make me do this?"

With her silence as confirmation, Casimir heaved the sweaty blanket to the end of the bed and exposed Seren, who was astonishingly still curled up and quiet.

"Gods, you're a heavy sleeper," he groaned, wrinkling his nose when a putrid smell rose from the disheveled sheets. He forced himself not to physically cover his nose and mouth as he leaned down and gently nudged her shoulder. When she still didn't move, he conceded to shaking her slightly, rolling her to her back as he said her name over and over.

Still, her eyes remained plastered shut, sunken in above dark purple rings that painted her pale cheeks. Her skin was flushed white and sticky beneath his touch, and a cold sweat covered her from head to toe despite the feverish heat radiating from her body.

"Seren," he said, his tone demanding. "Seren, wake up."

Panic threatened his throat and raised his voice, his magic surging as he shook her. He placed two fingers near the base of her jaw and hovered his other hand over her lips, his breath hitching before he whispered, "Thank the gods."

Weak, warm air floated to his palm, and he exhaled, his fear subsiding slightly. His magic called out to him, his every nerve lit with anxious energy as he placed a firm hand on her forehead, then allowed the faintest of power to ebb from his fingertips and seep into her skin. He watched her chest rise and fall quicker than before, her heartbeat fluttering in response to his healing magic.

Urging his magic to strengthen, he held his breath as silver light flickered across her skin, scouring her body for ailments, working quickly until silver tendrils clustered intensely over her left side. He pulled at the soaked cream sweater and cursed at the sight. The source of the smell: a fleshy gash that consumed her entire side, frayed at the edges where her skin refused to heal. "Dammit, Seren."

Casimir stilled, eyes wide as his magic flickered up her chest and down her back.

Not only did her body refuse to heal, but her wound was spreading dangerously fast, infection eating away quicker than his magic could even begin to help.

"Okay. Fuck." He paced the length of the bed and raked trembling hands through his hair. "Hold on, okay—I'm going to get help."

He barged from her room, his thunderous steps echoing through the corridor while he searched for the Verti. He pounded his fists against Rae's door first, shouting as he stomped down the hall, nearly breaking into a sprint as he shouted the guys' names. Tearing the skin across his knuckles as he beat on their doors. "DAX. CARR."

He yelled, surprised by the crack in his voice, "Get out here.

Now." His head spun, his attention caught by the click of Rae's lock.

"What's going on?" Rae demanded, standing in the doorway.

Casimir was in front of him in a heartbeat, the others on his heels as they registered the commotion. "Something is wrong with Seren."

Rae's eyes darkened and he clenched his fists at his side. Slamming his door, the scent of fear on his breath, he asked, "Where is she?"

"Come on." Casimir opened the door to Seren's room, the Verti right behind him, tense and prepared for whatever threat they were imagining as worst-case scenarios swarmed their minds. This time, the putrid smell was so strong their eyes watered instantly; the air saturated by the scent of rot. He said, "Seren and I were supposed to meet this morning. When she didn't show, I thought she was just sleeping in. But then I got worried…" He hurried to the bedside. "I found her like this."

Rae shoved past the prince and raced to Seren's side.

Carr took slow steps. "What's wrong with her?" Bunching his fists in the wrinkled sheets, he leaned over her pallid body.

Casimir shook his head, and Rae jerked his gaze to him, his voice laced with hatred. "What did you do to her?"

"I told you." He took a deep breath. "I found her like this."

Rae looked ready to rip his throat out, then reluctantly reverted his attention back to Seren, shaking her as he sat on the edge of the mattress. "Seren, wake up."

Casimir didn't care to hide his anger. "Don't you think I tried that already?" He slid between the others and reached for her sweater. "Look at this."

"What the fuck are you doing?" Rae barked, his hand wrapped firmly around Casimir's wrist.

"Easy." Casimir glared, his forearm taunt beneath Rae's clawed grasp, then peeled the soiled sweater from her chest. "Just look."

Carr gasped, his eyes landing on the bruised and bloodied wound devouring Seren's torso.

"It's getting worse. It wasn't this bad a few minutes ago."

Dax stilled. "Why isn't she healing?"

"Why didn't she tell us she was hurt?" Rae's gaze never left her face. "We could have helped her."

"She probably expected it to heal." Casimir fought the crack in his voice. "Or knew if she told us, we would have made her wait even longer before going to Stellean."

Carr took a step back. "Dammit, Seren."

The same ferocious warrior Casimir had seen take down tens of Lunaan soldiers alone, then even worse soldiers in Etiamella, now looked like he was going to be sick to his stomach. For the first time, Casimir realized just how much the Verti truly cared for their friend. Because despite the horrors the prince suspected the Verti had lived through, the sight of Seren—weak, ghastly, and vulnerable—was enough to terrify them all.

Rae wrapped a hand over Seren's small one, and Dax suggested, "We should find a healer." His dark eyes lifted to meet Casimir's. "You must know some of the best here, right?"

"I already tried." Casimir couldn't stand to meet their eyes. "My magic couldn't heal her."

Rae stood quicker than Casimir could react. The prince stumbled a step back, caught off guard when Rae slammed two heavy blows into his chest and shouted, "A real healer, you bastard! For all we know, you're the reason this happened. I don't trust you." Casimir stiffened at the sound of Rae's snapping teeth. "It was your brother who attacked us, after all." Rae moved to throw another punch. "Are you working with him?"

Dax and Carr were on Rae before he could attack the prince again, their arms wrapped around their friend to protect him from himself. Casimir's power surged at the accusation. Begged to be released. To show this foolish male exactly who he was messing with. Trust went both ways, and it appeared the bond between them was instead made of hate and suspicion. But Casimir conceded, exhaling slowly. He forced his magic to cool, and fortunately, it obeyed. Just enough to where it remained poised and prepared right beneath his flesh—a viper ready to spring if taunted again.

"Rae, we get it, we do. But now is not the time to tear each other apart." Carr kept his voice calm, tightened his grip around Rae's arm, and emphasized, "Seren needs us." He looked to the prince. "All of us. We can't lose our heads now."

Rae relaxed at the sound of her name; Seren, the anchor in the storm of his untamable emotions. Shaking off his friends' worried fists, Rae returned to Seren's side, shooting a dismissive glare over his shoulder with a huff.

Their fight was far from over.

His rebellious power stirred at the threat, and Casimir argued against his magic. But Carr was right. Seren needed them, now more than ever, and they couldn't help her if they ripped each other's throats out in the process. He could place his feelings aside long enough to help her, and he only hoped Rae could do the same. Seren would never forgive him if he killed her friend. Even if Rae was entirely deplorable. Casimir smoothed the wrinkles from his shirt and sharp expression and extended a branch of truce. "I'll find a real healer. There's a woman who checks in on my father from time to time. She's the best there is. She'll know what to do."

He turned sharply, not waiting to hear the Verti's response. If he was lucky, the woman would still be in the Lunaan court. She had come immediately when she got word of the assassination attempt on King Egil, then spent a few weeks ensuring his well-being.

Casimir turned at the end of the hall and sprinted up a swirling staircase, taking two, even three, steps at a time. When he reached the top, four elite Lunaan guards bowed their heads and let him slip into his father's chambers without question. His gaze locked solely on the massive doors dominating the end of the silver corridor.

For a second, he listened for any signs of company before he barged in, the heavy doors slamming shut behind him. King Egil's eyes snapped up from where he lay in the center of his bed, his skin flushed pale, almost violet, tucked beneath the heavy indigo quilt that likely now weighed even more than his ill father.

A sickly smile spread over his dry lips. "Son."

Casimir forced a grim smile. He didn't hate his father. Had even looked up to him more than anyone else in all of Clarallan prior to Quinlan's death. But a small part of the prince blamed the king for not saving her, and a larger part of him hated himself for feeling that way. His father loved Quinlan. More than Casimir had ever seen anyone love another in his entire life.

But it still wasn't enough.

"Father." Casimir approached him, his eyes scanning the room. His heart strained as he glanced at the painting that hung above the bed frame: a self-portrait his mother had finished just weeks before her death. She was the only person who had ever truly loved him for him. Yes, his father cared, loved him even. But deep down, Casimir knew it was because of his magic, the reason why Egil wanted him to be the next king. But Quinlan— she'd loved him simply because he lived.

So not only had he disappointed his mother by not being able to save her, he'd also disappointed his father for swearing off the crown after her death.

A true familial disappointment, Casimir huffed silently.

Liquid iron flooded his mouth from biting the inside of his cheeks, and shame caught in the back of his raw throat. His scowl deepened, and he refocused on why he had come to see his father in the first place. "I'm looking for the healer that was here yesterday. Where is she?"

Disappointment soured Egil's face. His eyes glanced down as he said, "Unfortunately, you just missed her. She left this morning."

Guilt bit at Casimir. He knew he should have visited his father more often, but each time he reached the top of the stairs, he turned around before the guards could even catch sight of him. Too ashamed to hear how disappointed his father was in his decisions over the years. He asked quickly, "Do you know where she went?"

Egil shook his head, stiff and slow. "She said something terrible had happened. That she was needed immediately."

Casimir placed a tense hand on the wooden frame. "Did she say where she was going?"

"No, son," Egil said, his breathing rough. "What happened?" He coughed, glancing up. "Why do you need her?"

Casimir looked at his father, truly looked for maybe the first time in years. The king's pale blue eyes—once a vibrant blue, before his magic was broken in the attack that left him so sick—sat deep above his sunken cheekbones. The same attack had killed Casimir's mother—their carriage ambushed by Fae rebels when the princes were children. Now his father's frail frame consisted of nothing but wrinkled skin and bones. With such little strength, it was impossible to keep muscle on his failing body. "It's nothing to worry about, father. Just get some rest." Casimir retreated a few steps. "I'm sorry, but I have to go."

"Casimir, wait."

Reluctantly, the prince shifted his weight and glanced back at the once powerful king—now constrained solely to his castle. Waiting, he lifted his expression.

"You know you can tell me anything." Egil's words were slow, forced out between coughs and deep breaths, as he gasped at the effort it took to keep air in his weak lungs. "Even this, whatever this is. Let me help, son."

Casimir tipped his chin, one side of his mouth curved up in a thin smile. "It's okay, Father. Get some rest."

Without looking back, Casimir marched from his father's room, not slowing down until he left the king's chambers far behind. His mind swirled with a lifetime of things he had kept hidden to protect his father, certain that even the best of his secrets would send the king to an early grave.

Cyclical questions consumed his focus as he raced back to Seren's room: Where was the healer? And if something terrible had happened, was it best to just find someone else? But who else did he know?

Back in his chambers, Casimir rounded a corner and ran chest first into Dax.

Groaning, Dax rubbed his sternum. "I was just coming to find you." He gestured to Seren's room. "The healer you sent thinks she knows what's wrong with Ser. We figured you'd want to hear."

"The healer?" Casimir went cold.

Dax twisted his head. "The woman you went to find? She showed up a little after you left—said she was sent to help. She knows Seren. We've met her before actually."

Without thinking, Casimir shot forward, accidentally shoving Dax in the process.

"Wait up," Dax hollered. "What's wrong?"

Casimir's voice shook the paintings on the walls. "I didn't send any healer."

Dax was on his heels as Casimir slammed into Seren's room, his panic rising to compete with the prince's anger.

Casimir launched himself to the edge of the bed, prepared to rip the head off anyone who dared lay a finger on Seren without his permission. He stopped himself as his recognition flared, just before he could shred the stranger in front of them. "You…" Casimir's voice was an intersection of relief and rage—the predator he could normally keep hidden, lurking just beneath his skin, its bloodthirst heavy on his breath.

"My favorite Child of the Moon. How nice of you to finally join us," the small woman cooed, ignoring the fact that Casimir had just wanted to kill her.

"I thought you were gone. My father said you left this morning. That you were needed because something terrible had happened."

"Not a lie, dear child." Prue's eyes fell over Seren's still body, her palms hovered over the spreading wound. If Casimir had to guess, it was sadness that tainted her usually melodic tone. "Something terrible has happened."

"Can you help her?" Rae asked, sitting at the end of the bed; not hiding the urgency that engulfed his words.

Prue shook her head, her jet-black hair twirling all the way to her hips. "No," she said, crumbling the last bit of hope that floated in the tense air. "I'm no healer."

"But—" Casimir started, and the Verti exchanged a confused look before turning their anger to the prince.

"I'm just a Seer," Prue said, a little too calmly.

"My father introduced you to me as his healer. Why?"

"Not all that is broken is visible." Prue stared at the prince.

"If you can't help, then why are you here?" Casimir's voice was jarring, the full force of his status and power raging behind his words. "You should know I don't take kindly to those who waste my time."

Prue waggled a small finger. "I didn't say I couldn't help. I might not be able to heal her physical injuries, but if I can get a look at how they happened, then maybe I can tell you how to save her."

"We already know how it happened—a fight at the last trial. Now she's dying and we need to do something now." Casimir ground his teeth, and for a second, the Verti actually looked nervous.

"Patience has never been your strong suit, has it, child?"

Casimir bared a wicked smile. "Don't act like you know everything about me."

"Oh, but I do. A Seer knows all, even about you," Prue nearly sang. "My magic reveals to me, the trials a key, I grow stronger each and every day."

"Can we get on with it already?" Rae asked, agitated, the others nodding their hasty agreement.

Prue's violet eyes gleamed at the prince before she returned her attention to Seren. She lifted her spindly hands above Seren's left side, her eyes glossed over as she called on her magic. A dense veil of gray magic shielded her hands from sight. Like the smoke of a raging forest fire, her magic spread quickly. Gray tendrils flicked toward the wound, like flames licking desperately at oxygen, as her magic searched for some unknown answers.

Sounds of war came to life, erupting from the smoke. Metal crashing against metal, cutting through flesh. Cries of death and fear.

Casimir's blood chilled as the Seer relived the battle that had nearly gotten them all killed. He ground his teeth, and the hair on his arms rose. He didn't want to think about the trial, about his brother. About Evander's final act of betrayal after tormenting the younger prince for years.

Prue's head snapped back, her eyes rolling, exposing their whites. Her hands shook violently when a scream burst from the smoke—Seren, her blood-curdling cry the moment she yelled Casimir's name.

He couldn't think about that again. The pain the sword caused as a soldier cut into his left side was incomparable to the agony that tore through him when Seren had cried out.

He felt the Verti stare at him, but he refused to look away from Seren's face. Her mouth twitched and her lashes fluttered—

the first sign of life since he had found her that morning. He took a step, afraid to disturb the Seer while she worked.

It looked like Prue was fighting against her magic, on the edge of losing control, when her melodic voice broke through the screams. "ENOUGH," she yelled. Sweat covered her ghastly skin, and still, her hands trembled as her eyes beamed a vibrant violet.

"What did you see?" "Did you see anything?" The Verti asked at once as Prue caught her breath.

Everyone had jolted at the Seer's command, everyone except Casimir. He wrapped a warm hand around Seren's and squeezed, allowing a fraction of his magic to flicker through his fingers. Her skin was cool to the touch, and shock clouded his worries—her fever had broken. He sighed, relief and regret waging a battle in his heart. He wanted to lean closer, bring his lips near her face and confess over and over how sorry he was. But he could do no such thing. Squaring his shoulders, he plastered on a neutral expression and turned to the others.

"You…" Prue whispered.

He looked at her, boldly meeting her startled stare as he willed his eyes to give nothing away. Something had happened in Etiamella that he didn't know how to explain. Something that he couldn't consider bad despite the gravity of their situation, because what he had felt between Seren and his magic was unlike anything before. They needed more time to discover what it meant—something she had to live for.

"Him what?" Carr asked. "Can someone explain what the hell is going on?"

"I'm with Carr," Dax added.

Prue shook her head from side to side. "There is nothing else I can do for her." She glanced at Seren, an unreadable emotion controlling her face, then back to Casimir. "Only you can be the one to save her now."

Rae interrupted, "Tell us what you saw." His nostrils flared.

Casimir knew the male didn't trust him, but there seemed to be more than that. He just didn't know quite what yet.

"How? How do I save her?" Normally, Casimir wasn't one to listen to the manic riddles of the Seer, but in that moment, he would have done anything.

"We're all connected by our magic." Prue waved a hand and continued with a *tsk*. "Some more than others. You must use that connection to save her."

"What does that mean?" Casimir was on the verge of destroying his pride.

"Let what you do not understand guide you, child. Your heart, your magic, the moons, and the stars. They all know the truth." Prue's harmonic voice rose quietly above the stirring fog of magic that swarmed at her feet, rising quickly like a shield of impenetrable gray.

Casimir lunged, shoving his hands into the mist. But Prue was already gone. When he pulled his hands back, his fair skin sparkled with tiny silver flecks, like a million tiny galaxies swirling in his palms. "Dammit," he cursed, unable to stop the string of obscenities.

"I still don't like Seers," Carr grumbled.

"Me neither." Rae slumped and shoved his hands through his golden hair.

Dax asked, "What do we do now?"

Casimir stepped to where Prue had stood, his boots kicking more silver specks into the air.

"Seren would know what to do." Rae frowned, more defeated than angry. "If one of us was hurt, she would know."

"Ser always has an idea—beauty and brains, you know." Carr smiled softly at Seren, his comment earning a jab to the side from Dax.

"Really, *really* not the time, Carr."

"And she appreciates my jokes." Carr scowled. "Unlike the rest of you."

Casimir could understand Carr's use of humor to deflect the weight of his emotions. He shared a similar tactic—but where Carr cracked jokes, Casimir preferred to crack bones. He'd been on his best behavior since the Lunaan trial, but his magic was growing restless; something would have to give, preferably when he saw Evander and the Stellean king again.

"Say that again," Casimir demanded of Rae.

Rae hesitated, scratching the side of his cheek. "Seren would know what to do if one of us was hurt?"

"That's it."

Carr leaned closer to Dax. "I don't follow."

"Me neither."

All three Verti stared at Casimir as if he had grown a tail. "We need to talk to Seren," Casimir said, pacing the length of the bed.

"Um, I know I'm not the smartest here," Carr said. "But I'm pretty sure if we could talk to her right now, we wouldn't exactly be in this situation."

"Prue said that we're all connected, right?" Casimir's heart raced. "Well, what if we could use our magic to talk to her? Even like this."

"That would be great, except how exactly are we going to do that?" Rae asked.

"I have an idea. But I have to be asleep for it to work."

Rae's hand shot straight up before Casimir could finish. "I call dibs on knocking you out."

Dax and Carr exchanged a coy look before giving into a fit of laughter.

Casimir scowled, but a hint of a smile crept over the corners of his lips, lifted by hope. "Unfortunately for you, that won't be necessary."

CHAPTER 39

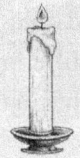

Seren sat beneath the dark sky, the stars slowly blinking out as she felt her magic fading.

She was stuck. Had been for a while now, in a barren landscape that narrowly resembled her dream realm—barring all its usual wonder and magic.

Darkness swarmed around her, seeped into her mind, and lured her to sleep. But a deep-rooted sense of fear prevented her from giving in—afraid of what would happen if she fell asleep while she was already dreaming. And what that would mean for the body she left behind in Clarallan.

Desperately, she held on to her heart's weak rhythm, her thoughts racing as she begged her magic to flicker to life; but if a fire needed oxygen to burn, all she had to give was the water from her unstoppable tears.

Her magic had left an empty hole in her chest, and her heart ached from the loneliness that flooded its vacancy. Having grown to accept her magic, she loved how it made her feel.

Powerful.

And hated how she felt without it. How vulnerable it made her to the unknown. She didn't understand what was happening, why her magic waned, and why she couldn't wake up. And still, her greatest question: How had she gotten hurt so badly in the first place?

Only the hope that her friends were on the other side—fighting for her as fiercely as she was for herself—kept her from breaking down completely.

Regret plagued her mind and haunted her with hopeless what-ifs. Would things be different if she had only told her friends she was hurt? Would they have been able to save her?

Was it already too late?

She couldn't bear to imagine their guilt if she didn't pull through. Their pain—that she had so desperately tried to protect them from—caused by her own flaws: her inability to ask for help, her severed branch of trust, too broken at the end to reach even her best of friends.

She squeezed her eyes shut. *If only I had told them...*

She would do things so differently if she could go back. Would force herself to lean on her friends, to ask for help. Even if her fear promised her vulnerability would stab her in the back. But look where trying to do everything on her own had gotten her...

She trusted her friends with her life, but didn't have the words to tell them before. Now, she feared she would never get the chance.

Her anger flared. One stupid mistake and it had cost her so much. Her friends' faces flashed in her mind—she had to get back to them. To tell them how sorry she was. That she would never scare them like that again. *But how?*

The answer had to be connected to how she had gotten hurt. But she had already spent hours trying to understand what happened at the fourth trial, and always came up empty. She forced herself to scour once more through her muddled memories of the Etiamella battle. But her heart kept circling back to just one.

THE WEIGHT OF WISHES

Crying out for Casimir and from the pain that had erupted at her side right before Evander attacked her again. Seconds before her magic burst across the sand—there was a spark that lit her power, something she was too afraid to try and understand. A match made of pain and struck against passion brought fire to her soul just before she let the flames engulf her. Welcomed them even, wrapped in the heat of an emotion she couldn't place.

Again, she held onto that spark. Needed its strength to keep her alive in the darkness. The accelerant, a striking set of silver-blue eyes that saw her, really saw her, as the scent of rain dampened the shadows that threatened to consume her. Closing her eyes, she basked in the memory's comfort, her lips moving to form words she would never say out loud.

"Seren?" A whisper sent chills down her spine.

No. No. No. She trembled. Afraid that the isolation had finally gotten to her, she wrapped her weak arms around her knees and rocked back and forth.

"Seren," the voice said again, louder this time.

But she refused to look, because if she did and no one was there, then not only would she be alone and terrified, but she would be hallucinating. A sure sign that her fight was almost over.

"Go away." Her voice shook.

"Seren, look at me, please." The melodic voice spoke softly in front of her, a warm breath caressing her face as large hands wrapped around her shoulders. It all felt so real: the sound of the prince's voice, the weight of his touch. She pinched her eyes tighter. "Please, Ser."

Eyes the color of kyanite sparkled as she forced herself to look. Her heart pounded and her lips wavered, her voice so quiet she could barely hear it herself. "Are you really here?"

Casimir's eyes glimmered with promise. "You need to wake up."

"I can't." She looked down.

He cupped her chin and lifted. "You must."

"I've tried...hundreds of times." Her voice was lathered with defeat. "Something is wrong, Cas."

A lump bulged in his throat as he swallowed, the sound deafening against the tense silence between them. His gaze slipped to her side and he sighed. "I know."

Blinking slowly, she asked, "Why can't I wake up?"

His lips twitched and he took a long breath. "You're hurt, Ser, terribly. And you're not healing." Something unreadable crossed his face and he looked away. "Why didn't you let us help you?"

"I wish I had," she rasped. "If I could take it back, I would. But I have to stop the king...and if I had told you, any of you, you would have tried to stop me."

When Casimir looked back, the guilt on his face was enough to stall her heart. "We would have helped you. Now—"

"Now, what?"

"Now we don't know how." His stare was piercing. "You're dying, Ser."

The gravity of his words pummeled into her, snatching the air from her lungs.

No. No. No.

She stared at him, fear constricting her throat as she begged him to step down, admit that he was wrong, that he was lying. His lips pressed firmly together, and she asked, "Why are you here, Cas? How?" Her voice was scratchy as her nervous words climbed out of her mouth.

"The Seer said there is *one* way to save you, but she didn't specify how."

"The Seer... Prue?"

Casimir's pupils dilated as recognition widened his eyes. "She bought us some time, said there was nothing else she could do. That it had to be us"—he shook his head—"or maybe just me to be the one to save you."

"What else did she say?"

"That we're all connected by our magic. That the only way to save you is to use that connection. But the guys and I...we don't know what that means."

"Tell me everything she said."

"We don't have time for that. You need to wake up now." Casimir's jaw tightened.

"Don't you understand? I can't just wake up." Her tongue was sharp as she spoke. "And we don't have any better ideas, so please," she begged, "tell me everything."

Casimir hesitated, then gave in, repeating everything Prue had told them with perfect recall. But Prue never spoke clearly, a fanatic for riddles and omniscient details. There was nothing that stood out until Casimir got to the end. "One last thing," he said. "Right before she disappeared, she told me to let what I do not understand guide me to the answer."

Seren gasped, her waning breath tight in her struggling lungs. "That's it." Prue had said that before, when they first met again in the forest. Seren always assumed it was only connected to the trials, but maybe it was more than that—the answer hidden right in front of them.

"Care to explain?" Casimir asked.

"Prue has said that to me before. I thought it was just about the trials, but maybe..." Seren's eyes fell from Casimir's face and trailed down his large frame. "There's one thing I've been trying to understand, but I just can't."

"What is it, Ser?"

"I figured the reason I couldn't wake up was because I was so hurt. But what has been driving me crazy wasn't the why, but the how. How did I get hurt, Cas?"

"What do you mean?" he asked, not looking at her. "It was the battle, Ser. It was a war zone. I watched you get hit countless of times."

Casimir's gaze fell to her side, and she placed a hand over

where her fatal wound festered. "But I was never struck here. I was never even hit hard enough to cause such an injury." She let her words hang in the unknown between them, waiting for him to answer her silent question. When he offered nothing but silence, Seren pushed harder. "You know something, Cas. You know something, and you're not telling me, and I don't understand why."

Seren shivered at how harshly the prince bit down on his lip, the tension in his jaw enough to draw blood. "What do you know?" she asked again.

Casimir shook his head, unable or just unwilling to meet her eyes. "You're right. There are things that I'm not telling you, but the reason—I don't understand them enough myself to explain."

Seren pushed down the ferocity of emotion that clawed at her heart at his admission. "Do you know how I got hurt?"

"I don't know." The coldness of his tone sent shivers rushing over her skin. He lifted his brilliant eyes, and suddenly everything was too much for her. Too much color, emotion, and especially too much fear as she waited for him to break the silence once more.

"Cas…" Goosebumps lifted the hair on her arms as she reached for him, and before her trepidation could stop her, she pressed her palm against his chest and felt his heartbeat raging beneath the contact. A spark lit in her core and heat swelled in her fingers, her magic sizzling as he leaned into her touch.

Just when she thought he was about to give in and shatter the walls between them, he said, "I can't, Ser. I just can't."

She dropped her hand, stirring the frigid air that replaced the prince's warmth. His words were like cold water, drenching her to her core, numbing her heart to the pain. "You're not even willing to try."

"That's not fair."

"Isn't it?" Her eyes fell to the shadows around them, and her voice cracked as she whispered, "I just want to go home, Cas."

"I want that too. We all do."

"Then tell me what you know."

"It's complicated."

"If you truly cared, you would do anything to help get me out of here. Anything." Her chest tightened. "Yet all you have to say is 'it's complicated'? That's bullshit and you know it."

"I know." Casimir's tone was guttural, sharp enough to pierce through the ice that froze her heart. She hadn't expected him to agree with her. "Seren, it's just that I look at you and I'm terrified. More so than I've ever been in my entire life."

She looked to him, overwhelmed by the devastating vulnerability that caressed the sharp features of his face.

His voice was softer this time, hesitation marking his words. "I'm terrified that if I tell you everything…about this darkness that lives inside of me, you won't look at me the way you do now. But what terrifies me the most is knowing what I would do for you—the only person who makes me feel like I can see the light."

Seren opened her mouth to respond, but all the wrong words wanted to fall out. She pressed her lips shut and stared at the prince, the sky—where two stars appeared in the pitch-black night, the first light since everything in her dream realm had gone dark. Heart racing, she took a deep breath, and more stars dotted the void, twirling and blinking in shades of silver and gold, filling the desolate world with hope.

A tingling sensation zipped across her cheeks and down her spine when Casimir brushed his fingertips over her jaw. The weight of his gaze spread across her skin, and she tore her eyes from the shooting stars.

"I've never been more scared," Seren confessed, admiring the intersection of light and shadows playing delicately over his features, softening his lingering torment. "But we can't let our fears stop us from doing what we have to do—what we want to do."

"You say it like it's easy." Casimir shook his head and his low laugh tickled her senses. "But trust me when I say I would do anything for you. Anything." He wrapped his rough hands around hers, and her heart stuttered as he tugged her close and looked down, his eyes shimmering. "Do you trust me, Seren?"

"We've been over this before."

He squeezed her hands. "I need to hear it again."

Despite everything she knew he was keeping from her, she let the words fall clumsily from her lips. "I trust you."

The air between them was tight, tense, too hot between their joined hands.

Casimir's gaze fluttered up and down before landing on her face, her lips. Her heartbeat lodged in her throat as she cracked her dry mouth to say something. But before she could do anything, he moved. Quick and gentle at the same time, his mouth brushed hers. Soft at first, a question only she could answer.

Terrified and excited, nothing mattered to her except the prince. She angled her chin upward to deepen the kiss. Giving him the permission he was so desperately waiting for. He tasted like darkness and rain, cold water and sparkling silver. He released her hands and placed his touch on the sensitive small of her back, wove the other hand through her hair, eliciting a heady thrill that rippled throughout her entire body as her magic sparked. She yielded to his touch fully, desire coating her skin as his hands found their home. Pulling her closer, his tongue swept into her mouth, moving in a way that made her entire body go limp.

Seren wrapped her arms around his neck, caught up in the intensity of it all, overdosing on the overwhelming feelings that flooded her system. She needed more, more of him, more of them. She didn't know anything could feel that way, and now that she did, she never wanted it to end. Her magic, a weak flame at first, flared to life as the prince deepened the kiss further, the heat of her power catching fire in her veins.

She pulled away, breathless, leaving only enough space between their lips for her to force air into her burning lungs. Casimir groaned at the new distance between them. His hands pressed firmly around her waist as he brushed soft kisses to her neck, slowly dragging his lips over her skin, his touch a match struck against her smoldering magic—she was liquid in his hands as the air twined fiercely around them. She melted into the warmth and pleasure as he held her so tight it felt like he would never let go.

He was the Prince of the Moons, and like all the other stars in his dark sky, she felt the pull of his magic begging her to shine.

"Seren." The sound of her name on Casimir's lips stirred something deep inside of her.

Afraid that it had all been a dream—her mind's last-ditch effort at peace before death devoured her—she cracked her eyes open in the Lunaan castle, blinking slowly as a warm, bright light gleamed across the silver bedroom. Her skin glowed, radiating strength and power as golden tendrils fluttered from her fingertips.

Lifting her gaze, her eyes bounced from the magic on her fingers, to the bed, her best friends. To the prince, sunlight illuminating the storm in his eyes as a relieved smile split his expression. Without a second thought, Seren threw herself from the bed, Casimir there in a heartbeat to draw her into his trembling arms. "You did it," she breathed, her voice muffled as she pressed her face against his chest.

"We did it."

She pulled her head away. "How?"

"I had an idea." Casimir smiled, releasing her. "And luckily it worked."

"UH-hum," Carr grumbled, and Seren snapped her head to the Verti with an untamable grin that made her cheeks hurt. "You two could at least get a room," Carr chided, taking two large steps before hauling Seren into the tightest hug of her life—without any pain from her side. He spun her around, and her feet lifted off the ground as he chuckled.

Seren coughed as he set her down, her voice scratchy as she laughed. "Last I checked, this *was* my room."

Carr rolled his eyes and clutched her shoulder once more. "We missed you too, Ser." He stepped aside for Dax and Rae to get their turn.

"You did it." Rae's eyes were glued on Seren despite directing his words to Casimir. "I can't believe you actually did it."

"Like I said"—a coy smile tilted Casimir's lips—"we did it."

"So you're okay?" Rae asked and she smirked, patting her side without a flinch.

"Appears so."

"But how?" Dax asked, always searching for more answers. To the prince, "What was your idea?"

"We just had to get Ser's magic back," Casimir answered, his expression boringly neutral.

Not a lie, and not the full truth. But in that moment, Seren was grateful for the prince's strict self-control, his sly ability to keep things hidden from others.

The Verti waited for more explanation, but to Casimir, the conversation was over.

"It's a long story and I'm pretty tired," Seren added, a weak attempt at lessening the thick tension suffocating the room. "I can tell you guys more later."

Rae lowered his eyes. "You must be exhausted," he said, his voice apologetic.

She nodded. "But I'm going to be okay...because of all of you." Her voice cracked. "I can't thank you all enough for not giving up."

"We would never give up on you," Casimir and Carr said together, Dax and Rae adding their encouragements.

"Thank you," she repeated, stifling a yawn. Now that the adrenaline of nearly dying had worn off, her exhaustion was all-consuming. Given the chance, she could have slept for a hundred years. But despite how tired she was, a spark of magic remained lit in her core.

"You should get some rest," Casimir said, the heat of his gaze on her skin.

He might have been the most confusing, aggravating male she had ever met, but he had saved her. And the way he made her feel...it was enough to override anything. She couldn't have been more thankful.

If he hadn't come to rescue her, she was certain she wouldn't have made it out.

"I will," she said, focused on her friends' company as they asked her a string of questions: Where were you? What was it like? But her exhaustion gripped tightly around her mind, demanding rest, and her overwhelming feelings around her heart, demanding time alone. When her blinks grew too heavy, she could no longer control her irresistible thoughts about what had happened right before she woke up. Something she didn't want to think about in front of her friends, wanting complete privacy to imagine that kiss again.

Casimir interrupted, "We should let Seren get some rest." He stood at the edge of the group, his eyes never staying in one place for too long.

The others hesitated, and Seren guessed they likely didn't want to leave her alone after what happened. Smiling, she squeezed Carr's knee gently where their legs touched as they sat on the end of the bed. Slowly, the Verti came to an agreement and took turns hugging Seren one last time before sulking to the door.

"We're glad you're okay, Seren," Rae said, stepping into the hall.

Carr smiled. "We'll see you in a bit, okay?"

She nodded, watched her friends leave, and waited for Casimir to speak as he stood at the edge of the doorway, hoping he would say something, anything really, to acknowledge what happened between them.

But the prince simply glanced at her with a half smile, his sterling eyes darker than before, before he stepped into the hall and left Seren alone.

She couldn't help but feel her heart stutter as he closed the door in silence.

CHAPTER 40

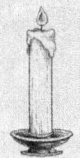

Seren woke up to afternoon sunlight glittering through the open space of her bedroom. In her rough estimate, she'd slept for over twenty-four hours. Her stomach growled its protests as she pushed the covers away from her legs and sat up. She hadn't meant to sleep for so long, but both her body and mind needed it after forcing herself to stay awake through her latest near-death experience.

Gently, she rubbed the crusty sleep from her eyes and looked around the quiet room. To her surprise, sprawled over the far table was a fresh spread of fruits, breads, and cheese, with something hidden under a silver platter and a steaming mug to its left. Nausea did cartwheels in her throat as she realized how hungry she was. When she actually thought about it, she realized it had been days since she'd last eaten.

Aware of that fact, Seren forced herself to start slow while she lounged on the plush bed and sipped the warm liquid from the white mug. A laugh itched its way up her throat as she noticed gold words etched into the side of the cup, next to a large yellow star and an upward pointing arrow.

"This is what a star looks like," she read aloud.

She made a mental note to harass the prince about the mug later, assuming he was the one who brought her the delicious breakfast. Careful not to stuff herself sick, Seren picked through the meal and waited for her stomach to settle. Her personal favorite: the well-aged Bellelay cheese, which paired exquisitely well with the sweet fruits, particularly the syrupy pears.

After lounging in the sun's warmth while her heavenly meal digested, she decided to go find the others. She changed into something more appropriate, landing on a comfortable set of workout clothes. To her surprise, her side was completely healed. No scar, not even a scratch where the vile wound had been. Casimir's theory had done more than just rescue her. It had restored her magic to its full potency, and with that, her body felt brand new. Magically healed, she figured she could maybe even go for a walk or a run or possibly even get some training in to test the limits of her body after nearly dying. She would need to be at her strongest if she was going to face the Stellean trial soon.

And it had to be soon. Because of her unfortunate delay, they had already wasted too much time, and if they waited too long, Seren worried they were going to be too late.

She fastened on her boots with a newfound determination. Coming so close to death made her realize how much she truly had to lose. How much the kingdom of Clarallan had to lose, when she really thought about it.

The hallway was empty when she slipped out of her room. She followed a slight sound of commotion from down the hall that rang through the air. Eventually, the pattern of groans and clanging metal led her to a courtyard on an outside balcony of the prince's floor, where she spotted her friends enjoying the warm day with some sparring.

She kept her distance at first, allowing herself a little time to watch without them knowing she was there. She had seen the Verti train more times than she could count, but besides when they were truly fighting for their lives, this was the first time she got to watch the prince join in.

He wore nothing besides a tight pair of black shorts that clung closely to his thighs, his skin slick with sweat and tattoo-covered chest on full display while he sparred against Dax. All four of them were drenched, their muscles flexed and taut while they fought one another relentlessly. Seren could barely keep up, watching as they took hit after hit, never backing down. They fought as if it were the real deal, like lives were genuinely at stake. Seren was in awe of all of them, each a seasoned warrior with years of experience, skills, and strength to back them up. Anyone would have been able to tell that these four males were far from ordinary soldiers. They moved with mechanical instinct, as if fighting were as natural to them as breathing.

Seren's eyes kept riveting back to Casimir: the seamless agility he used to dodge any unnecessary blows before pivoting and taking down his opponent so quickly she couldn't believe that it happened before her very eyes. Watching him was captivating—almost too surreal to believe or appreciate fully.

Eventually, the males noticed her lurking. Carr hollered first, claiming she was being a real creep by standing so far away, and invited her to join them. Seren kindly declined, but took the opportunity to catch up as they took what she guessed was their first break for any water or rest. As they talked, she flicked her eyes back and forth between the prince and the others. Her mouth parched, she gulped, not too subtly, when she watched Casimir swiftly drain his entire glass of water, while her gaze tracked the sweat that dripped down his neck as he swallowed. She shook herself from a daze right when Dax asked, "Do you want to get some training in?"

Seren declined once more. "I think I'm actually just going to go on a walk. Taking it easy getting back."

They all agreed that was a good idea and were equally

surprised that Seren had even been the one to propose it, with her habit of rushing into things.

"Do you want any company?" Rae asked from where he lounged against the balcony railing.

Seren shook her head, hoping she wouldn't hurt their feelings too badly, and replied, "No, no, you guys keep at it. I wouldn't mind some time alone anyway."

Her smiling friends waved her off, all eager to return to their training, except for Rae, whose intense gaze remained on her until she walked completely out of sight. She wasn't sure where she should go as the Lunaan court was massive, and she certainly didn't want to end up in any trouble as she explored.

She eventually decided to wander the castle a bit more, uninterested in explaining herself to anyone she might run into in the city. She followed hall after hall, took turn after turn, lingering near every piece of artwork that caught her attention, before she realized she'd been walking for well over an hour. She had no idea where she was or how to get back to the prince's floor, but she wasn't ready to go back yet, anyway.

She took another left turn and came face-to-face with a staircase that she couldn't see the end of. Her steps echoed against the white marble stairs as she followed the hanging gold lights illuminating the path up the steps. After climbing over one hundred stairs, Seren was greeted by a large glass door that appeared to lead onto the roof. Hesitation held her back from opening the door, but after a few minutes she gave in and pressed on the cool metal handles.

The view from the rooftop was more incredible than anything Seren had discovered in the castle. Eight strategically placed dark marble pillars lined the outer edges of the rooftop, defying logic where they split in the center, exposing the perfect view of the moon phases orbiting through the Lunaan sky, day and night. They stood so tall that Seren had to crank her neck upward to get a glimpse of where they ended against the vibrant sky. To her surprise, a frail, hunched figure with short, graying hair and dressed in fine navy robes leaned precariously against one of the huge marble pedestals on the far side. His back was turned to Seren, and his small frame was just barely a speck against the astounding architecture, making him appear even more vulnerable as he sat alone in the quiet.

Seren didn't want to disturb the male, especially as she wasn't certain she was even permitted to be on the rooftop unaccompanied. But as she turned to walk back toward the doors, her steps echoed against the sparkling floors, and a faint voice beckoned her from afar.

She thought about ignoring it, pretending she hadn't heard him, and dashing through the doors before anyone recognized her. But a comforting sensation coursed through her veins as her magic sent its warmth through her every limb, urging her to answer its call.

She held onto the courage her power gave her and dampened her anxiety as she swiveled to look back at the unknown male. He faced her then but was still too far away for Seren to recognize, and he offered a gentle smile as she approached. His face was cast half in the light and half in the shadows, distorting his features as Seren beheld him.

By the time they stood facing one another, recognition flashed through the front of her mind, and she instantly fell into a polite curtsy with a tip of her head as a sign of deep respect. The pallid male before her, shoulders hunched forward with a lifetime's weight of hardship, and deep wrinkles worn across his ghastly face, was none other than the Lunaan king himself.

Her eyes widened—Casimir's father.

Once, King Egil had been the kindest Fae ruler in the entire kingdom of Clarallan. He ruled with a gentle fist, and believed in using his power for good, unlike many of the courts' other rulers. The Lunaan court prospered under his authority for decades, and everyone believed that their heirs would help save the kingdom one day. That was, until the unfortunate loss of his beloved queen, the dear Queen Quinlan, who died a tragic death far too early, leaving Egil behind along with their two sons.

That was as much of the story as Seren knew, despite having grown closer to his youngest son over the past few weeks. Casimir was rarely the vulnerable type, and his mother was the touchiest subject of them all.

They stood in silence for so long that Seren was convinced neither of them were going to say anything at all, but eventually Egil broke the quiet.

"Seren, it's lovely to finally meet you." His voice was youthful and caught Seren by surprise as he beamed the most genuine smile he could muster, despite his illness. She was baffled as to how the king recognized her or even knew her name, but his presence was comforting, and she deduced her bafflement was likely the least of her worries. Seren offered her best smile in return as she took his outreached hand and shook it gingerly. His skin was cold and his grip weak. But her heart swelled at the interaction, grateful to know that the king was still trying his best after everything he had been through. Her thoughts fell to the most recent tragedy involving King Egil—Hellevi's failed assassination attempt—and she couldn't stop the sorrow that overwhelmed her as her mind wandered to thoughts of the prince and his family.

"It's lovely to meet you too, Your Majesty. But I didn't mean to disturb you, and I'm very sorry if I did. I thought the roof was empty." Seren prepared herself to leave as she waited for the king to respond. But Egil, weak with illness and age, simply sat down against the cool marble steps and patted the open space next to him.

"Sit with me, will you?"

Seren beamed and joined him, the marble cool beneath her clothes as she leaned against the towering pillar. She crossed her legs and placed her joined hands in her lap, unsure of what to say or do. When it was clear to Egil that Seren had no intention of speaking, he continued, breaking their silence once more.

"It's beautiful out here, isn't it? It's even more magnificent at night, if you can believe it."

Seren agreed immediately; the Lunaan court continued to amaze her with every new thing she learned or incredible sight she saw. "It's lovely, truly. What brought you out here today?"

He sighed and rubbed his hands together slowly. "It's no secret that my health is not what it used to be. My magic is long gone, and I'm dying. There is nothing anyone can do for me. But I'm determined to spend my last days living, rather than waiting for death." He paused to catch his breath, already winded by their short conversation. Once he gathered himself again, he continued, Seren hanging on his every word. "This spot has always been my favorite. My beloved Quinlan and I used to come out here every evening and watch the sunset together. I guess the habit never went away, even after she passed."

"I'm very sorry for your loss." Seren didn't know if that was the appropriate thing to say considering how long it had been, but she didn't want to be impolite and she appreciated how vulnerable Egil was being with her. Her voice wavered. "I know what it's like to lose someone you love."

"Death is not a good thing to hold in common with anyone, and I'm so sorry that we share it. My heart broke when your mother was killed. I still think about her nearly every day."

Seren's brows lifted as curiosity took a hold of her. "You knew my mother?"

King Egil nodded deliberately. "Very well, actually. Adora was one of my dearest friends and Quinlan's best even, like a sister she used to say."

Disappointment weighed heavily on Seren. "Oh, I think there's been a mistake, Your Majesty. My mother's name was Aleah, not Adora."

"No, no. There's been no such thing. Yes, your mother went

by the name Aleah, but only because she had to protect you both in Stellean. Before that, she grew up in Lunaan, just like Quinlan and me. We'd known each other since we were children, around nine years old if my memory holds. And she and Quinlan were friends years before I ever met your mother. That, child, is the truth."

Seren's mind raced with so many incoherent questions it was useless to try and sort through them all, so she started with the first one that came to mind. "How come I never knew that? My mother told me very little about her time in Lunaan, and she never mentioned being friends with a king or queen. I think I would have remembered all that."

Egil loosened a disconcerted chuckle. "Oh, my dear child, there is so much history to the kingdom of Clarallan it can be truly overwhelming. Especially when my kind have made it so difficult to discover the truth—the Fae and their need for power." He smiled weakly, warm sunlight reflecting in his pale icy eyes. "Do you want to hear a story?"

Seren looked around, her stomach growling as she watched the lowering sun. But if Egil could help her learn more about the truth—it was worth it. "Yes, please. If you have time."

"Of course, dear." He took a few deep breaths. "The story I'm about to tell you is the truth and nothing but, exactly as I lived it. But you will find no record of it in the history books. King Hellevi made sure of that, determined to rewrite our history so that it favors only his greatest desire."

"Please...tell me everything," she urged him on. "I want the truth. Even if it hurts, it hurts worse to not know." Seren didn't care if she sounded desperate. She was sick of being fed nothing but lies. It shouldn't have surprised her to learn that even more of her life was a complete lie, but somehow, she couldn't help but be upset that her mother helped hide the truth from her, even if she had been too young to fully understand. She knew her mother was trying to protect her, but she couldn't help but feel betrayed.

With his illness, it was difficult to believe the Lunaan king fully as he rambled on, but a large part of her was certain that he believed his every word. She could only hope his illness had yet to spread to his mind, that his memory was preserved and clear as he recalled the story of her mother.

Egil took frequent breaks between sentences to catch his breath, but Seren didn't mind. She used the extra time to ponder what he shared. Her thoughts raced faster than she could keep up with as her mind tried to piece together the bigger picture between the lies and half-truths she had grown up on. Seren used one of Egil's particularly lengthy pauses to remember anything that she could about her mother, not that there was a lot to remember. It wasn't until Egil said her mother's name again that Seren remembered the letter she had found in the Stellean castle. It had been addressed to a woman named Adora and signed by Q.

Suddenly, everything started to make sense. The letter she had found, the recurring nightmares she had about the two women she couldn't recognize, and what the Seer had tried to show her. Adora truly was her mother, and Queen Quinlan had been there that unfortunate night. As the pieces fell together, Seren was overwhelmed with an urgent need to know everything —she had gotten just a taste, her truth-starved soul desperate to feast on Egil's wisdom. She hung onto his every breathy word and leaned closer to not miss a single thing.

"Your mother was an amazing woman. Human, yes, but one of the strongest women I've ever had the pleasure of knowing. She refused to let the Fae push her around and used every opportunity to prove herself—a trait I see reflected in your soul as well."

Seren's heart beamed at the king's compliment. It was a good change of pace to hear her mother discussed in such a positive manner. Her lips curved in a genuine smile, and she continued to listen.

"Adora's strength was inspiring. When I took over as king, Quinlan my queen, we offered her a chance to work with us. She was strategic and intelligent. But around the time that she'd been working with us for a few years, Hellevi planned a series of attacks. You see, Hellevi has always wanted to rule Clarallan, that's nothing new. We needed your mother's help in preparing our court for when Hellevi decided to make his move against us. Adora was incredibly skilled at information collection, and we'd hoped that she could discover the truth. Eventually, your mother learned of Hellevi's plans, but it was already too late. We didn't have enough time to prepare the court." For a moment, Seren thought she saw Egil's faded eyes flash a vibrant color. But when she looked closer, they were simply an ashen blue.

Egil's shoulders drooped as he leaned forward on bent knees. Seren guessed sharing this story was incredibly difficult, but he didn't appear interested in stopping. The king's voice darkened as he continued, "Hellevi's troops descended upon the Lunaan court in broad daylight with the help of Etiamella soldiers. They swarmed my territory and ravaged our land. The city, the castle. Nothing was safe from him, not even our temple. He encouraged his soldiers to do their worst. We were lucky to get out alive, but many of our citizens did not share the same fate. The death toll that day was crushing. It nearly destroyed Quinlan and me. Over one thousand of our people, Fae and humans alike, were dead. And even more of them were injured or taken, stolen by Hellevi and his troops to work in his court."

"My mother," Seren gasped. "She was one of the taken?" Everything came into focus, the blurred edges of her vision cleared as the lies she had been fed her entire life were replaced with the gut-wrenching truth.

With a sigh, Egil pushed his head back and his shoulders fell forward, and Seren could see the pain that flashed in his eyes as he relived such melancholic memories. She tried and failed not to feel too guilty about the whole conversation and reminded herself that he was the one who had brought it up. But still her heart ached as they were both reminded of the beautiful soul they had lost to Hellevi's cruelty.

Egil offered a grim smile. "Your mother was a fighter, and in the end, I think that's what caught Hellevi's interest. He couldn't believe that I'd given a human woman such responsibility within my court, especially regarding our politics. When he came across Adora during the raid, he knew instantly that he wanted her for himself. I don't know if he thought he could break her or if he genuinely favored the fire in her soul, but Adora never stood a chance. Once Hellevi has made up his mind, it is nearly impossible to change."

Seren knew that firsthand. She had personal experience dealing with the worst of Hellevi. For a second, it felt like she couldn't breathe, imagining the hurt her mother had gone through at the hands of such evil.

Fortunately, King Egil's voice broke through Seren's thoughts before she could envision the worst of it. "It's one of the biggest regrets of my life that I was not with your mother when she was taken. To know that she was alone and vulnerable, and that I'd left her that way. I will never forgive myself for letting that happen to her or what happened to my court. It was one of the worst days of my life, and I never imagined it could've gotten any worse. Until after a short time went by, and Adora confessed to Quinlan by dream-walking that she was pregnant with you."

"It isn't your fault," Seren offered kindly, but she knew her words were of little condolence to the heartbroken king. She smiled grimly and asked, "Do you know what happened to her after she was taken? And what of my father? Did you know him?"

"Adora never told me the details of your father. And if she

told Quinlan, I never knew. All they ever said to me was that he died in Hellevi's raids."

"Oh." Seren couldn't hide her disappointment; even though she had spent her entire life believing her father was dead, it was ten times worse knowing it was true. Seren shoved her grief to the dark depths of her mind. "Back in Stellean, I found a letter to Adora, signed by Q. Do you know anything about that?"

Egil kept his eyes locked on a faraway point in the city beyond the edge of the roof. "Quinlan and your mother attempted to stay in contact, mainly through dream-walking and the occasional letter. But they had to be careful. If Hellevi ever learned of what we were up to, he would have killed you both immediately. Over the years, we devised so many rescue plans, but every single one failed. We spent years trying to get you and your mother out of the Stellean court, but it was impossible. When Adora mentioned Hellevi had taken an interest in you, we knew we had to act immediately, even if it was the last thing we ever did. But after failing so many times, it took a while for us to breach Stellean's security again. Hellevi has that court locked up tighter than any other ruler I've ever seen."

Seren knew how much money Hellevi allotted to his militant security. The entire court was overrun by soldiers and guards, each adorned with a multitude of the deadliest weapons in Clarallan. It was impossible to look anywhere without seeing Hellevi's soldiers. A near-inescapable cage.

"We grew desperate, and our plan was nowhere near complete, but Quinlan couldn't let it go. Not when her best friend and her child were still in the hands of Clarallan's worst monster." Egil's tone exuded so much palpable shame, Seren could almost taste it. "Not that I blame Quinlan, of course, nor do I wish she had let it go. I just wish we could have done things differently. I tried to get her to wait, to give us more time to perfect our plan before we traveled to Stellean. But Quinlan lost contact with your mother for a few days and feared the worst, around the time you were just a few years old. This sent Quinlan over the edge. She was half-hysterical when she came to me with her plan to finally rescue you and Adora. I begged her not to go, but her decision was final." He shook his head, coughing as he caught his breath. "See, it wasn't up to me whether I let Quinlan go, only whether or not I let her go alone."

Seren nodded, nervous as the king continued.

He took a moment to catch his breath and gathered his composure. "Of course, I would never leave Quinlan alone, especially with her plan to break into the Stellean court. And Adora, she was my friend too. I couldn't give up on them, not when you all needed me the most.

"The next night, Quinlan and I traveled to Stellean. She got information about the tunnels beneath the castle and planned on breaking Adora and you out that way. And actually, the plan almost worked. Quinlan and I breached the castle despite the challenges, and I waited in the tunnels for her to find you and your mother. She did just that, and it didn't take long before the three of you were running toward me. The worst part of the whole thing is that we believed we'd made it, only to be caught right before we were free."

Since Seren had been so young when the story actually took place, she could only imagine how excruciating it must have been. To be so close but still fail. That was one of her greatest fears regarding the trials. She didn't want to think about that happening to her when she finally faced the Stellean king again. Her voice cracked with worry as she said, "That must've been awful. I can't imagine."

"It was the worst day of my life." Egil paused. "I don't remember many of the details after that. Hellevi attacked me first, knocked me out, and beat me senseless. I was unconscious for such a long time that I honestly don't know what all he did to me. I only know that when I finally woke, you and your mother were gone, and my magic, it was broken beyond repair. And

Quinlan..." The king sniffled and wiped clumsily at his face as tears welled in the poor elder's eyes.

Seren's voice cracked, mirroring her heart, and she choked out her next words. "You don't have to continue. I can only imagine how painful the memories are. I'm so sorry for making you relive that." And she was sorry, more than Egil would ever know. She knew it was illogical, that she was just a kid caught up in a cruel mess that was completely out of her control, but somehow, she still felt responsible.

"You have nothing to be sorry for, dear. Quinlan's death was a tragedy, but a senseless one at that, one that never should've happened. But the past is simply the past, and any shame and guilt regarding her death or your mother's should be saved only for Hellevi. It is not our cross to bear. Only his."

Seren appreciated his efforts to comfort her, but they were fruitless. She had always known that Hellevi killed her mother, but to learn the real reason it happened left her empty inside. She didn't know how to feel, knew even less what to say. Learning the truth was more difficult than she had ever imagined it to be, and she couldn't quite understand why it left her feeling the way it did.

Her throat ached with a burning sensation as tears threatened to transform into what she knew would be uncontrollable sobs. She forced herself to swallow the lump that formed in the back of her throat and looked up through dewy lashes at the king. Her voice burned as she spoke. "I know the fault falls solely on Hellevi, but that doesn't make it any easier. He's the worst monster I've ever met, and my heart breaks to know how many people he has hurt over the years, including your family. Do Evander and Casimir know the truth?"

Egil shook his head as guilt crept over his expression. "Neither of my sons know the truth behind their mother's death. I never had the heart to tell them how badly I failed that day. How I let them and their mother down in the worst way possible, and the same goes for you and Adora. And not to make excuses, but honestly, Hellevi screwed with my mind so violently that I was lost for many years after the incident. It wasn't even until the boys grew up that I discovered the truth of what happened. And by then, I was too cowardly to confess my mistakes. I knew how much the truth would hurt them. At least with the story they grew up with, their mother died a quick death, and I can live knowing that provides them with at least a little comfort."

Seren pushed, her voice soft, not accusatory. "But Casimir blames himself... You must see that. The loss of his mother destroyed him. Don't you think he deserves a chance at peace? The lies you've told can't save him." Seren's heart cracked at the thought of the prince. All the things he told her about blaming himself, how his mother's death had ruined him, left him feeling like he had no choice but to pursue the darkness within. Seren felt like she was going to be sick. "You know it's possible that if Casimir learned the truth, that maybe he wouldn't carry so much shame. The story you just shared, the events that you know to be true, that could help set Cas free." Egil's gaze settled on her face. "Maybe it would help him stop living beneath the weight of such self-hatred. The weight that has crushed him ever since his mother died. Doesn't he deserve the chance to forgive himself for something that was never his fault? To know the truth, just like you and I do?"

Seren was baffled as to where she got the courage to talk to the king that way. But maybe it wasn't courage, rather just an overwhelming need to protect those she cared about. She knew what it was like to be lied to her entire life, and it was a torment so wicked she wouldn't wish it on anyone, let alone someone as good as the prince—even if he couldn't see it.

Egil's face lifted and his voice shook. "It's up to you whether you disclose what I've told you to my son. At this age, and with how ill I am, I know my heart can't take the burden of that confession. The stress of it would surely kill me. But if you believe the truth could help Casimir, I give you my permission to share this story with him. I would do anything to help after failing him so miserably."

Guilt stirred in her gut as she beheld the king after her rant. At that moment, he eerily resembled his son: his sharp features, and eyes that held so much raw emotion. She hadn't meant to make him feel bad, at least not entirely, but she had to get that off her chest. Slightly ashamed, she lowered eyes. "I'm sorry if I came across too harshly. I don't blame you for not telling them, not at all. But as someone who was lied to for so long, I can't help but wish the freedom of truth for your sons as well. Please don't get me wrong, I'm so grateful for the story you shared. There aren't enough ways for me to thank you for the gift you have given me today."

Egil placed a gentle hand on her knee—such a fatherly gesture that she couldn't help but wonder what it would have been like to grow up anywhere that wasn't the Stellean castle.

Egil squeezed her knee and gave her an avuncular smile that captured his entire face. "You have given me a great gift as well, Seren. You've given me hope that one day our kingdom will prosper again. That it won't be afflicted by the cruelties of Hellevi and his terror much longer. That our curse will finally be lifted, and Clarallan may return to the kingdom it once was. I wish you the best moving forward, and I wish that I could be there when you win. But just know, if I am no longer with us then, that I'm watching from above with your mother. And she would be so incredibly proud of you."

Seren couldn't stop the tears that fell at Egil's kindness; she was a mess, but she couldn't bring herself to care. Her entire life had passed by without her ever hearing those words before, and she didn't realize how long she had waited to hear someone say they were proud of her. A lifetime's worth of emotion flooded within her, washing away the anger she had held onto for so long. What Egil shared with her not only gave her clarity about herself but also restored the picture of her mother that Hellevi had tried to ruin for so long. She no longer had to think of her mother as a thief or a criminal, and that was one of the greatest things Egil could have ever done for her. Even if it meant her mother's death had no good reason, Seren could move forward knowing the truth about her. And she was proud to know that Adora spent her last day trying to save her only daughter.

After Seren escaped, she had never felt truly ready to face the Stellean king again. Not until she learned the truth. The story that Egil shared did more than just wash away the lies of her life. It gave her a newfound sense of purpose and determination. She was certain she felt the way it would feel to be reborn after having spent hundreds of years learning the secrets of life.

She was more ready than ever.

Soon, she would face Hellevi for what she hoped was the last time. With the strength of her mother and the kindness of King Egil on her side. With the bravery of her friends and the heart of the prince.

Nothing would stop her.

When Seren left Egil's side, they had tears in their eyes as they said their goodbyes. There was only one thing left for her to do. Before Seren lost her courage, she ran all the way to the prince's floor, not slowing down until she stood outside his room.

Taking a deep breath, Seren lifted her hand.

Then knocked.

CHAPTER 41

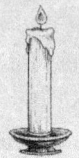

"Seren, what are you doing here?" Casimir asked, his broad stature filling the doorway as he leaned casually against the silver frame. His voice was gruff, as if he had been asleep when she knocked. "Is everything okay? Did something happen?"

Seren's mouth went dry at the thought of why she was there. "I have something important to tell you." Her eyes scurried nervously to a point behind him, allowing her a glimpse into his room. She dipped her head. "Can we talk?"

Casimir swallowed tensely, but gestured for her to come in. By the tightness in his jaw, she guessed he rarely allowed anyone into his personal room. But Seren didn't care. What she came to tell him was too important.

"So, what do you want to talk about?"

Okay, then. Right to the point.

Seren scanned the massive room—so large, she wagered he could fit an entire kingdom inside if he really put his back into it. Her eyes lingered on the far wall. Above his bed, a painting dominated the entire side, hauntingly similar to the one in her guest room and beautifully illuminated by pools of moonlight that shimmered through the navy curtains. Not entirely ready to confess her reason for being there, Seren ignored his question and pointed at the artwork. "What does the painting mean?"

Sighing softly, Casimir's expression soured. "It's my mother's work."

Seren's breath hitched. Of course her plan to delay the inevitable failed miserably. Taking a deep breath, she forced as much oxygen into her lungs as they could hold. "That's actually what I came to talk to you about."

"My artwork?"

"Your mother." Her words fell into the tense silence between them.

She risked looking at him and instantly regretted it. His sharp features were pulled tightly into a lethal expression. *If looks could kill*, she mocked nervously to herself, despite the fear that grabbed her by the throat.

"I don't like talking about her," he said softly, with a hint of kindness that Seren hadn't expected.

"I understand." She approached the prince the way she would a wounded predator. No sudden movements, no loud sounds. "But this is important. And I think you need to hear it."

He scowled darkly. "Go on, then," he demanded, obviously not a fan of being told what he did and did not need.

"Okay." Seren's heart raced. "But you might want to sit down for this."

"I thought you said it was important. Now you're making it sound like you have something terrible to tell me."

"I never said it wasn't bad," Seren clarified, her throat scratchy. "But it is important, and I would take a seat if I were you."

There was a long pause before he said anything else. "I have a different idea."

Her brows lifted. "What is it?"

"What if, for old times' sake—" He made it sound like they'd been friends forever. It was difficult for Seren to remind herself they'd only known each other for a few weeks, and honestly, been friends for even fewer. "We talk somewhere else, in our usual spot."

She didn't understand what he was getting at, and they certainly didn't have a usual spot.

He explained. "Dream-walking. You and I, one more time, in case we never get the chance..." His tone was light despite the gravity of what he implied—that they might not survive the final trial. Seren agreed. One last thing they could share together, just the two of them.

"I like that idea." She beamed. That way, no one else could hear what she told the secretive prince.

Casimir smiled, his white teeth flashing in the shadows that flickered across his sharp face. He gestured with an open palm toward the king-sized bed. "After you."

Seren shot him her sharpest glare. "Don't get any ideas, princeling."

Her old nickname earned the most genuine laugh she had ever heard come from the serious prince. "I wouldn't dream of it." He winked.

Rolling her eyes violently, she couldn't help giggling as she crawled onto the most comfortable mattress she had ever felt. She adjusted the plush pillows until she was satisfied and chided, "No wonder you always complain about missing your beauty sleep. I would too if this was my bed."

Casimir shrugged before lowering himself onto the plush mattress. "Only the best for a prince."

Seren's breath caught as she watched him slide back until his head leaned against the silk pillows and he hauled the weighted covers over them. There was plenty of cool space between them on the large mattress, yet the heat radiating from the prince was overwhelming. Distracting herself, Seren craned her neck back and peered at the ghostly painting above them. Like the one in her room, the painting displayed a ghastly cliffside cast in shadows and moonlight while a figure hung precariously near the edge.

Despite the intensity of Casimir's gaze, she kept her eyes riveted to the painting's details. She couldn't meet his eyes just yet, not without giving away how nervous she was. Willing her voice to be steady, she whispered, "Will you tell me more about your mother? Just as we fall asleep?"

The mattress gave way beneath them as Casimir took a deep breath and stared at the scattering moonbeams that slipped through the glass windows.

"My mother was beautiful. Her beauty comparable only to something as grand as our Moons—something to be worshiped. She believed in true love and using magic for good, and she lit up any room that she walked into. And her smile…" Casimir paused, his voice gruff with painful remembrance. "Sometimes when I close my eyes and think about her, I can still remember her smile the best. The way it always reached her violet eyes and how brightly she beamed when she told us children she loved us."

Without thinking, Seren turned to her side and gazed at Casimir. Soft moonlight poured through the fluttering curtains and warped his sharp features beneath the velvety shadows, breaking up the harshness that devoured his tense expression. Her voice heavy with sleep, she murmured, "She sounds wonderful. I think I would've liked her very much."

"You would've loved her," Casimir mused, running his fingers through his disheveled hair. Seren's eyelids grew heavy but she couldn't help but think he'd never stared at her like this before; as if she were the final thread that kept him from unraveling. "But not nearly as much as she would've loved you."

Knowing how much his mother meant to him, there was nothing Seren could say to describe how much his compliment meant to her. To hear his praise through the eyes of his mother—

it was the kindest thing anyone had ever said to her, which only made what she had to tell him that much more devastating.

BURIED DEEP within her resting mind, Seren felt a tugging sensation she had never experienced before; slight at first, it morphed into an overwhelming feeling she couldn't deny. She followed the pull of her thoughts until she reached what felt like the end. Everything complete darkness had consumed, replaced by a devastatingly bright light.

When she opened her eyes to the dream realm, she was stunned to discover it wasn't her own. Every time she had dream-walked with Casimir, it had taken place in her own mind. But this time, that wasn't the case.

Unlike her dreamworld, which ebbed and changed on her every chaotic whim, Casimir's remained mostly stagnant. But that wasn't to say his was any less extraordinary.

If anything, Casimir's dreamland was nothing short of incredible. To the right, as far as she could see, the land swept away to towering mountain ranges that eclipsed the entire horizon; and to her left, beyond the sturdy land at her feet, was a dark sea thriving far beneath the breathtaking cliffside.

Somehow, the world around her was both entirely overwhelming and peaceful at the same time. Mirroring exactly how she felt in Casimir's presence.

She couldn't place the familiar feeling in her chest, having never seen such a landscape in her life, but as she thought back to the paintings in the Lunaan castle, she couldn't help but wonder if Casimir had ever shared his dream realm with his mother.

She walked along the cliff's edge as she waited for the prince to arrive, her steps stirring up hints of blossoming flowers and salt, carried by the brisk sea breeze. The sound of powerful wings pressing against the wind drew her attention to the sky, and Seren's gaze immediately landed on a flock of jet-black birds, casually soaring against the vibrant blue. Despite the sunlight, eight moons of various phases hung delicately around the horizon, each accompanied by a few visible stars.

A harsh commotion crashed directly behind her with a loud thud. Immediately, she looked over her shoulder, only to be met by her favorite pair of silver-blue eyes, vibrant against a stirring cloud of thick dust that swarmed at his feet.

She waited a moment, then asked, "Where have you been?"

Shaking his dark hair loose, Casimir casually flicked the dust off his black shirt before taking a step toward her. As he did, Seren's eyes fell to a milky white feather that fluttered up and over his boots. She stared curiously at the feather before Casimir's voice drew her attention. "Around."

"I haven't seen you."

"Like I said, I've been around."

"Why did you wait so long to find me?"

"I never needed to find you. I've been watching this entire time."

"Creep," Seren scolded. "But seriously, why were you watching me?"

"I wanted to see what you would do. Mainly, since this is your first time in a dreamworld that isn't your own."

"And?" Seren's curiosity piqued. "Did I pass?"

"It wasn't a test. Think of it rather as a simple opportunity of observation."

His words left an uneasy sensation within her. "Well, I'm glad you're finally here. Now that you're not off being some freaky stalker and gods know what else."

Casimir cocked his chin quizzically before allowing his expression to glaze back to neutrality. "So, what's so important that you need to tell me?"

Never the subtle type, Seren mocked. She'd had plenty of

time to think about the words she needed to say, yet now that the time had come, her mind was completely blank. Not that there was any good way to start, but Seren had hoped she would come up with something better than what practically tumbled out of her mouth. "I met your father today."

"Oh?" Casimir mused. "Don't just leave me hanging, Ser."

"He told me a lot of interesting things. Things I think you need to know."

"And? What kind of things?"

"Well, first, he told me about my mother, and explained how there is still so much that I don't know. After the past few weeks, I foolishly thought I'd escaped the cycle of lies that characterized my life for so long. But seemingly, that wasn't the case. Even the only name that I've known for my mother for the past twenty years was a lie."

"I can't imagine how that feels." Casimir's breathing deepened. "What was her name?"

Her heart ached at the thought that she might cause the same type of pain in him with her next declaration, but it was too late for any doubt. Still, she wasn't used to hurting those she cared for. A lifelong sin-eater of pain, Seren would rather break her own heart than let others know what it felt like to feast on the vile tastes of trauma. The spoiled feelings that would rot in their gut, killing them slowly from the inside out. She reminded herself that yes, what she had to tell the prince may hurt, but the path he was on because he never knew the truth would get him killed anyway.

Seren cleared her throat and said proudly, "Her name was Adora."

Casimir's brows tied together in thought, but all he said was, "That's a lovely name."

"It is," Seren agreed, and her mind wandered to the abstract memories of her mother's face from when she was a little girl. "Apparently, she and your parents were friends before she died, even worked in the castle with them. And actually, she and your mother were the best of friends, as your father put it. They'd known each other ever since they were children and were like family until the bitter end."

"I'm sorry, but I've never heard of her before," Casimir said. "Which I don't understand if they were truly so close. Why wouldn't my family talk about her?"

Seren shook her head. "I don't want to put words into the king's mouth, but as he told me the story, the one thing he kept reiterating was how guilty he feels. He blames himself for everything that happened."

Casimir crackled his knuckles, annoyed.

Seren didn't wait for him to respond and jumped right back into the story. "Before I tell you the rest, I want you to know that I understand exactly how it feels to find out everything that you believed to be true was a lie. So please know I'm not doing this to hurt you—the opposite, rather. Everyone deserves the chance to know the truth and decide for themselves what to do with it." The prince stared at her, and it felt like the intensity of his gaze could have burned right through her skin; his expression ravaged by conflicted emotions waging a war behind his eyes. Seren softened her voice and added, "Especially you, Cas."

His eyes nearly glowed. "If your plan was to scare me, Ser, it's not working. I can handle whatever you have to say. Just spit it out already."

Seren wanted to believe that, but her voice wavered anyway. "When my mother still lived in Lunaan, a few years before she died, there was an attack by the Stellean court. Apparently, Hellevi has been trying to take over Clarallan as the High King for decades now. But around this time, he orchestrated a series of attacks on the Lunaan and Sollian courts. I don't think he planned to start a war back then; rather he just wanted to make it clear to everyone what his intentions were. To spark fear in the citizens of Clarallan and assure everyone that if they tried to stop him, they would regret it."

Casimir stared at her impatiently while she rambled, clenching his jaw when Seren paused to catch her breath.

"During these attacks, Hellevi instructed his and Etiamella's soldiers to do their worst. To kill and injure as many Fae as they could. Then steal as many humans as they wanted, so they could take them back to their own courts to use as servants. My mother was taken during one of the raids. Stolen by Hellevi personally and forced to endure his tortures for the last few years of her life."

Seren's voice was hoarse as she denied the urge to cry upon thinking about the horrible things her mother had gone through.

Attentive, Casimir noticed and said warmly, to give her a minute, "I've heard about those raids before. My father never told me personally, but Evander and I used to sneak around the castle when we were younger. We always stumbled upon information we weren't supposed to. But I never learned the whole story." Casimir shook his head, his dark hair cascading over his tense features. "I'm honestly surprised my father told you."

Guilt bit at her heart as she recognized the hurt in his tone. He'd never admit it, but Seren knew how badly it stung to know his father kept so many things from him—a familial trait, it seemed. "I'm sure your father never meant to hurt you. And I know it's of little condolence, but I think he did everything with the intention of protecting you."

Casimir's fists clenched at his sides while he waited for her to continue.

She walked him through the rest of King Egil's story, right up to the point it involved his mother. She told him how Adora found out she was pregnant with her shortly after arriving in Stellean and how the Lunaan king and queen planned to rescue them. The prince followed along easily enough, but was unusually quiet throughout the entire conversation—presumably waiting for Seren to get to the point.

It was difficult to spit out her next words. She focused on his silver-blue eyes, the sharpness they beamed as he beheld her. "There's not an easy way to tell you this, Cas. But the story you know, the one about how your mother died..." Her voice trembled violently as she dropped her gaze. "It's all a lie."

Her confession tumbled into the silence that fell between them. It felt like she waited years for the prince to say anything about the bomb she had just dropped on his life.

"Cas," she started, but he interrupted her.

"Don't lie to me, Seren." His voice was as dark as the night that fell upon his dreamworld. The sun shifted above them suddenly as darkness devoured the entire sky, eclipsing the pools of light coming from the eight moons.

It took physical effort to keep her teeth from chattering as the temperature dropped dramatically. "I would never lie to you."

"Tell me more, then," Casimir said coldly. "I want to know everything."

Seren did exactly as he demanded without missing a single detail. She began right where she had left off and told him how their parents planned to free Adora and Seren. She explained how they had grown desperate, his parents' plan left incomplete before the day they broke into the Stellean castle. She was grateful her voice remained steady even as she described how Hellevi caught them in the act. But she couldn't look at the prince too intensely as she described what happened next.

"Your father was attacked first, knocked unconscious even. But from what he told me after he woke up, there was nothing he could've done. Hellevi had nearly beaten him to death, and when he finally woke up, your mother was already gone. Hellevi killed her the same day that he sentenced my mother to death."

Casimir said nothing, not even after she finished the whole

story. Seren waited until she couldn't take the silence any longer. "I'm so sorry, Cas."

He blinked slowly. "Thank you for telling me."

Seren nodded. There was nothing else she could say. As the unbearable silence dragged on, she contemplated pinching herself awake to give him the space he needed. Then his voice broke through the quiet.

"I'm sorry as well, Ser." He took a step closer, his tone bolder than before as he towered over her. "For your mother and for the way I've been treating you. This entire time, I've been acting like I'm the only one who just learned the truth. The story my father told you, it had to have hurt you as badly as it does me, maybe even more."

The weight of his apology slammed into her like a punch to the gut, stealing her breath away. Seren wanted to cut out her beating heart and remove her overwhelming emotions with it. She couldn't handle the way the prince looked at her or the softness in his voice as he apologized. She had never seen him so vulnerable, and although her feelings frightened her terribly, she couldn't deny them any longer.

In seconds, the walls that had taken a lifetime to build, the ones that had protected her heart, threatened to crumble. Her mind spun illogically, not comprehending how something that required so much strength to build could dissolve with such softness.

"Thank you." Tears welled in her eyes as she squeezed them shut. "You don't know how much that means to me."

"The same goes for you. You didn't have to tell me anything, and I know that story had to have been difficult to relive. But your faith in me"—Casimir's shoulders rolled forward with defeat—"I don't deserve it."

With a tingling hand, Seren lifted his chin and placed the other delicately on his face. "Everyone deserves to know the truth, Cas. And no one deserves to blame themselves for the consequences of others."

"How can you be so certain I don't deserve to blame myself? You don't know the things I've done."

"Maybe not all of them," Seren countered. "But ever since we met, I've seen the good in you and I believe in the good you can still do."

"But what about all the bad things I have already done?"

Lifting her eyes to the dim moons hanging above, she gestured with her chin and Casimir's gaze followed. "We can learn a lot from the worlds around us, Cas. Just like the moons, we all go through phases—some light, some dark. But sometimes we have to live through the darkness before we get to feel the light again. And just because we've done bad things doesn't mean we're bad people."

Casimir looked at her so clearly, she could have been made of glass. He saw her, really saw her and everything she'd kept hidden for so many years—the reason she spoke with such conviction, the dark memories she had lived through and the ones she knew still waited for her. The times when she felt worthless, lonely, incomplete even. She would turn to the sky and wait for the stars' advice. Like the moon, she always kept pieces of herself hidden away, too afraid to show people the darkness that lived within her. But there was no beauty without fear, and even when she felt incomplete, the moon taught her that she was still enough—no matter what phase of life she was in. And she believed the same for Casimir.

"You can tell me anything, Cas. Whenever, and if ever, you're ready, I'll be here. Always."

Casimir smiled genuinely for the first time since they arrived, and his dreamworld mirrored his emotions simultaneously. The encroaching darkness slowly dissolved, the surrounding shadows retreated swiftly. The air tasted like hope, like citrus candies and spring blossoms, and ripe pears drenched in honey. It wasn't long before the entire sky was encrusted with a velvety blanket of the brightest shining stars Seren had ever seen.

"The man that I have been doesn't deserve your kindness." Casimir's voice was charged with passion, and the way he looked at her—as if she had personally hung the stars. She couldn't breathe properly as he continued in a tone that made her entire body buzz. "But I promise you, I will do everything in my power to become him."

Seren kissed him then.

She didn't think before doing it or what it might mean for the two of them if they survived the final trial. But she didn't care. Not as the magic of their collision devoured her entire being. His touch filled her mind with colors as he wrapped his hands low around her waist and pulled her hips closer with each greedy breath—wanting her nearly as much as she needed him. Her mind grew dizzy with need, and nothing else mattered. Everything they didn't understand they could figure out later. Casting her worries away, her body completely melted into his. She let go of everything—her doubts, and fear—her heart liquid in his hands as she let the prince deepen the kiss.

In that moment, she was nothing but stardust.

Their souls cut from the very same star.

CHAPTER 42

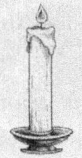

Seren stood before her reflection, holding her star-encrusted dagger as she admired the Verti craftsman's handiwork. She brushed her fingers over the familiar star pendant fixed securely at the base of the blade—the one from her mother's necklace. Her heart fluttered; she was grateful she would have a piece of Adora with her when she finally faced the Stellean king.

Her magic flicked from her fingertips and she let it grow, the empty void in her chest pleased to have it back, thankful that not only was she alive, but that she had the strength of her heart, and her power back.

Ready to complete the final trial.

After spending a week in the Lunaan court, the day that Seren had both wished for and feared had finally come. Yet despite what she would face in just a few hours, a strange sense of serenity swept through her. She had her magic, her friends, and almost the whole truth at her sides, and a brightness within her that reminded her how direly she needed to succeed, and why.

The fate of Clarallan rode on one last test.

Seren had survived the last few weeks by learning from her kingdom, its history and life, and most importantly, by discovering things about herself. Things she never expected she was capable of.

She still had so many questions, but no longer were any of them whether she was worthy. That, she already knew. Now, it was up to her to prove it one last time, by earning the respect of the Star God.

She didn't let herself think about what would happen if she failed. She couldn't have any doubt if she was going to stop Hellevi.

What came after was still uncertain. But thus far, Prue's words had yet to let her down. Seren knew that after completing the final trial, whatever unknown emerged would guide her and Clarallan to a better life—her greatest wish since the day Hellevi destined her to nothing but pain.

For years, Seren had dreamed of escaping the king, his torture, of living a vibrant life beyond the cold walls of the Stellean castle. But what Seren knew now that she hadn't before was that wishes are granted to those who fight for them.

And that was what she was going to do.

Fight.

With everything she had. She was going to stop the king. No matter what it took. Everyone had the power to grant their own wishes if they were daring enough to fight for them.

"I'm worthy," she said to her reflection, and the magic of four Clarallan courts hummed within her, gifted by seven gods, as she prepared to face just one more.

Seren and the prince stood alone, waiting for Rae, as rested and ready as they would ever be.

Casimir crossed his arms, dressed in a fine navy suit that made his eyes glow. "How much longer do we wait, Seren?"

"I don't know, but he has to be here any second." She kept her eyes on the ground, worried about her friend. She hadn't gotten the chance to talk to Rae since their fight, and it was impossible to stop her mind from feasting on her fear. Was he still mad at her? The prince? How were they supposed to face Hellevi together when she wasn't even sure he could look at her without anger in his eyes? She shook her head, exhaled slowly, then repeated, "He has to."

"Do you think he's going to show? It's been over an hour, and we need to get going." Casimir's voice was calm and composed, no sense of urgency in his tone despite his words.

"I know."

They were all supposed to meet at dawn in the same room they had originally arrived in so that Seren could *velis* their group to Stellean after saying farewell to Carr and Dax. Seren had offered to take them directly to the Verti village, but Casimir had argued that she needed as much strength as she could get before the final trial. So he had taken the responsibility of setting them up with horses and rations for their long ride home.

Rae hadn't been there when they said goodbye to the others either. Carr had tried to assure her that he was okay, and Dax explained that they had said their see-you-laters beforehand. But Seren wasn't convinced. Because if that was the case, where was Rae now?

She looked at the closed door. "I'm going to go check his room."

"I'll come with you."

"No, it's okay. I'll be right back."

The handle was cool under her touch as she opened the door, bracing her hand for balance as a sense of déjà vu washed over her.

Rae stood in the hallway, head hung low, right outside the meeting room.

Neither of them said anything, the palpable silence

dampening the air between them. There was so much and nothing to be said at the same time. Seren wondered if the right words even existed to fix what was broken.

"About damn time," Casimir said from behind.

Seren jolted, the silence broken. She looked over her shoulder at the prince, then said quietly to Rae, "We need to go."

It took physical effort to force her steps toward Casimir, a small piece of her begging to stop, turn around, and never return to Stellean. After she had escaped, she never thought that she would return, let alone willingly and of her own choice.

But plans change.

"Let me get this straight," the prince said after Seren finished explaining her plan. "You expect us to just wait outside while you waltz into the castle alone? What's the point in even bringing us then?"

"I know I'm not one to normally agree with the prince, but he's right, Seren. You're nuts if you think we're not going to help."

"I get that you think you're protecting us, that for some unknown reason you need to do this all by yourself." Casimir blew out a breath. "But what you just told us isn't a plan, Seren. It's a death wish."

"We go in together," Rae demanded, "or we don't go at all."

"Last I checked, I'm the only one who can *velis*," Seren countered, and the guys glared at her.

"Seriously, we're seeing this to the end. All of us. Together."

"Fine." Seren crossed her arms. "But if either of you get hurt, or..." She glared at them both, unable to say the words out loud. "Just know I'll kill you."

Casimir raised his hands in front of him and a wicked grin tugged at the corners of his mouth. "Understood."

Rae bobbed his head in agreement.

"Do you have the journal?" Seren turned to Rae, studying the purple circles that darkened his cheeks. Apparently, she wasn't the only one unrested.

Rae slid his pack over his shoulder, unfastened the ties, and reached for the leather-bound notebook. She took it from him, careful not to let their hands touch with the exchange.

"Thank you," she said, immediately flipping through the pages to find the final map.

Unlike the other trials, the Stellean map marked a vague location around the castle's highest tower—the king's personal floor. Luckily for them, Seren knew the layout better than anyone. A lifetime as Hellevi's servant forced her to learn every hallway, hidden door, safe zone, and places to avoid at all costs.

She knew it was foolish to think she could avoid returning to the place that was once her prison, her cage, her personal nightmare. But now that it was really happening, her heart sputtered in her chest.

"The trial is in the castle, but I won't know exactly where until we're in Stellean and I can use my magic." Seren's tone darkened. "We'll be going in blind."

STELLEAN WAS A WAR ZONE. Cold. Dark. A place that celebrated torture and death. Seren couldn't remember if it had always been that bad, or if in the past few weeks, the court had transformed from a bad dream to a nightmare.

Casimir's steady hand wrapped around hers as they landed in the small, cramped closet that had once been her room, the smell of fear amping her nerves. His strength was comforting, and she let herself admit that she was thankful her friends had come with her.

She couldn't shake the tremor of her hands even as Casimir squeezed tighter. Being back in Stellean, in the castle... Every breath burned, as if she could taste the memories of her past screams.

Rae paced back and forth, one step left, one step right, the entire length of the tiny room. It had been a risk landing there, but Seren had wagered that even if someone new occupied her room, they would be busy working. Luckily, she was right.

She had begged the guys to let her try and find Mare before the final trial, desperate to know if her friend was okay. But they risked detection every minute they were in the castle. They had no time to waste.

"Everyone knows the plan?" Seren asked, determined that when it was all over, she would do anything to free her friend.

The two males nodded, and she repeated the plan back to herself in simple terms, making it easier to face:

Complete the fifth trial. Stop the king. Get out alive.

Just three things they had to do. Three steps between Seren and the truth, dreams and nightmares, life and death.

"Then let's go." She kept her breathing tight as she cracked open the wooden door and peered into the empty hallway. Whispering over her shoulder, she said, "All clear. Time to move."

It was easy to guide them out of sight from the servant quarters to Hellevi's personal floor. She had every back door and hidden corridor committed to memory from her time trying to survive in Stellean. And the closer they got, the stronger her magic hummed.

Turning down the last hall, they saw two guards posted outside the entrance of Hellevi's golden chambers, each readily armed and attentive.

"Here goes nothing," Casimir said and gave Seren a thin smile. "See y'all on the other side."

The three of them had said their piece in Lunaan, and she couldn't help but feel like she had to say goodbye then. It wasn't like her to be so pessimistic, but she hadn't wanted to miss the chance.

Casimir held her gaze before marching toward the guards.

Once, Seren had believed him to be some arrogant prince, aloof and brazen, ignorant even, as the rumors said. But now as she watched him, sure-footed, long-strided, and chin held high, she recognized his reputation for what it really was—a shield.

She marveled at the strength beneath his mask, the courage in him that he wouldn't admit to. And although she wouldn't tell him yet, she liked the darker parts of him too; how they were the bones of his confidence, and because of his past, she knew there was little that could harm him. She felt safe around him, even from afar. He drew his broad shoulders high, stretching the dark blue suit across his back, his size and the casual air around him creating an imposing silhouette as he stalked forward.

"I need to speak with your king." Casimir's thunderous voice echoed through the hall and skittered across her skin.

"He's out," the guard on the left said, his eyes looking at a point beyond the prince, dismissiveness lathering his tone.

"No," Casimir demanded. "No, I don't believe he is."

A bluff. But it got their attention.

Both guards dragged their eyes over Casimir, a grave expression mirrored on their faces as they looked at him for the first time.

"He's busy," the other guard spit.

Casimir loosened a low chuckle. "I don't care."

A chill bit at Seren's neck, flushing goosebumps across her skin. Her breath quickened. "It's not working."

"Give him a minute," Rae said. "It's going to work."

Seren didn't hear the rest of their conversation, her heartbeat drumming in a rhythm with her eager magic that drowned out their words.

She watched as one guard sheathed his sword and reached his hands to open the door inward, while the other guard remained armed, the sharp tip of his weapon pointed directly at Casimir's back as the three of them walked in. The heavy doors clicked shut behind them.

They were gone.

Seren counted her breaths in tandem with how many steps it would take for Casimir and the guards to reach Hellevi's study—for the hall to hopefully be clear, for their chance.

"Now," Seren whispered, already walking toward the doors. She and Rae moved as quickly and quietly as possible and dashed into the king's chambers. They slowed down once inside, aware they had to blend in.

It had been Seren's idea to dress them in old servants' clothes, coarse brunette rags that helped them seem as if they truly belonged. A small part of her hadn't wanted to suggest it, resistant to the idea of ever having to reshackle herself through her old clothes, but it was the smart thing to do.

They kept their eyes low and walked swiftly down the main corridor. Seren let her magic guide her, turn after turn, fully singing in her chest, until they reached a grand two-door archway.

"This has to be the place," Seren whispered, studying the grand door she had never seen the inside of.

Rae's golden face paled, as if the grave reality of everything they were doing finally dawned on him.

She added, "Remember, if something goes wrong, you run." She offered a grim half smile. "Save yourself. We'll find each other later."

Even after everything that happened between them, Seren knew if worse came to worst, Rae wouldn't do as he was told. Her heart threatened to crack, but she willed the pieces to stay together just a little while longer.

He squeezed a lingering hand on her shoulder and said, "Be careful, Seren."

"You too." Seren forced a real smile this time. "Time to make a wish."

CHAPTER 43

Seren walked into the unknown room alone, her steps echoing against the chilling, star-encrusted stone floor as the golden doors sealed behind her.

She swallowed, the audible gulp loud against the ghastly silence. In scale, it reminded her of the king's throne room, with high-vaulted ceilings, intricately carved statues, and columns lining the walls. But where the throne room was dark and confined, this colossal space was airy and well lit, the entire far wall built of intersecting clear and stained-glass windows, all surrounding an open arched doorway that led to a balcony outside.

The light of an overcast day, soft and hazy, slipped through the colored glass, illuminating the reflective floors cast in stars and moons and suns. Seren looked up, her lips gaping at the divine artwork.

The entire ceiling depicted a grandiose mural of an unearthly galaxy. Night and day. Suns and moons. Stars and comets. All intertwined by the delicate strokes of a paintbrush.

It was the most beautiful thing Seren had ever seen.

Her heart raced, and she could have sworn her magic sang

through her veins in response to the magnificent sight. It felt like the kind of thing people dropped to their knees and worshiped, its magic and beauty too overwhelming not to praise and adore.

She stepped forward, knees wobbly, drew her mind back to the task at hand, and scanned the room again.

Nothing seemed out of the ordinary, but it had to be the right place. The floor glowed at her feet as she walked toward the balcony. Her magic beat against the walls of her chest as she stood beneath the towering frame—as if in answer to the question of what she was looking for. Her eyes drifted up the tall arches. Squinting slightly, she tried to make out the elegantly carved inscriptions, distorted by long, abstract cracks in the stone. But where the previous trials had two quotes, the stone she now read had only one.

Her lips moved to form the words as she spoke quietly. "The Stars grant the final feat; make a wish and all is complete."

The exact words from the journal, the ones that marked the Stellean trial.

She waited for something to happen. For the test to begin, the room to change, or the Star God to appear.

But nothing did.

She tugged on her magic, urged it to answer her questions. Still, nothing happened.

"Come on," Seren whispered. "Please."

She was missing something, the final piece of the trial.

But what?

She was wasting time. Time she and her friends and the kingdom didn't have.

Slight tremors rose goosebumps over her skin as she read the words again and stepped onto the balcony. Her eyes tracked a large bestial silhouette flying through the clouds as she gazed across the Stellean court, which was darkened by somber clouds, the city void of saturation and life. Then she looked up at the stars, but they too hid beneath a blanket of gloom and gray.

She wrapped her hands around the balcony railing and nausea roiled in her stomach, threatening the back of her throat as she remembered what Nephein had made her confess. She hated this place. Its king, even more.

"Make a wish," Seren scoffed. Could it really be that easy?

The previous trials had nearly killed her, shattered her soul into pieces that grew harder and harder to put back together.

In Sollian, she found the will to see the light.

In Lunaan, she conquered her greatest fears.

Out at Sea in Ocealla, she found the power of her mind, and in Etiamella, the strength of her body.

Every trial had taught her something. She thought they had been preparing her for this very moment. But now...she was supposed to just make a wish?

"I wish to stop the war." Seren's voice cracked with a hint of shame.

She blinked slowly, her eyes scanning the court once more.

Nothing changed.

Maybe she wasn't specific enough?

She gathered her voice, squeezed her eyes shut, and said, steadier this time, "I wish to stop Hellevi from ever hurting anyone again."

She cracked one eye open, then the next. Everything was still the same.

"Dammit." Seren wanted to scream. She rattled her fist against the cool railing. It shook and the reverberating metal sent a chill coiling down her spine.

Behind her, a thunderous *boom* rocked through the other side of the grand room as soldiers barged through the large doors, their violent force shaking the walls. They filled the space between Seren and her escape as the king stalked in after them. He wore his darkest war robes, his eyes like two golden stars against the blanket of evil that consumed his face, his chin held high, a cruel grin splitting his thin lips. He held a short sword at his side, twirling it around as if out of boredom. He halted in the center of the room, his eyes casually searching, stalling for a moment to let her panic build, until his gaze finally stilled.

Seren felt the blood drain from her face, the onset of dizziness that swirled her mind as she gripped the balcony railing, unable to shake the blinding anger that strangled her heart. A surge of that vile rage coursed through her veins and begged her to kill him.

The trial might be a failure, but she could at least end it all with his blood on her hands.

She did a quick head count of how many soldiers occupied the room, calculating how long it would take for her to reach Hellevi before one of them ultimately cut her down.

Her dagger was in her hands as she took a few steps forward.

Hellevi loosened a dark chuckle, his hand raised in front of him. "I wouldn't do that just yet, Seren." He paused. "Bring him in."

Seren's stomach dropped so quickly she thought she was going to be sick.

Four soldiers marched forward, dragging a restrained, beaten, and bloody male behind them. His hands were bound behind his back in the same metal manacles that Seren recognized as powerful enough to snuff out even the strongest of Fae magic.

The soldiers dropped the male. One kicked a booted foot into his back, sending the prisoner falling to his knees.

"Cas…" Seren whispered.

She assessed him from afar while every part of her begged her to run to him. The prince lifted his head, his beautiful face almost unrecognizable. He struggled to say something, but Hellevi's magic compelled his lips shut, the prince's magic useless beneath the manacles' power. His silver-blue eyes, wild and apologetic, pleaded for her to save herself. Black-red blood matted his long hair, staining his fair skin as it dripped down his forehead. A deep gash split open his left cheek, while the other already wore a gruesome bruise, its purple-and-yellow color contrasting with his fresh black eye.

Seren shook, unable to control the anger and fear that seared her veins.

This is what she wanted to avoid. She cursed herself for giving in, for letting her friends come with her.

Look at what good it did. Seren still hadn't figured out the final trial. Casimir looked like death had chewed him up and spit him out. And Rae...she hoped, for once, he listened to her, that he ran and saved himself, that he was okay wherever he was.

"Sad, isn't it? That a prince of such power would align himself with someone like you." Hellevi stepped closer to the prince, his eyes lathered in disgust as he kicked a booted foot into Casimir's stomach. Casimir didn't react, his face steeled over, his lips pressed into a thin, flat line. Hellevi lifted his gaze to Seren and continued, pointing at Casimir. "If you're wondering why he looks like this...he did this to himself, really. I had to figure out what he knew about you...the trials. He could have chosen the winning side, chosen to align himself with me, like his smarter older brother did." Hellevi's sneer flicked a switch in Seren. "I even gave him a second chance, tried to cut a deal—his life for yours. But nevertheless, you both chose to die."

Seren's magic flared inside her, so hot against her sorrow she thought she was going to burst with anger and rip the king's heart out.

"I'm going to kill you," Seren said, her threat vibrating throughout the entire room.

"No. I don't think that you are." Hellevi gestured around the room with an open palm. "Look around you, Seren. I've already won."

No.

No. No. No.

She wouldn't accept that. After everything she had been through. She couldn't.

She had to keep fighting. For herself.

For Casimir...and Rae. The family she had found and would do anything to protect. For Dax and Carr and the other Verti, and the entire kingdom of Clarallan, which deserved a chance at something better.

"You really thought that you could beat me?" The king's booming voice echoed against her pounding temples. "It's over, Seren. And with your magic, I have everything I need to become the next High King of Clarallan."

With my magic?

Her thoughts twined around her throat, and Hellevi must have seen the confusion written boldly across her blanched face because he answered before she could say anything. "I know everything, Seren. About the trials. The kingdom's rules. A High King cannot be forged through war, only through tests and proving one's worth. And you have done just that."

"What does any of that have to do with me?" Seren asked.

"You see, there's one loophole in Clarallan's ridiculous rules... Family." Hellevi tapped his hand casually along his sword. "I may not be able to take what I want from Clarallan... the trials prevent that. But what I can do is take what I want from you. Of course, you must die first, but after that, I can take over as the High King of Clarallan."

Seren stared and stared.

Hellevi's yellow eyes glowed. "And as your father, it is my right."

His words cut through her like a sword to the chest, straight through her middle as if her world had been cleaved in two, as Hellevi's confession echoed in her mind. *Hellevi's my father?* She couldn't believe that. A crack rang through her ears, the sound of her heart breaking. It felt like her insides were flayed open for everyone to see.

"You're a liar." Seren's voice wasn't entirely her own as she yelled. "Was this all part of your sick plan?"

The king merely waved a hand and shook his head as he said, "Foolish child, you know the Fae cannot lie." Seren's heart sputtered as she listened to the monster standing before her. He continued, "I was never certain you had magic until the day you ran from this castle, but I always suspected it. Why do you think I punished you so much?"

"Because you're a monster." Seren's voice cracked. Of all the terrible truths she had discovered, this was the worst of them all.

He shook his head, clicked a *tsk,* and said, "To test you. I thought if you had magic, it would want to protect you. That threatening your life would be enough for it to reveal itself. But when it never did, I realized I'd been wrong, that you were merely human...just like Adora."

Her mind went completely blank, unhearing, as Hellevi spoke about her mother. Seren charged the king, her dagger stretched out in front of her. She didn't believe him, but she still wanted him dead. She only made it a few barreling steps before the rough hands of soldiers caught around her waist, her shoulders, in her hair, ripping her backward and pinning her in place. She wrestled against their grip, but it was useless.

"Enough," Hellevi roared.

Seren whipped her head to the king. He towered over Casimir, the tip of his sword pricked against his chest. She needed to think of something, do anything to stop him. Now.

"Your plan will never work," Seren admitted.

His face flashed with anger, then contorted into a cruel grin. "You can't manipulate me, Seren. I see right through you."

"It won't work because...because I never completed the trials."

"You stupid girl. All you had to do was make a wish and you couldn't even do that?"

Seren felt her magic pulse at the king's words, and a whisper crept up the back of her neck: *Wish for what your heart most desires...*

"I wish—" Seren began, her eyes locked on Casimir's. Hellevi's face twisted between rage and fear as he realized his mistake. He plunged his sword into Casimir's chest before Seren could finish.

Casimir gasped and his glowing silver-blue eyes dimmed, his mouth gaping open as if to say something, before his head rolled forward.

A scream pierced the room, and it took a minute for Seren to realize it was coming from her. She thrashed against the soldiers' unyielding grasp as tears burned down her cheeks.

"I wish to defeat the king," Seren cried out.

Nothing happened.

"I wish to stop the war." She tried again. She could hear the desperation in her voice, felt it ravage her body. "I wish to save Clarallan."

Hellevi's wicked laugh echoed throughout the room as he dropped Casimir's body to the floor.

Thud.

Seren's throat was raw from screaming.

How did I fail so horribly?

She kicked and clawed at the soldiers, until one had enough and yanked her head back and another smashed his armored fist into her jaw. Her head rolled, and she blinked until white dots disappeared from her vision, but the stars she saw were not from pain or whiplash.

She stared at the galaxy on the ceiling, her eyes flickering back and forth from star to star until they landed on the fine golden brush strokes of a shooting star. It glowed, and Seren didn't know if it was a consequence of her throbbing skull until she heard the whisper again.

"Take her away," Hellevi ordered.

Right. He couldn't kill her yet. Not with the trials incomplete. He needed her alive for his plan to work.

The soldiers started to drag her limp body away, but she kept her eyes on the sole shooting star, its golden color glowing brightly, as she listened to what her heart cried out for.

She thought of all the things she wanted and let her magic guide her mind to where it intersected with her heart...

To what it desired most.

Seren hesitated before giving herself over to her greatest wish. If she completed the final trial, Hellevi had no reason to keep her alive. But if she didn't, her magic wouldn't be strong enough to fight him. It was her only chance.

"I wish..." Seren paused, lips agape, as her mind battled against logic and feeling. Desires and thoughts tangled as they raced through her, until they all circled back to just one. Her gaze fell to the prince's crumpled body, his cold cheek pressed into the stone floor, his eyes closed, unseeing. She stared at his tragic face. She would let the unknown guide her. *This has to work*, she begged. Her words fell from her cracked lips: "I wish for Cas."

A flash of pure light erupted from her chest, blinding everyone in the room. The soldiers dropped her, and she fell to her knees. A searing pain captured her entire body as she recognized the familiar burn of the fifth and final tattoo.

"Grab her." She barely heard the king's command above the agony ringing through her body. She felt the tough hands of the soldiers reach for her, felt them wrap around her shoulders and ankles as they tried to haul her out of the room.

She couldn't fight them, her body ravaged by the power that took over her every limb, the surge of flames that coursed through her veins. They dragged her numb body over the stone floors, through the doorway.

Her wish had worked.

The trial was complete.

Her eyes remained locked on Casimir as she slid farther and farther away from him.

The first door swung shut and Seren let out a small cry. She reached with tingling arms to shove the second door open before it could click shut completely. The soldiers froze, even the king.

And before her magic erupted as a flash of light that burned throughout the entire room—

All Seren saw was blue.

CHAPTER 44

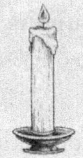

"SEREN." A familiar voice barreled through the fire.

Izzac? Her mind spun violently, her every nerve lit with unbelievable energy. Panting, she crawled forward, clumsily stumbling over the armored bodies scattered across the smoldering floor.

Get up. She clenched her fists, unable to clear the ash from her panicked mind. *Get up.*

A burning haze dominated the room, heavy with magic that fried her senses. She stood, trembling with the amount of power that coursed her veins, unable to see through the flames and devastation that her magic had caused. She yelled for Cas, whirling when rough hands caught her by surprise.

"Seren, we have to go." Izzac wrapped taloned fingers around her arms, unflinching at the flames that licked her glowing skin. "Now."

"Izzac?" She couldn't believe her eyes. Maybe she really was dead. But the searing burn across her sternum told her otherwise as her magic drummed in her chest. "What are you doing here?"

"Saving you."

Her eyes narrowed. Of everyone she expected to save her, Izzac was near the bottom of the list. "How did you find us?"

"Seriously, now is not the time for so many questions. We need to get out of here. If anyone survived, we don't want to be here when they wake up."

Hopefully, the king and his soldiers were dead, but—

She jerked her head, squinting as she scoured the room, barely able to see the soldiers' sizzling bodies that littered the floor. She shouted, coughing on smoke. "CAS—" Cut off with a cry when Izzac's unyielding talons pierced her skin. Struggling, she yelped. "What about the others?"

"I can't take more than one." Izzac gritted his teeth and tugged her toward the balcony. "We have to go."

"But Cas—"

Izzac's sharp teeth snapped. "Now." He ran, and she lurched after him, his firm grip impossible to shake.

Dazed and disoriented, Seren didn't have enough time to stop Izzac's Verti strength before he wrapped his arms around her waist and threw them both off the balcony.

Screaming, the wind caught in her raw lungs as they fell headfirst, hurtling hundreds of feet toward the hard ground. The pressure built in her temples, wind screaming in her ears as loudly as the cries that rang from her body, frozen with fear as she clung to Izzac.

Her neck jerked and joints wailed from whiplash when powerful red wings erupted behind Izzac and dragged them higher into the dark sky. As her mind raced to fathom seeing his Verti form for the first time, fear and anger shook her words against the wind. "We have to go back for them," she yelled.

"No."

Seren sucked in a breath and pleaded, her voice nearly lost over the powerful flap of his feathered wings. "Please, Izzac. We can't just leave them."

"They might not even be alive, Seren."

Her heart stilled at his callousness. "They have to be."

"You don't know that," Izzac roared against the storm clouds filling the sky with thunder. "And I can only carry one of you."

"Then get me somewhere safe and go back." Her voice broke. "Please."

"It's too risky." His tone made her blood chill. "There are things you don't know, Seren. Reasons why I can't go back."

"Tell me," she shouted.

"I will." He gripped her tight and dove through the damp mist, then his wings wrapped around them before cutting through the rain clouds. "Just not right now. Okay?"

Seren nodded against his chest, her magic sizzling with defeat at the thought of leaving Casimir and Rae behind. If the king was still alive…

She couldn't let herself think like that. Didn't even dare to finish that thought.

If her friends were still alive—which she believed they were—she would save them. With or without Izzac's help.

She shook down to her bones, fear causing the worst of it despite the cold rain that poured from the dark clouds. Her eyes glued to Izzac's wings, she asked, "What are you? Your Verti form, I mean."

A haunted look filled his eyes. "A phoenix."

She gasped. "But Rae said they were extinct."

"They are," he said quickly. "My Verti form is one of a kind."

"How?" Seren asked, but she knew Izzac well enough to not expect too much of an explanation.

"It's a long story, and a complicated one at that." He lowered his voice. "No one understands how my Verti form came to be."

She glanced over his shoulder, in awe of the strength woven into his body. "I don't understand."

"No one does." His strong wings beat through the storm, carrying them away from the Stellean court, now soaring high above the Galaxius Forest. A haunting clatter of sound burst through the trees as deafening roars reached into the sky, stuttering Seren's heart despite the distance.

Her voice wavered, panicked. "What was that?"

"You completed the final trial, right?"

She tensed. "Yeah…"

Izzac's throat bulged. "Then Clarallan's magic has been restored."

"What are you getting at?"

"That there will be greater consequences than we ever could have imagined."

"Like what?"

"The kingdom's magic has been tempered for centuries, nowhere near as strong as when the gods walked the lands. But now—"

"Spit it out."

"Let's just say, the Fae are not the strongest predators in Clarallan anymore."

Seren's eyes dropped, her heart thundering. "I'm guessing that's not a good thing."

"Depends on how you look at it."

"Seriously, Izzac."

"If you thought Hellevi was the worst monster you would ever face, you've been sadly mistaken."

Afraid to ask, Seren forced out shaky words. "Do you think he's alive?"

Izzac's tone was as dark as the escalating storm. "I don't know."

Quivering, Seren squinted through the rain, scanning the dense trees as they trembled and cracked. Her mind was a mess too tangled to sort through as they flew through the frigid air. The creatures that lived in Galaxius—the Caripers, the Khaous, and gods knew what else… She didn't want to think about what Izzac's words truly meant.

Quietly, Seren asked, "What have I done?"

"What you had to."

"Do you really believe that?"

"Yes." Izzac glided them quickly away from an ear-shattering crack of lighting. Doubt doused her heart, and he added, "We all do."

Her mind raced. "The others—Dax and Carr..." She swallowed, unable to get the words out.

"They're both safe. All the Verti are."

Nearly thanking the gods, Seren stopped short, unsure after what Izzac had just said about the consequences of their trials. *Why did no one warn me?*

"Okay," she breathed. At least some of her friends were safe. For now. "I wish Rae would have gone with them."

Izzac gulped, and his eyes snapped to the sky.

"What?" she asked. "What aren't you telling me?"

A pause.

"Izzac, come on," she demanded.

"Like I said, there's a lot you don't know."

Seren could have sworn Izzac almost sounded sorry. She asked, not wanting to hear his answer, "About Rae?"

"Yes." He wet his lips and his arms tensed around her, and her heart cracked as loudly as the lightning that split the dark sky. "But also about everything else."

She knew the Verti had their secrets. Rae more than anyone. But he had saved her countless times, and she trusted him with her life. Yet the way Izzac spoke made her feel like his secrets were bad enough to bring her whole world crashing down.

"Please, tell me."

"I will," he said, and Seren followed his eyes as he glanced down through the mist. "Just not up here. I don't need you causing us to fall out of the sky."

Her heart clamored. "Is it that bad?"

"It'll be okay."

"That's not what I asked."

"I know." He chewed on his thin, cracked lips, his answer planting dread in her gut.

She asked, "Where are you taking us?"

Izzac's red-rimmed eyes met hers, his voice much softer than before. "Home."

EPILOGUE

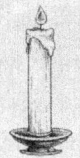

Casimir gritted his teeth as he strained his wrists against the sharp metal shackles and painted another bloody line on the cracked dungeon wall, marking his thirtieth day beneath the Stellean castle. Nearly a month since things had gone so terribly wrong at the last trial. Nearly a month since he had last seen Seren.

His stomach twisted at the thought of her. Was she okay? Was she even alive? It was difficult to remember what happened after Hellevi had plunged his sword into Casimir's chest. His only thought was that he had let Seren down. Disappointed her in the worst way possible.

He tried not to imagine the worst, but after a month in isolation, it was difficult to control the darkness that plagued his mind. His only company was his guilt, his shame and regret. He had to believe she was alive. That he would feel it if she wasn't—somehow, with that unearthly connection between them. Since Etiamella, it had grown so powerful that he could feel her heartbeat without even seeing her. But now, without his magic, he couldn't feel anything—his heart was an empty pit in his chest that filled him with dread. It was impossible to know.

With red-stained nails, he clawed at the metal shackles. He would have done anything to free himself, to not be so helpless and vulnerable. The manacles did more than hinder his magic. They drained him of it.

A slow and miserable torture.

When he wasn't thinking about Seren, Casimir passed most of the time imagining what he would do to the Stellean king when he saw him again. Because when he did, only one of them was going to live to see another day.

Interrupting his favorite part of the daydream—right before the prince ripped Hellevi to shreds—approaching footsteps slapped against the wet stone floor. Casimir pressed his back to the cell wall and stifled a groan as his numb limbs resisted. He strained his stiff neck to the left and glimpsed the back of two large males dragging a small redheaded woman into the cell next to him. With a clang of metal, they shoved the woman roughly inside and slammed the gate closed, locking it immediately.

The prince's vision blurred with rage as he recognized the two males. "You bastards," he shouted, his voice hoarse as he used it for the first time in weeks. "I'm going to kill both of you."

The one closest to him *tsked*, wrapping his large hands around the metal grates. "And how are you going to do that, brother?" Evander gestured at the shackles before throwing his gaze around the cell. "Because from where I stand... Well, you'll never get the chance."

"Don't doubt me, Evander," Casimir said with a dark voice that promised pain. "When I get out—"

"*If* you get out," Evander sneered. "Which will never happen."

"You think you're better than me, Evander. You always have." Casimir bared his teeth with a sinister grin, years of hatred festering in his chest. The eldest Lunaan prince had resented him since the day their father said the crown would wait for his golden son. He took every vile emotion out on Casimir, angry that Egil would choose his *weak* younger brother over him —*the prince who deserved to be king*, Evander had said, *would do anything to be king*. Casimir's eyes darkened in remembrance of his brother's rage. "But you're nothing and everybody knows it."

"It's good your opinions mean nothing to me, little brother. Hellevi and I have a plan, a great one. And, spoiler, you and all your foolish friends don't survive." Evander chuckled, a raucous sound that boiled Casimir's blood. "Except this one, of course." Evander waved the second male closer. "Who I guess was never your friend after all, was he?"

Evander slapped a heavy hand on Rae's shoulder. "You see, Cas. There's so much you don't know. Like how your little friend has been betraying you since the beginning."

"He's not my friend."

"Obviously," Rae groused.

Evander raised his brows. "Details aside, did you know Rae has been working with Hellevi and me since before you two even met?"

His brother's words constricted the vessels around Casimir's breaking heart. Did Seren know? The Verti? He couldn't believe that any of them were in on it. And Rae—Casimir hadn't liked him from the start... But he never would have guessed he would cross Seren like that. "How could you do that to her?"

"How could I not?" Rae tapped his claws against the gate. "Hellevi promised me something. A deal I couldn't refuse."

"What's worth turning on her? What could Hellevi possibly have offered you?" Casimir's heart stormed with rage. He'd always known he didn't like Rae, but he never thought the male was capable of something like this. "I thought you cared about her."

Rae's expression curled and he shifted his weight uncomfortably. "She was...unexpected collateral. I made my deal with Hellevi before I met her. But I suppose fate was on our side the day I found her in the Galaxius Forest."

For a second, Casimir's anger was so strong he swore he could feel his power rumble in his chest. "What deal?"

"He's going to help me find someone." Rae lowered his eyes, and Casimir thought it was guilt that weighed down his expression. "Someone I've been looking for for years."

"You're both more idiotic than I thought if you believe Hellevi will keep his promises. He's selfish, and as soon as you no longer serve him, he'll toss you out with the rest of the dead."

The two of them snorted.

"I won't waste another breath on you." Evander turned and said over his shoulder, "I hope you rot down here, Casimir."

Neither looked back as they walked to the exit, and Casimir refused to give them the satisfaction of groveling. He shoved his anger deep within and sealed his cracked lips, his fists clenched tight enough to draw blood.

"Are you okay?" A quiet voice carried through the darkness and Casimir jerked. In the heat of seeing his brother and Rae, he had completely forgotten about the woman they had thrown into the neighboring cell.

"I'm fine," Casimir bit out. He didn't have a reason to be rude, but after everything he had just learned, he really wasn't in the mood.

"So that was your brother, huh? That must make you the other Lunaan prince." She paused. "Casimir, right?"

Casimir mumbled his confirmation and hoped she would take the hint soon enough.

"You're not much of a talker, are you?"

In response, Casimir let a thick silence fill the cells. It lasted less than a minute before the sweet voice spoke again.

"Are you going to ask for my name?"

"No."

Casimir heard her bristle against her cuffs. "Okay... Well, are you always in such a bad mood?"

"Are you always this annoying?" he retorted.

Ignoring his question, she said, "I'm Mare, in case you were wondering."

Casimir swallowed—a heavy knot of recognition and relief. "Do you know Seren?"

A heavy pause. "She was my best friend."

"Was?"

"I haven't seen her in months." Her voice cracked.

"I know it's not much, but Ser talked about you all the time. She always wanted to find a way to save you."

Quiet gasps echoed against the stone. "How do you know her?"

Casimir's heart beat an erratic rhythm. "I was trying to help her."

"Was?" Mare mirrored his sorrow.

His voice fell. "I failed her."

"Is that how you ended up down here?"

"Yes."

"Do you know where she is?"

"No," Casimir said. "Why are you down here?"

Pain lathered Mare's tone. "A few months ago, when Seren was still in Stellean, we had this plan. Long story short, it was a complete disaster. And I don't know what happened to Ser, but I was caught and locked up, have been ever since." Choking back tears, Mare went on to explain to the prince what happened the day Seren ran away from Stellean. How she had spent every day since wearing those damn manacles.

Which explained why every time he and Seren had tried to dream-walk to Mare, they couldn't reach her. Always met by a raging, dark sea, which made Seren fear the worst. Casimir had tried to comfort her by saying that if Mare wasn't alive, they wouldn't see anything at all. But he wasn't sure Seren ever believed him.

When Mare finished, Casimir asked, "Why haven't I seen you down here before?"

"For weeks, Hellevi kept me close to get information about Seren. But I don't know anything. I guess he finally believed me today because he sentenced me to the isolation cells."

Hope lightened his tone. "So Hellevi doesn't know where Seren is?"

"Nope. And I hope he never finds her."

Relief washed over him, and Casimir agreed. Seren had to be alive. And that meant they still had a chance. "We have to get out of here."

"You don't have to tell me twice, but um…how exactly are we going to do that?"

"First, we need to get out of these chains."

"Way to state the obvious. But if you haven't had any luck already, what makes you think you will now?"

She was right. Casimir didn't know how he could remove the shackles himself in his state, but that didn't mean it was impossible.

And if it was the last thing he did, the prince would do whatever it took to see Seren again.

A CLARALLAN PLAYLIST

If you know me, you know I couldn't write a book and not include a playlist. So, for everyone who loves music and wants to experience Clarallan a little better—I hope you enjoy!

Best wishes,
TW

"My Blood"—Ellie Goulding

"Bad Dream"—Ruelle

"Sky Full Of Song"—Florence + The Machine

"Runaway"—AURORA

"Flaws"—Bastille

"You Got Friends"—Ashley Singh

"Counting Stars"—OneRepublic

A CLARALLAN PLAYLIST

"This Is A War"—Losers

"Outnumbered"—Dermot Kennedy

"Restless"—Cold War Kids

"Achilles Come Down"—Gang of Youths

"Atlantis"—Seafret

"Dreams"—Gabrielle Aplin, Bastille

"Where You're Coming From"—Vincent Lima

"Arsonist's Lullabye"—Hozier

"Power"—Isak Danielson

"Play with Fire (feat. Yacht Money)"—Sam Tinnesz, Yacht Money

"Blood // Water"—grandson

"Cosmic Love"—Florence + The Machine

"Power Over Me"—Dermot Kennedy

"Orpheus"—Vincent Lima

Find me (@toriweed) and the playlist (Reading TWoW) on Spotify.

ACKNOWLEDGMENTS

To be honest, I don't even know where to begin my acknowledgments, because the fact that this book exists is proof that wishes do come true, and although not granted by real magic, it was made possible by the dedication and passion of everyone who helped bring this story to life over the years. And for that, thank you all for allowing me to experience what magic feels like in this lifetime:

David Gardias, Designer extraordinaire. Thank you for having a vision for this story from the start. You brought this book to life in a way that no one else ever could and I am so honored to have your talent on this journey. You are a brilliant designer and the kindest to work with, and I can't wait to see what we do next.

To my many editors, critique partners, and beta readers: What ever would I do without every single one of you? All of you are the reason this book shines for its readers. Thank each and every one of you for your time and love dedicated to bringing this story to life. I couldn't do it without you.

To my friends and family, to whom I owe each and every one of you for your tireless support. This book would not exist without you guys.

Mackenzie Johnson and Savannah Danenhauer: Thank you for the endless hours you both gave me through this long (and I mean very long) journey. From Wyoming to Mykonos, this story has grown with us over the years and I can't wait to see where our stories continue to take us. You both have my gratitude forever.

Juliana Davidson, #1 Fan Club Leader. Juju, thank you for always being my biggest cheerleader. I couldn't do this without you and our special coffee breaks.

To my mom: Thank you for encouraging me to go forth and chase anything that helps bring dreams to life. I owe everything to your unconditional love and support. I love you.

To Ayden, Nathan, Aubrey, Connor, Reid, Chariss, Kayleigh, Natalie and to every single person who ever let me bounce ideas off them, ask for their opinions and advice, or to just read some pages—THANK YOU. I valued every minute of your time spent reading, talking about, or even just thinking about this story. It wouldn't have been possible without everyone's support.

Love always and best wishes,
Tori

ABOUT THE AUTHOR

Tori Weed is the author behind The Weight of Wishes, the first book in her debut fantasy series that she began writing as a psychology student still in university. She is a writer, equestrian, photographer, an ENFJ, and a creator from Denver, CO.

For more information about Tori and her books you can visit her online at https://toriweedauthor.com/

Printed in Great Britain
by Amazon